Beasts of
UPTON
PUDDLE

The Beasts of UPTON PUDDLE

Simon West-Bulford

MEDALLION
P R E S S
Medallion Press, Inc.

Printed in USA

Published 2013 by Medallion Press, Inc.

The MEDALLION PRESS LOGO
is a registered trademark of Medallion Press, Inc.

Copyright © 2013 by Simon West-Bulford
Cover illustration by Chase Stone | © Chase Stone, 2013
Edited by Emily Steele
Illustrations by James Tampa

Typeset in Adobe Garamond Pro
Printed in the United States of America

ISBN# 978-160542520-7

10 9 8 7 6 5 4 3 2 1
First Edition

ACKNOWLEDGMENTS

With special thanks to my wife, Ruth, and also to Kirstie, Charlotte, Carrie-Ann and Andy, Jenny, Gill, Jennie, Bev, Michelle, Mo, and a whole host of other friends too numerous to mention. Your encouragement and enthusiasm when I first wrote this book have always stayed with me.

Also a massive thanks to everyone at Write Club, especially Jason Heim, Caleb Ross, Paul Eckert, Anthony David Jaques, Richard Thomas, Mlaz Corbier, and Nik Korpon. Your encouragement, advice, and critiquing were amazing.

Thanks also to everyone at Chronicles, where the world of Pyronesia first blossomed.

And also a huge thanks to Medallion, especially Emily Steele, who put the sparkle into my words and is fantastic to work with.

Thank you!

PROLOGUE

1962—Location Unknown

One more minute and Ronnie would be free from the stifling heat of the cavern. Five more minutes after that and she would be back on the boat, sailing home.

Safe. Alive.

But that was not going to happen now. There was a terrible moment when Ronnie thought she might actually pretend that she heard nothing—that she was the only one left alive and could run away to safety.

But the cry was unmistakable.

"Ronnie! Help!" It was weaker the second time, with subtle tones of defeat.

Shielding her eyes from the sun, she stole a final glimpse of the island she loved so dearly. Framed perfectly by the cavern mouth, the bay stood, gentle waves lapping on its virgin-white beach. And sweeping back in a huge rocky crescent, the swelling green hills that nurtured the untroubled wildlife tempted her to abandon any remaining hope. In a place of such unspoiled beauty, the horror of the past two hours could almost be considered a lie. But the truth forced her back into the cavern with terrible cruelty.

A coiling jet of fire seared the air above. A warning shot.

"I'm coming, Heinrich," she called.

It was on the tip of her tongue to ask if he was hurt, but the answer was obvious. She saw exactly what happened, and it was a miracle he was still alive at all.

A roar like the sound of a freight train rushing through a tunnel shook the cave walls, but she carried on. No turning back. She'd rescue Heinrich or die trying. Probably the latter.

The mouth of the larger cavern loomed ahead—a hub area connecting a series of vast underground tunnels and caves, richly embedded with diamond deposits and lush natural architecture. Earlier that day it was a place of popping champagne corks and snapping group photographs. Now all she expected to find when she got back inside were smouldering bones and the stench of death.

Testing not only her balance but her nerves too, she grabbed at the rock face to steady herself, ready to bite back the pain radiating from her torn ankle before running inside. Her skin blistered when she touched the hard surface, and at once she pulled away, feeling a rush of cold adrenaline as her foot took all her weight. She conceded a small yelp, but the ache was bearable, and without pausing for thought, Ronnie half ran, half hobbled toward the hub area.

Great rhythmic thuds crashed somewhere ahead and above her, each one followed by a fiery snort of breath. It was coming.

"Ronnie!" It was more a scream than a cry for help that time.

"Almost there! Don't move! If you can see it, don't provoke it!"

"Quickly!"

Ronnie tripped as she entered the area. Cursing at the sudden pain, she glanced back at the cause and saw the jutting handle of a barrow they had brought in earlier. It was full to the brim with diamonds, each one sparkling with fiery brilliance, illuminated by the tiny flames lapping the roof.

The roar came again.

Flinching, Ronnie glanced around the cavern, desperate to find Heinrich. All she could see were the charred remains of their equipment blasted across the ground. Oscilloscopes and clinometers smashed; notebooks, specimen bags, and tools scattered. And, of course, the bodies.

Then she saw him. A hulk of a man now reduced to a battered wreck, Heinrich lay sprawled in the blackened dirt next to some storage cases, a red sheen covering one side of his face, one leg twisted underneath him. Something was huddled between his shuddering arms beneath his burnt trench coat.

"Heinrich!" She scrambled across ash and broken glass to reach him, suppressing a shriek when he revealed what hid beneath his coat. A small boy, streaked with dirt, lay there shivering. He stared directly ahead—the look of shell shock Ronnie had seen so many times as a girl in the war—but then she saw. Two bodies, burned almost beyond recognition, lay against another barrow filled with diamonds.

"There were supposed to be no children on this expedition." Heinrich sobbed. "He hid himself away to be with . . . to be with . . ."

Ronnie could not look at the bodies for another moment. She fought back a surge of despair as she closed her stinging eyes.

"Get him out of here, Ronnie. Before—"

The dull thud of something heavy impacting the ground interrupted them, and Ronnie, knowing precisely what she would see, turned to look.

A fluttering of ash churned around a huge reptilian head, larger than a truck, dark red like congealed blood. Two great eyes, each a river-green vortex of light, shone through the settling cloud.

Ronnie drew in a faltering breath and stifled it, as though some primal instinct told her any movement might be the last she made.

As if it sensed her fear, the beast slowly lifted the top half of its jaw to reveal a pink thorny tongue and an explosion of twisted grey fangs. A blast of earthy breath ruffled Ronnie's hair as another roar blasted out.

Behind Ronnie, Heinrich moaned, but she dared not turn.

The jaws clamped shut, and the head, still pressed to the ground, began a fluid zigzag motion toward them. A thick scaly neck trailed behind it, leading into one of the connecting caverns ten feet above. It was then that Ronnie realized just how huge this creature was.

Two sizeable forearms dragged a huge body out from the hole, and with a sound not unlike the snapping of a hundred wet branches, an intimidating set of leathery wings unfolded. With its head still flat to the ground, back arched, and wings fully extended, the enormous lizard was a terrifying sight.

"Such a sudden end for so magnificent a venture," Heinrich said quietly.

From somewhere, Ronnie managed to find the strength to steady her shaking as she said what might be her final words. "Ah, Heinrich, but how many people can say they have lived to see a real dragon?"

"Don't you mean dragons, Ronnie?"

Ronnie was about to ask what he meant when two more reptilian heads, much smaller than the first, appeared from behind the enormous wings, hissing in defiance.

"Hatchlings," she gasped. "No wonder it attacked so ferociously."

"A breeding colony?"

"Exactly."

"Could we have stumbled upon a more dangerous place?"

"We have only one chance to survive this," she said, staring at the boy cowering within Heinrich's coat.

"No!"

"Bring the boy. Now."

Guardian of the Nesting Caverns

ONE

Joe Copper yawned a fourth time, switched off his mobile phone, and listened for birdsong, bemused. Most Sunday mornings, he would finish his paper round by five thirty, drag his old trolley into the woods, slump against his favorite tree stump, and fall asleep listening to the unhurried noises of nature. Most of the other twelve-year-old boys he knew couldn't care less about wildlife. But to Joe, Ringwood Forest, aglow with the blush of first light and alive with the dawn chorus, was the most wonderful place on earth.

This Sunday was different. The lull of sleep beckoned him as it always did, but not a single chirp or whistle could be heard. A brooding silence smothered the forest, as if everything living had paused to stare at something in astonishment.

And that wasn't the only mystery Joe had encountered since he started his day. At exactly three minutes past five every Sunday, Joe delivered the *Telegraph* to the Gordon residence. Today he did just that. Peering cautiously through the black bars of the gate, as always, he pushed the newspaper into the letterbox and braced for the inevitable maniacal barking from their oversized rottweiler. As far back as he could remember, it was the only animal that had ever disliked him. On several occasions, the ferocious dog almost took a chunk out of him as it rammed its spittle-covered jaws through the gate, but oddly enough, there was no sign of the animal today.

Joe fought his sagging eyelids, sucked in another yawn, and smiled despite the strange atmosphere. The aroma of baking bread from Mrs. Parkin's home bakery near the edge of the woods reminded him that Upton Puddle would always hold fond memories—especially on a Sunday. Collecting rejected loaves from her backyard was one of the many things that made his paper round such a pleasurable routine. He stared through the trees, straining for a glimpse of the puffy clouds rising from her chimney, but these days it was hard to see. A huge tower block loomed on the far side of the woods, swallowing the sunrise and spoiling Joe's view. It soared far above the tips of the ancient oak trees, glowering at the forest with its deep red brickwork and long shadow. Joe hated it.

Less than a year ago, Redwar Industries—a research company with a monstrous appetite—had turned its hungry eye on the unassuming village of Upton Puddle and built its head office right in the heart of the community. Each passing month the industrial park chewed its way through the woodland, replacing trees with scaffolding and ponds with concrete and parking lots. Maybe it was Redwar Industrial Park that had frightened off all the animals.

Joe kept his smile, trying to ignore the presence of the Redwar building. He rubbed the heel of a hand into one eye and relaxed into a final yawn before the early morning snooze took him.

Perhaps it was the uncanny silence or the lingering thoughts of Redwar's building that caused Joe's dreams to be so strange. Whatever the reason, Joe was startled by how real it all seemed. But even more startling was the fact that he actually *knew* he was dreaming—it was a rare treat. Having never left the shores of England, Joe didn't recognize the tropical surroundings of his dream world, but he instinctively knew he was walking on the beach of an island far from home. Scorching sand burned the soles of his bare feet, and a hot gale tugged at his ragged clothes as he pressed forward. Squinting through fierce sunlight, Joe took in the impressive landscape. Gaping caverns lined the edges of a crescent-shaped cliff edge to his left. Ruling the horizon above the caves, a structure stood that Joe knew from the world outside his dreams.

A vast tower, wider and taller than any he had seen before, weaved a twisted path into the sky, its tip obscured by clouds. Enormous extensions reached at crooked angles from the walls, and it was then that Joe realized the whole thing looked exactly like a gigantic, leafless tree. It was even made of wood, as if the designers had decided to cut down all the trees on the island to construct one monstrous imitation in the center. Even knowing he was in the middle of a dream, Joe was curious and quickened his pace, determined to find out who or what lived inside before he woke up.

Joe stopped, aghast, when the details became clearer. At the end of each branch, objects that looked like bunched grapes from a distance revealed themselves to be clumps of bulbous eyes, all staring intently at Joe. Then came a series of terrible sounds. A roar of fire belched from the caverns, forcing Joe to stagger backwards, shielding himself from the heat. A thundering vibration of galloping feet and terrified yelps drove Joe into a panicking sprint away from the cliffs and toward the sea. He could not see the source of the sounds, but it was enough to know they were heading his way. It was time to wake up.

Joe lurched from the tree stump, half dazed and still raw with alarm and bewilderment. It took a second to realize that some of the sounds still echoing in his thoughts were not just creations of his imagination but were actually happening in the woods surrounding him. The silence had been shattered by the yelps and growls of one wild animal being attacked by another.

Joe rubbed his eyes and scrambled to his feet, glancing between the trunks of large oaks, looking for signs of the struggle. Perhaps Mr. Gordon's rottweiler had escaped and was running, crazed, through the woods. Perhaps he would be next!

The commotion paused and Joe crouched, holding his breath, staying as still as he possibly could. Bulky steps came from behind, too heavy to belong to a dog, even one as large as the Gordons'. Joe turned his head slowly, hoping his movement would not draw attention to whatever was lurking. Something dark and hairy moved behind a tree less than thirty feet away.

It was hard to see properly in the half light, but Joe was convinced it was taller than a man. It slouched like an ape and, with massive hairy feet, prodded at something motionless on the ground that looked like a badger. It shuffled as if in confusion, scratching its side with long spindly fingers, then stretched its mouth wide to reveal a set of decayed fangs. The roar that followed was cut short when Joe jumped in shock. The ape thing snapped its mouth shut with a loud clack and ducked as it stared in Joe's direction.

With a mop of straw-colored hair and a bright blue T-shirt to match his eyes, Joe knew he would not be well camouflaged, and sure enough, the creature saw him.

Great emerald eyes glared at Joe as the creature's lips curled into a snarl.

Joe swallowed hard. His throat felt as dry as the sand he had been dreaming about only moments ago, and cold shock froze him as he stared at the thing crouching between the trees. The staring continued for several long seconds, and as each moment passed, Joe chided himself for not looking away. He'd read enough books to know that maintaining eye contact was a sign of aggression for most animals, but Joe couldn't help himself.

Astoundingly, the creature seemed to lose interest. It turned away, loped off a few steps into the forest, and shuffled down into a mound of earth, disappearing from view.

Joe waited a full minute before making another move. Watching his surroundings, he crept toward the creature's victim, dragging his trolley with him, and found that his suspicions were right—it was a badger. The poor animal was on its side, breathing slowly and making no attempt to escape from Joe as he approached. Taking great care not to make sudden moves, Joe edged closer, holding a thick stick near the badger's mouth in case it decided to bite. If the animal was badly injured, it probably wouldn't attack, but Joe knew not to take any chances.

After a few awkward maneuvers, Joe had safely wrapped the injured badger in his jacket and placed it in his trolley. It was time to wake up Mr. Wheeler, the vet.

Three raps on Argoyle Redwar's office door announced the arrival of another doomed employee. The director frowned at the wooden panels, then at his secretary, who stared back at him through disturbingly thick glasses.

"Who's that?" he growled.

The small woman, semiconsumed by a leather chair, continued to gawk. Her eyes widened only slightly as she tilted her head and mumbled something about not seeing through walls.

"Come in," Redwar boomed.

The door opened, and a well-groomed man wearing a cautious but friendly smile stepped inside, clasping a folder against his chest.

"I do apolo—"

"Door!" Redwar thumbed his way through a planner, hardly interested in the visitor.

The man hesitated, then closed the door and smiled nervously at the secretary, who squinted back. An embarrassing silence followed as the employee glanced around the huge windowless office, the mahogany paneling, the meager lighting, and the long line of animal heads gazing down with lifeless eyes. There were only three chairs: one at the far end of the room, another for the secretary, and behind a monstrous desk, the throne-like chair for Argoyle Redwar.

Redwar shifted in his seat. This was the third replacement chair since his office had been refurbished. Having fired the last two employees for cautiously suggesting it might be his weight causing the chair to groan, Redwar had decided a director's chair was probably supposed to do that.

"I don't have an eleven o'clock in my planner," said

Redwar, not looking up.

"Yes, sir. The name's Brant. Gregory Brant from archives? I was due to see you at nine, but I'm afraid we had an emergency. Dr. Golding collapsed, and I had to call an ambu—"

"You didn't think to warn me you'd be late?"

"I left a message with Ms. Burrowdown. She said—"

Redwar finally looked up. "Did he?"

Ms. Burrowdown nodded.

Redwar eyed his employee. "So you're Gregory Brant."

"Yes, sir."

"Know why I called you in here?"

"No, sir."

"You've been putting a lot of hours in this week, haven't you, Brant?"

The man's shoulders relaxed slightly. "Erm, yes, sir. There are a lot of projects which needed—"

"And you didn't think we'd notice?"

Brant looked confused. "Well . . . I had hoped that I'd earn a little recognition for my efforts since—"

"I'm not a fool." Redwar picked up his planner and slammed it down, causing the employee to wince. "You know what I'm talking about."

"I'm sorry, sir. I—"

"Theft is a very serious thing, especially for a man on a salary as large as yours."

"Sir, I can assure you, I—"

"Don't even *think* about denying it. The security cameras showed you stacking several boxes of confidential files into the boot of your car after hours yesterday."

"Well, of course, sir, the planning department instructed me to—"

"To what? To steal?"

Brant, his mouth agape, said nothing.

Redwar glowered. "I'll have security escort you off-site, and your personal effects will be posted to you in the morning along with your official letter of dismissal. I'm a reasonable man, so I won't be reporting this to the police on this occasion, but rest assured, I won't hesitate to contact them if you go whining to your union representative. Understood?"

"No, sir. I—"

"Good day, Mr. Brant."

Redwar returned to his planner, angrily thumbing through the pages.

Brant remained where he was, openmouthed.

"Well? Why are you still here?"

"Sir, I really must protest. I was not stealing anything. I—"

"I said good day, Mr. Brant."

Brant carefully placed his folder on the desk in front of Redwar and, after a puzzled glance at Ms. Burrowdown, walked silently out of the office. The door clicked shut behind him.

Ms. Burrowdown approached the desk and uttered

something unintelligible just as Redwar punched a button. A ring sounded on the speakerphone.

"What? Speak up, woman."

Ms. Burrowdown took Brant's folder and waved it at him.

He waved back dismissively. "Oh, just file it away. I'll look at it later."

She stepped back from the desk and opened the folder.

A voice crackled on Redwar's phone. "Hello, sir. Security here."

Ms. Burrowdown thrust the open file under Redwar's nose. "Yooshd takeylook."

"A moment, please," he said at the phone before turning on his secretary. "What?"

She jabbed a bony finger at the paperwork, and Redwar glared at it.

PLANNING DEPARTMENT—REF:65KT175

ORDER FOR DESTRUCTION OF DOCUMENTATION TO MR. G BRANT.

DOCUMENTATION FOR DESTRUCTION:
Architectural Designs, Planning Applications, Surveyor Reports, Budget Plans.

REASON:
Purchase offer to Merrynether estate rejected by owner.

Planning permission for extended building contracts denied. Expansion plans into Ringwood Forest rejected. Architectural designs no longer required.

Redwar shifted his glare to Ms. Burrowdown. "The planning department abandoned my expansion plans because of that Merrynether woman?"

Ms. Burrowdown stared back.

Redwar huffed. "I want the head of the planning department fired too. Get him up here after lunch."

"Sir? Did you need a security guard?" repeated the voice on the phone.

Redwar pushed the file aside. "Yes. Send someone up here immediately. I need to have an employee escorted off-site."

Ms. Burrowdown continued to stare as he switched off the speakerphone.

"What? You think Brant's innocent? So what?" Redwar jabbed a finger at her. "The man had no backbone. If an employee of mine can't stand up for himself, I don't want him on my payroll. I despise cowardice, Ms. Burrowdown. Remember that."

Mr. Wheeler observed Joe sympathetically over the top of his gold-rimmed spectacles and scratched his head through a clump of grey hair that had not long ago left a pillow. "I'm afraid there's nothing I can do for you,

Joe. We're just too busy this morning. We already have two cats and a rabbit to deal with. And a few minutes ago, I got a call from the Gordons. Their rottweiler's had a nasty bite. I'm not even supposed to open for another two hours." The old man smiled an apology toward a queue of people seated behind Joe.

Joe turned to look at the array of frowning men and women, each clutching a shivering animal or a small cage to which they were murmuring words of baby-talk comfort. "But you always help out, Mr. Wheeler." Joe pushed his trolley closer and offered him the badger and an expectant smile.

"I know. And it's commendable of you to keep your eyes open for injured animals, but this is a business, you know. I can't help you every time."

Joe looked at him silently.

A forlorn look held long enough might normally have swayed the old vet, but Mr. Wheeler smiled all the more. "I have to give priority to paying customers, see?"

"I'll pay," said Joe, rummaging through his pockets.

"I'm sure you would." Mr. Wheeler smiled and ruffled Joe's tangled hair. "Truth is, lad, things have been a little crazy in the last couple of weeks. Maybe it's the Beast, eh?"

"Beast?"

"Yes, the Beast of Upton Puddle. You deliver papers every morning. Haven't you heard of it?"

"No."

"It was on the front page yesterday. Some people even think it's bigfoot; others say it's a wolf. But ever since the first sighting two weeks ago, we've been run off our feet here with pets and livestock."

"I think I saw it half an hour ago in Ringwood Forest."

"You did, huh?" The vet looked over the top of his glasses.

"Yes, I think so. It looked a bit like an ape or something, but it was huge."

"Well, I'd better ring the police," the vet said, reaching for the phone. "Whatever it is, they'll need to cordon off the area."

"My badger?"

Mr. Wheeler paused as he picked up the receiver and looked at the motionless mammal. With his free hand, he picked up a large book from a pile near the phone and placed it on the counter. "Here. This is a directory of all the veterinary practices, wildlife sanctuaries, and animal keepers in the county. Take a look through there. One of them might be able to help you if you're lucky."

"Thanks."

Joe flopped the directory open and leafed through the thin pages while the vet spoke with a police officer.

Carmichael Veterinary Practice . . . Farringdon Dogs Home . . . Haltsworth Rescue Center. Joe stopped there and traced the writing with his finger, reading aloud.

"Specializing in the rescue and shelter of a wide variety of animals, great and small. Members of the ADCH and practitioners of the Merrynether Techniques."

The name *Merrynether* seemed familiar. Joe thought carefully as he scanned through the directory. Several other entries also made mention of the Merrynether Technique, and then the thought came to him: it was a name engraved on a plaque decorating the gate of a mansion he'd seen on his paper round. Could this be the same person?

Mr. Wheeler was still busy on the phone when a flustered Mr. Gordon burst in, dragged along by his insane rottweiler. The slavering monster spotted Joe instantly. Drawing in a rattling breath, it exploded into a psychotic episode of barking.

Joe decided it was way past time to leave. He placed the book on the counter, waved to Mr. Wheeler, and pulled his trolley and badger out of the building.

Wrapped snug and warm inside Joe's jacket, the badger seemed untroubled by the bumpy trolley ride as they neared the end of Merrynether Mansion's long driveway. Joe took a moment to admire the grandeur of the building as it came into view. The magnificent Elizabethan house was eclipsed by enormous oak trees and obscured by untamed creepers, as if in submission to nature. An overabundance of leaves and colorful blossoms almost overwhelmed its ancient red bricks and dark beams. At the base of the mansion was the main entrance, also under threat by an array of unruly plant life. Had it not been for the white van parked by the side of the building, Joe could have imagined he'd been transported to a time when the owners would walk the grounds dressed in medieval garb and speaking the kind of language heard only in dated movies.

Joe left his trolley by the entrance and tentatively peered around the corner at the van. The engine was running. "Hello?" he called.

No answer.

Joe walked to the mansion's front door and, seeing a pull cord, tugged it. A deep chime sounded from somewhere within the house. Joe waited, feeling oddly nervous.

A minute passed before the door swung open. For a split second, Joe expected to see a tall butler with a pale, thin face, but he was greeted by somebody completely different.

"Yes, young man? Can I help you?"

For some reason that Joe could not fathom, he simply stared, unable to answer. An old lady stood before him. She was even shorter than he was, dressed in a bright red gown, almost royal in appearance. Her head was crowned with a rich hive of black hair in which not a single white strand could be seen. Her twinkling grey eyes acknowledged him from behind a pair of huge spectacles. There were so many lines carved into her skin that Joe wondered if she even needed ears to support her glasses at all.

"Young man?" she tried again with a friendly smile that miraculously produced even more lines on her face.

"I . . . Badger!" Joe pointed at the trolley, feeling extremely stupid.

"Excuse me?"

Joe's cheeks flushed. Why he felt so odd, he was not sure, but the strangest of premonitions crossed his mind as he looked at this unusual old lady—as though he were about to step inside the house and into a world that would turn his life upside down and inside out.

"I'm very sorry," he said, finally shaking the peculiar feeling. "Are you Mrs. Merrynether?"

"That's the name on the gate." She continued to smile.

"Then I'm sorry to disturb you, but—"

A loud crash, the sound of something very heavy slamming into metal, came from the direction of the van.

"Do come in," the old lady said suddenly. And before Joe knew what was happening, she pulled him inside with his trolley and closed the door. "Badger, you say? In the trolley? Hurt, is it?"

"Um . . . yes. Can you—?"

"Oh, dear me, no, young man. What's your name?"

"I'm, uh, Joe Copper," he said, being bustled through another door and into a huge leather armchair.

"Well, what brings you here, Master Copper? Oh, yes . . . the badger. Would you like a cup of tea?" She was rubbing her hands together now, looking every-where in the room except at Joe, as if he were a distraction she needed to remove in a hurry.

"Actually, I—"

"Well, good. Good! I'll get you one."

There was another crash, farther inside the house, followed by the muffled yowl of something that sounded very much like a giant cat being stuffed into a sack.

This time she looked at him, eyes wide, lips pursed.

Joe stared back.

A silent agreement passed between them that the noise was not to be mentioned.

"The badger," they both blurted at the same time, then paused.

"Well, young man, how about this? I'll help your badger if you help me. I need some things from the local store."

"Really?"

"Yes. Now wait just there, and I'll fetch some money and write you a list." She hurried from the room.

Joe sat in the chair, fingers digging into the soft leather.

Like the outside of the house, the inside was sub-dued. Tiny arched windows covered in ivy allowed only the thinnest rays of light to enter the room, and flickering candles illuminated areas the sun could not reach. Tall bookcases and antiquated cupboards were filled with dusty tomes and tatty encyclopedias. A bat-tered grandfather clock ticktocked in one corner, and a round card table with a chipped decanter, half filled with ruby-red drink, was placed by the chair.

"Here you are, Joseph," she said, returning almost as quickly as she had left. She stuffed three crumpled pieces of paper into his right hand.

"Now off you go, and I'll have that pot of tea nicely brewed by the time you come back." She hurried him out of the room, through the hall, and out of the house with his badgerless trolley, then slammed the door.

Joe opened his hand to look at the pieces of paper. One was a list:

> 1 pot of strawberry jam
> 20 liters of Irish whiskey
> 10 bags of natural clay cat litter
> 14 hot water bottles
> Toothpaste

The other two pieces of paper were fifty-pound notes!

TWO

By the time Joe had returned to Merrynether Mansion, his arms burned. He'd dragged his trolley and its heavy cargo all the way through the village, along the country lane, and up the bumpy driveway. Angry blisters stung his fingers, but the job would have been impossible without his set of wheels.

He let go of the handle and yanked the bellpull, grimacing as the rope bit into his sore hand. The low chime sounded, and Joe took another look at the contents of his trolley. What on earth would anybody want with so many hot water bottles, and what kind of mammoth feline would need so much litter? Joe ran the numbers in his head, calculating the volume of cat litter, duration of use, and possible weight of such an animal. He grinned as he imagined a twenty-foot kitten squatting in a bathtub. Then he remembered the feral yowl within the house less than an hour before. What exactly did Mrs. Merrynether have in there?

The five bags of cat litter loaded onto his trolley cushioned the bottles of Irish whiskey. In most towns, no responsible retailer would ever sell alcohol to a twelve-year-old boy, but Upton Puddle was a small village with a close community. Reginald Bacon, the village storekeeper, knew a customer's list when he saw one, and apparently he was accustomed to seeing bizarre requests from the Merrynether residence.

Joe tugged at the rope again, wondering why there had been no response. Again the chime sounded, and he waited patiently for another minute, picturing more outlandish visions of giant saber-toothed tigers eating bucketfuls of cat food and playing with yarn coils the size of bowling balls.

Still no one came to the door. If the old woman didn't show up and he didn't leave soon, he'd be in a lot of trouble when he got home. He was already late, and his mother would be wondering where he was.

He walked around the side of the house where the white van had been parked. In the ground was an old, square oak door. A latch and a rusty padlock held it shut, but its subtle angle told Joe the padlock had not been closed properly. After glancing around, he knelt and, with a little help from his penknife and his overactive sense of curiosity, worked the padlock free from the door. A pang of guilt interrupted him, but for a boy like Joe, it was too late to worry about something so trivial.

He'd made his mind up. He was going inside—just to look around; that was all.

The door creaked so horrendously that he almost dropped it. He continued anyway, and peculiar odors wafted up as he opened it fully. Raspberry mixed with creosote, cheese with a hint of freshly cut grass, wet dog and a sour smell he could not identify—all these assaulted him as he peered into the gloomy cellar.

A set of brick steps beckoned. Ignoring a squirming sensation in his stomach and the pumping in his chest, Joe crept inside. By now the cat in his mind was a monstrous black moggy waiting in a corner, licking its teeth, ready to pounce. He expected a huge pair of green eyes to blink open right in front of his face, and it was precisely then that he remembered his encounter in Ringwood Forest. He was about to turn back when a voice yelled out. It was the shout of someone very annoyed, very Irish, and possibly very drunk.

"Torn dat loight out, would ya? Can't a fella get a little shut-oy when 'e wants ta?"

Joe froze. His eyes were adjusting to the darkness of the cellar, but his nerves were not as eager to follow suit. The words almost stuck in his throat as he called, "Hello?"

"Hello! Hello!" the voice spat back in a mocking tone. "Six horse loads of graveyard clay on top o' ya! Would ya clorse dat bloody door!"

"Uh . . . yes, sorry!" Joe rushed back, wondering

why he was shutting himself in a dank cellar with an abusive Irishman.

The door slammed shut. Without the glaring daylight spoiling his peripheral vision, Joe could see his surroundings. The cellar was far bigger than he expected, packed with an array of tools, workbenches, wooden cages, clockwork contraptions, outrageous apparatuses, tables and chairs, boxes and books, crates and cartons, bottles and bags. The only open spaces were where doors were set into the brickwork. At the center of the cellar was yet another large trapdoor, but it was a wooden cage placed next to it that really grabbed Joe's attention. His mouth hung open.

"Wot are ya gawpin' at, ya snotty-norsed little ankle boiter!" With tiny pink hands gripping the wooden bars, a man no more than a foot in height and dressed in a sky-blue waistcoat and pantaloons, puffed out his shiny red cheeks in frustration. He chewed on a smoker's pipe with his miniature white teeth and stared at Joe with fiery eyes.

Joe's feelings of apprehension fell away instantly as he looked down at the angry creature. A huge grin split Joe's face. "You're calling *me* an ankle biter? You're a pixie!"

"Pixie? A bloody pixie?" The little man almost swallowed his pipe in rage as he jumped up and down inside his apparent prison. "How dare ya! How *dare* ya! Pixie, me granny's armpit. Don't ya know a cluricaun when ya sees one?"

"A what? A loony corn?"

"Let me outa here and oi'l stick dis fist up ya nostril."

Joe laughed and sat in front of the cage, watching the tirade.

"Oi'l slap seven bails of—"

The sound of a clicking padlock came from behind Joe. A wave of cold shock stifled his laughing. He was locked in! But was it an accident, or did somebody do that on purpose?

The tiny Irishman ceased his ranting, watching Joe with his mouth forming a ridiculing O. "Oh, dearie, dearie me! Da little boy's a goner!"

"But I haven't done anything. I only wanted to—"

"He-he, yes, indeedee. A goner he is." The tiny man's anger had suddenly turned to glee.

"Which one of these doors gets me upstairs?"

"Oooo, dat'll cost ya," he said, removing the pipe from his mouth and casually tapping the tobacco out. "Oi'm a little thirsty. A bit droy in de old cake horl, if ya take me meaning."

"But I don't have anything to drink. Just tell me how to get out."

The little man raised his eyebrows as he settled his gaze upon a cobwebbed wine rack in the far corner.

"Wine? You want wine?"

"Of course oi want some woine, ya stoopid boy. Now let me outa dis cage, would ya?"

Joe eyed him. "I think I'll just pick one of those

Simon West-Bulford

doors and try my luck."

"Oooo, oi wouldn't do dat if oi were you."

"Why?"

"Troo one door, da way out. Troo de udder door," he whispered in tones of melodrama, "certain death."

Joe raised an eyebrow. "Certain death? Which one?"

"Get me outa dis bloody cage, and oi'l tells ya," he screamed back.

"Tell me first, and *then* I'll let you out."

"All roight, all roight. Go troo da green door, but never go troo da red door."

"Got it. The green door takes me upstairs."

"Aye, now let a little fella out, would ya?"

"I'd like to check first, if you don't mind."

The angry man rolled his eyes.

Joe edged to the red door and pressed his ear against the cold wood. No sound came from behind it. Joe looked at the black doorknob.

"Oi said da green door!"

"I know. I'm just curious."

"Curiosity killed da cat, ya knor."

"Is there a cat in there? A big one, I mean?" Joe was still looking at the red door, his hand poised above the knob.

The cluricaun crossed his arms. "Moi lips are sealed."

Joe eyed the knob for a few more seconds before forcing his attention to the green door. With his breath held, he turned the knob and pushed. Sure enough, a

32

set of carpeted stairs greeted him, and he let out a sigh of relief.

Perhaps he could get back to the entrance of the house unnoticed. But what would he say to Mrs. Merrynether? Was it she who had locked the padlock? And what was she doing with a cluricaun in her cellar? With each question wriggling like a worm in his stomach, Joe decided it was no use staying in the cellar. He had no choice but to take his chances.

He made a move for the stairs.

"Oi! Ya little tadpole, where d'ya tink you're goin'? Let me out!"

Joe looked at the little man and grinned. "I didn't say *when* I'd let you out, did I?"

And with that, he closed the door and sneaked up the stairs.

Behind him, through the closed door, echoed the ranting of a betrayed midget about to burst a blood vessel. "Ya backstabbin', slippery son of a pig farmer's poop shoveler. If oi ever foind ya, oi'l stick my pointy red boot roight up yer . . ."

The bellowing faded as Joe passed through another door into a cold pantry with a single door at the far end. Quickly but silently, he closed the trapdoor, tiptoed out of the room, crept along a hallway, and to his great relief found himself near the familiar entrance.

Joe hesitated, his fingers on the door handle. The events of the last ten minutes should have been enough to convince him to restrain his inquisitive nature, yet the same curiosity that drew him into the cellar ached for more information about Mrs. Merrynether and her ill-tempered tenant.

"Did you manage to get everything?"

Joe jumped when he heard the voice behind him. Breathless, he turned to see Mrs. Merrynether standing at the end of the hallway. Mrs. Merrynether's left forearm was wrapped tightly with a bandage; four distinct crimson lines, looking very much like a claw wound, bled through. Nestling by Mrs. Merrynether's feet and looking up at her was, unmistakably, a black potbellied pig.

Mrs. Merrynether continued to wrap linen around her arm as she watched Joe expectantly. "Well, Master Copper? Has the cat got your tongue?"

"Cat?" Joe stared at the pig.

Mrs. Merrynether followed his line of sight and smiled down at her friend. It was still looking at her, its snout wrinkling slightly as if it hoped for a morsel.

"Oh, don't worry about Archibald. He won't hurt you. Archy, go and say hello."

The small pig, apparently understanding her completely, turned his attention to Joe, snorted, and then half-skipped, half-trotted toward him. He butted Joe's leg and stared up with tiny eyes barely visible between great folds of skin.

"Hello," said Joe, scratching behind one of Archibald's ears.

The pig squealed and ran to Mrs. Merrynether's side.

"He likes you," she said, "but he's rather shy, I'm afraid."

"Oh . . . is he—?"

"Did you manage to get everything on the list?" she repeated.

"Um, no . . . not quite. Mr. Bacon has to order a few things in."

"Oh, dear. Did you get the water bottles?"

"Yes."

"The jam?"

"Yes."

"Out of cat litter, was he?"

"Yes, but I did get five bags."

"Hmm, well, that'll have to do. Can you bring it inside for me? As you can see, I'm not able to lift anything for the time being," she said, motioning to her injured arm.

"Right away, Mrs. Merrynether."

Joe was astounded she hadn't asked how he had entered the house. Perhaps she was coming to that. He opened the door and brought the trolley inside.

Mrs. Merrynether examined the contents briefly. With a mumble of approval, she wheeled it into another room out of sight.

"How did you hurt your arm?" Joe called after her. "Is my badger okay?"

"As you seem to have discovered, Joseph," she said

as she returned, "I spend much of my time attending to a great many different species. Some animals are less amiable than others when receiving treatment. Thankfully, your badger friend was less of a trial than . . . than my *other* patient I dealt with this morning. She's fine, by the way."

"Thank you."

"No. Thank *you*, young man," she said, ushering him toward the room he had sat in earlier.

On the small table, Joe saw a silver tray on which sat an old brown teapot, a jug of milk, and two teacups. The excited pig followed them in, found his way to a tatty tartan cushion, and flopped onto it with a satisfied grunt.

"I simply don't have the time or desire to go shopping for things these days. And it looks like I won't even be able to for a week or two anyway." She looked at the bandage on her arm with apparent irritation, as someone might look at a wasp that had landed on their sandwich.

Still nervous about being found out, Joe felt an uncontrollable urge to prove his good intentions. The words spilled from his mouth: "I come this way most days, Mrs. Merrynether. I can help you with your shopping."

"My! We *are* feeling enthusiastic, aren't we?" Her gaze was fixed firmly on Joe as she poured tea into the cups; it was a miracle it didn't spill everywhere.

"I just want to help."

"I'm sure you do. Did Mr. Bacon give you any change?"

"Oh! Yes. Sorry. I completely forgot. Hold on . . ." Joe rummaged in his pocket and pulled out two screwed-up notes and some loose change. At the precise moment he handed them to Mrs. Merrynether, a chill of fear almost choked him.

Something was missing from his pocket.

"Very well," she said, making her way to another chair close to the snoring pig. "You can start next Sunday. Come back here at the same time, and I'll have another list for you. It'll be quite a novelty having someone fetch my groceries for me. Is twenty pounds a reasonable payment? If not, we could always . . ."

Joe didn't hear the rest as hot panic surged through his stomach to his chest. He fished deeper in his pocket, then dug into another one. No doubt, it was gone. He searched the floor with rapid but furtive glances.

"Is something the matter, young man?"

Joe gulped, knowing his face was flushed yet again. He had no answer. Deep down, he knew exactly what had happened. The sneaky little man in the cellar had stolen his penknife!

*T*HREE

The week dragged by like a zombie with arthritis. A flood of worries saturated Joe's mind the whole time, and just as his face had so often been dunked in the toilet by the school's godfather of torture, Kurt Duggan, the events of each day were drowned in one long blur of embarrassment. He left his school books at home, he wore odd socks, and many lengthy moments of staring into space were captured by sniggering classmates on mobile phones. He even managed to wear a note on his blazer for two whole days that read, *Donkey rides—£1.*

And it was all because the same tormenting questions remained unanswered.

Had the cluricaun taken his penknife and escaped? What if Mrs. Merrynether knew? He hadn't let on that it was missing, but what if she found out? Surely she would. And what would she do about it if she *did* know? Should he go back early and confess all or just wait to see what would happen on Sunday? What other creatures was she hiding in that house?

Not one fact from any of his school lessons sunk in as he agonized over the possibilities, and his finger-wagging teachers had even felt the need to discuss Joe's distracted state with his mother. Naturally she was concerned, but to Joe's relief, her only action so far was to watch him with a concerned frown and ask if he felt ill.

But Sunday morning at last arrived, and with a hurricane of conflicting thoughts still jostling for control, Joe found himself standing outside the main door of Merrynether Mansion, waiting nervously for it to open.

The seconds seemed to drag almost as long as the last seven days had. Joe eyed the bellpull, chewing his lip like someone about to pull the stinger from a bee. His fingers teetered at the edge of the cord—and then his eyes focused on something he hadn't noticed before: an old plaque, obscured by dead vine leaves, directly behind the cord.

It read:

Tradesmen: Please use side entrance—Turn left.
Deliveries: Please use side entrance—Turn right.

As was always the case with Joe, curiosity lured him, and he found himself heading left to look for the trade entrance. It was not difficult to find. Not only was it revealed by a conspicuous door and sign, but Joe also heard a voice bellowing from inside. Though he could not see who was shouting, the thick and pompous tones, punctuated by occasional puffing and wheezing, suggested it was an incredibly fat businessman. The door was slightly ajar but not enough to see inside.

". . . And furthermore Mrs. Merrynether, if you continue to ignore my solicitors, I shall be forced to involve the police."

Then came the familiar voice of the old woman, considerably calmer than the other and laced with more than a hint of sarcasm. "Mr. Redwar—or may I call you Argoyle? Is it really so hard to understand my previous replies to your office? There is no need for these legalities; therefore, I shall not respond to them. And *do* stop shouting—surely a man with such a low IQ ought to have a low voice to match."

Joe expected a returning tirade, but instead, the voice took on a quiet and far more menacing tone. "Need I remind you, Mrs. Merrynether, that I know enough about your little . . . menagerie here to have you imprisoned for the rest of your life? My secretary has a detailed portfolio. Isn't that right, Ms. Burrowdown?"

There was a mumbling response that Joe could not hear clearly, and his curiosity ballooned like a puffer fish on steroids. He had to see what was going on.

Gingerly, he pushed the door open. "Hello?"

Four faces turned toward him.

Mrs. Merrynether was standing, hands clasped,

behind a worn mahogany serving counter surrounded by dusty bottles and books, an antique cash register, and an old bell that had evidently been untouched for years. The bandage that covered her arm the day before had been replaced by a smaller one but still revealed the stains of what must have been a nasty wound underneath. Despite that and the obvious hostility directed toward her a moment ago, she wore a sweet smile and seemed perfectly relaxed, which was more than could be said of the ogre directly in front of her.

Mr. Redwar was exactly as Joe imagined from his voice. The towering mountain of blubber squeezed into an immaculate suit was topped with an equally bloated face resembling an oversized tomato on the brink of explosion. A large toothy mouth exaggerated by a bushy moustache dominated his features, but the man's eyes drew Joe's attention most. Though they were small, they expressed a riot of emotions—none of them positive: anger, greed, impatience. Joe could read all of that.

A woman even smaller than Mrs. Merrynether stood close to Redwar. Joe decided this must have been the puffing man's secretary, Ms. Burrowdown, whose appearance seemed to fit her name. She resembled a mole in human form wearing glasses with lenses as thick and wide as the bottoms of pint glasses. Even with such magnification, her eyes were mere slits, and it appeared she was straining her neck with maximum effort to scrutinize Joe. In her tiny hands she clutched a notepad and pen that looked as if they might spring into the air if she relaxed her grip.

Archy the pig stood in a doorway directly behind the counter. His curly tail wiggled, and his ears perked up at the sight of a new and exciting entrant.

Joe looked at the peculiar group and could not stop an involuntary snort of laughter. Whether it was amusement or nerves, he was unsure, but the result was a hush that smothered even the silence accompanied by the staring. Fortunately that silence was brief. Brief because Mr. Redwar was not about to allow such an intrusion to be overlooked.

"Something amuses you, boy?"

"I . . . er . . ." Joe fumbled for a reply but was quickly rescued by a recognizable voice from a hidden source.

"Ah! Well, you're makin' me laff, fatty! Anyone wit a nose loik dat ought not underloin it wit whiskers."

The awkward silence descended once again, and for a few tense seconds, all eyes were still locked on Joe as he bit down on another laugh.

Redwar, shocked and outraged, could not contain his temper. "Who said that? Who's there?"

But the cluricaun made no more taunts.

"I will not be mocked in this way, Merrynether," Redwar said. "I came here in good faith to offer you a very reasonable resolution to our mutual problem, and you choose to respond in a most unprofessional manner. Now, either accept my generous terms or cooperate with my solicitors. Your only other alternative is to submit to the authorities, and neither of us want that, do we?"

The response was equally resolute. "Firstly, Mr. Redwar, I need do nothing of the kind. There is no mutual problem. The problem is yours alone; I am perfectly within my rights to stay here. And secondly, shouting and ranting is not something *I* would deem to be professional conduct. If you continue in this manner, I will be the one who calls the police. Do I make myself clear?"

Ms. Burrowdown wagged her pen at Mrs. Merrynether. As the woman spoke, Joe realized it was not the door that had prevented him from hearing what she had to say earlier. "You shud beshamed self. Mr. Redwar only try telp people."

"What?" Redwar turned on her. "How many times do I have to tell you? Speak up, woman!" He turned back to the counter, placed a great sausage finger on a brown envelope, and shoved it closer to Mrs. Merrynether. "You have no more than two weeks for a satisfactory reply. Redwar Industries is the fastest-growing industry in this country, and I do not take kindly to obstructions of its progress. Do *I* make myself clear?"

"I'll not open it," she said, pushing the envelope back.

Redwar leaned over the counter, using his full bulk to look as intimidating as possible. "I think you will, Merrynether. In fact"—he appeared to be making the decision there and then as he pointed a threatening finger at her face—"I'll not leave here until I see you reading it."

Redwar had gone one step too far for one of the observers. At the sight of the threat leaning over the counter, Archy squealed, raced from the doorway, and charged with head bowed at his unsuspecting victim. The hairy head connected with Redwar's leg, producing a satisfying thud, and the bulky man staggered back with a cry of shock. Archy squealed again and prepared for another charge.

Redwar regained his balance, grabbed Ms. Burrowdown by the arm, and moved with unexpected speed for the door.

Archy stopped short at a command from Mrs. Merrynether, but the deed was done and the startled duo were already out of sight.

Redwar's angry but wheezing retort sounded from the grounds outside. "Two weeks, Merrynether . . . Two weeks!"

After a long sigh of relief, she replied, "Obnoxious oaf."

"That was Argoyle Redwar? The man who owns that massive factory behind Ringwood Forest?"

"Quite so, Joseph, but please don't concern yourself with that unfortunate conversation. It was most unprofessional of him to approach me like that."

Joe was about to ask what it was all about anyway when Mrs. Merrynether's expression suddenly sharpened. She glanced about and waved a fist. "And you're not helping matters either, Lilly. Making Mr. Redwar angry will only make things worse."

"Ah, stoff 'im. If 'e comes back again, oi'l climb up 'is trouser leg and boite 'is—"

"So, Joseph," Mrs. Merrynether said, "this is your second week in my service. I'm very pleased to see that you've returned. Are you ready for the next list?"

Joe measured her expression. Either she had an expert poker face or she suspected nothing about the events of last Sunday. Whichever, he decided it would seem suspicious if he didn't at least ask about Redwar's antagonist.

"Mrs. Merrynether, who's Lilly?"

She sighed and rolled her eyes. "Oh, dear, I was so hoping to avoid this . . . See what you've done, Lilly?" She stabbed a finger toward Joe while addressing the ceiling. "One more word out of place, and I'll set Archy on you."

The cluricaun remained silent.

With a satisfied shrug, Mrs. Merrynether returned her attention to Joe. A curious twinkle flashed in her eyes. Her look stretched into a gaze and then to a penetrating stare. And all the while, as Joe's vision tunneled on Mrs. Merrynether's face, the strange sense of premonition he experienced when he first met her returned with all the mystique of a long lost destiny tapping at the edge of his soul.

"Tell me, Joseph, do you think you are special?"

The question jolted him but not enough to dampen the atmosphere.

"Isn't everyone special?"

"Ah, yes. But there's special and there's . . . *special*. Do *you* think you're special?"

"I don't know what you mean."

"Well, to be special you have to think you're special. Some people will say that you're arrogant if you dare to think of yourself that way, but did you know, Joseph, that to be special is a choice? That's all it is."

Joe smiled.

"I'm perfectly serious. Do you know what an epiphany is?"

Joe shook his head.

The old woman gently placed her hands upon his shoulders. Her voice lowered almost to a whisper. "Then I'll tell you. There comes a time in a person's life when that choice to be special hits them square between the eyes. It's a wonderful moment but a terrible moment too. Most people look away and go back to their boring lives, frightened of what might happen, but some people . . . some people *seize* that moment and see life for what it really is. *That's* an epiphany, Joseph."

She paused, squeezing his shoulders a little tighter. "You're a little younger than most, but I have a feeling about you, and I'm giving you the chance to seize the moment right now. How do you feel about that?"

Joe was breathless and more than a little taken aback. He had no idea what she was talking about, but with such an overwhelming sense of fate and curiosity tugging at his innards, Joe knew there was only one choice to be made. "You mean right now, as in . . . *right* now?"

"Most certainly. I think you can be trusted, and I know Lilly likes you."

"Do not!"

Joe ignored the voice. "Here?"

"Not quite. As a matter of fact, it's through a door in my cellar. Are you ready?"

"Yes."

"Then follow me."

And with that, Mrs. Merrynether took one of Joe's hands and led him out of the room.

Instinctively, Joe knew exactly where they were heading.

FOUR

Fragrances, whether foul or fair, often have the effect of bringing past events to the forefront of one's thoughts with startling clarity. That was exactly the experience Joe had when he stepped back into Mrs. Merrynether's cellar. Anxiety and wonder wrestled within him as he breathed the same peculiar odors that greeted him the first time he set foot there.

Mrs. Merrynether muttered curses over a set of rusty keys as she hunched before the ominous red door. Joe glanced around, reacquainting himself with the cellar, and his gaze settled on the wooden cage at the center of the room. It was empty. He knew it would be, but the clear evidence that he'd aided the escape of a mad Irish midget knotted his stomach. A fresh impulse to come clean about his part in the affair ballooned within him but was quickly deflated by an exclamation from the old woman.

"Ah! Here we are. Key nine—always forget."

She inserted the key, turned it, and opened the door. A set of stone steps, at least forty of them, beckoned them farther underground and Mrs. Merrynether led the way in silence to another red door. With her fingers on the handle, she paused and looked at Joe over the top of her spectacles.

"Your epiphany awaits. Are you ready?"

"I—"

"Too bad if you aren't. It's coming anyway." And without delay, she pushed the door open to reveal not a cupboard or a storeroom but a huge vault, much larger than the cellar they had just left. Merrynether walked in, stepped to one side, and watched Joe with obvious anticipation.

Joe edged inside, slightly stooping, mouth agape and eyes wide as though he had stepped onto holy ground.

Stone walls, almost hidden by a vast array of shoddy crates, tall cages, and a host of old unfamiliar machinery, stretched out far ahead of him. At regular intervals along the vault, dusty shafts of sunlight filtered through latticed hatchways in the high ceiling, providing just enough illumination for a number of large pens. Joe caught teasing glimpses of shuffling shadows within most of them, but the enclosure closest to him was what really captured his attention.

It was the size of a small garden. Turf, grass, wildflowers, and ornamental rocks decorated it, and there was even a quaint water feature trickling a gentle melody at the back. It was exactly the sort of sculptured display Joe had seen at a zoo he'd visited recently with his school. The animal on display in Merrynether's vault, however, was a completely different matter.

At first Joe thought he was looking at a tiger or a lion leaning against a pile of hot water bottles, fast asleep. But that, Joe realized, was his mind's instant attempt to make sense of what he was looking at; this beast was nothing like either of those animals. Sure, it had a silky coat and, yes, a large head with a shaggy mane, but most tigers have golden fur with black stripes. This beast's coat was dark red, mottled with black rings of various sizes, and glistened with a curious waxy sheen. But most of all, tigers are not usually known to have a set of enormous crimson-feathered wings.

A surge of excitement, starting from his toes and ending as a buzzing sensation tickling his scalp, caused Joe to suck in a long faltering breath. Discovering a cluricaun the previous week was astonishing enough, but somehow that tiny man with his thick Irish accent and human characteristics still seemed like something that could be explained away—like someone you'd see in the *Guinness World Records* or maybe at a carnival. But this? Whatever Joe was staring at now had trespassed well over the line separating fantasy from reality.

As if sensing Joe's awe, the creature lifted its head from its grassy pillow and looked directly at him. Joe's first impression was of a cat waking lazily from a long sleep to make a halfhearted attempt at detecting what sort of noise had woken it. But Joe's breath halted in his lungs when he saw its features. The face, sharing the deep red tone of its fur, had undeniable human qualities. Nose, lips, ears, even the structure of its cheekbones and chin—all looked human. Even the eyes, though distinctly yellow with slitted catlike pupils, had a human quality about them—a hint of intelligence not normally seen in the expression of animals. The teeth, on the other hand, were not so human in form. The creature yawned, unhinging a set of interlocking fangs that looked like they could rip through a car and then chomp on it as if it were a Gummy Bear. For several seconds, the creature proudly displayed the depths of its cavernous throat. A curious melodic sound gargled outward, as if it had swallowed a drowning opera singer. After a lick of its lips with a black, forked tongue, it snapped its mouth shut and stared nonchalantly at Joe.

"He's a little worse than yesterday," said Mrs. Merrynether. "By this time, he's usually pacing around his pen expecting his supper."

"Oh," was all Joe could manage.

"Yes, in fact he hardly ate a thing yesterday. If I can't diagnose his problem soon, I have grave concerns about my ability to treat him at all."

The creature flopped its head down, releasing a deep sigh.

Mrs. Merrynether walked to the wall next to the

pen and pulled on a length of rope. A metallic rumbling sounded from nearby, and through a hatch in the roof, several lumps of raw meat came tumbling out.

"Cornelius?" called Mrs. Merrynether. "Din-dins."

The beast didn't even lift its head. Instead it swooshed its long tail through the air as if annoyed by the disturbance and thwacked it down to the ground, sending up a spray of earth. Joe took a step back when he saw why the tail had made such a hard thump in the turf. Rather than a fur tip, the tail ended with a brown, pinecone-shaped growth, barbed with hundreds of long white needles.

"Mrs. Merrynether," said Joe, finally finding his voice. "What *is* that?"

"I thought you'd never ask," she said with a sly smile. "This species is known as Antathalicus respudicus Nimbrosii—better known to the world of mythology as . . . a manticore."

"Manticore," whispered Joe, not taking his eyes from the wonder before him.

The beast unfolded a wing and scratched its rump.

"Is it—?"

"Dangerous? Oh, goodness me, it's positively lethal. How do you think this happened?"

Still unable to tear his gaze from the creature, Joe was vaguely aware of Mrs. Merrynether lifting her bandaged arm. He took a step back from the enclosure and could feel the old woman's stare tunneling into the side of his head, scrutinizing him.

An unexpected euphoria flooded through Joe like ice water.

"How are you feeling?" the old woman said.

Joe's attempt at an answer erupted in the form of a delirious chuckle.

"Well, good. I'm pleased to see you aren't disappointed. I reacted much the same way when I saw my first . . . beastie."

Joe finally turned his attention away from the manticore. "You mean there are more of these?"

"Well, I certainly hope so. I wouldn't want Cornelius to be nursed back to health to spend the rest of his life in solitude."

"But didn't you say it was dangerous? How are you supposed to help something like that? It's got claws bigger than a bear's. How come it didn't kill you?"

Mrs. Merrynether walked to the enclosure. Her good arm reached through the bars. Looking away from the creature to stare confidently at Joe, she patted, stroked, and scratched the beast's side.

The singing noise gargled from somewhere inside the manticore as it unfurled a wing to expose more of its underside and receive Mrs. Merrynether's affection.

"Ah, well, that's the question, isn't it, Joseph? Do you remember why you came to me in the first place?"

"I found an injured badger."

"Yes, but what convinced you *I* could help?"

"I found your name mentioned in Mr. Wheeler's

veterinary directory."

"Go on." She turned back to the manticore.

"Something about the Merrynether Technique."

"Exactly," she said, selecting a large chunk of meat from the grass and waving it near the beast's jaws. "And I suppose a curious boy like you wants to know exactly what that is, don't you? Care to have a guess?"

Joe thought for a moment as he watched the creature lift its head and test the meat with its leathery tongue. It raised its huge paw and, with a tenderness that surprised Joe, gently pushed Mrs. Merrynether's arm aside. The beast and its keeper stared at each other through the bars. The look in the animal's eyes was more than an instinctual plea for help, and Mrs. Merrynether's expression revealed something deeper than sympathy. There was a profound understanding between them.

"Are you . . . Can you read its thoughts?"

"No." She seemed distant, distracted. "But you're very close. You might call it a heightened gift of empathy. I have a finely tuned instinct when it comes to diagnosing illnesses. Sometimes, on a good day like today . . . I can feel what *they* feel."

Joe stayed silent, watching the strange connection between woman and beast.

"Cornelius is dying." She sighed, withdrawing from the enclosure. "He has a powerful poison in his bloodstream that seems to be increasing in volume every day, and I have no idea where it's coming from."

"Perhaps it's the food?"

"No. That was our first thought, but his diet has been thoroughly tested. It isn't that."

"I wish I could help."

Mrs. Merrynether smiled ruefully. "Cornelius may be beyond our help." She lifted her chin, forcing a wider smile. "But next week I have a very special guest coming, and I will most certainly need your help then."

Joe opened his mouth to ask the first of a long list of questions, but he was distracted by a tall, stooping shadow emerging from the far end of the vault. It spoke with a slight German accent as it strolled toward them. "This is the fourth time in a week, Ronnie. We will have to find a new place for the wine, or we will have none left by . . . Oh, I am so sorry, I did not realize you had company."

Joe gawped at the man who appeared from the shadows. At least seven feet high and burly enough to bulge through his long, black overcoat, he dwarfed Mrs. Merrynether like a vulture looming over a shrew. In one hand he held a bucket filled with scraps of meat, and in the other was a large wooden chair carved into the form of interlocking swans.

Immediately after the man made eye contact with Joe, his pockmarked face twisted into an expression of alarm, as if he had just remembered something terrible. The bucket crashed to the floor, spilling its morbid contents onto the concrete, and the man shrank away, fumbling for the hood at the back of his coat. It took several pains-taking seconds for him to cover his aged features but not before Joe saw why he tried to hide them. One side of the man's face looked raw and scarred, horribly dis-figured by what must have been a fire.

"Oh, Heinrich, forgive me, I should have warned you. This is Joseph Copper—the boy I told you about?"

Heinrich had stepped back into the shadows, one hand desperately holding the hood across his face, the other hand still clutching the chair. "Joseph Copper?"

"Yes. Or you can call me Joe." Joe edged forward. "It's all right . . . I saw you. And I don't mind. Honestly."

"Really?"

"Of course. Do you mind me asking what hap-pened?" Joe cursed his curiosity for the hundredth time. That was not the wisest thing to ask under the circumstances.

"It was a very long time ago . . . I—"

"He was trapped in a . . . in a forest fire," Mrs. Merrynether blurted.

"A forest fire? Was it Ringwood Forest?"

"No." Mrs. Merrynether turned quickly to the cowering man, who tentatively lowered his hood while staring apprehensively at Joe. "What was it you were saying, Heinrich? The wine? We're running out?"

"Yes. It must be Lilly again."

"Lilly?" asked Joe. "The person who was shouting at Redwar earlier?"

"Yes, that's him," said Mrs. Merrynether. "He escaped about a week ago, and he's been causing havoc every day since then. Stealing wine, teasing Cornelius, shouting at night—"

"Making chairs," Heinrich interrupted.

"Making chairs?" Mrs. Merrynether balked.

"Yes." The huge German lifted the chair for her to see. "Making chairs."

She squinted at it. "Goodness me! Where did that come from?"

"I think it's been made from one of the old wine racks."

"That little . . . Heinrich, are you quite sure you locked his cage door? It wouldn't be the first—"

"I swear it wasn't me! He must have picked the lock."

"And how did he do that, hmm?"

"Perhaps he made himself a key?" Joe offered, feeling the sickly guilt stir little circles in his gut.

Mrs. Merrynether released a deep sigh and turned back to the manticore. "Well, however it happened, it's history now. What matters is Cornelius. Unless I find an antidote to the toxin in his blood, I don't believe he'll last another week."

"I cannot believe it." Heinrich shook his head. "He is so young." He set the chair in front of the enclosure.

"How old is he?" Joe asked.

"Sixteen in human years; eight in manticore years," Mrs. Merrynether answered, sitting in the chair.

"How do you know?"

"Several ways. Manticores grow a second set of teeth in their fifth year; plus there are subtle changes to their markings. And I'm also told that you can tell their exact age by their tails."

"Their tails?"

"Yes. See the tip of his tail there?" She pointed. "Manticores are ferocious carnivores, and they shoot those quills at their prey to capture them. And, much like domestic cats, they're obsessed by routine, so they feed according to a precise schedule. One kill every three months as soon as they're able, which is not long after they're born."

"I get it. So you can tell how old they are by counting how many quills they have."

"Exactly, yes, but it's an arduous task. There are so many."

"Can you get Cornelius to show me his tail?"

Mrs. Merrynether reached in and gently patted Cornelius's side. He lifted his head to look at her. A moment later, Joe saw the barbed tail suspended just behind the bars. The spikes jutted out in complicated clumps pointing in all directions.

"How old did you say Cornelius is?"

"Sixteen."

"And how many quills are they born with?"

"Six hundred."

"He has five hundred ninety-eight. That would make him six months old."

"That's not possible. Manticores don't have any black markings on their hide until a year. And anyway, how could you know that? You looked at his tail for only a few seconds."

"I have a way with numbers. I can see things quicker and work things out in my head faster than most people." Joe looked at the floor. "It gets me in trouble at school sometimes."

"The boy could be right, Ronnie. Those barbs are poisonous. What if Cornelius is sick because he has not fired enough of his quills?"

"My goodness," said Mrs. Merrynether, snapping her fingers and jumping out of the chair. "That's it, isn't it?"

She stared again into the manticore's eyes. "Don't worry, Cornelius. I know just what to do. Heinrich? Bring me my notepad. It's time for Joseph's next shopping list."

FIVE

Reginald Bacon forced a smile that was more like a grimace, as though he'd just eaten a slug and pretended to like it. He spoke with a hoarse voice as he leaned over the counter. "I'm very sorry, Joe, but we're all out of meat today. There's no steak, no beef, no lamb, no chicken, no pork, not even any fish. It's all gone."

Joe smiled back at the shopkeeper, unable to keep himself from counting how many unshaved follicles greyed his haggard face.

"Mr. Bacon?" yelled a girl from the stockroom behind him. "Angus won't help me with the eggs."

"Not touchin' no eggs, sir," squawked a boy. "They gots spit on 'em."

Mr. Bacon sucked in a long breath as if through a straw and clamped his eyes shut. Joe guessed he was counting to ten. "Excuse me a moment, would you, Joe? We've had a . . . disturbance this morning, and those two are about as much use as a pair of solar-powered foghorns."

Mr. Bacon turned to exit through the back door and collided with a spiky-haired teen in dark blue overalls.

"Sorry, sir," said the boy, clutching a hair dryer and a soggy black book. "I found this under the fridge. Soaked in milk, it was. Tried to dry it out with this hair dryer, but it's gone a bit—"

"Oh, for the love of . . . Put it down, Angus, and help Jennie with those eggs, would you? We've got a customer, and I need to get everything in order before the next delivery. And don't forget the police will be here in half an hour too."

"Told you, sir. Ain't touching them eggs." Angus leaned closer. "We reckons that monster licked 'em."

"I don't care if the thing laid them, boy. Just put them in the larder, sweep the yard, and get that stock check done."

"But—"

"No buts, Angus. Just get back in there and earn your pay."

Angus slumped and shuffled back through the door.

Mr. Bacon drew another labored breath, turned to Joe, and opened his mouth. A cacophony of clattering pans, accompanied by a thunder of falling boxes, stopped him. He shut his eyes again as twin screams followed.

"Sunday staff," he whispered apologetically to Joe. "I'll be back in a moment. Don't go anywhere. I'm sure there's—"

Crash!

"Some other—"

Boom!

"Items on—"

More screams.

"That list I can help you with."

Mr. Bacon rushed out the back, yelling as he went.

Joe took another look at the crumpled paper in his hand.

3 bottles of Irish whiskey
4 bottles of red wine (preferably Chilean)
3 kilograms of finest steak
1 bag of sugar
1 large church candle
1 lightbulb (filament removed)
1 pocket mirror

"A lightbulb without a filament?" Joe mused. "Why?"

Mr. Bacon's voice exploded from the stockroom. "Are you holding what I think you're holding? Because if you are, Angus, you'd better get rid of it right now before I—"

"Don't shout at him," protested the girl's voice. "You know how it affects his acne."

"Not there, boy! In the bin outside!"

Joe flinched as the sound of smashing crockery drowned out the boy's whining response.

The shopkeeper returned to the counter, shaking his head. "So sorry. Been a bit of a stressful morning, and Angus has a habit of bringing out the worst in me at times like this."

"Should I come back a bit later?"

"No, no! There's not much more they can break out back, so it'll probably all calm down in a couple of minutes anyway."

"So what happened? Was there an accident or something? Angus was talking about a monster."

"Monster, me granny!" Mr. Bacon scoffed. "Everyone's been blaming the Beast of Upton Puddle for everything these past few weeks. Nope, I reckon it was a break-in—a rather bad one too. We got here this morning to open up shop, and the stockroom was a right mess— like a tornado had hit the place. Door was ripped clean off its hinges."

"They must have been pretty strong to do that."

"Well, Angus swears blind he saw the Beast. Says a huge hairy man or a bear was running up the path toward the forest with a big lamb chop in its mouth, and then it jumped into a big hole. Got a big imagination, that boy, and he's as thick as a duck plucker's wick. Last summer he thought he saw aliens in the oven, until he remembered he was baking gingerbread men in there."

"Easy mistake to make." Joe chuckled.

Mr. Bacon rolled his eyes. "Well, let's take another look at that list of yours, shall we? I'm sure you don't want to hear me jabbering on all day."

Joe passed the list to Mr. Bacon.

The shopkeeper flattened out the creases and examined the words. "The sugar, wine, whiskey, and mirror are no problem, and I have one candle left in stock, but what the devil does she want with a lightbulb that doesn't have a filament?"

"Search me."

"Well, I can sell you a lightbulb, but good luck with getting the workings out of it without breaking it."

"I'll figure something out."

Mr. Bacon nodded thoughtfully. "I bet you will too. You're a bright little spark, aren't you?"

With the commotion in the stockroom and the arrival of the police ten minutes early, Mr. Bacon took quite a while to work his way through the list, so Joe returned to Merrynether Mansion much later than he expected.

Back in the vault, he found Mrs. Merrynether inside the manticore's enclosure. She was stroking the creature gently along its side. A purr gargled from its cavernous chest.

"Is he any better?" asked Joe, struggling with several carrier bags.

"No change, I'm afraid. Did you manage to get everything?"

"Mr. Bacon's totally out of meat. I got everything else, though. Not sure where else we can get steak on a Sunday unless we go outside the village."

Heinrich emerged from one of the other enclosures, hiding his features with the hood of his coat. "Here. Let me help you with those."

The giant man relieved Joe of his bags and skulked away.

"Be sure to bring the candle with you," Mrs. Merrynether called.

"Of course."

"He has no meat at all?" Mrs. Merrynether asked Joe, leaving the manticore and stepping out of the enclosure. "He's running a supermarket, and he doesn't have any meat?"

"He had a break-in. The whole place is upside down."

She tapped a finger against her lips and scanned the floor as if the answer might present itself in the concrete.

Joe watched her, considering whether this was the right opportunity to pursue one of his suspicions. "One of his Sunday staff thinks the Beast of Upton Puddle did it."

Mrs. Merrynether's gaze flicked upward to meet Joe's for an instant before she returned her attention to the floor.

"Do you think there are apes or bears in Ringwood Forest, Mrs. Merrynether?"

"Hmm, perhaps I could call Derek Sunderland over at Oakridge Farm. He might have some fresh meat."

"It's just that I saw something in the woods last week. I couldn't see it very well, but it looked too big to be even a bear. And bears don't live in England, do they? Except maybe in zoos or . . . or places like this."

The tiny woman placed her hands on her hips. "I beg your pardon. Are you fishing, young man?"

"Well, I . . ."

"If you have something to say, say it. Let's see if you've got the gumption."

He could almost feel himself shrinking to the size of a gnome. "It's just that . . . you said yourself Cornelius was very dangerous, and for all I know, you could have other creatures in here that are even worse. What if . . . what if one of them—?"

"Escaped?"

"Yes." Joe gulped.

"Do you really think I would be irresponsible enough to allow that to happen?" She folded her arms and lifted her chin. "Well, do you, Joseph?"

"Go easy on him, Ronnie," Heinrich said, shuffling from the shadows with five empty wine bottles. "I for one can understand his suspicions. We already have an inebriated cluricaun on the loose, after all."

Mrs. Merrynether drew a long breath, released it slowly, and offered Joe an apologetic smile. "Heinrich's right, of course. I should apologize. I'm worried about Cornelius, and I took it out on you. Do forgive me."

Joe smiled. "Don't worry about it."

She nodded and squeezed his shoulder. "If there is a creature stalking Ringwood Forest, I'm afraid I have no idea what it is or how it came to be here, but I will tell you this: I'm not unmindful of what's been happening in Upton Puddle, and I intend to get to the bottom of it. Now, we need to do something about our manticore. Heinrich?"

Heinrich had set up a workbench near the enclosure. A Bunsen burner fired its flickering blue flame onto the underside of a black ceramic bowl, and Joe watched as the tall man placed the church candle on it.

"That'll take a minute or two to melt," Mrs. Merrynether said. "I have no idea if this will work, but I'm not sure what else to try at the moment."

"What are you going to do?"

"You'll see soon enough."

Joe looked at the huge red beast sleeping in the enclosure. His paws twitched, and every so often, the cactus-like end of his tail stirred, making thin lines in the soil.

"I still can't believe what I'm looking at."

"You'd better get used to it. You're likely to see other creatures far stranger than Cornelius in the weeks and months to come."

"Stranger than a giant red cat with wings and a spiked club for a tail?"

The old woman smiled wistfully. "There are beasts in this world so bizarre and so fantastic they defy reason. Some are so terrifying they'd turn every hair on your head white if you just looked at them. Others are too beautiful to describe.

"Did you know, for example, there are colonies of

creatures alive today that hide themselves away in great underground caverns? Fearsome, black monsters that spit acid and can crush any intruder twenty times their own size with scissorlike mandibles.

"And still other creatures with two sets of wings as delicate as paper-thin glass that communicate with each other by dancing. And when they aren't doing that, they spend a great deal of their time producing a substance I find rather delicious on toast . . . I have a few jars at the back of this vault."

Joe's jaw was dropping lower with each word Mrs. Merrynether spoke. "Will I ever get to see any of those?"

"What? You've never set eyes on a common garden ant or a honey bee, lad?" She winked. "My point is that every creature is amazing. We're just so familiar with them that eventually we forget to appreciate how magnificent they are."

Joe smiled and nodded. "I didn't know bees talked to each other by dancing, though!"

"The wax is ready," Heinrich called.

"Good! Be careful, Heinrich. Cornelius is asleep, but he might not take kindly to a dose of hot wax."

The huge man stepped inside the enclosure, knelt beside the manticore's tail, and with gentle precision, he grasped it just below the spikes. Glancing at the tail and the beast's head, Heinrich poured the wax carefully over a portion of the quills.

They all watched as the wax hardened.

A few tense seconds passed before Heinrich started prying the wax free. There was a soft crackling noise as a cluster of quills popped out from the manticore's tail. "It's working, Ronnie. A lot of them are coming free."

"That's good news."

Still watching the sleeping animal, Heinrich stepped out of the enclosure, holding a formidable lump of thorny wax.

Mrs. Merrynether sat in the chair and sighed as she looked mournfully at the sleeping beast. "All we can do now is wait. Hold on, Cornelius. Hold on."

SIX

Joe was distracted when he arrived home. Thoughts of the manticore and how it was suffering squeezed everything else out of his mind, and he traipsed from the porch and into the living room with a distant expression that caught not only his mum's eye but his aunt's too. His mum sat in one armchair talking on the phone, and his aunt sat in another clasping a copy of *Wrestling Today* in her chubby fingers.

As Joe slumped loudly onto the sofa, the pages of his aunt's magazine flicked up and launched crumbs into the air. Hardened cake debris pitter-pattered against the glossy paper.

Joe smiled for an instant, mostly because of Aunt Rose's look of surprise.

She licked one of her thumbs and set to work jabbing at each morsel so she could have another taste. "Waste not, want not," she said with a sunshine grin taking over her podgy face.

Joe liked Aunt Rose. In truth, she wasn't actually his aunt but such a close friend of the family that Joe's mum had always called her that, and so had Joe. She was like a nightclub bouncer squashed into the body of a Victorian cook who had helped herself to a few too many currant buns over the years.

For as long as he could remember, Aunt Rose had always been around, looking out for him. When he was five years old, Aunt Rose took him to Mr. Bacon's petting farm every Thursday afternoon. Joe would drive his toy tractor about the grassy mounds, pretending to be a farmer rounding up livestock. But one particular Thursday, Mr. Bacon had hired a new farmhand— a man in his early thirties, built like a bulldozer and with a temperament to match. New to the job, the man had forgotten to close one of the chicken hutches, and Joe found himself rounding up livestock for real. It was something of a shock when the farmhand, not knowing his mistake, came running and shouting at Joe to stop frightening the chickens. Aunt Rose had shouted back, telling the man exactly where he could put his chickens, if he were even capable of catching them. Two abusive words from the man ensured he'd never work for Mr. Bacon again—or wake up for the next thirty minutes. Aunt Rose had planted a perfect uppercut to his chin.

Yet, despite her formidable powers among humans,

a spider had to merely poke its spindly leg from a gap in the skirting board to send Aunt Rose into hysteria. On those occasions, it would be Joe jumping to her rescue for a change.

Joe smiled at her briefly again but found his mind wandering back and forth to Merrynether Mansion and the mysterious creatures it housed.

His distraction was not lost on either of the two adults.

Aunt Rose's smile gave way to pouting lips and squinting eyes.

Joe's mum leaned toward the phone cradle, trying to break off a conversation. "Sorry, Mum, I have to go. Joe's just got back," she said, casting a concerned look at her son. "Yes, I'll give him your love. Yes, I'll call you tomorrow . . . Sure . . . Okay . . . Yes, have a great time . . . Bye." She placed the handset on the receiver.

Joe stared into space, chewing the inside of his mouth.

"You're home late again, Joe. Is everything okay?"

"Girls . . . I'll bet he's got himself a girlfriend," Aunt Rose said.

Joe stared, only half aware of their chatter.

"Earth to Joe. Is anybody there?" his mum said.

Joe snapped from his thoughts, looked at them, and smiled again. "Sorry, Mum. Yeah, everything's all right. I was miles away."

"And where exactly was that?" she asked, getting out of the armchair and picking up a pair of oven gloves she'd left hanging by the mantelpiece.

It was then that Joe noticed the aroma wafting from the kitchen. "Are you making cakes?"

"Aunt Rose has made coffee walnut muffins. They'll be ready in about ten minutes," she said, walking out of eyeshot into the kitchen.

"And they'll be eaten in five." Aunt Rose winked.

Joe licked his lips. "Awesome!"

"So where have you been?" his mum called. "Usually it takes you two and a half hours to deliver those papers, but you came back well after eleven last week, and this week . . . well, look at the time."

Joe had been so consumed by the events at Merrynether Mansion during the week that he hadn't even considered how to reply to such an obvious question. But what would he say? If he told them the truth, neither of them would believe him. On the other hand, lying didn't sit comfortably with him either.

"D'you know who Mrs. Merrynether is?" he blurted.

His mum came out from the kitchen and leaned against the wall.

"I know *of* her, but I've never actually met her. Doesn't she live in that big mansion somewhere in Ringwood Forest?" she said, directing the question to Aunt Rose.

"Merrynether Mansion," Aunt Rose confirmed. "She's a recluse, she is. Hardly ever sets foot outside her door."

"That's her," said Joe. "She hurt her arm last week,

so I've been helping her with some shopping."

Joe's mum nodded, then inclined her chin and smiled. "How did you know she'd hurt her arm if she hardly ever leaves her home?"

"I rescued an injured badger in the woods, and I found out from Mr. Wheeler's directories that Mrs. Merrynether's a vet—so I went to see her and that's when she asked me if I could help her with some shopping."

"She's got a nerve," said Aunt Rose.

"I don't mind."

"Shopping or not," his mum said, "that doesn't explain why you've been in a daydream all week, does it?"

"You can ask Mr. Bacon if you like."

"Oh, I believe you, Joe. But there's more, isn't there? You've been in a world of your own, and I could hardly believe it when Mr. Henderson called. The school never calls, so you must have really got his attention."

"Definitely girls," Aunt Rose insisted.

Joe gazed at the carpet, counting the black swirls in the pattern.

"I'm not angry," his mum continued. "I'm just worried. I thought at first you were ill. Is that what it is?"

"No."

Aunt Rose opened her mouth to speak.

Joe beat her to it. "It's got nothing to do with girls."

Joe's mum walked from the kitchen and sat beside Joe on the sofa. "Didn't we say we would talk to each other about anything?" She brushed a hand through his hair and offered a smile of encouragement, lowering her head to catch his eye.

Thoughts of the suffering manticore filled Joe's mind yet again. There was no way he could tell her—was there? "Mum," he said quietly as he met her gaze. "Do you think heaven is a real place?"

Joe's mum glanced at Aunt Rose.

Aunt Rose lifted her magazine.

"Heaven? Honestly, Joe, I really don't know." She released a breath slowly. "Joe . . . is this about your father? Is that what's on your mind? It's been almost three years now since he passed away."

Joe remembered those days all too well. His father's death had been so sudden; road accidents usually were. With no chance to prepare, no chance to say good-bye, and so much left undone, nobody in the family knew how to handle the grief. Joe's mum almost had a breakdown. If it weren't for Aunt Rose, she probably would have. Joe took the longest to recover, and he knew his mum believed he never had.

But it wasn't his father's death that was on his mind. "No, this isn't about Dad."

"Then what brought this on?"

"Nothing, really." He looked at the carpet again.

"Come on. Something's obviously shaken you up. Can't you tell me?"

Joe thought before answering. "Promise you won't laugh?"

"Joe!"

"Well, Mrs. Merrynether has this . . . pet, and it's really ill. I think it might die, and it started me thinking. First I wondered if animals go to heaven; then I started thinking about if heaven was actually a real place."

"Why would I laugh at that? Some of the greatest thinkers who ever lived have been arguing over that since the year dot."

Joe shrugged. "It's just that some people might think it's a stupid idea that animals go to heaven when they die. I mean, can you imagine how many flies there'd be? Or where they'd put all the dinosaurs?"

Joe's mum smiled. "I suppose if heaven *is* a real place, it would have to be pretty big, wouldn't it? But I don't think that'd be a problem for God, would it?"

"Yeah . . . So do you think it's a real place, then?"

Aunt Rose rustled her magazine and cleared her throat, a look of mild concern on her face.

"I'd like to think it is." His mum shrugged. "It'd be a pointless life without a heaven, wouldn't it?"

But Joe saw a different answer in her eyes. "I suppose so."

Monday came. It was the second Monday since Joe had discovered some fairy tales are real.

A trifle more than seven days.

A little over one hundred seventy-two hours.

Ten thousand three hundred fifty-eight minutes.

Six hundred twenty-one thousand four hundred eighty seconds.

Or thereabouts.

Joe stared through the huge white clock on the wall, vaguely aware of the second hand as it began a new minute.

Only another five hundred seven thousand seconds to go before he could find out if Cornelius had recovered.

Ninety-nine . . . ninety-eight . . . ninety-seven . . .

An eternity. Perhaps he could risk going there one afternoon after school. Joe turned the idea around in his mind, thinking about what he would say to his mum about why he was home late again. Hopeless. It wasn't going to happen. He'd have to wait until Sunday.

Seventy-three . . . seventy-two . . . seventy-one . . .

All Joe could hear was the relentless ticktock of the clock, which was indifferent to the torture it inflicted. Something wasn't quite right. It shouldn't be this quiet.

"The wheel is still turning," said Mrs. Conway, "but it would seem the hamster died at the beginning of the lesson."

The sound of the clock was replaced by a scattered sniggering, and it took a few more ticks of the second hand before Joe remembered where he was.

Mrs. Conway stood next to her whiteboard, arms crossed, her pristine white jacket complementing a red blouse. Her expression reminded Joe of a startled lemur's. "Have you been with us for *any* of today's lesson on matrices, Copper?"

Joe glanced around.

Thirty students stared back, all clearly waiting gleefully for what they knew would be a futile answer.

"Sorry. Can you repeat the question, Mrs. Conway?"

A voice hissed behind him. "Sorry. Can you repeat the question, Mrs. Conway? Prat!"

The last word provoked stifled snickering from either side.

"I heard that, Duggan. One more smart remark comes out of that foul hole you call a mouth, and you'll be back in detention—tonight!"

"Geek!" came another attack in an even quieter whisper.

The sharp end of a pencil dug into the back of Joe's neck, causing him to cry out.

"Duggan! That was quite uncalled for, and I *am* able to read lips, you know. Detention!"

The class continued without further incident.

When everybody shoved each other outside for break, Joe knew if he switched on his mobile, a threatening text message from Kurt Duggan would be waiting for him. He also knew his daydreaming would not go unreported; his mum had already been hearing reports from his teachers.

"Dead," the ape-faced bully whispered as he muscled ahead through the crowd.

Once out of the classroom, Joe had nowhere to go except through the double doors that opened into the school yard. Sure enough, there was Neanderthal Kurt Duggan leaning against the wall, accompanied by his three sneering minions.

"Oi! Brain boy!"

With his gaze directed firmly on the tarmac, Joe strode ahead, trying to blend in with the rest of the dispersing herd, pretending he hadn't heard a thing. He knew exactly what would happen. The same scene had played out time and again on every boy labeled a brainiac. The hunting ape-men would circle the flock, looking for the weakest victim, and then close in so the alpha male could draw first blood.

"Where you going, Copper?" One of Duggan's lackeys blocked Joe's path.

The other two closed in like velociraptors as Duggan strolled forward.

Joe said nothing. He studied Duggan's face, hoping to find something in the bully's features that would distract him from the fluttering in his stomach. Nothing.

The cold grey eyes stared back at him from underneath a caveman ridge. "I got another detention coz of you."

Joe stayed silent, knowing the slightest tremor in his voice would betray any illusion of composure. A few stragglers from the herd watched from a distance, and he knew they were waiting for the inevitable.

"D'you think that's fair, geek?"

Joe shrugged. Inside he felt the adrenaline surge,

and it was hard not to run away.

Duggan's hands balled slowly into fists, and a series of images flooded Joe's mind. The manticore leaping and roaring, the great Beast howling in the woods, and Mrs. Merrynether staring at him with eyes of fire. The memory of her words flashed in his head like a floodlight in a cavern: *There comes a time in a person's life when that choice to be special hits them square between the eyes. It's a wonderful moment but a terrible moment too. Most people look away and go back to their boring lives, frightened of what might happen, but some people . . . some people seize that moment and see life for what it really is.*

Another opportunity to seize the moment.

With a speed that shocked him, Joe planted his fist squarely in Duggan's left cheek. There was a moment of slow motion as Joe saw a snapshot of the bully's contorted face. The rubbery lips twisted into a bizarre crescent shape, and his ape-man eyes squeezed shut from obvious pain.

Joe's jaw dropped. He could hardly believe what he'd done. He'd been told many times most bullies were cowards and if someone stood up to them they'd show their true colors. Joe hoped more than anything that was true.

A dull ache throbbed through Joe's hand, and he stifled the urge to cry out, not least because of the stunned silence that had settled in the school yard.

The hush was broken by one of Duggan's meatheads. "Woooo, Duggan, it's an uprising." He grinned.

Duggan did not turn out to be the whimpering wreck that Joe had desperately hoped for. Instead, the face that had squinted in pain mere moments ago now twisted with rage.

The tribe exchanged excited looks while the rest of the school watched with wide eyes like a troop of nervous monkeys sheltering in the high branches of a tree.

With a nod to the others, Duggan grabbed Joe's hair and waited. One of his henchmen removed his tie and used it to blindfold Joe.

Joe was dragged away in darkness.

"We're going to be late back from break today," grunted Duggan. "Go and tell Edmonds to have our cover story ready for Lardy. That fat sod'll come looking for us otherwise."

For several minutes, Joe bumped into corners and railings, stumbled up steps and across what seemed like a field, guided by the unsympathetic hands of his executioner, taunted by the whoops of the other apes and the pounding of his heart. Finally he was thrust through a set of double doors into an area that stunk of stale cigarette smoke and spilled beer.

Somebody yanked the tie away from his eyes, and Joe saw a burnt-out classroom occupied by a gang of kids much older than him. Under the glare of naked fluorescent lights, several faces stared at him through a haze, some smirking, some frowning, but most looking uninterested.

"This one got brave," Duggan said, releasing Joe's hair and then jabbing the back of his head. "Gave me a slap right in front of the whole school."

Two boys and one of the girls laughed.

"Oh, funny, is it? Perhaps I'll use wiener boy here for a bit of practice before I start on you, eh?"

The kids stopped laughing, and Joe wondered how a boy at least three years their junior had such influence. It was true that Duggan was well-built for his age, but that wasn't enough to gain a reputation as the school kingpin.

Joe glanced around him. The fact that he'd been blindfolded meant they were trying to keep this place a secret, yet it was obviously somewhere within the school building. Clarkdale School was not very big, so the hideout could not remain concealed for very long. On one of the benches a deck of cards was surrounded by cans of lager and a pile of money. On one of the doors numerous darts hung on a dartboard. The charcoaled walls were covered with blisters and peeling paint, and the windows were boarded up. There'd been a fire here.

This was the old chemistry block that had been gutted by last year's blaze, no doubt.

"You're going to get such a beating," Duggan said, pushing his face into Joe's.

"Do I get a final request?" Joe asked.

The question roused a howl of belly laughs from the others, followed by a whistling chorus from *The Great*

Escape. From the back of the room, a lanky kid rushed forward and shoved a cigarette in his mouth.

"I believe it's the custom for a condemned man to have a final smoke, what?" he said like an English gentleman. "May I give you a light, old chap?"

Deciding he had nothing left to lose, Joe rolled the cigarette inside his mouth with his tongue, chewed on it, and then opened his mouth, allowing the mangled paper and tobacco to drop to the floor in soggy brown pools of saliva. The whole time, he looked at Duggan.

"Hey! That was a perfectly good smoke," said the lanky kid. "When Duggan's done, I'll give you a good pounding myself."

Duggan glared. "Five minutes ain't enough time for you to take the sort of punishment I'm gonna dish out to you, Copper. Tell you what," he said, putting the tie back round his neck and tightening it into an impossibly small knot, "I'm gonna let you go now, but when that last bell rings today, you'd better know I'll be waiting right outside those school gates. And then we'll have all the time in the world, won't we, geek boy?"

"No problem." Joe beamed, realizing Duggan was stupid enough not to remember he'd still be on detention while Joe was safely strolling home.

Duggan gave him the briefest of confused looks before barking at one of his cronies to drag Joe back to the main school yard.

"What about the blindfold?" Joe asked.

Duggan pursed his lips and shot a glance at the tie he'd just tightened. "Just close your eyes. If you open them, I'll know, and then I'll be waiting by those gates for you every day for a whole month. Got it?"

"Got it." Joe smiled, though inside he was still fighting back his fear.

Duggan glowered at him, then waved dismissively at nobody in particular. "Just get rid of him."

Joe clamped his eyes shut as two grinning apes grabbed his arms and dragged him out of the room. After a few minutes of stumbling, Joe was dumped in the school yard. He puffed out a huge sigh as the school bell signaled the end of his nightmare. But Joe knew his relief would be short-lived. Duggan's long list of detentions would be enough to prevent a monumental battering outside the school gates for a while, but sooner or later, it was bound to happen.

Joe shrugged, massaged his aching knuckles, and joined the herd shuffling into the classrooms.

SEVEN

Argoyle Redwar lumbered through the animal block, though he did his best to make it look more like marching. He lifted his flab-swaddled chin and clasped his hands behind his back while casting a haughty gaze on his nervous employees. Behind him, armed with her notepad and pen, Ms. Burrowdown trotted in his shadow.

The constant whining of caged dogs competed with the moan of overworked air-conditioning units, and the throat-choking reek of ferrets saturated the air. It was a place widely avoided and detested by all the employees, not least Redwar. The law stated that companies in his line of business had to test their products on animals, and though Redwar despised that law, it was not because of any moral objections.

Redwar stopped to look inside one of the cages and traded a glare with a chimpanzee. It rocked from side to side, blowing raspberries at its captor.

"Not happy in there? Well, I'm not happy about paying to keep you either. If I had my way, you'd be back in a jungle somewhere, hiding from hunters in the trees and dodging bullets."

The chimp grinned, looked around at nothing in particular, then held out an open hand through the bars of his cage.

"No, George!" A pale stick of a man came rushing out from among the employees. "You mustn't do that to Mr. Redwar." Then with a whisper, "He doesn't like animals."

"Are you Gumble?" snapped Redwar.

"Yes, sir. Arthur Gumble—the animal block supervisor. I do apologize for George's behavior. He thought you were going to feed him. He likes—"

"Never mind that. Let's get this over with. I want to see what all the fuss is about."

"Of course, sir. This way. We've moved her to the quarantine area."

Gumble hurried to the end of the room and held a pass card against a reader in the wall next to a set of double doors. The doors swung inwards with a hiss, and the skinny man beckoned Redwar and Burrowdown inside. A cacophony of barking and howling assaulted them as they entered, but the noise came from only three animals, all of them dogs. Most of the other cages were empty.

"Can't you do anything about this infernal stench,

Gumble?" Redwar covered his nose.

"I'm sorry, sir. Bessy has an infection, so—"

"Never mind. Where's . . . where's . . ." Redwar twirled his free hand in frustration.

"Lucy?"

"Yes, yes, Lucy. What's the matter with her?"

"Here she is." Gumble pointed to a sullen beagle in the cage closest to him.

"Well? What's wrong with her?" Redwar barked.

"We don't know, sir. She's on our most important trial, but she's very sick. Toxicology reports show—"

"Is the testing making her ill?"

"No, no. I was just about to say that this has nothing to do with the trial, Mr. Redwar. But if we aren't able to help her soon, it may affect the results. Four years of—"

"You have qualified vets here, don't you, Gumble? Why are you involving me in this?"

"None of our vets have been able to help. I need your authorization to go outside the company. We were—"

"There are proper channels for such requests," Redwar scolded. "Why on God's green earth did you have me dragged down here, wasting my valuable time?"

"You . . . wouldn't answer my—"

"Did he place any formal requests?" Redwar turned on Burrowdown.

Her response came out as a confused murmur.

"What? Speak up, woman!"

She stared back at him.

Gumble lifted his hands in apology. "If I may, sir?"

"What?" Redwar spun round on his heel.

"We heard you were trying to buy out a veterinary practice in the area. Apparently Mrs. Merrynether has a very good reputation. Perhaps we—"

"Merrynether?" Redwar's eyes bulged. "*Never* mention her to me."

Gumble cowered at the outburst, which was exaggerated, even for Redwar.

"That woman," Redwar continued, growling more to himself than anyone else, "is a thorn in my side, a fly in my soup, a . . . a . . . cantankerous old witch!"

Silence followed. Even the dogs had stopped barking.

"Oh, and Gumble?" Redwar said eventually.

"Sir?"

"You're fired!"

Cold sparks tingled under Joe's skin as he stood outside the door of Merrynether Mansion with his trolley. For an entire week he had struggled so desperately to be patient, resisting the urge to visit after school, fighting a compulsive need to rejoin the new world he'd discovered. And now that Sunday had arrived, he could hardly bear the anticipation.

The moments ached by, but eventually the door

creaked open. Joe was greeted by a welcoming snort from Archy the pig and the hasty beckoning of Mrs. Merrynether.

"Come in." Tension bristled in Mrs. Merrynether's voice. She had her back to Joe and was stomping through the hallway toward the study.

Joe lifted his trolley inside before closing the door, wondering what unexpected shopping items would fill it this week. The rustling of paper and the rasp of sliding drawers came from Mrs. Merrynether's direction.

"How's Cornelius?" called Joe.

There was a brief silence from the study as if the old woman had stopped whatever she was doing to consider her answer.

"Why don't you go down to the vault, Joseph?" she called back. "I have one or two chores to attend to up here before I can join you. Heinrich's down there. He'll see to you while you're waiting."

Joe's stomach sank. Mrs. Merrynether's mood didn't sound good, and she had deliberately not answered his question, which could mean only one thing. After all the waiting and bottled excitement, the vault was now the last place on earth Joe wanted to be. But he knew he had to go down there, despite his fear of what he might find.

"Here goes," Joe said to Archy. With a deep breath, he walked alongside the trotting pig into the pantry, through the end door, down the steps, and into the cellar where he had first met the cluricaun. His hand hovered over the knob of the red door that would lead down to the vault. A vision flashed in his mind's eye with sudden clarity: the manticore's lifeless body stretched out inside the enclosure with lolling tongue and glassy expression. Joe snatched his hand back.

A gentle nudge from a soft snout caught Joe's leg.

"I can't, Archy."

The pig looked at him insistently.

Joe clenched his teeth and looked at the doorknob.

"Looks loike da boy needs a . . . hic . . . wee tipple of de orlde Dutch courage," came a slurring voice from somewhere in the cellar, the word *courage* belched rather than spoken.

Joe peered into the cellar, looking for the source.

"Lilly? Is that you?"

The hollow chinking of empty bottles falling and rolling along the cellar floor came with the reply. "Oh, Danny boooooy. Oooooh, Danny boooooooy!"

"Lilly?"

"Da poipes, da poipes are a carllin' from glen ta glen, and down da mountainsoide."

Archy snorted loudly and ran into the middle of the cellar.

"Da sommer's gorne, and orle da flowers are a dyin' . . ."

The tune continued in off-key notes from the blowing of bottle rims.

Joe thought he glimpsed the cluricaun's sky-blue

waistcoat in a gloomy corner obscured by old rags and boxes. He crept toward it, hoping for a chance to catch the tiny man.

"Oooo, quick, quick . . . hic . . . da boy's comin' ta gets me."

The smell of wine filled Joe's nostrils as he neared the tiny item of clothing, and with squinting eyes and bated breath, he reached for the troublemaker.

A howl of drunken hysterics echoed in the cellar as Joe looked at the empty waistcoat in his hand.

"Oooo, did ye want me pants too?" A tiny pair of baggy slacks were thrown from somewhere close by, hitting Joe square in the face. "Oi didn't knor orlde Merrynedder would be . . . hic . . . sending you down ta collect me washin'. Could ya polish me little shoes too?"

The hysterical laughter continued, and Joe suppressed a smile as he put the miniature clothes on top of a nearby crate.

Archy scampered off, skidding into some boxes as a small pair of shoes flew through the air and clattered close by.

"Are you going to show yourself?"

"Heheeee, have it your way, boy. Take a look at da moon. It's broight tonoight!"

Realizing what the cluricaun was about to do, Joe focused on the floor rather than have his eyes assaulted. "No, thank you. I didn't bring my telescope."

"Why, ya cheeky . . . hic . . . little snot farmer! Tells

ya what, Lilly'll make ya a teshlescope . . . with—" The sentence ended with another clattering of glass followed by loud snoring.

Sufficiently distracted from his fears by the cluricaun's interruption, Joe turned his attention back to the red door and marched to it. "Right. That's it." He turned the knob and, finding it unlocked, walked down the stairs and barged through the vault door before he could change his mind.

He was unprepared for the shock.

The manticore enclosure was exactly as it was the last time Joe saw it. Mossy floor, ornamental rocks, decorative water features, and there, lying motionless on its side with its back pressed against the bars of the cage, was Cornelius.

Joe felt the blood drain from his face. "No," he whispered, ignoring the minor commotion he'd caused to his left when he burst in.

Seated at an old desk facing the wall, a startled Heinrich hurriedly swept sheets of paper and a stack of small envelopes into a drawer before slamming it shut and fumbling in vain to lock it with a fountain pen. Joe watched as Heinrich quickly stuffed the pen in his pocket and pulled out a key instead. He locked the drawer and glanced back at Joe, offering a nervous, lopsided smile.

"Hi, Heinrich."

Heinrich opened his mouth to provide what Joe

assumed would be an excuse for something he obviously felt guilty about.

Light footsteps tapped on the concrete stairs behind them.

Mrs. Merrynether walked inside and slammed the door so hard that the key fell out and clattered onto the floor.

"Pompous, irritating, self-important . . . ugly brute of a man!"

Heinrich's mouth, which was already open, stretched wider as his fearful eyes met hers.

"Not you," she grumbled. "That ignoramus Argoyle Redwar. If there weren't laws against it, I'd sincerely think about chopping him up into tiny kibbles and feeding him to Cornelius . . . though I think the poor creature has already had his fill of poison." Her last sentence was tinged with remorse.

"Oh, I see," said Heinrich. "You finally decided to read those letters he's been sending us all week, then? What are they?"

"You mean, what *were* they? I've just spent the last ten minutes reading and burning three revised offers for the purchase of Merrynether Mansion, two requests for my presence at that abominable factory, and two letters threatening to reveal what I do here. Hasn't that obnoxious secretary of his got anything better to do than write me letters every day?"

"Redwar's desperate, Ronnie," Heinrich said to Mrs. Merrynether in a low voice. "And desperation is the last weapon of a man who craves control he cannot have. Try not to worry about him."

"I'm not worried, Heinrich. I'm—"

"Is Cornelius alive?" Joe interrupted, too choked with surprise to wait for their conversation to end. "I thought he was . . . dead."

"Dead?" Mrs. Merrynether swung round to face Joe. "Heavens above, whatever gave you that idea?"

"Well, you didn't answer me upstairs when I—"

"Oh, pay no attention to an ignorant old woman. I was too busy fuming over Redwar's letters. Cornelius is still alive."

"He's asleep, then?"

Mrs. Merrynether shot a glance at Heinrich. "For now, yes, but he's still very sick, Joseph. In truth, he may not last more than a week unless we find a way to help him."

"But I thought you were taking the poison quills out. Didn't that work?"

"I'm afraid not."

Heinrich left the desk and walked to the enclosure. He brushed a large hand against the beast's fur. "Plucking the quills from his tail does not release the poison. I believe a manticore must actively fire its quills to do that. When the muscles tighten in its tail, the venom is injected into the quill at the moment of ejection. Simply plucking the quills will not remove the venom."

"Then he needs something to shoot at. Something to attack?" Joe asked.

"Yes, motivation is the key," said Heinrich, "but I fear he is too exhausted to respond now."

"There's still time," Mrs. Merrynether said. "We've managed to help creatures in a much worse state than this. Remember that epileptic bunyip that swallowed a bag of hand grenades? And that ogre with Tourette's syndrome?"

"How could I forget?" Heinrich said, standing and glancing back at his desk as if checking for something he might have missed. "I still say it was a terrible idea to treat both of them at the same time." He walked to his desk.

"But we helped them, didn't we?" Mrs. Merrynether said. She approached the sleeping beast to take her turn at stroking him.

Joe saw a wastepaper bin at the side of the desk. Several balls of crumpled paper were inside, and there was surely something written on them that was supposed to be kept secret. Heinrich looked at him pleadingly, and the weight of another secret burdened Joe. The guilt of his involvement with Lilly's escape was uncomfortable enough, but now what should he do about Heinrich? It was obvious that Mrs. Merrynether and Heinrich had a relationship with a long history. How could he interfere with that?

With a cautious foot nudge and a well-timed clearing of his throat, Heinrich slid the bin behind his desk while Mrs. Merrynether's attention was on the manticore. He directed another look of earnest at Joe before he spoke. "You're right, of course, Ronnie. We will think of something. We've never let any of our patients down yet . . . er . . . which reminds me: perhaps it is time we told Joe why he has been chosen to help us."

Mrs. Merrynether straightened and turned to Joe, a thoughtful expression on her face. "Yes, Heinrich, though it seems we already have our answer."

Joe looked at Mrs. Merrynether, then at Heinrich, then back at Mrs. Merrynether. Heinrich had obviously done this not only to keep Mrs. Merrynether's attention away from his desk but also to divert Joe's attention.

"Chosen? For what?" Joe asked. "I thought I was just doing your shopping for you."

"I'm afraid I have a confession to make, Joseph. Do you remember when I told you that I have a particular gift that allows me to empathize with animals?"

"Sure. The Merrynether Technique."

"Do you think that gift is limited to animals?"

"I hadn't thought about it." Joe braced himself for the punch line.

"Well, it isn't. Do you remember that powerful feeling of purpose and destiny when you first came to my door? I'm afraid that was my doing." She raised a hand. "But please don't jump to conclusions. It wasn't meant as a deception. Rather, it was intended to present you with a choice. Remember I told you that being special *is* a choice? Not everyone would have responded to such a call, but you did."

Joe felt the walls of the vault closing in on him, a sense of unease accompanied by the slow realization of a wakeup call. He was a young boy standing in an underground vault with two people he knew nothing about, and not a single soul knew where he was. Could he really be that stupid?

"It took courage to reach this point," she continued. "Not just for you but for me. You placed your trust in me, and now I am trusting you. I didn't have to tell you any of that."

All three exchanged looks of uncertainty.

Somewhere at the back of the vault, a creature stirred, and Joe was suddenly aware of the peculiar sounds made by a host of other unidentified animals. From one side, a soft whisper like sand being shaken through a sieve; from the other, a rhythmic breathing like distant wind passing through the tubes of a great church organ. He could turn his back on all of this and be safe. But he would never know what was making those strange noises, and he may never have an opportunity like this again. It was worth the risk.

"Why?" Joe asked Mrs. Merrynether.

"Why what?"

"Why did you choose me?"

"I . . . we had a feeling about you. But more importantly, we needed you for a very special patient we've been expecting for several weeks . . . It's time you were introduced."

EIGHT

Mrs. Merrynether walked away, deeper into the vault, leaving Joe and Heinrich to watch each other with uncertain smiles.

"Who were you writing to?" Joe asked once Mrs. Merrynether was out of earshot.

Heinrich's smile fell. His eyes twitched and swiveled, looking anywhere except into Joe's.

"Please don't tell Ronnie. She . . . she wouldn't understand."

"Is it really that bad?"

"Yes . . . No . . . She . . ." Heinrich's face twisted in confusion, and Joe was about to tell Heinrich to forget it when a brilliant blue-white light emerged from behind Cornelius's cage.

The entire vault was exposed, and Joe was treated to a spectacle of tentacle and claw, a parade of cherry reds and lizard greens as a host of animals were gloriously revealed within their enclosures. The black silhouette of Mrs. Merrynether was at the center of it all, stooping over a casket, lifting something out. Then the glare diminished, and Mrs. Merrynether walked toward Joe and Heinrich, an enigmatic smile curling her lips. She cupped in her hands something small, the source of the light.

"The more excited she gets, the brighter she glows," she said. "I take it you saw that little outburst, Joseph?"

"Uh . . . yes. I could hardly miss it." Stunned, Joe looked at the object in her hands. It was the lightbulb he'd bought from Mr. Bacon a week before, and now it was obvious why she wanted to have the filament removed. Something living shifted inside it.

Carefully, Mrs. Merrynether unscrewed the cap of the bulb. "Out you come," she whispered. "Time to stretch those beautiful wings."

Two milk-white arms as delicate as matchsticks yawned outward from the opening, and the tiniest fingers Joe had ever seen grasped the edge of the bulb. A petite head, crowned with wisps of sapphire-blue hair, stretched up gracefully. With two diamond eyes, it gazed at its surroundings, eventually setting its sight upon Joe. It smiled and, with a gentle squeeze, pulled the rest of its body from its glass home. Around its frame was a lattice of tiny crystals, which Joe assumed was some kind of clothing. Two sets of dovelike wings unfolded, sending out ripples of light with each slow beat as it drifted on the air toward him.

"Is it an angel?" Joe asked, his gaze firmly locked on the miniature wonder.

The reply came from the creature as it floated at Joe's eye level. Its voice, undoubtedly female, seemed to be right inside his ear, tickling like a blade of grass.

"Some call us angels; some call us fairies. I am a seraph."

"A seraph?" Joe poked at one of his ears.

"Yes."

"So you *are* an angel, then. Like the seraphim and cherubim? I heard about them in a church once."

"If you like." The seraph laughed, spun in a graceful arc, and glided down into the enclosure, settling on the side of the manticore. Her tiny fingers splayed as she pushed her hands into the crimson fur. Joe could hear her humming as she turned onto her back and stretched, apparently enjoying Cornelius as though he were a luxurious cushion.

"You can see her without any difficulty?" asked Mrs. Merrynether.

"Of course," Joe said. "Why? Shouldn't I?"

"Actually, no. Nobody should be able to see a seraph. They're usually invisible to the naked eye. The seraphim feed on light, a bit like plants, and once they've absorbed what they need, the rest is radiated back at a very specific wavelength unique to each seraph. No two seraphim ever radiate light at the same wavelength, you know. And it's always out of the range of the human eye."

"So how is it we can see her?"

"Ah, that's the question, isn't it? It's why she's here, and it's why you're here too, Joseph. I had to know for sure if she really has a problem."

"I don't understand."

"Well, there are specific situations where a human being *can*, in fact, see a seraph. First, you have to believe they exist and, second, you have to know the name of the seraph. Don't ask me how that works. We're still trying to sort out the science behind it, but somehow those two things tune you in. Only under those circumstances can a human being hope to see a seraph."

"A bit like remote central locking on my mum's car, then? Our key is the only one tuned in to our car."

"As good analogy as any, I suppose." Mrs. Merrynether smiled. "Heinrich and I knew of the existence of seraphim a long time ago. We both know her name," she said, motioning toward the creature as it crawled along Cornelius's back. "So there was no question that she would be visible to us. She came to us with her ailment, hoping to be cured, and we attempted a variety of remedies, but unless we could find someone who should not be able to see her, we couldn't know if we were successful."

"Sorry, but I didn't know they existed until today, and I definitely don't know her name."

"Yes, but from the moment you walked into the vault, I knew you would be able to see her."

"How?"

"Do you see any other sources of light in here today?"

Joe looked around him. All the lamps and ceiling lights were off, and the skylights had shutters bolted across them, yet for a radius of at least fifteen feet, everything was bathed in light.

"There's no artificial light in here," said Mrs. Merrynether, "and no daylight either. She's providing the illumination, and she even shines straight through solid objects just as X-rays do. If you were unable to see her, you wouldn't be able to see anything at all in here today."

"So that means if I can see her, anyone can see her? There's no way to hide her unless she stays down here?"

"That's why we have this lightbulb. It may be the only way to disguise her. I admit that her light isn't exactly normal, but at least if it's seen to be coming from a lightbulb it might not warrant a second look. We don't expect anyone down here, but we like to be prepared—just in case."

Joe shrugged and watched the seraph. She had worked her way up to the manticore's mane, wading through the fur like an excited butterfly hunter walking through long grass. Then with an elegant sweep of her four wings, the seraph launched into the air, bursting with blue-white brilliance.

"He is proud and beautiful," she said, flittering in circles around Mrs. Merrynether's head. "Why doesn't he sing as a manticore should?"

"Cornelius is very ill, Danariel," Mrs. Merrynether replied.

Heinrich slapped his forehead and then shot a pained look at her. "Did you really want Joe to know her name? Now even if we cure her, Joe will still be able to see her."

"Oh, goodness!" Mrs. Merrynether clapped her hands to her mouth.

"Danariel? That's a lovely name," Joe said.

The seraph drifted in a spiral motion toward Joe, smiling and beaming rays of white. "I know," she said. "Someone lovely named me."

"Your mother?"

"We seraphim do not have mothers and fathers. We are . . . thought into being by—"

"Danariel." Mrs. Merrynether stepped forward. "It would be best if young Joseph does not know everything. He—"

"Nonsense. In fact, would you both please leave us alone for a few minutes? Joe and I have things to discuss, and I would rather not have either of you interrupt."

Mrs. Merrynether and Heinrich shot astonished glances at each other. Joe was equally astounded when they agreed and headed for the door. They stopped before leaving the vault and looked at Danariel, who had settled on the edge of Heinrich's desk, smiling sweetly and swinging her legs. She lifted a hand to shoo them off, and both of them left.

"Sit down, Joe." She nodded at the chair Lilly had made.

Joe sat obediently, and Danariel wiggled her fingers at him, beckoning him to drag the chair closer.

The sound of the wood scraping the stone floor was louder than Joe expected, and from the back of the vault, strange gurglings and rumblings sang out in reply. He peered into the darkness, wondering whether the other creatures could see Danariel too and if any of them were as ill as Cornelius. He looked at the sleeping red giant. There was no change. Joe frowned.

A gentle tap on the side of his face, like the pattering of rain, caught his attention. He turned to see Danariel, floating inches from his head, staring intently at him.

"You are worried about the manticore?"

Joe nodded. "Mrs. Merrynether thinks he might—"

"He may die, yes."

Joe fell silent and stared at the floor. Danariel glided downward, intercepting his line of sight, making it impossible for him to avoid her eyes.

"There are many who fear death, but most are afraid of *how* they will die, not of death itself. Yet I sense you are different. You are a happy soul. Why does it trouble you so?"

"That's just it. I'm happy, and I don't want it to ever end. There are so many things to see," he said, waving both hands. "I'm afraid of what I might miss out on once I'm dead. All the discoveries. All the crazy inventions.

People landing on Mars or . . . or being able to watch holographic movies."

"Dream recorders or telescopic contact lenses," Danariel added with a wide smile.

"Yes, or what about teleportation?" Joe grinned as he allowed his imagination to run riot.

Danariel was caught up in Joe's momentary thrill too. The light in the vault had intensified, and her sparkling eyes shone.

They stared at each other for almost a full minute, sharing a quiet joy.

Joe sighed, the brief excitement melting away. "I can't bear the thought of missing so many amazing things. One day I'll be gone. I won't see any of it."

A quiet settled in the vault.

"Tell me, Joe," Danariel mused, "what was it like for you before you were born?"

"Before?"

"Yes."

Joe thought for a moment. "It wasn't like anything. I didn't know anything, and I couldn't feel anything."

"Just like how it will be after you die."

"I suppose so," Joe nodded slowly, "but I still can't help thinking about the things I'll miss."

"Then weep for today also."

The second deep frown of the day knitted Joe's brow.

The tiny creature closed her eyes, apparently concentrating, and the aura of light surrounding her softened into a calmer hue. "At this very moment," she whispered, as if careful not to disturb something delicate in the air, "there is an old man in Bulgaria who has heard the funniest joke ever told. He has been laughing for over three hours now.

"In Japan a young woman is crying. Two hours ago she finished composing a piece of music, and it was the most beautiful symphony ever crafted. Ten minutes ago it was accidentally destroyed by a candle flame.

"Right now, there are ten people living in different parts of the world, gasping in awe at revelations most will never understand. There are two hundred seventy people breaking world records, fifty thousand people being reunited with loved ones they believed were dead, twenty-eight million people laughing hysterically at something unexpected.

"And, Joe, you had no idea any of it was happening at this moment. You will never experience those things yourself."

Joe was listening intently, entranced by her words.

"We are always missing out on amazing things," she continued. "Dead or alive, it is the same. What matters is that you hold on tightly to the miracles that belong to *you*. Learn to find value in those things that exist *now*."

Joe opened his mouth to speak, but nothing came out.

"But there is more to this than you say." Danariel left the desk and hovered closer to Joe. "Death is a greater burden to your heart than it is for most boys your age. I wonder if it has touched you in a deeper way."

The seraph's diamond eyes were suddenly all Joe could see, and a yearning to pour out every trouble and fear swept through him. But in equal measure, Joe felt the need to stay silent, to resist this longing that somehow did not feel real. He rubbed his eyes, as though waking from a heavy daydream.

"Not only happy but strong." She smiled. "You will confide in me when you're ready. I cannot pry where I am not allowed to go." She danced through the air to find her place on the desk.

Joe drew a long breath. "Did Mrs. Merrynether teach you her technique too?"

At that, the seraph laughed, sending out a pulse of light between each breath.

"Veronica learned it from *me* many years ago. Of course, she cannot read minds, as the seraphim can, but she has embraced the simple skills of a novice. She can impress feelings upon man or beast, and she can discern the feelings of a troubled mind, but she is still only a human. She will never go further."

"You can read minds?"

"Only if I am given permission," Danariel said, "and even then, there can often be barriers."

"Can you teach me what you taught Mrs. Merrynether?"

"If I wished to, but I have another purpose for you.

A greater purpose."

A fresh skin-prickling excitement accompanied the seraph's words and Joe clutched at the chair in anticipation. "Mrs. Merrynether said my purpose was to meet you, to see if I could . . . see you."

"Just a little fib on my part." She tilted her head. "I did not come here wishing for a cure, though it would not be unwelcome. I came here because I've picked you out as someone special. I impressed on Veronica's mind what to look for, and when you came, she knew you were the one, but she is unaware that this is my idea."

"Oh!" Joe scratched his head. "I see . . . I think. So why do you need me?"

"Not just you. There will be a gathering of champions. A group that will play a vital role in a struggle against a great enemy. When all are assembled, I will reveal everything. But until then, I will say nothing more."

Questions erupted in Joe's mind. "Tell me now!"

"No," she snapped playfully. "Now go to the door and call Veronica and Heinrich back to the vault. I imagine our hosts are becoming quite restless by now."

Biting his bottom lip, Joe obeyed. He had to go home soon. With an inward groan, he opened the door.

Waiting for Sunday would be even harder this week.

NINE

Joe didn't feel much like a champion. Champions were not in the habit of crouching behind school dustbins to evade a good beating. Despite the seraph's inspiring words of destiny, Joe did not feel any compulsion to face Kurt Duggan and his thug friends. Half an hour had passed since he'd tucked himself behind the bins, knees clutched to his chest. The three silver silos were large enough to hide a horse, but that didn't mean he wouldn't be discovered.

He'd switched off his mobile phone again for fear of being given away by the loud alert of a new abusive text from Duggan. These days he hardly ever switched it on. He tried to keep his breathing as shallow as possible, not just to avoid detection but also to minimize the stench. The tang of rotting fruit and a month's worth of soured milk clung to the back of his throat, but that wasn't as bad as the cold dampness soaked into the backside of his trousers. Joe had no interest in finding out what he'd sat in.

Pressed against his chest was the thing that had brought down the wrath of the school bully upon him. Had he not taken it, Duggan would have forgotten about the incident in the playground eventually, but there was no way Joe was going to get away with this one.

Desperation and a fanciful idea had forced Joe to retrace the steps he'd memorized to get into the bully's lair. He'd sneaked out of his history lesson to find the burnt-out chemistry section, pried off some of the boards from one of the windows, and clambered inside. It wasn't long before he had the dartboard in his hands and was running to the school gates.

But he'd been spotted. It had been a mistake to assume everyone would be in lessons—especially Kurt Duggan. Duggan had screamed at him across the school yard before sprinting toward him in blind rage. Joe knew it wasn't really the dartboard that had incensed his enemy but the fact that the hideout had been compromised. There'd be a royal battering if Joe got caught. With a healthy dose of panic boosting him, he'd run like a ferret down a rabbit hole and out of sight.

Joe looked at the dartboard and set it down beside him, shaking his head at his own stupidity. From Monday through Wednesday, he had suffered the usual torture of wanting to break away from school to go back to

Merrynether Mansion. By Thursday, he could bear to wait no longer. He had to know if Cornelius was still alive.

In an impulsive flash of misguided heroism and inspiration, Joe decided to pit himself against the evil Kurt Duggan, break into his hideout, take the dartboard, rush to Mrs. Merrynether, and hand over the one item that would bring salvation to the manticore. Joe's determination had been galvanized by thoughts that if the creature opened a sleepy eye and saw the bright colors of the dartboard, it would feel compelled to fire its quills at the target and recover.

Feeling tears welling in his eyes, Joe stared at the dartboard. It was a ridiculous fantasy. But sitting behind the bins and hoping to escape a pummelling was not a fantasy. That was very real.

Joe punched the tarmac. Even if the dartboard *was* a realistic idea, he could've just bought one with all the money he'd been earning recently. He didn't have to be sitting here now, hiding among the black banana skins and sticky sweet wrappers.

A rustling came from underneath one of the silos, and a hedgehog snuffled into view, poking at an empty carton.

Joe heaved a sigh and smiled as he watched the animal. "It's no good me sitting here feeling sorry for myself," he said absently to the creature. "I'll just have to face up to things."

Grimacing at the ache in his legs from sitting in a

cramped position for too long, Joe struggled up and felt the damp back of his trousers. With a jolt, he remembered what was in his back pocket—the next shopping list for Mrs. Merrynether. As carefully as he could, he pulled out the soggy paper and unfolded it. Thankfully, though the ink had run slightly, he could still read what was on it.

> 2 bottles of Irish whiskey
> 1 perfume atomizer or spray can
> 4 bottles of decongestant syrup
> 2 bottles of window cleaner

He hadn't been to see Mr. Bacon for these items yet. They were closed for the week for a stock check and refurbishment following the break-in, but Joe had planned on getting it all Saturday. He folded the paper, put it in his front pocket, and with a last glance at the discarded dartboard, Joe stepped out from behind the bins to accept his fate.

To his great relief, there were no fists waiting for him. Break had come and gone, and the rest of his class had probably left for their next lesson, Duggan with them, he hoped. It was too late to sneak into class now, and turning up in this state wasn't a good idea. No, he'd at least do some of what he planned. Even if he didn't use the dartboard, he could go to Merrynether Mansion and find out how Cornelius was doing.

Ringwood Forest bordered the edge of the playing fields. If Joe was lucky, he could run in there without being spotted.

He waited, mustering up courage, and took off past the music block, across the field, over the fence, and into the woods. Once he was far enough inside, he slumped against an oak tree and checked his watch. Ten forty-seven. He'd have enough time to get to Merrynether Mansion, check on Cornelius, rush home to change, and get back in time for the day's final lesson. The only problem would be Duggan. His stomach lurched, and he caught his breath at the sound of crunching footsteps nearby.

"Perhaps he's turned commando and camouflaged himself under one of those blanket things they cover with dirt and leaves." One laughed.

"Yeah, or maybe he's got all the brainy boys trained and they're gonna throw sharp pencils at us from the trees," said another.

"Just shut it." That was Duggan. "The little turd's caused us a lot of . . ."

The bully's voice trailed off as the crackling of foliage became softer and slower.

Joe stiffened.

From behind the tree on both sides came four boys, three with openmouthed grins and Duggan with his bottom lip twitching.

For an endless silence, Joe stared into his enemy's

eyes, waiting for the thrashing of his life.

When Duggan eventually spoke, it was loud enough to make one of his friends jump, though Joe managed to keep his cool. "D'you know how long it took me to get that chemistry room, Copper?"

Joe shrugged.

His nemesis crossed his arms, maximizing his bulging biceps. "I've got connections, see? My dad knows people in the school. And that means I get special privileges, but it won't stay that way if little prats like you keep interfering."

"So?" It slipped out.

One of the boys grinned even bigger and was swiftly jabbed.

Another inhaled through his teeth, as though he'd just witnessed a hideous accident, which wasn't far from reality.

Duggan snarled, and a guttural rumble sharpened into an ominous growl. "You think that'll scare me off, brainiac?"

"What?" Joe said.

"Growling like a dog. What, you gonna give me rabies or something?"

"I thought that was *you*."

The throaty warning came closer, and Joe was suddenly aware Duggan was not the only predator at large in the woods. One of the boys tugged at their leader's arm, muttering and staring at something Joe could not see.

There was a mad flurry as the other two almost fell over themselves to sprint away. Duggan's expression changed from irritation to horror as a hulking black shape came out of the dark depths of the trees.

Stalking forward on piston-like legs, the Beast of Upton Puddle fixed its gleaming green eyes on the fleeing boys. Fangs bared, it launched after the floundering runners. Joe could almost feel the thud of its paws matching the hammering of his heart.

All was screaming confusion as Joe took off into the woods, fearing for not only his own life but also Duggan's and the others'. Branches, sky, and dirt became a blur of motion as he raced through the forest, crashing through leaf and twig, slamming into trees, screaming and tripping. Joe risked a backward glance, expecting to see bloody yellow fangs close on him, but there was no sign that the Beast was on his trail.

Fifteen minutes of running took Joe to the drive of Merrynether Mansion, and with pain stabbing his lungs, he collapsed against the main doors, yanking the bellpull. Joe leaned against the door, gulping air, waiting for an answer. None came. He pried his phone from his pocket and suppressed a cry of despair when he saw a crack across the display. Another tug at the rope drew no response. Joe, now desperate to find a working phone to call the police, decided there was only one other thing he could do—make for the cellar entrance again.

With the air still coarse in his throat, Joe tore

around the side of the house, wondering how he would get inside if the cellar trapdoor was padlocked properly this time. But today he was in luck. It was wide open, and parked beside it was the same white van he had seen when he'd first found the mansion.

As Joe skidded to a halt by the cellar entrance, Heinrich's panicked voice sounded from inside the back of the vehicle. The whole van shook.

"Please, Flarp, don't excite yourself. Ronnie needs us to stay out of sight until he's gone. Please calm down!"

But the frantic ruckus continued as though an enraged lunatic was throwing a basketball inside.

Though he was desperate to find out who or what Flarp was, Joe had other priorities and made for the cellar as fast as he could. Three steps at a time, he bounded inwards, rushing into Mrs. Merrynether's voluminous store of bric-a-brac. Still panting, Joe scanned the enormous room before making for the door that would take him up into the house, just in case there happened to be a phone handy. Boxes, piles of books, old crates, a strange-looking wooden contraption that resembled a telescope. A telescope? Surely Lilly hadn't actually made one, had he? Scattered wine bottles, battered kegs, gardening tools. Ah! A dusty phone hooked onto the wall above a gnarled table. It looked old, but with any luck, it was still connected. Joe rushed over, snatched at the receiver, and set it against his ear. The familiar trill of a ringtone greeted him and, without a thought for the trouble he was about to get himself into, he rung the school's reception desk.

"Good morning. Clarkdale Secondary Education. Can I help you?"

"Yes," said Joe, breathless. "I'd like to speak to Mr. Graves as quickly as possible, please. It's an emergency."

"I'll see if he's available. Who should I say is calling?"

"It's Joe Copper. I'm in his class. Please get him quickly. I think some other boys in my class might have been . . . hurt. We were in the woods, and a great big— I think it was the Beast—it . . ."

"Whoa! Slow down, slow down. Was Kurt Duggan one of those boys?"

"Yes, yes! He might've been—"

"He's fine. He and three others are in the headmaster's office right now. He's asked me to find a replacement for his lessons this afternoon, so I think they're in quite a bit of trouble."

"But they're okay?"

"A little shaken up at being caught truanting, but yes, they're fine . . . Were you with them? Where are you now?"

"I'm . . . safe," was all Joe could think to say before thrusting the handset back on the cradle with his eyes crinkled shut.

His hand remained on the phone as he thought through the possible scenarios. Whatever happened, he was probably going to get into a lot of trouble when he got back, but at least nobody was hurt. That was the important thing.

Joe breathed a huge sigh of relief and tried to get his bearings again. Outside, Heinrich was apparently still wrestling with the psychotic basketball as it pounded away inside the van. It was probably not the best time to stick his nose in uninvited, but perhaps now Joe could find Mrs. Merrynether and ask her if he could see Cornelius.

Despite the continued thonk and thunk of the mysterious Flarp bouncing around inside its temporary prison, Joe heard the van door slide open and then slam shut. Within seconds Heinrich had burst into the cellar, slammed the trapdoor, and raced down the steps. He halted, startled when he saw Joe standing before him. Beads of sweat clung to the good side of his face, while the burned side oddly remained dry, and green goo clumped in his hair.

With a shudder, Joe wondered what sort of a creature he'd been grappling with. "Hello?" he said awkwardly.

"What are you doing here? No, never mind," Heinrich said, exasperated. "Tell me later. Just follow me quickly. The inspector will be down here any minute, and if he finds out what we do here, it will all be over."

The Beast of Upton Puddle

*T*EN

Muffled voices came from behind the door leading to the pantry. Joe recognized one of those as Mrs. Merrynether's. The other belonged to that of an officious, gruff-sounding man. Probably the inspector that Heinrich had mentioned.

Joe felt one of Heinrich's large hands planted gently but firmly on his back, pushing him toward the vault.

"Through the door, quick. If he comes into the vault, God forbid, and sees us, you're my nephew visiting for the week. Understood?"

"But—" Joe protested as he was thrust through the door and manhandled down the steps.

"Understood?"

Argument was obviously not an option.

"Yes, but won't the inspector see all the—?" Joe stopped short as he entered the vault.

It appeared that a great deal of effort had gone into

disguising the Merrynether menagerie. The manticore's enclosure, as well as all the other cages, were hidden behind huge wooden screens made to look like walls. The vault seemed a lot smaller than before but was considerably brighter than usual—so much so that Joe found himself squinting at the blue-white glare flooding the area. Shielding his eyes, he looked up to the stony ceiling and saw a lightbulb dangling on a piece of black string disguised as an electric cable. It was too bright to see Danariel's slender form inside the glass, but Joe knew she was in there.

All possible signs of beast life had been completely hidden, but the visual trickery hadn't done anything to conceal the strange whoops and cackles or the pungent smells.

"Louder than usual, aren't they?" Joe commented to Heinrich.

The man paced around in no particular direction. "Louder? Yes. Oh, yes! Thank you." Heinrich rushed past Joe to his desk, shoved unfinished letters into a drawer, and rushed to switch on an enormous flat-screen TV recently mounted on the wall. He stabbed at the buttons at the bottom of the screen until a wildlife channel portrayed jungle scenes. A cacophony of squawking parrots, roaring lions, and screaming chimps competed with the excited noise of Mrs. Merrynether's beasts and Heinrich gave a quick thumbs-up to Joe.

"And the stench?" Joe asked.

"Oh!" Heinrich froze, then grabbed an aerosol by

his desk and began running around the vault spraying liberally.

The vault door swung open, and in stepped Mrs. Merrynether accompanied by Archy the pig and a pristinely suited man.

Joe instantly disliked the man. He had the expression of someone who had accidentally placed his hand into a soiled nappy. With his nose lifted and nostrils flared, the inspector cast his heavy-lidded gaze around the vault. Archy rubbed his snout against the man's crisp trousers and snorted when the man sharply nudged him aside.

Mrs. Merrynether glanced at Joe. If she was surprised at his unexpected presence, she hid it well.

"Somewhat bright in here, isn't it?" The man sneered as he raised his voice above the jungle racket.

Mrs. Merrynether pierced Heinrich with a hard stare as he scuffed to a stop, hiding the aerosol can behind his back and smiling nervously.

"Heinrich, would you be so kind as to dim"—the blue-white glare softened suddenly as she spoke—"the lights?"

Heinrich's nervous smile widened into an embarrassed grimace. He shrugged as though he'd somehow lowered the lights by using an unseen command. The inspector's drooping eyelids narrowed.

Joe crept to the side, beckoning Archy, hoping not to draw attention.

"Is it absolutely necessary to assault my ears with

this terrible noise?" The man's gruff voice was barely audible above the animals' sounds.

"Mr. Huffney, I'm afraid our Heinrich does enjoy his surround sound. And he's a little on the deaf side, you see."

Huffney waved a pen at Heinrich. "Could you turn it down a little, please?"

"Eh?" Heinrich replied, looking perplexed.

"I said, could you turn it down, please?"

"What?"

"I . . . Oh, never mind."

The inspector, clearly irritated by everything around him, scribbled on the paper in his clipboard. He turned sharply to Mrs. Merrynether. "It would appear that extensive refurbishment has been carried out here." He flicked some papers over. "According to standard council procedure, you should have completed a D974 renovations form to make any changes to a government-standard nuclear bunker." He stared down his long nose at Mrs. Merrynether, and a brief but icy silence ensued. "Has this been actioned, Mrs. Merrynether?"

"Eh?" shouted Heinrich.

"Not you!"

Mrs. Merrynether pointed at the inspector. "I can assure you that I went through all the appropriate channels when Merrynether Mansion was renovated."

"There is no record of any government-sanctioned builders contracted to do work here. Whom did you employ?"

"I don't trust any layabouts employed by Upton Puddle Council; I did it privately."

"That just won't do. Any work of this nature must be performed by government-approved—"

"Oh, poppycock! It's my mansion. I'll do as I please."

Huffney's expression twisted from general disdain to a picture of squirming indignation.

Heinrich, apparently suffering from extreme nervous tension, unwittingly pressed the nozzle behind his back. A loud hiss ripped through the air, joining the shriek of monkeys from the jungle documentary. With an apologetic expression, Heinrich showed them his aerosol can.

The inspector stared at him as if he were looking at a dog that had just defecated on his lawn.

"He has a few . . . digestive problems," Mrs. Merrynether improvised. "He takes air freshener with him everywhere."

"Eh?" barked Heinrich.

Huffney shook his head. "A deaf and flatulent assistant? How charming."

And then with timing that caused everyone's stomach to leap, a loud Irish shout boomed out, and the light in the room was mysteriously dampened to a dim blue glow.

"It's da horle family. Even da boy can't horld it in. Look at da little ankle boiter's backsoide. He's wet himself! You'd better get out before you drown in muck."

Joe checked the back of his trousers. It was only an hour ago he'd been hiding behind the school dustbins, sitting in filth.

"Who the devil was that, and who turned the lights down?" screamed Huffney.

Joe couldn't be sure if it was rage or shock that drove the exclamation, but either way, he could tell that the man was close to snapping.

At the sound of the cluricaun's voice, Archy yanked himself away from Joe and ran toward the back of the vault. No doubt the pig would be as unsuccessful in catching the Irish pest as everyone else had been.

"Come and get me, little piggy."

"I said, who was that?"

"Please stay calm, Mr. Huffney," said Mrs. Merrynether, "I'm sure that—"

"Didn't ya hear me, deafy? There must be a village somewhere deproived of its idiot. Oi said, you'd better go away before ya gets covered in muck. Dat gores for arl of yaz!" The last sentence was growled rather than shouted.

Archy came running back, squealing. A large patch of dark brown gunk had been splattered over his head. Two balls of what looked suspiciously like excrement whistled through the air. They splattered close to Huffney's shiny shoes. His eyes were open almost as wide as his mouth as another barrage flew past, hitting the vault door, apparently in anticipation of Archy scrambling up the stairs. At the far end of the vault, where the light was dimmest, Joe thought he could see the sky-blue color of Lilly's waistcoat and a line of devices like miniature trebuchets made with old wooden spoons and clothes pegs.

"This is preposterous! Whoever you are, stop this immediately. You are threatening a civil servant!"

"Ah, shot ya horle, ya rotten faker. And may da seven terriers of hell sit on ya shorlders and bark in at ya soul-case!"

Huffney's mouth opened even wider, which Joe considered to be extremely unwise as another shower of dung rained around them.

The panicked inspector pulled his jacket over his head and rushed for the vault door. "I'll see myself out. You'll be hearing from the county court, Mrs. Merrynether."

Thwak! A particularly large dung packet struck Huffney square in the back, and the inspector almost tripped as he ran from the vault. Joe could still hear his screams as the man fled from the mansion.

As soon as Huffney had left, the excremental onslaught ceased and the light came up to a normal level.

Heinrich stepped carefully around brown puddles and switched off the TV. Oddly, the hidden creatures had quieted down, and all that could be heard was the cluricaun laughing hysterically.

"Lilly," yelled Mrs. Merrynether, "you've gone too far this time. That's no whiskey for three weeks!"

The laughter continued.

Mrs. Merrynether turned on Heinrich, who flinched. "Every time something like this happens, it reminds me of your shabby security measures. If ever I find out how he got out of that cage, I'll—" She pursed her lips and drew a deep breath through her nose.

"I'm sorry, Ronnie. I already told you it wasn't me. What more can I do?" Heinrich said plaintively.

She nodded firmly.

Joe stepped forward, a surge of fresh guilt welling in his stomach as he approached Mrs. Merrynether. She turned to look at him, her wrinkled brow making her look like a furious walnut.

"And as for you, young man, why aren't you at school? What do you think you're doing here?"

"I . . ."

"Well?"

Joe wanted so desperately to tell her that it was his fault the cluricaun had escaped. That he was sorry for all the trouble he'd caused. But as each moment passed, he found it harder to speak. Then the memory of panic in the forest rushed like a hot wind through his mind.

"The Beast of Upton Puddle—I saw it again in the woods, so I ran here as fast as I could."

A flush of concern reddened her cheeks, but suspicion remained in her eyes. "The Beast? The one you saw before? The same one that raided Mr. Bacon's store?"

"Yes."

"Can you describe it?"

"Sure, it's—"

"Good. Then we can discuss this Beast of yours later. Right now I'm more concerned about getting everything ready for our next patient. It's a terrible mess in here."

"Can I help you clean up?" Joe asked.

"That's not for you to do," she said, turning to squint at the back of the vault.

The laughter had stopped.

"You have an hour's grace before you have to clean up this disaster, Lilly. As soon as we've settled Flarp inside, you'll have to get to work. Do you hear me?" she shouted. "I hope you realize what you've done. We'll have the council, the police, and goodness knows who else coming down here in no time, thanks to you."

"I don't believe so," came a whisper from the lightbulb.

"Danariel?" Mrs. Merrynether looked up at the light.

"Don't be so harsh on Lilly," Danariel said, pulling herself out of her glass home and fluttering to Mrs. Merrynether's level. "I warned him about Mr. Huffney."

"You warned him?"

"Yes, Mr. Huffney is not what he appears to be. Didn't you sense it? Have I not trained you well enough?"

"I sensed some deception, but I sense that in everyone—even in Heinrich and Joseph here."

Joe, still feeling guilty about Lilly's escape, stepped closer. "Is that why Lilly called him a rotten faker?"

"Yes, Joe," Danariel said, with a gentle smile. "Mr. Huffney was not from the council as he claimed."

"Redwar!" Heinrich punched the air. "I bet my socks that Redwar sent him."

"How clever," said Danariel, swimming up to the old giant of a man and brushing his cheek with her wings. "Yes, Argoyle Redwar sent him. Though I could not pry deeply into his mind, I sensed Redwar's . . . impression on him."

"So what's Redwar up to?" Joe asked.

"More scare tactics," Mrs. Merrynether said. "He wants this place, and he seems to know something of what we do here—enough to realize he mustn't get the *real* authorities involved. Can you imagine what would happen if the government found out that manticores and cluricauns are real? This place would be shut down and sealed off by scientists and black suits galore; then Redwar would never get his grubby hands on anything."

"But how does Redwar know?"

"That's what concerns me most, Joseph. I chose this mansion in this village because it is so well concealed. Not even the locals know what I do here, so it's a mystery to me that he knows anything at all."

Heinrich shuffled. "I too would like to know the answer, but we should discuss this later. Flarp was very excited when I left him in the van. We should get him inside."

"Ah, yes." Mrs. Merrynether put an arm around Joe's shoulders. "Are you ready to see our next patient? I think you'll like him."

ELEVEN

Heinrich loped over to the wall where the TV had been mounted and pulled at several levers sticking out of the floor, grunting with the effort needed to move each one. With the slow grinding and squealing of pulleys, each of the fake wooden walls raised into the ceiling. Like a dizzy firefly, Danariel flitted from one cage to another, apparently interested in how each of the animals was doing.

Much to Joe's relief, Cornelius the manticore was in his enclosure, still clinging to life.

"Is he any better, Mrs. Merrynether?"

Her arm dropped from around his shoulders, and her voice was no more than a whisper. "No change. There's nothing more we can do for him other than make him comfortable."

Joe felt all his sadness press itself into a tight ball in his throat. "Can I go in and see him?"

Joe saw the word *no* form on Mrs. Merrynether's lips, but then she paused.

"Please? Surely he's not dangerous anymore."

Heinrich came back to them with a grimace, rubbing his right bicep and rolling his shoulder. The levers were obviously quite stiff.

"Ronnie, we must see to Flarp." His tone was gentle but insistent. "I hate to think what he has done to our van in the last fifteen minutes."

"Yes. But first, open Cornelius's enclosure for Joseph, would you?"

He nodded, produced a weighty set of keys from the pocket of his huge coat, and unlocked the cage.

"We'll be two minutes," said Mrs. Merrynether.

Danariel was busy circling the horns of something large and grey in one of the other cages.

"Danariel?" Mrs. Merrynether called. "Joseph is going to spend a few minutes with Cornelius. Would you be so kind as to watch over him? We won't be long."

"Of course," the seraph replied. She fluttered to Joe and settled on his shoulder.

Mrs. Merrynether and Heinrich left the vault.

Joe pulled the barred door of the manticore enclosure open. A thrill ran through him as his foot crossed the border and touched the moss. Under the sole of his shoe, Joe felt the subtle snap of a quill belonging to a scarlet feather; the whole enclosure was littered with them. Though Cornelius was completely still, the reality that he was sharing a cage with something more dangerous than a lion struck Joe with sudden intensity.

With trembling hands and a racing heartbeat, he knelt beside the creature and pressed one palm against his side. He slid his fingers through the crimson fur and over the flowing bump of the manticore's ribs, the silky texture smooth against his skin.

A low moan gurgled from the beast's chest.

Joe quickly withdrew his hand.

"He will not hurt you." Danariel's voice tickled Joe's ear. "He likes affection."

As if to agree with the seraph, the animal's great head lifted from the rock he was resting against and turned toward Joe, its pupils no longer revealed as cat-like slits but wide wells of pain. Something that sounded like a complaint gurgled from Cornelius's chest again, and his barbed tail thumped against the turf.

"He likes affection," Danariel repeated.

Tentatively, Joe returned a hand to Cornelius's side and began to stroke him again. The red head, with its disturbingly humanlike face expressing weary satisfaction, returned to rest against the rock.

Three more minutes passed as Joe sat silently with Cornelius, watching his chest heave, listening to the soft, deep hum of what he believed to be purring. Joe wanted to stay there forever.

Just as Joe was about to lay his head against the manticore's side, the sound of splintering wood and smashing glass erupted from the cellar outside the vault. The equally loud shrieking of Mrs. Merrynether firing irritated commands at Heinrich followed immediately, and then Joe heard the giant man stumbling, almost falling down the steps. He too was shouting in panicked response, but the short outbursts sounded muffled to Joe, as if Heinrich had a bag over his head.

The sight of Heinrich bursting into the vault, staggering like Frankenstein's monster on a pub crawl was as shocking as it was comical—not because of the way the huge man's arms were outstretched in zombielike desperation and not even because of the German's cursing but because of the extraordinary thing covering his head.

Joe could do nothing apart from open his mouth wide and scream, more from shock than fear. Upon Heinrich's broad shoulders, completely surrounding the man's head, was a massive, pea-green ball of translucent slime. Dead center of the blob, the most enormous eyeball Joe had ever seen stared outward emoting what could be nothing other than delirious excitement. Snotty tendrils lapped around its floppy base as the eyeball swiveled, looking at everything with the frenzy of an unrestrained dog in a butcher's shop.

Joe's scream gave way to laughter as the riot continued.

Danariel shot to the safety of her lightbulb.

Sucking, plopping noises drowned out Heinrich's muted pleas as the eyeball drove him farther into the vault. It appeared to be all he could do to not slip in the muck that still coated the floor.

Right behind him, Mrs. Merrynether jabbed a broomstick at the hapless man's back. "I told you to calm down, Heinrich. You'll just make him worse. You know how excited this species can get."

A stream of gargled German swear words erupted from within the slimy eyeball before Heinrich lost his balance and fell backwards against his desk. With a loud pop and gasp of air, the jellylike creature flew upward, leaving Heinrich to spit and scoop off lumps of gloop from his face.

The creature was on the loose. Like a deflating party balloon, it spun and raced through the air, eagerly seeking something new and interesting to look at.

"Get up, Heinrich. Catch it before it gets away." Mrs. Merrynether jabbed him again.

With all the commotion, Joe hadn't been watching the manticore. Now he saw that Cornelius had lifted his head. A look of ruffled annoyance distorted the animal's proud features as he watched the slimy intruder whoosh around the vault. It was a look Joe had seen before on a stray cat he'd tried to befriend, and it wasn't a good sign. Cautiously, Joe stood and backed out of the enclosure, shutting the door behind him. He sidled up to Mrs. Merrynether, who was squinting intensely at Heinrich.

"What *is* that?" Joe asked.

"That, dear boy, is a globble." She gave Heinrich

one more nudge as he strode toward the eye, arms lifted. "He's got about as much chance as an elephant catching a fly," she whispered to Joe gleefully, leaning on her broom. "But it'll be amusing to watch him for a while, won't it? And perhaps it'll teach him to tighten up his security methods."

Heinrich, covered in slime, his grey hair sticking out in all directions, staggered after the blob. To Joe he looked like a man who had narrowly escaped an explosion in a hair gel factory.

"What did you say that thing is?" Joe asked again.

"A globble. His name is Flarp."

"I've never heard of one of those."

"Well, I'm not surprised. You won't find them in any encyclopedia, not even under the mythology section."

"Where did it *come* from?" Joe asked. "Actually, where do *any* of these animals come from?"

"That is a secret, but I will tell you this: Every single one of the creatures treated at Merrynether Mansion comes from an island—a protected island. Only I and Heinrich—"

"Ronnie, look," Heinrich shouted.

The globble was hovering outside Cornelius's enclosure, apparently fascinated by the manticore, and Joe had the distinct impression that this strange ball of slime was desperate to make friends. Unfortunately for Flarp, the feeling was not mutual.

The disgruntled manticore whipped his barbed tail

in the air, and with a deadly swing, a poisonous dart shot out at the jelly beast.

Flarp deftly avoided the poisonous projectile.

"Get back," said Mrs. Merrynether to Joe. "If one of those barbs hits you, I'll be spending the rest of the day saving your life. The venom is extremely potent."

With undampened enthusiasm, the globble flew back to the enclosure. Its enormous eyeball strained, looking like it was about to burst with the excitement of meeting a new friend. With a rhythmic sloshing motion, it weaved and dodged quill after quill as Cornelius tried to rid himself of this new intruder.

"Still want me to catch it?" Heinrich grinned.

"Of course not." Mrs. Merrynether waved him over. "Just back away to a safe distance, and let's see what happens. This could be the answer we've been waiting for."

Joe marveled at the speed of the green blob as it zipped around the enclosure, never taking its focus off Cornelius and easily dodging each attack. "Are you sure the globble won't get hurt?"

"It may get unlucky," Mrs. Merrynether answered, "but globbles are notoriously unresponsive to toxins of any kind. No circulatory system, you see."

"That's why it couldn't be sedated for the journey here," Heinrich cut in. "No, Flarp will be fine. The worst that will happen is a tiny cut. And he will heal quickly."

Mrs. Merrynether shook her head. "Strange beasties,

these. No sense of smell, hearing, touch, or taste. They just suck in air, feed on bacteria, and float around all day long, looking at things. Essentially, the globble is nothing more than a conscious eyeball."

"So what's wrong with it?" Joe asked.

Mrs. Merrynether smiled back. "It's blind."

Joe gazed at the creature bobbing like a hyperactive jellyfish, still avoiding darts with incredible agility. "It looks like it can see perfectly," Joe said. "It *must* be seeing those darts, especially if it doesn't have any other senses."

Mrs. Merrynether removed her glasses and gave them to Joe. "Put these on for a moment."

Joe obeyed and was immediately confronted by a world so blurred and distorted he couldn't even distinguish Mrs. Merrynether from Heinrich. He could just about see her lips moving as she spoke.

"Even now, Flarp can see far better than you or I, but in comparison to others of its kind, Flarp's vision is no better than what you see through my spectacles."

Joe took the glasses off and handed them back.

"So he's a super eye?"

"In a manner of speaking, yes. Our vision is limited to a narrow spectrum of light and relatively short distances, but a normal globble can see the fleas on a cat's back a thousand miles away through a ten-foot wall of lead."

"Wow! Really? Can they see other planets and stars and things if they look at the sky?"

"D'you know, I've never thought about that," she

answered. "I'll have to ask him one day."

"Ask him? How do you talk to a floating eyeball?"

"I can't, but Danariel can."

As if she sensed she was needed, Danariel popped out of her lightbulb and drifted to Mrs. Merrynether, careful to stay out of the line of fire. "You'd like me to talk with the globble?"

"If you wouldn't mind. Though I'm certain Flarp's provocation is going to help Cornelius, the manticore is still very weak, and too much antagonism may not be beneficial. We need to calm our new guest down and get him settled into his own enclosure."

"I will do what I can, but these are not the brightest of nature's creations."

Danariel flittered as close as she could to the green ball and danced around it. Flarp's attention instantly transferred to this new curiosity with equal interest. With little regard for the seraph's personal space, the globble pushed as close to her as he could get.

For the first time since its arrival, the globble stopped rushing around, and the two oddities drifted in graceful orbit together, sharing in what Joe assumed was some sort of private conversation.

"What does it say?" Joe asked.

Danariel was silent for a moment or two before moving away from Flarp, whose unrelenting stare was still trained on its new playmate. "He said, 'Me! Me! Me! Red thing. Blue thing. Me green. Me! Me! Me! Happy thing.'"

Mrs. Merrynether and Heinrich exchanged knowing looks.

"I believe Flarp understands me," Danariel continued, "but whether he is willing to calm down and behave himself in an enclosure is another matter. He's still very excited."

As she spoke, Joe could see the globble spinning around and around, its snotty extremities stretching outwards. Joe smiled. He was reminded of how other kids in his class would often sit on swivel chairs in the common room when they were bored, spinning as fast as they could until they collapsed in laughing heaps.

Mrs. Merrynether sighed. "Perhaps we should have waited a little longer before agreeing to treat Flarp. We already have our hands full with the cluricaun."

"Perhaps," said Heinrich, "but at least with him, we have a chance to save Cornelius."

"True." She smiled. "Well, enough dillydallying. We have to get our new patient tucked away."

Joe stared at the muck-covered floor, still feeling a certain responsibility for the fact that Lilly had caused so much devastation. "I can get started clearing this up, if you like."

"I think not, young man. That's Lilly's job, and you shouldn't even be here. Return to school at once. I don't want teachers and parents as well as fake council inspectors knocking on my door, do I?"

"But I can come back Sunday?"

"Of course. The shopping won't do itself, will it?"

Joe grinned and stole another glance at the manticore before leaving.

Cornelius had returned to his former sleeping position, but at least now there was hope for the beast to pull through.

TWELVE

Joe had not seen his mum so angry in quite some time. She said nothing as he walked through the front door, but the look in her eyes told Joe she wouldn't stay silent for long. The deputy head of Clarkdale School, Mr. Henderson, sat in one of the armchairs taking tiny sips from a cup of tea.

Aunt Rose passed Joe on her way out of the house, buttoning her coat in a hurry and tossing him a look that an army general might give a cadet who was about to be exposed to the front line on a battlefield. "I'll see you later, Jane. And it was nice to meet you, Mr. Henderson."

She smiled and left the house.

Henderson looked like his eyes had given up smiling long before his mouth, which was half disguised by a patchy greying beard. One ear stuck out a little more than the other, and one eye pointed slightly inward, giving Henderson an appearance that terrified younger students and sent older ones into stifled hysterics. Adding to those his tweed suit that was a size too small and his bouncy walk, the deputy head was a continual source of amusement at Clarkdale. Nevertheless, Joe liked him.

"Hello, Joe," Mr. Henderson said in a higher pitch than usual. The greeting sounded friendly enough, but being called by his first name instead of the usual *Copper* made Joe instantly uncomfortable.

"Hello." Joe stood perfectly still, unsure which of Mr. Henderson's eyes to look at.

Mr. Henderson placed his teacup on the coffee table and glanced at Joe's mum expectantly.

She nodded back, tight-lipped.

"Sit down, Joe," he said with a sigh. "Do you mind if we talk about what happened today?"

Joe decided not to reply as he sat in the armchair opposite Mr. Henderson. He could already feel his throat waiting to betray his guilt with a telltale swallow halfway through a sentence.

"It's no secret your concentration in *all* your classes has been lacking for the past few weeks, but today's events are not what I . . . or your mother expected from you."

Joe stared at the carpet.

"Lack of concentration is one thing, but leading several other students into truancy and then trying to use the Beast of Upton Puddle as an excuse for your behavior is quite unacceptable."

"What? That's not true!" Joe looked up.

Henderson adopted a much harder tone. "There were several witnesses who saw you run through the yard with school property during lesson time. Mr. Graves has also spoken to Kurt Duggan, and it's now apparent that you coerced him and several other boys to leave the school grounds."

"Who? Mr. Graves?"

"What? No, of course not! Kurt Duggan. You coerced Duggan into skipping class."

"But the Beast! It was—"

"The other boys say there was no Beast."

"But—"

Henderson leaned forward, his ears turning a deep shade of red. "Did you or did you not enter a restricted classroom area during lesson time and take an item that does not belong to you?"

Joe looked away from the deputy head and into his mum's pleading eyes.

"Yes," he whispered.

Joe's mum pressed both her hands against her mouth.

"Why, Joe?" Henderson asked, lowering his voice.

Joe chewed at his top lip, desperate to think of a way to explain everything, but how could he tell them the truth—the truth that would make him sound insane? Joe couldn't bear to look at either of them, so he focused on the carpet again. "I . . . don't know."

The deputy head sighed. "You're one of our brightest. Up until the last few weeks, you've been a model student, and I don't want to see you throw away a promising future."

"If you think I'm such a model student, why do you take Duggan's word over mine?"

"The groundskeeper vouched for him on this occasion. Besides, you haven't offered any explanation."

Joe's mum could hold her silence no longer. "Please tell me what's going on, Joe. Why did you do it? Why have you been so distant lately?"

The tightly controlled emotion in her voice hurt Joe, but no reasonable answer came as he opened his mouth to speak. Should he tell her of manticores and cluricauns? Of globbles and seraphim?

Tears trembled on the edges of his mum's lids. "It's that place you told me about last week, isn't it? Merrynether Mansion? Ever since you've been going there, you've been acting differently. Is that where you've just come back from?"

Joe hesitated.

"Is it?" Her voice sounded much louder than usual.

Joe searched her eyes, then looked at Mr. Henderson. The deputy squinted at his student as though stumped by a particularly hard equation. Joe felt the weight of regret press on him as he looked back at his mum. He knew what would follow his reply. "Yes."

She stared at him for several seconds, the decision

hardening in her eyes. "I want you to promise me you won't go back to that place. I don't know what's really been going on, and I know you're not going to tell me, but it's obviously having a bad effect on you."

"But Mrs. Merrynether needs me. I get her shopping for her."

"Yes, so you've told me, but that doesn't—"

"Here," said Joe, eagerly pulling the latest list from his back pocket and handing it to his mum.

She unfolded it. Her mouth opened wider as she read. "A shopping list for an elderly lady? This?"

"Some of the things are a bit strange, but—"

"Strange? That isn't the word I would use. There's almost every alcoholic drink I can think of listed here. And why is she asking for a packet of Cuban cigars and a poster calendar of Belfast's Best Buxom Bikini Booty Beauties?"

Mr. Henderson, who had just taken the opportunity for another sip of his drink, coughed out a spray of tea.

"Lilly!" Joe said. "He must have swapped the list somehow when I wasn't looking."

"Lilly? Who's Lilly?"

Joe shook his head and made a grab for the list, but his mum quickly folded and pocketed it.

"But that isn't . . . That wasn't Mrs. Merrynether's list. I swear! There was a . . . a bag of apples, a muzzle, and . . ."

"I'm not going to argue with you. You are *never* to

go to that place again. I mean it. Never again."

"But—"

"No! Now go to your room."

Cold despondency dragged all his dreams into the pit of his stomach when he saw the resolve in her eyes. Reluctantly, he left the living room and headed upstairs.

Mr. Huffney pressed down his pin-striped suit, smoothing out creases as he stood before Argoyle Redwar, wishing he had a chair to sit in. He fixed his gaze directly upward, waiting for his employer to speak, the plain white of the ceiling being the least uncomfortable place to look. If he were to focus any lower, the ugly stuffed animal heads would be staring right back at him. Looking to his right would place him firmly under the scrutiny of Ms. Burrowdown and her fearsome notebook, but the worst place to look would be into Redwar's beady eyes. The fat director had been kept waiting for much longer than he would have liked, but after fleeing from Merrynether Mansion resembling a human cow pie, Huffney needed time to freshen up, calm down, and change into a new suit before facing his employer.

Redwar leaned across his desk, interlaced his fingers, and scowled. "I trust this delay means you have a profitable report for me, Mr. Huffney?"

Huffney shuffled. "I regret that my report will not be as profitable as you might have hoped, sir. In fact—"

"What do you mean 'will not be,' Huffney? What have you been doing since you left Merrynether Mansion? I expected a report on my desk an hour ago."

"There was . . . an incident involving—"

"Incident? What sort of incident? Did you get into the vault? Did you see any of the animals?"

"No, sir, but there may have been a . . . pygmy."

"A pygmy?"

"Yes, sir. It was quite dark, but I thought it may have been an Irish pygmy wearing a little blue—"

"Never mind. My informant has told me exactly what she has in that vault, but that's not what I need." Redwar leaned farther over his desk, his piggy eyes scrunching in what might have been discomfort from the hard edge of the wood cutting into his voluminous stomach but was more likely avarice. He licked his lips. "I'll forgive the report, Huffney, if you provide me with the files I asked for."

Huffney found the courage to look at Redwar. "I am afraid I was unable to confiscate anything. I was attacked, sir."

Redwar's hands shot up, throttling an invisible neck. "I gave you explicit orders to bring back every piece of documentation she has in her possession, and you're telling me you came back with *nothing*?"

Huffney took a step back. "Sir, didn't you hear me? I said I was—"

"Nothing?"

"I didn't have a chance to—"

"You actually got into her vault and came back empty-handed? No map? Nothing?"

All Huffney could do was blink.

Redwar stood and slammed his palms on the desk. "Get out of my office, Huffney. As of tomorrow you can look for employment elsewhere. I am not in the habit of employing people who are unable to deliver upon a simple request."

"You're . . . you're firing me?" Huffney blinked some more.

"Ms. Burrowdown," he bellowed, "I've tried patience, kindness, bribery, infiltration, threats, and even sending *this* imbecile to get the information I need, but still I don't have it. Do I have to fire every single employee to get the location of that island?"

"I'm fired?" Huffney stood frozen like a rabbit caught in the headlights.

"Yes! Get out!"

Ms. Burrowdown garbled something.

"What? Speak up, woman."

"Sepshun?" she mumbled a little louder.

"Reception? Why would I want to call reception?"

"Fired?" Huffney was still mesmerized.

"Security. That's what I need. Not reception." Redwar stabbed a thumb at his phone while drilling a hateful look into his ex-employee.

"You need someone escorted off-site, sir?" came a

drab voice over the speakerphone.

"Don't preempt me, young man. People have been sacked for less."

"Sorry, sir. What can I do for you?"

"I need someone escorted off-site."

"On our way, sir."

Huffney straightened his tie and made for the door. "You will be hearing from my—"

"Oh, save your breath, Huffney. A word or two in the right place, and I'll have your lawyers fired too."

"Not sepshun," Ms. Burrowdown muttered, "*Sep*shun."

Redwar frowned at her. His eyebrows raised as enlightenment followed. "Ah! Deception! Yes, indeed, but what?"

Ms. Burrowdown's face twitched into a new pattern of wrinkles as her lips curved into a wicked smile.

"Now I know why you've been in my service for so long, Ms. Burrowdown. You have an idea, don't you?"

As curious as Huffney was to hear the end of their conversation, he had no desire to suffer the indignity of being dragged off-site by security guards. He slammed the door on his way out.

THIRTEEN

The toughest question in the world ached in Joe's head for two whole days and nights. Should he defy his mother? He had never done that before. Not to the extent he considered now. To ignore her order to never go to Merrynether Mansion again, to betray her trust and hurt her like that, would change everything between them. When his father had died, Joe had decided he would never let his mum down but would always obey and trust her. Until now, he had never needed to question that.

But he had been chosen, hadn't he? Danariel said he would be a champion among champions, fighting a great enemy. Could he really turn his back on such a destiny? Could he walk away from this newly discovered world of wondrous beasts and adventure?

Agony! Joe pressed his palms into his forehead and tried to stare holes through his bedroom ceiling. If only he could see into the future and know which decision was right. With a deep sigh, Joe flopped his arms by his sides and glimpsed the red numbers of his alarm clock: 03:17. If only he could sleep.

Joe closed his eyes tight, wishing he could doze off, but the sounds of night denied him that relief. The refrigerator downstairs gurgled, then clicked. The boiler in the cupboard hissed. The weather vane on the roof groaned as the light rain tapped its rhythm on the window, excited briefly by each gust. Every sound reminded Joe of a different animal hidden away in Mrs. Merrynether's vault.

Ten more minutes and he could stand the torture no more. Half past three in the morning or not, sensible or not, Joe decided not to turn his back on destiny. He would go there now, risk a trip through Ringwood Forest, and deal with the consequences later.

By the time Joe reached Merrynether Mansion, it was four thirty in the morning. The ocean blue of early light washed the sky through the trees, and soft rain pattered against their leaves. The gothic silhouette of Mrs. Merrynether's home was a welcome sight, especially after Joe had trudged through the woods in the early hours, terrified the Beast of Upton Puddle may be lurking behind any tree.

Joe pulled his hood tighter around his head and squinted up at the mansion through the rain. What was he supposed to do now? Ringing the doorbell at this hour wouldn't do him any favors.

Scolding himself for yet another stupid decision, Joe headed toward the side of the mansion. Perhaps he'd be lucky with the trapdoor again. But as he approached and saw the padlock fastened securely against the wooden boards, Joe knew there was no way of sneaking inside. The dead weight of decision tormented him once again as he imagined pulling the bell cord.

"Pssst!"

Joe ducked and glanced around.

"Pssst! Oi! Spam fer brains, over here!" The harsh Irish whisper came from an open window on the first floor, and the tiny man in his pale blue waistcoat stood with his stubby hands splayed against the panes.

"Lilly?" Joe whispered back.

"Oi can't believe ya came! Did ya bring da booze, boy?"

"Booze?"

"Me list! Why else would ya be sneakin' around in da wee hours? Ya saw me list and tort ya'd take pity on a poor tirsty cluricaun. I didn't tink ya'd actually get da stoff, but here ya are!"

"How did you know I was here?"

As if in answer to his question, an enormous eyeball squidged against the window next to Lilly, pressing so hard to get out that Joe could see every vein flattened against the glass.

"Dis ting is me new best friend. Flarp can see troo walls, ya knor! I saw him get excoited dat someone was comin', so I followed him. Dat's when I saw ya, boy."

"Wow! He could see me from in there?"

Lilly pushed the window open a little wider and threw something shiny onto the driveway near Joe's feet: a copper key.

"Dat's da key to da padlock, so stop yackin' and get yaself insoide widdat drink. Oim on me last dregs of Jameson and gettin moity tirsty."

Without waiting for an answer, Lilly left the window, dragging the reluctant Flarp by his snotty edges.

Joe picked up the key and stared at it. It may as well have been a crowbar or a brick. Joe was about to break in to the Merrynether vaults for the second time. But surely if he explained everything to Mrs. Merrynether, she would understand, wouldn't she? What would he tell his mum? Sickening guilt and worry anchored Joe to the spot.

"I can't do it," he whispered. He squeezed the key and took one final look at the mansion before turning back to the forest.

"Where d'ya tink you're goin'?" It was more of a screech than a whisper.

Though startled, Joe hesitated and then turned around.

Still accompanied by Flarp, the cluricaun had returned to the window, leaning into the rain while shaking his fist. The globble looked a lot less excited than it had a few minutes before, and Joe wondered if it was actually disappointed to see him leave, or perhaps it could see the look of dejection in his face.

"I'm going home."

"Home? But ya can't. What about me whiskey?"

"I didn't bring your stupid whiskey," Joe shouted back, the hurt obvious in his voice. Flarp turned to stare at Lilly, and it was the first time Joe had seen the great eyeball look annoyed. It quivered in irritation and then drifted off somewhere out of sight as if in disgust. The cluricaun seemed unconcerned by Flarp's protest.

"No booze?"

Joe shook his head, his shoulders slumping as he sulked into the forest. He chose to ignore the frustrated curse that Lilly fired into the wind behind him.

"A witch's itch on ya bum, and may ya have no nails ta scratch it with!"

Joe's alarm clock read 05:34, which meant he had a mere twenty-six minutes before his mum came in with tea and cereal. Joe lay on his bed again, staring at the ceiling again, thinking about the creatures he would never see . . . again.

Bright Friday morning sunlight invaded the room through the ruffled gaps in his curtains, and Joe watched the slow twirl of tiny dust particles in the light. Usually that would fascinate him. He'd calculate the subtle fractal patterns, count the visible specs, and imagine what it would be like to be a microscopic bacterium swept along in the currents. But today all the magic had gone.

Nothing compared to Merrynether Mansion. The same choice tormented him, and now he faced a new temptation to disobey his mum: the key. He'd resisted the first urge to use it, but how long would he be able to keep that up?

Joe lifted it into the light and stared at it, feeling numb. Free entry to a world of wonder that so few others would see, and he could do nothing about it. Still, he'd keep the key with him all the time . . . just in case.

At six o'clock, Joe's mum came in with a tray and a smile. "I made you something special today."

Joe looked at the tray as she placed it on the bed and sat next to him. "I made this last night. I know how much you like it."

The scents of toasted fruit bread lightly buttered and spread with damson jam wafted under Joe's nose. "But I thought I was being punished."

"I saw that look in your eyes when I sent you to your room yesterday, and I realized just how important that place is to you."

Joe sat upright with the speed of someone who had been woken with a cattle prod. "I'm allowed to go back?"

"I didn't say that."

Joe slumped.

"I just want you to know I'm not doing this to upset

you." She touched his shoulder. "And I need you to understand I'm stopping these visits to Mrs. Merrynether's for your own good."

Joe nodded but avoided eye contact. "I know."

"Will you tell me what's really going on? We don't usually keep secrets from each other, do we?"

Joe stayed silent, frowning at his breakfast, sifting through ideas. He wanted to tell his mum about all of it, even confess the pointless trip in the middle of the night, but surely she would think him a liar. At least she wasn't mad at him, which meant he still had a chance to turn things around.

"If you don't tell me, I can't help you, Joe. Is it something to do with bullying at school? Is that why you haven't been switching on your mobile?"

Joe couldn't believe his luck. She'd served him the answer right alongside his breakfast. All he had to do was take the truth and sprinkle it with a little seasoning—just to make it more palatable. A second or two of silence and a brief but timorous glimpse into his mum's eyes were all he needed.

"I knew it!" she said. "Someone's been picking on you, haven't they?"

Joe held his silence a little longer.

"You don't have to tell me who it is, but if that's what's happening, I can have a word with Mr. Henderson and he can do something about it."

"Well"—Joe lifted his head—"I *was* chased into

the woods, but I didn't actually get beaten up. I didn't mean to stay away from school. It's just that I was a bit . . . frightened."

Joe's mum nodded. "That explains a lot."

"And that's when I ran to Merrynether Mansion. I knew I'd be safe there and that there'd be a phone. I busted mine when I was trying to get away. I had to know if the others were okay."

"So you really did see the Beast?"

"Yes." Joe nodded furiously.

His mum sighed. "I believe you, but I'm still concerned about this Merrynether woman. That list was hardly the sort of thing she should be getting a young boy to collect for her."

"But it really wasn't her list. That was somebody's idea of a joke. Why would an old lady want a calendar full of Belfast's Best Buxom—?"

"Yes, I remember what it said. No, I don't think she would have put that on a shopping list." She stared at Joe thoughtfully.

"Please, Mum. Don't stop me going there. I've learned so much. Please?"

A smile formed on her lips. "All right, but on one condition," she said, raising her voice above Joe's whoop of joy. "I want to see a marked improvement at school in the next few weeks. Understood?"

"Understood." Joe grinned.

She stroked his hair and stood. "Enjoy your fruit

bread. Don't let me down." She left the room, still smiling.

Throughout the next week at school, Joe became the new center of attention but not in a good way. The teachers acted the same, apart from a noticeable suspicion in their eyes when they spoke to him, but the others in his class taunted him with growls and impressions of the Beast in the woods. Predictably, Duggan was the worst, and Joe found it impossible to resist a cutting remark every time the bully targeted him.

By Friday, it was obvious to everyone that Duggan had had enough. When the final bell sounded, a hungry group of spectators gawped at Joe as he endured a week's worth of frustration in the form of a severe pounding outside the school gates. It didn't last long—Duggan clearly knew a crowd would draw unwanted attention from any number of nosy teachers—but it was, nevertheless, a thorough battering.

As the sneering bully wandered off with the dispersing mob, Joe staggered into Ringwood Forest. Bruised by Duggan's knuckles and feeling sick to his socks with the hammering in his head, he collapsed at his favorite tree stump, not caring about how long he'd have to sit there. At home his mum would press a pack of frozen peas against his eye and try to comfort him, but Joe wanted the soft sway of leafy branches and the open air. He wanted the healing warmth of nature.

"I'll be missing my kicking fix for Saturday and Sunday, won't I, brain boy?"

Joe opened his eyes to see his nemesis standing over him, holding a thick branch. Apparently, Duggan wasn't satisfied with his brief clash outside the school and had followed Joe into the woods. He hoped Duggan couldn't read the surprise or fear in his face, but it would make little difference anyway. The whites of the bully's eyes contained the usual psychotic excitement that told Joe he was about to feel a sting of bark on his skin. He may as well make Duggan earn it.

"That's a nice stick," Joe said. "Why don't you throw it and go play fetch with yourself?"

Then came the angry smile and a whoosh of stick across the side of Joe's head. His ears rang.

"Think you're really clever, don't you?"

Whump! The stick connected with the other side of Joe's head. He scrambled away on hands and knees.

"Think you can keep it up if I break your jaw?"

The stick fell across his back, followed by a boot to the ribs. Joe groaned and turned over, looking into the sunlight, wishing someone somewhere would intervene, wishing he'd decided to go home instead. Images blurred and swam as if he'd put on a pair of water-filled goggles.

Duggan's figure darkened Joe's view as he stooped over him like a gorilla about to swat a chimp from his den.

"What's that?" Duggan stopped moving.

For a second, Joe hoped they'd been disturbed by

the Beast of Upton Puddle, but Duggan was staring at the ground a few feet away from the tree stump. "This yours?" he said, picking up a shiny object and showing it to Joe.

Joe squinted, battling with his vision. It was the padlock key. He stared at it for a second or two, trying to look unconcerned. "Never seen it before."

Duggan's teeth flashed in a sadistic grin. "It *is* yours. What does it open?"

Joe shrugged and shook his head.

"You'd better tell me, 'cause if you don't, I'll have to take it to Gravesy the groundskeeper. Me and him are like that." Duggan crossed two fingers. "He used to be a locksmith, and he'll be able to tell me what lock this fits."

Joe knew that was a lie, but it didn't matter. His stomach tied in knots. He stared at the key, then at Duggan, gritting his teeth. There was no way he could allow this thug to walk away with it. Though he knew there'd be little chance of success, Joe launched himself at the yob, screaming his tonsils out.

Joe's head connected with Duggan's chest, almost toppling him, but he responded with a sharp lunge. Joe no longer had the advantage of surprise, and Duggan was ready for the next try. He came at the bully with a wild windmill of fists, but Duggan met each swing with a jarring block and drove him back to the ground. Two knees pressed Joe's aching arms, and he knew his face would be the next target.

"All right, all right," Joe gasped. "I'll tell you what the key's for, but you *have* to keep it a secret."

Duggan grinned. "I don't *have* to do anything. How about you tell me, and I don't finish off this kicking?"

"Fair enough. Just get it over with, then, but you'll never find out what it opens."

Duggan squinted, his tiny brain obviously calculating the odds. With a slow nod, he opened his fist to look at the key, then pocketed it. "I'm keeping the key, but, yeah, okay—I'll keep it a secret."

Joe knew that was a lie too, but it didn't matter. "It's the key to my savings box, which I buried out here in the forest."

"Savings? How much?"

"Two hundred fifty quid."

"Really?" Duggan almost drooled the next question. "Where did you hide it?"

"I made a map, but I don't have it on me. That would be stupid, wouldn't it?"

"Yeah, I s'pose so. So where's the map?"

Joe was tempted to tell the thug there was another map for that map but decided not to push his luck. "It's at home."

"Well, go and get it, then. I'll be waiting here."

"I won't be able to come back out once my mum sees I'm home. I'll bring the map to school on Monday, but you have to promise you won't beat me up again."

"All right, but if you forget it, I'll make sure you won't be able to walk for a week. Get it?" Duggan shifted more of his weight onto his knees to emphasize his point.

"Got it." Joe winced.

Duggan eyed him, then got up. "Monday, brain boy. Don't forget," he said before he strolled off.

Joe struggled to his feet. There was no choice now. He had to get to Merrynether Mansion fast. There was little chance that Duggan would ever find out what the key was for, but that was not his chance to take. He had to warn Mrs. Merrynether.

FOURTEEN

By the time Joe had pulled the bell cord the fourth time, he knew nobody was coming to let him in. Joe made his way around the side of the mansion, thinking this was getting to be a bit of a habit. He doubted the trapdoor would be open this time, especially since Lilly had stolen the padlock key, but perhaps the tradesman's entrance would be a possibility.

Both were shut. The tradesman's entrance displayed a sign saying *Closed until Monday*, and a shiny new padlock secured the trapdoor to its frame. At least there was no chance of Duggan getting inside with the old key, but Joe was desperate to know how things were coming along with the manticore. The last time he stood in the vault, there came the glimmer of hope that Flarp's chaotic arrival would help him recover.

Something small and sharp bounced off Joe's head.

He yelped and rubbed furiously at his scalp.

A screw chunked in the grass by his feet.

Lilly leaned out of a window, his beetroot face wrinkled in anger and his little teeth chomping down on his pipe as he waved his fists in the air. "Get ye gone, ya backshtabbin' yellow-bellied turncort." His eyebrows rose. "Unless a course ya brought me drink dis toime?" The cluricaun paused, his teeth clacking on the end of his pipe as he passed it from one side of his mouth to the other.

Joe grinned. "Are you going to let me in?"

"Get me a bloody drink, boy! That woman's new beasty is drivin' me ta misery—I needs me some relief."

"I thought you liked Flarp."

"No, not him. She got a new one yesterday. Horrible little ting, ruder than a nude at a queen's tea party . . . and twoice as ogly!"

"You two should get along just fine, then."

"Why, ya little—" Lilly almost fell out of the window.

"So where's Mrs. Merrynether?"

Lilly ducked inside, slammed the window, and screamed a torrent of Irish curses as one of the panes smashed.

Joe cupped his hands around his mouth, "You all right up there, Lilly?"

A loud raspberry sounded in return.

"Thanks!" Joe laughed. "So is Mrs. Merrynether in or not? I'll keep on until you tell me."

More curses accompanied the scrunching of tiny

clogs on glass. A hand shot out of the window, pointed toward the back of the house, and then made a V sign before darting inside again.

"Thanks, Lilly." Smiling, Joe walked past the trapdoor and around the back of the mansion, realizing he'd never actually been there before. He wondered what he might find.

An explosion of color and grandeur stole Joe's breath as he turned the corner. A huge garden, bursting with sunny pineapple broom and vibrant lilies painted like cherry-red lips, greeted him. Ancient oaks lined a perfect circle of grass the size of a small lake. From their branches hung baskets of snowy petals that splashed outward like frozen fountains. Central to the ground's grassy expanse, moss-smothered statues dominated the view, each fantastic creature swathed in wild vines. Joe recognized a manticore sculpture rearing on two legs as if in battle, the tail arched and the fearsome talons extended like knives. But commanding even greater attention, standing on a plinth at the very center, stood the proud figure of a dragon, its long neck searching upwards and its arrow-shaped head lifted to the sky. Joe worked out that from the base to the tip of its snout it stood at exactly twenty-three feet and seven inches.

Impressed by the workmanship, Joe took a few more moments to gaze at it and then noticed the strange figurines circling the plinth. At first he thought they were simple stone funnels spouting jets of water over the base, but a closer look revealed them to be a ring of flabby men covered with warts and seated with their heads pressed into their palms: they were crying over the dragon's feet. A few paces in front, completing the display, was the likeness of a seraph with both its arms and wings stretched in abandon, its face also tilted skyward like the dragon's.

Joe studied all this for a while longer, wondering what it was supposed to represent, before turning his attention back to why he had come. At the far end of the grounds, Joe saw Mrs. Merrynether dressed in muddy, green overalls and crouched over a large rectangle of soil and a long line of canes supporting a crowded array of bulbous fruit. Her back was to him, and her shoulders pumped as lumps of dirt and weeds flew from either side of her.

In contrast to Mrs. Merrynether's sprightly action, Archy the pig lay next to her on his back, snoring with an occasional twitch.

"Mrs. Merrynether?" Joe called.

Her head turned, and she squinted through her enormous lenses. "Ah, Joseph. Good to see you, boy. Come over here and give me a hand, would you? My back's not what it used to be."

Joe hurried over, sat beside her, and looked at the plants on display: things he'd never seen in the fruit and veg section of the local grocery store before. Knobbly fruit like pink golf balls hung from one bush; long yellow things with black hooks and hairy tips sprouted from thick roots too. And then he noticed a fat pea-green mushroom that looked like it had split into four separate heads, each entwined with its neighbor.

"What are they?" breathed Joe. "I've never seen plants like these before. Where did you get them?"

Mrs. Merrynether picked a golf ball from the closest bush and inspected it. "This one is called baby moons' blight."

She tossed it into a basket to her left and picked another. "They're very good for your health, you know—strengthen the arteries. Want a bite? This one's perfect."

Joe wrinkled his nose but accepted it anyway. Being sure to watch her reaction, Joe had a tentative sniff, then bit into it. The skin popped, and a fine mist of clear juices sprayed into the air as the pulp savaged his taste buds. Joe wasted no time in spitting it out and gargling his disapproval. "Urgh! It tastes like vindaloo. They're horrible."

"You don't like a good curry?" Mrs. Merrynether chortled.

"No, I do not. I had a bit of my mum's takeout a few months ago. It was gross."

"Shame. I've got some daddy moons' blight growing in the conservatory. That's the *really* hot stuff. Heinrich made some stew with it a few weeks back and couldn't speak for three days after he'd eaten it." She chuckled.

"And what's that?" Joe pointed at the twisty mushroom.

"That? Oh, that's Minutis explosus, or midget's puffball."

"And you can eat it?"

"Well, yes, if you like, but they taste vile. It's the spores you want."

"The spores?"

"Yes, watch." She picked up what looked like a small butterfly net and held it over the top of the mushroom. Leaning closer to it, she hummed a melody as if whispering a lullaby to an infant. Within a few seconds the mushroom bulged like a pair of green cheeks stifling a sneeze, and then, following an unsightly shudder, an inky cloud containing miniscule black seeds wheezed into the air surrounding it.

"Here," Mrs. Merrynether said, removing the net. "Try one of these. It's not spicy, I promise you."

Joe frowned but decided that however foul it could be, it would be better than the curry-tasting nightmare still tainting his tongue. He popped one of the seeds in his mouth and crunched it down between his teeth.

"Popcorn! It tastes like popcorn."

"Lovely, aren't they?"

"They're great. Where do you *get* these?"

"Aha. That would be telling, wouldn't it?"

"Is it the same place as the animals?"

Mrs. Merrynether tapped the side of her nose. "Why don't you go inside the house—the back door through the glasshouse is open. Heinrich will be in the vault as usual, and I'm sure you want to see how Cornelius is getting on, don't you?"

"Yes, and can I see the new creature? What is it?"

Mrs. Merrynether's chin jerked forward. "How did you know we have a new patient?"

"I . . . er . . . Lilly told me?"

"Lilly?" Mrs. Merrynether's spectacles slipped down her nose, and a vein stood out on her forehead. "You saw that little nuisance? Where? We've been trying to catch him ever since Heinrich let him escape."

"He was on the second floor a few minutes ago." Joe grimaced. "I think he broke one of your windows . . . by accident."

Mrs. Merrynether shut her eyes and took a deep breath. "Thank you, Joseph. Please go inside the house and see Heinrich. He will have a new shopping list for you."

"Ah . . . about the other list. I sort of—"

"Oh, the old list? Don't worry about that. Snappel, the scheduled patient, is going to be delayed by a week or two. We need some items for our newest guest instead." Mrs. Merrynether got to her feet and passed the basket to Joe. "Take these inside and give them to Heinrich. He'll give you the list, all right? I'll see you in a while." She shooed him away with muddy hands and then turned back to her plants.

"Okay." Joe balked under the weight of the basket and turned his head as the golf balls wafted curry smells at him. "See you soon."

Passing through the glasshouse, Joe saw yet more botanical oddities. One plant, perhaps because of its resemblance to the fruit in his basket, might have been the daddy moons' blight that Mrs. Merrynether mentioned, but most of the others looked even more bizarre than the ones outside. He didn't stop to look at them for long, mainly because he wanted to get rid of his heavy load but partly because at least one of the inhabitants didn't seem to like him very much. The offended vegetable, not unlike a bunch of uprooted carrots with a collective beard, puckered up and rustled an array of wide yellow leaves at him. If Joe didn't know better, he could have sworn they had somehow scrunched together in a way that imitated an irritated version of his face as he stepped through the exit and into the mansion.

Joe closed the door behind him, pausing to collect his thoughts and process the last few moments of bewilderment, then made his way along the passageway to find the entrance to the cellar. He entered the vault a minute later, feeling the familiar buzz of excitement at what he might find. The same unusual smells and sounds greeted him as he set the basket down just inside the door, but Cornelius's enclosure had been cleaned out and there was no sign of Flarp or Danariel either. Joe looked around for Heinrich.

The tall man, dressed as usual in his heavy overcoat, was at his desk again, asleep this time, slumped over a pad of writing paper, somehow oblivious to Joe's entrance and the sounds of the animals. A fountain pen balanced on the thumb of his right hand, threatening to clatter onto the desk, and a half-full mug of tea rested on a slab of well-used blotting paper. It was the second time Joe had caught him writing. A fresh wave of curiosity possessed Joe's feet, and before he knew it, he had tiptoed up to the desk, determined to see exactly what Heinrich was writing that was so secret.

Heinrich's left elbow and face obscured most of the sheet he had been writing on, but the first few lines of the letter were clearly visible—if he could just get a little closer. A musky odor drifted from the old coat, and Joe held his breath as he leaned in, momentarily fascinated by the stretch of shiny skin twisting the old man's burnt features. Heinrich stirred. Joe froze.

A trembling nerve fidgeted on one of Heinrich's eyelids, and for one numbing second, Joe feared they would be staring eye to eye. But Heinrich remained still.

Joe looked at the paper.

Dear Jimmy,

I am, as always, thrilled that you wrote back to me again, though I am sorry to learn that your mother's health has deteriorated. I know money does not solve everything, but I hope that my gifts continue to keep her in comfort. I enclose two more this time. Please do not hesitate to ask for more if you need to.

I know that my stories always help to cheer you up, so you will be pleased to hear that Cornelius has made a full recovery and that we have another new patient today. His name is Kiyoshi, and he's quite a —

Heinrich's elbow hid the rest. Joe considered sliding the sheet upwards so that he could read a little more. Touching his top lip with his tongue, Joe held the sheet between finger and thumb. Before making his delicate move, he noticed a small felt pouch near the cup of tea. Something glimmered just inside the opening. Distracted by this new discovery, Joe left the letter and prodded at the pouch. Three sparkling diamonds tumbled out, and Joe could not help but release a sudden gasp at the sight of them. Was Heinrich really going to send two of these in the post to this Jimmy person? And who was Jimmy anyway?

But Joe had no time to speculate.

An iron grip clamped the top of his arm, and Heinrich's eyes flicked open.

$\mathcal{F}$IFTEEN

"Thief!" Heinrich rasped. "Come for the diamonds, have you?"

"I . . . No!" Joe tried to move, but the old man's fingers tightened like pliers. "Mrs. Merrynether sent me down for the next shopping list."

With a slight wobble, Heinrich raised himself from his chair, still holding Joe firmly by the arm. "And you thought you would help yourself to some valuables while you were at it, hmm?"

"I didn't even know you *had* any diamonds until a minute ago," Joe protested, still struggling. "And who's Jimmy anyway? I saw your letter."

Heinrich's fingers loosened, and his eyes flickered as if he'd been slapped across the cheek.

Taking full advantage of Heinrich's momentary shock, Joe wrenched his arm as hard as he could and managed to free himself.

Heinrich made no further attempt to grab Joe but swayed slightly, as though groggy from a day's worth of sleeping. He shook his head, gave Joe a studious look as if mulling over a difficult clue for a crossword puzzle, then turned back to his desk to snatch the letter away.

The phone rang, startling them both.

Heinrich huffed with frustration, looking from Joe to the letter in his hand to the phone hanging on the wall not far from his desk.

"Who's Jimmy?" Joe said.

Heinrich stuffed the letter into his coat pocket and, with his bleary gaze still on Joe, lurched to pick up the receiver. "Merrynether Veterinary Practice."

Joe heard a monotone female voice.

Heinrich pinched the bridge of his nose. "No, I have already told you for the fourth time today: Mrs. Merrynether does not wish to see Mr. Redwar and will *not* be arranging an appointment."

The female voice droned again.

"No. As I said, she will not be available."

More droning, and Heinrich moved his attention from Joe fully to the conversation.

Feeling like he was waiting for a headmaster's detention, Joe shifted his feet, rubbing his sore arm. He was about to sit in Heinrich's chair when a familiar blue light shone through the door leading from the cellar. It intensified around the handle, and a moment later, the door swung open to reveal Danariel fluttering in her usual butterfly-like fashion.

Directly behind her, Flarp bobbed, his euphoric stare directly upon the seraph.

"Danariel! Flarp!" Joe beamed.

"Hello, Joe. Can't stop, I'm afraid. There's mischief afoot in the mansion that Mrs. Merrynether needs to know about." And with a brief smile, Danariel flitted past him and out through the door to the glasshouse, pursued by the eager globble.

Heinrich slammed the phone onto its hook and stared at the floor, balling his fists, breathing hard.

Joe backed away and resisted the urge to run.

"Why won't they leave her alone?" Heinrich ranted.

"Who?"

Heinrich looked up, shocked, as if he'd forgotten Joe was there. With a disgruntled sigh, he frowned back at the stone floor. Again Joe noticed a slight unsteadiness in his posture.

"Redwar's people. They still want to buy the mansion from her."

"But surely they can't force—"

"Why won't they leave us alone?" Heinrich groaned, apparently distracted by a number of worrying thoughts. He rattled his head for a second time, as if trying to flush a foreign object from his ear.

"Are you all right, Heinrich?"

"I feel a little . . . tired." Then with a sheepish glance at Joe, he said, "I did not mean to hurt you. I'm sorry if I did."

"It's okay. I honestly wasn't trying to take your diamonds, you know."

Danariel's blue aura returned through the glass-house door, trailed as before by the indomitable Flarp and hotly followed by a furious Mrs. Merrynether. She glared at Heinrich as she stomped past, and Joe heard the cellar door slam after she exited the other side of the vault.

Heinrich's eyes widened, and he nodded slowly. "I think she is angry."

"With you?"

"It certainly looks that way, but I do not—" His mouth twisted into the horrified expression of a man who sneezed into a vicar's dinner. "Cornelius. I don't hear Cornelius," he said with a gulp.

Joe took a step back.

Heinrich spun on his heels, almost falling over. Like a man with his feet on fire, he staggered around the other side of the enclosure, dropping to examine a large iron ring fastened to a concrete slab. "Oh no!"

"What is it?" Joe asked, almost afraid of the answer.

"There was a rope tied to this. And tied to the rope was . . ."

"Cornelius?"

Heinrich nodded grimly.

"Where is he?" Joe glanced tentatively around the vault. "He couldn't have got outside, could he?"

The befuddled keeper stared at Joe with his lips

flapping, but all he could do was shrug.

"How could you have slept through—?" Joe almost choked on the end of his sentence.

The door to the vault smashed open and shuddered against the wall. Danariel and Flarp shot through the opening, and Joe saw for the first time a look of alarm on the seraph's face. She sped in several tight circles like a burst balloon and darted all the way to the other end of the vault, apparently trying to hide. It was then that Joe noticed at least three of the previously occupied enclosures were empty, their doors wide open. Flarp decided to make one of them his own hideout and flopped his shaking amorphous form under a pile of straw.

The source of their panic became apparent as the sound of Mrs. Merrynether's stamping feet and furious shouting echoed down the stairs. "Heinrich Krieger! You have gone *much* too far this time. Have you seen what that maddening midget has done?"

Despite her size, she seemed to fill the entire door frame as she entered. In one hand she held a coiled rope and in the other an empty wine bottle, which she wielded by its neck like a mace. "Have you, Heinrich?" her screeching reached an entirely new octave.

"I—"

"Lilly has not only constructed an entire drinking bar in room sixteen under your very nose, using every last bottle of our vintage collection, but he has done so using items from inside this very vault!" Her tone sank into a dangerous whisper. "Do you recognize this, Heinrich?"

Heinrich stared at the rope. "Yes," he mumbled.

"Lilly used it to construct a pulley system with which to haul heavy crates of alcohol. The fact that he managed to untie the manticore without being maimed is beyond belief, but what is even more remarkable is that you didn't even notice." She paused for effect, then continued very slowly. "Do you, by some random stroke of luck, happen to know where Cornelius might actually be at this precise moment in time?"

Heinrich squinted, as if he had been asked a trick question, then shook his head nervously.

"He's in the driveway of the mansion in plain view with one leg in the air cleaning his . . . his . . ." She waved the bottle in the air. "And the whole wide world could watch if they wanted to."

Joe stifled a laugh with a snort. Whether it was out of hilarity or fear, Joe was uncertain, but the urge to chuckle fell away instantly as Mrs. Merrynether lanced him with a withering look.

He avoided her glare and turned quickly to look at Heinrich, who was shrinking away. To Joe he looked like an old tortoise who had made a tentative attempt to come out of hibernation, only to be beaten back into his shell by an icy wind. If he could have retracted his entire head below his shoulders and left only a shell, Heinrich surely would have tried.

Mrs. Merrynether was not about to let Heinrich off so easily. "Do you know what else I found up there?"

"Uh . . . no."

"Cage locks."

"Cage locks?"

"Yes, cage locks," she snapped.

Moving nothing but his eyes, which slowly looked toward the open enclosures, Heinrich breathed out a short gasp.

"That impudent cluricaun took at least four cage locks from our enclosures and fitted them to his own crates full of our wine."

Heinrich groaned as she continued.

"None of this would ever have happened if you hadn't let him escape in the first place." She threw the rope at him. "You can start by bringing that manticore back into the vault. Then you can go and find the other five creatures, and you'd better not come back until you've rounded up each and every one of them."

"Other five?" Heinrich asked. "I thought there were only four others."

"Not if you include that meddlesome Irish nightmare. I want him back here and locked up too. Am I clear?"

Heinrich nodded ruefully and scooped up the rope from the floor, casting Joe a fearful look as he coiled it. At first Joe thought the look was just part of his reaction to Mrs. Merrynether's verbal hammering, but then he saw the pleading expression showing through and knew that, even in the midst of this emergency, Heinrich was still thinking of the letters.

"And where is Kiyoshi?" Mrs. Merrynether looked around and scowled. "If you've lost him too, I'll—"

"He is safe," said Heinrich, nodding toward his desk.

Mrs. Merrynether walked to the desk, then looked at the floor into an antique mahogany box that appeared to be about the right size to hold a person's head. Joe watched, eager to see what kind of creature it was. How could he have missed it earlier?

Mrs. Merrynether sighed with relief after looking inside and was just about to turn away from the desk when she caught sight of something. Both Joe and Heinrich held their breath, wondering if any evidence of secret letter writing was visible. Fortunately for Heinrich, she picked up his mug of tea instead and held it under her nose. "How was it that Lilly was able to get away with all of this?" she asked, dipping her little finger into the cold beverage.

"I fell asleep, Ronnie." He shook his head, as if he knew it was not a good enough reason.

"A cluricaun enters the vault, steals a manticore, frees several more creatures, and you slept through that?"

She sucked her wet finger and smacked her lips several times, testing the tea. "I knew it. I can taste a hint of St. Martha's lullaby. I thought some of it had gone missing from my crop. Lilly drugged you."

Heinrich straightened, apparently hoping to be

exonerated. "I do feel very tired."

"No excuse," she barked. "Lilly should not still be running free."

A little deflated, Heinrich tried something else. "Redwar Industries called trying to make an appointment with you. I told them you are unavailable."

"Redwar? Calling here again?" She waved the wine bottle. "Oh, I'm in the perfect mood to be dealing with *him*."

She marched toward the phone, then paused. "Why are you still here?" she shouted. "Get outside and bring in those animals. Now!"

Heinrich almost dropped the rope as he muddled his way out of the vault in a panic.

"Should I come back later?" offered Joe.

Mrs. Merrynether hesitated again as she picked up the receiver and glanced at the open box. "I'm afraid you will have to wait until another time before you can meet Kiyoshi. Would you be so kind as to run upstairs to room sixteen? I'm afraid Lilly has made a terrible mess in a very short space of time. I'll join you as soon as I've had a word with this fat buffoon. It's up the stairs, last door on the right."

Pushing aside his frustration at not seeing the new creature, but relieved to escape the charged atmosphere, Joe nodded and left the vault to head upstairs.

Finding room sixteen was a simple matter; the task of clearing up the mess was not. Joe stared at the aftermath of a drunken marathon. Smashed beer glasses littered the stained wooden floor, the unidentifiable remains of various fruit adorned the walls in the form of smeared graffiti, and every piece of furniture had been either dismantled or smashed. Various sharp objects dangled from the ceiling as if some bizarre dare game had been played, and across the length of the walls, Joe could see the remnants of an intricate pulley system which looked like it had been used as some sort of alcohol delivery system. A few broken bottles were still attached to frayed bits of rope.

"Where on earth do I start?" Joe said to himself.

Picking a path through the debris, he made his way to the back of the room where a splintered bookcase leaned precariously against an equally abused crate. One nudge and there would be an avalanche of planks.

Joe decided his first job would be to rescue the bookcase. He slipped on something hideous and pushed his arm toward an overturned table to steady himself. His fingers connected with something soft, whose scream was drowned out by the clatter of collapsing furniture.

The flash of a pale green waistcoat told Joe that he'd almost bagged the infamous cluricaun. Joe clambered across the wreckage to shut the door and prevent any chance of Lilly's escape. The door's slam preceded a silence that only the drip-drip-drip of a half-empty beer bottle dared to interrupt. Joe scanned the room, hunting for any sign of the elusive party animal, but as usual, the only clue to his existence came in the form of an Irish voice.

"A hangorver loike ya wouldn't believe, and den some idjit sticks his hand in ya gonads! Well, if it's a foight ya want, it's a foight ya'll get, boy."

The sting of something wet and rotten bit into Joe's cheek as a series of items flew at him from a variety of directions.

"Victory or death!" yelled the tiny man.

The sound of at least a dozen chuckles followed Lilly's war cry. The cluricaun was not alone.

Sixteen

Joe looked around the room, surveying the broken furniture, beer stains, and sliding remains of a food fight on the walls.

"There's more than one of you?" he asked, hoping for a glimpse of another cluricaun.

"He's broight, dis one," came a voice near the bookcase.

"And ogly too," said another.

"Hey! I'm not ugly."

"Are too! I bet you were even oglier as a baby. I bet ya mammy had to pull the covers up orver ya head at noight so dat sleep would have da courage ta creep up on yaz," came Lilly's voice.

"Well, at least I don't have a girl's name . . . Lilly!"

Joe's comeback provoked some hearty laughter from one of the corners.

"What loike . . . Josephine, ya mean."

"It's Joseph."

The laughing from the corner hadn't stopped, and more cackling came from the other side.

"Heh . . . Lilly? He torld us his name was Maximus."

"Shot ya face!"

"Don't tell me ta shot me face, ya fat tart."

"How dares ya! And may the devil swallow me soideways if oi ever invoites ya ta me house again."

An uproar of swearing and shouting, punctuated by the crash of flying bottles, soon escalated into a full-scale riot. Joe imagined there had been a continuous cycle of drinking, fighting, and passing out like this for the last several hours while Heinrich had been drugged and Mrs. Merrynether labored in the garden. Ducking below an expensive-looking bottle as it exploded into the door, Joe reached for a chair, fumbled to open the door, and fell into the corridor, dragging the chair with him. He slammed the door and wedged the chair underneath the handle. With a little luck, Joe could get either Heinrich or Mrs. Merrynether upstairs before the fight had finished and the cluricauns realized they had been trapped inside.

Joe saw a window at the end of the corridor and ran to it, knowing Heinrich had been sent outside to catch the escaped animals. Perhaps if he saw Heinrich, Joe could shout down to him to come up while he guarded room sixteen. Breathless from his narrow escape, Joe undid the latch and lifted the window to look outside.

Sure enough, there was Heinrich in the garden, but

the situation looked far from under control. Yowling and hissing coupled with excited cheering spoiled the otherwise peaceful atmosphere of the grounds as Cornelius the manticore leapt and bucked across the grass, contending with several little men clinging to his mane for dear life. The cheesy grins, distinctive clothes, and drunken laughter revealed them to be more of Lilly's friends. Heinrich ran behind the panicked beast as he wailed at the cluricauns to get off, but it was clear they were having far too much fun to take any notice.

Joe cupped his hands around his mouth and leaned out of the window. "Heinrich!"

Heinrich looked up. "Joe?"

"I've caught Lilly."

"What?"

"I've caught the cluricaun."

A stray sprout hit Heinrich in the side of the head as one of the tiny men catapulted out from a bush and then dashed out of sight again.

"I cannot hear you," he shouted, rubbing his temple.

"I'll come down."

Joe took off along the corridor, down the stairs, into the hallway, out the main entrance, and around the back to the garden. The cluricauns' cheers still echoed through the grounds as Joe approached.

Heinrich stood by one of the statues, hands on knees, panting. "I . . . don't know what . . . to do. Look." He pointed and shook his head.

Cornelius bucked and reared as he tore a muddy path through the grass. The curiously human face contorted in frustration as he beat his wings and thrashed his tail, but even as the manticore roared, the sound of Irish jeering drowned him out. At least six tiny men clung to the beast's red fur, two of them swinging from his mane.

"Apart from Lilly, Cornelius is the last. All the others were easy to catch . . . but him . . . them?"

"I've got an idea. Play along, and this might work." Joe winked, then spoke as loud as he could—enough that the cluricauns would hear. "I've got Maximus and some of his friends trapped in room sixteen. I think we've got plenty of time to get him, though, Heinrich. I heard him say they had all day to drink the whiskey because the lightweights had gone outside."

"Who's Maximus?" whispered Heinrich.

"Long story. I'll tell you—"

"Loightweights?" spluttered a furious voice. "Da swoine carled os loightweights! We'll shor *him* who da loightweight is."

Joe suppressed a grin as a host of roaring cluricauns jumped out from behind trees and bushes, led by the six who had leapt off the manticore in anger.

Heinrich made an unsuccessful attempt to snatch some as they shot past and then threw himself to the ground with a shout, "Get down, Joe!"

"What? What is—?" But Joe was too late. A pain

like the thrust of a red-hot poker lanced his shoulder, and he staggered back, stunned by the blow. The next thing he felt as he turned to see where the attack had come from was a peculiar heat traveling from his shoulder, into his chest, and down his side. He slumped and, through blurred vision, saw Cornelius thrashing his tail, spraying spikes toward the fleeing cluricauns.

Then came the numbness with nausea as Joe tried in vain to move his stiffening limbs. A cry from Heinrich echoed somewhere distant as another stray dart powered into his leg. The heavy blackness of unconsciousness sucked away his fading thoughts.

Joe woke in a groggy stupor. A curious odor, like apples fermenting in a bucket of lavender, reached his nostrils as he breathed in, but it was not unpleasant. In fact, it was quite soothing. He felt soft bedcovers as the pins and needles subsided in his fingers and, through a watery haze, he saw deep blue walls and a collection of Victorian furniture, including an old grandfather clock that clunked its peaceful rhythm in the corner closest to him.

Joe squinted at two blurry figures. One was Mrs. Merrynether, and the other was Danariel, whose ethereal light bathed the room in what looked like moonbeams. Their muffled voices discussed something in conspiracy at the end of the bed. He thought the splintering throbs in his head might drown out their whispers, but as the fog of sleep lifted, their words became clearer.

"If you really are right about him, Danariel, then we must keep him safe. This cannot happen again."

"I understand your fear, but you should trust me, Veronica. I am rarely wrong about these things."

"Rarely wrong? So you *have* been wrong before, then."

A brief silence gave Joe the opportunity to test his voice.

"Hello?" the word rasped through his throat as though he hadn't drunk water for a month.

Mrs. Merrynether turned to look at Joe, a kaleidoscope of emotions crossing her features. "How are you feeling?"

"I've got a headache. What's that smell?"

"It's a special ointment we're using on your shoulder." She smiled. "A little something I dug out of my medicine cabinet, and I'll get Heinrich to fetch you some aspirin for that headache."

"Is he all right? We were hit by Cornelius's quills."

"Heinrich didn't get hit. Only you did. If Heinrich hadn't got you to me as quickly as he did, you'd be . . ." Her prune-like lips tightened.

"You would not be talking with us now," Danariel finished as she hovered to the side of Mrs. Merrynether's face and placed gentle hands on her cheek.

"Thank you, Danariel. She's right, Joseph. I should never have left you unsupervised with such dangerous creatures on the loose." She looked away. "I have been grossly negligent."

"But you've got them back now?" Joe asked.

"All but Lilly."

"Lilly? But I had him trapped in room sixteen."

"I'm sure you did, but cluricauns are highly skilled at evasion, and it's extremely rare to see one at all. The room was empty when Heinrich checked it."

"So where did they all come from? There were so many of them." Joe tried to sit up but felt a lurch in his stomach and a hammering through his brain.

"Never mind them," said Mrs. Merrynether, easing him back onto the sheets. "You need to rest awhile."

"There is a cluricaun in almost every home," Danariel explained, sitting at the end of the bed, "especially homes with wine cellars. Nobody knows how they communicate with each other, but on rare occasions they do get together like this, and the results are always chaotic."

"Oh," said Joe, rubbing his head. "Look. What time is it? I should call my mum. She'll be wondering where I am."

"Already done," said Mrs. Merrynether. "I told her you had a bit of an accident with one of our animals but that you were fine."

"And she was okay with that?"

"Well . . ." Mrs. Merrynether drew a deep breath. "Your aunt Rose is coming to collect you now. Both she and your mother are very concerned, and to be truthful with you, so am I."

"Did I do something wrong?"

"Oh, no, no, no! The fault is entirely mine. You see,

it was very irresponsible of me to get you involved in this situation. In my anger, it didn't cross my mind for a moment that you may be in considerable danger with so many wild beasts on the loose. I should have sent you home immediately."

"But I'm all right now, aren't I?" Joe felt another wave of nausea.

"You will be fine. But it could easily have been different, and you may not be so fortunate if something similar were to happen again."

Danariel flew in front of her face. "No, Veronica."

She wagged a finger at the seraph. "Don't you try that on me, Danariel. I won't have it."

"What is it?" Joe asked.

"Danariel can sense what I am about to say, and she is trying her hardest to dissuade me." Mrs. Merrynether sighed and looked away. Her next sentence was filled with defeat. "I am afraid I shall have to ask you never to return once you leave today."

Joe's stomach lurched as though he'd been driven over the edge of a cliff. "I . . . can't . . . come back?"

"Reconsider, Veronica." Danariel's light had diminished. "Think of the future."

"I am," she whispered. "I'm thinking of his."

"Don't I get a say in this?" A lump hardened in Joe's throat.

"It isn't just the danger of the animals," she said. "I was on the phone with Argoyle Redwar earlier." Her lips twitched in disgust. "Aside from his usual venom when trying to persuade me to sell my home, he again threatened to reveal the true nature of our work. He knows all about Cornelius's recovery. He knows about Danariel here, and he even knows that we have a globble in our care."

"How?"

"I don't know. But it's clear somebody close to us is disclosing very sensitive information . . . It may not be safe."

"You don't think it's me, do you?"

For a flash of a second, suspicion seemed apparent in Mrs. Merrynether's watery eyes. "Of course not," she said a little too quickly. "But it's just one more thing that convinces me you may be better off not being involved. I don't know where all of this will lead, but you must also promise not to tell anyone about what you have seen here."

Joe nodded reluctantly. The whole world had been screwed up into a tiny ball, and he was crushed inside, unable to feel or think.

Danariel sank onto the bed, settling between Joe's side and the crook of his elbow.

He stared at her tiny form, wondering if this would be the last time he ever saw her.

SEVENTEEN

Argoyle Redwar rapped on the window of the animal block and peered through at the panicking employees within. Even through the thick doors, he heard muffled barks and the rattle-clang of slamming cage gates.

"Blast their rancid hides. What are they doing in there? I gave them ample time, didn't I? This is a research facility, not a church jumble sale."

"—fteen mints," mumbled the hunched woman behind him.

"What? Oh, never mind. I detest this place, Ms. Burrowdown. Detest it," he said, still snarling through the window and creating a misty patch. "But I suppose if that blasted Merrynether isn't going to budge, I have no choice but to go ahead with your idea."

"Fanyou, Mr. Redwar."

"Yes, well, it had better work." He turned to point a stubby finger at her. "There are too many things about this plan that could go—"

The double doors swung inwards with a loud metallic moan, and the barking crescendoed.

The gaunt figure of Arthur Gumble in an oversized lab coat, along with a generous helping of ferret stench, greeted Redwar. Gumble rubbed his hands together nervously as a twitching smile crossed his pallid features. Redwar squinted at the man, his currant-like eyes looking even smaller than usual.

"Gumble?"

"Uh . . . yes, Mr. Redwar, sir."

"Didn't I fire you a few weeks back?"

"You did, sir, yes, but—"

"Didn't I fire him a few weeks back?" he said, now looking at Burrowdown.

"Yes-did. Scorted off-site nineteenf July."

"What? Speak up, woman! Oh, never mind. Gumble," he said, turning back to him, "what are you still doing here?"

"I, er . . . reapplied for the job, sir."

"You did what?"

"Yes, sir. The post was advertised the following Monday, and I just . . . reapplied. Had my interview that Wednesday, and they—"

Redwar turned on Burrowdown again. "Who's the imbecile in charge of personnel now? Is it still Katherine Carling?"

"No. You fired 'er six munfs go. It's Graham Chatterly

now."

"Chatterly, eh? Fire him."

Burrowdown scribbled something in her notepad.

"Mr. Redwar?" Gumble asked. "Would you like to come inside? I can show you to—"

"Yes, yes!" He dismissed the cowering man with a wave and strode into the area. The doors groaned shut behind them. "But don't think you're getting away with this, Gumble. You can collect your hat and coat at the end of the day."

"I, er . . . always do, sir."

"Don't get funny with me. You know precisely what I meant. You're fired!"

"Begging your pardon, Mr. Redwar, but . . . may I ask why?" There was a tremble in his voice.

Redwar's eyes narrowed. "You're still fired from last time."

"But I'm on a new contract now, sir."

Redwar glowered at him, his rubbery lips pressed together and moving as though he were chewing a very sharp sweet.

The other workers stared wide-eyed at their boss, carrying out their tasks in slow motion.

"Very well, Gumble. You can stay."

"Sir?"

"You want me to change my mind?"

"No, no! Er . . . I think you wanted to be shown to the restricted section." Gumble was already on his way to the next set of doors, inviting Redwar and Burrow-down to follow.

"I did, yes."

Gumble pressed his card against the reader, and the doors swung open to reveal another room with more stench, more barking dogs, and more nervous employees. He took them through another set of doors and into a corridor, through more doors and corridors, more rooms, a lift, and then another corridor.

Eventually they stood before a set of menacing black doors. At the top, bold yellow letters identified the entrance of a restricted area into which only the managing director and the chief veterinary officer were allowed.

Gumble pressed his pass against the reader, and the sound of heavy bolts receding into concrete vibrated through the walls. The doors labored inward to reveal a darkened room.

"Back to work, Gumble."

"Thank you, Mr. Redwar," said Gumble. Then he scuttled off.

Redwar and Burrowdown stepped inside, and the doors thunked shut behind them. The tap of their shoes echoed against the tall black walls, and hidden sensors triggered embedded spotlights to raise the lighting by a fraction. The walls at the far end were still shrouded in darkness, but the groaning and snuffling were enough to confirm that living things lurked there.

"I hate this room most of all."

"Why?"

"What? Oh, it smells, Ms. Burrowdown. The stink is unbearable."

"Whiffy."

"Indeed." Redwar rubbed his fingers under his nose as if it might cover the stench. "I loathe animal smells, but this room is the worst. However, it is also the most private place in the whole of this building. Even I have enemies, Ms. Burrowdown. There are unwelcome ears in the offices, so absolute secrecy is paramount, and this is the perfect place for us to discuss what must be done. What is spoken within these walls stays between you, me, and these pathetic beasts. Now, to business."

"Merrynether?"

"Yes. She thinks she's so safe, tucked away in the middle of Ringwood Forest, taking care of all those stupid creatures in secret. She has to go."

"An accident?"

"Whatever it takes, but obviously, the trail must not lead to us, understand?"

She nodded.

Redwar raised his voice to proclaim, "Yes, we no longer need Merrynether now that we know precisely where that island is. As soon as preparations are ready, we can go there and our real work can begin."

Ms. Burrowdown grinned as she looked up.

Redwar smirked as he looked down. "Now here's what we'll do . . ."

And in the darkness, another pair of ears listened intently.

Coming to terms with Mrs. Merrynether's instruction not to return to the mansion threw Joe into a spiral of gloom. His next week passed like a distant dream. Classes, meals, watching TV, dodging difficult questions from his mum, running errands for his aunt, even the bullying—all of it blurred past him as if he were watching it happen to someone else.

Even as Aunt Rose arrived at Merrynether Mansion that fateful day to collect him, Joe was still trying to persuade Mrs. Merrynether to let him come back Sunday, but she insisted to his aunt that, for his own safety, he must not be allowed to return. And when Aunt Rose took Joe home and told his mum, he knew his fairy-tale days of adventure had come to an abrupt end. To add to his woes, Kurt Duggan targeted him for not providing the nonexistent map to the nonexistent stash of money buried in the woods. Life had never been so glum.

But as the following Monday lunch break reached its end, something happened that stirred Joe from his doldrums. He had been sitting in the corner of the common room with his nose in a Greek mythology book, and a full twenty minutes passed before he'd realized he had been left on his own. Most of the other students, apart from Duggan and his thugs, didn't pay him much

attention anyway, but there would usually be at least
ten others in there with him during lunch.

Joe put the book back in his bag and left the common room, hoping to find out where everybody else
had gone. The first hint came when the flashing glare
of red-and-blue lights colored the sports block. Either
someone had been hurt or there'd been some sort of
terrible incident that required the police. The picture
became clearer as Joe rounded the gymnasium.

At the back of the school grounds, where the playing
fields met Ringwood Forest, a busy crowd of students
had gathered around something. Three teachers were
doing their best to herd them back toward the school
but with little success. Two police officers stood with
one of the other teachers, taking down notes.

Joe caught nuggets of conversation as he pushed
his way into the crowd, ignoring the protests of Mr.
Henderson.

" . . . blood everywhere. Mrs. Hedley is in the first
aid room with him now . . ."

" . . . glimpsed its back, but Doherty said he saw it
full-on. Looked like a big gorilla with long nails . . ."

" . . . and then about twelve coppers with rifles ran
past the gates . . ."

" . . . smelled like Henderson's armpits . . ."

Joe managed to scramble to the front. He half expected to see a mangled body, but what presented itself
instead was a gaping hole in the ground. The tangled

roots of one of the beech trees had been torn upward to make way for the entrance of a wide tunnel. Something enormous had dug its way through there, and at the edge there was evidence of a fight. A combination of boot prints and claw marks were smeared into the soil, and the tattered remains of a bloody glove lay there too.

Frantic whispering and chattering continued to bubble around Joe as he stared into the hole. To his left, three girls from the class ahead of him were huddled in terrified gossip.

"What happened?" Joe asked.

They stopped talking and turned to him, their eyes fearful.

"It was Gravesy, the groundskeeper. The Beast of Upton Puddle got him," one of them said.

"Yes," said another girl. "Apparently he was mowing the borders when it just jumped out of the woods and bit his arm right off!"

"No, it didn't!" The other one smacked her arm. "It just scratched him. That's all."

"They don't call out ambulances for a scratch."

"I'm just telling you what Lisa said Ian said Graham saw. If he—"

"Yaaaaaa! Monster! There! Monster behind those trees," shouted somebody a few feet away.

The three girls shrieked, provoking a parade of screaming, flapping, and crying all around them.

Seconds later Joe picked out the hysterical laughing of

Kurt Duggan. He and his minions were huddled in a small group not far from the hole, doubled over with laughter.

"All right, that's quite enough," screeched Mr. Henderson, his high-pitched voice conveying precisely no authority whatsoever.

By now, all the teachers had arrived and were busy rounding up their students while the police stuck metal pikes in the ground and cordoned off the area with stripy tape.

Deep in thought, Joe was bustled along with the crowd toward the main assembly hall. With everything else that had been going on, he hadn't given nearly enough thought to the Beast stalking the village. This was the first time a real attack on a person had happened. Until now, there had been damage to property and even some livestock and pets, but the situation had never been this bad. Mrs. Merrynether insisted the creature had nothing to do with them, but for Joe, this was far too much of a coincidence. Even during the time that Joe visited, at least five different creatures had escaped.

Uneasiness seeped in as the noisy crowd shoved Joe along the main corridor to the assembly hall. He'd promised Mrs. Merrynether that he would say nothing to anyone about what she was doing, but perhaps it was his responsibility now to tell the police what he knew before someone really got hurt . . . or worse.

Joe caught sight of Mr. Henderson at the back of the mob and fought his way against the flow to see him.

"Mr. Henderson?" he said, pulling alongside.

"If you're going to ask what happened, you'll have to wait with everyone else. That's why I've called an assembly."

"Is Mr. Graves all right?"

Henderson looked down at Joe with one of his eyes. The other one didn't quite make the journey away from the crowd.

"You mean you're not interested in the Beast like the rest of these little monsters?"

"Is he badly hurt?"

"He's fine, Copper. The nurse is attending to him in the first aid room."

"Thanks." Joe squeezed his way through the back of the line before Henderson could grab him.

A few students were gathered outside the first aid room when Joe arrived. Two of them pressed their ears against the door while the others bustled to get their turn.

"What's going on in there?" Joe asked.

"Shh!" hissed a lanky student with long hair. "We've already been sent away once."

Joe walked right to the door, opened it, and walked inside while the others stared agog.

Mr. Graves, the groundskeeper, sat in a chair next to the nurse, Mrs. Hedley. One of his arms had been wrapped with a bandage and, although there was no sign of any serious injury, his face was bleached with shock as he looked straight ahead.

A police officer stood by the window scribbling into a notepad and promptly stopped when Joe barged in.

"Are you all right, Mr. Graves?"

Mrs. Hedley stood, her fists on her hips. "Get out of here right now, boy. This is—"

Joe heard the eavesdroppers outside scuffle away quickly.

"Did you really see the Beast?"

"I said—"

"Big shaggy thing, really long fingers? I've seen it too."

Mrs. Hedley grabbed Joe's arm.

The groundskeeper looked straight at Joe. "That's it! It came right out of the ground, it did. Big green eyes and . . . and claws like . . . like eagle's claws, they were, but hairy."

"Hold on, Mrs. Hedley," said the officer. "It sounds like this lad knows something."

She let go of him.

Graves was still talking. "Scared the bejeezus out of me. I'm tellin' you, boy, the sooner I get out of this job, the better. The Duggan boy—he's my ticket out of Clarkdale. His old man works for Redwar Industries, you know. Head of security, he is. He's going to get me a nice little cushy job at the gatehouse . . ."

Graves, obviously still in shock, rambled on, but Joe had seen enough. The groundskeeper wasn't seriously hurt, but . . .

"What's your name, son?" said the officer.

"Joe . . . Joe Copper."

"So it sounds like you're another eyewitness to this creature. Are you prepared to make a statement?"

Joe looked at the officer and thought about his promise to Mrs. Merrynether. Her future depended on his next words, but so did the safety of the village. Joe took a deep breath before deciding on his answer.

EIGHTEEN

Each tick of the clock accused Joe of betrayal.

Tic. Nine hours, fifty-nine minutes, and fifty-eight seconds since he'd told a police officer that Merrynether Mansion might be where the Beast of Upton Puddle came from.

Toc. Nine hours, fifty-nine minutes, and fifty-nine seconds since he'd felt the sickening weight of treachery line his stomach like a bag of heavy stones.

Tic. Ten hours since that same police officer smirked at Joe's confession.

But it didn't matter to Joe that nobody, not even his mum, believed him. He had still broken his promise.

The night closed in on Joe as he stared at the expensive new clock his mum had bought to cheer him up. She knew exactly how much it hurt Joe to be kept away from the new world he'd discovered, and she'd left it on his bed, wrapped and with a bow and card ready for his return from school. The clock face glowed in the dark, illuminated by a million pixels to show off a digital picture of something mystical or mythological. Normally Joe would have been thrilled by it. He had a bizarre fascination with clocks, but this one only reminded him of what he'd lost.

Each hour the picture changed into something new and spectacular. At one in the morning, the bright green hands moved across the figure of a stomping cyclops. Joe stared at it. It reminded him of something. Something he'd been dreaming about earlier in the night, perhaps?

Joe switched his lamp on. Rubbing his eyes, he fought to remember images from the sleep he'd been woken from a few minutes ago. Was it sand? A beach maybe? Yes, a beach. The same beach he'd dreamed about a few weeks ago in the forest. And that colossal tree-shaped tower with all the eyes attached to its branches. That's why the Cyclops reminded him of his dreams. But what did it mean? Was it a real place? A few months ago the idea that such a place existed would have been ridiculous, but since then he'd seen things that defied explanation. And he'd been told he had a destiny.

A sudden chill of excitement flushed his tiredness away as he thought about it all. How could he get back to sleep now? But what woke him in the first place? He listened for a moment but only heard the usual night noises.

Tic. Six hours, twenty-seven minutes, and forty-one seconds until he'd have to get up.

Toc. Six hours, twenty-seven minutes, and forty seconds of lying there thinking.

Tic. Plink! At the window.

Toc. Creak. Something pressing at the windowpanes.

Holding his breath, Joe crept to the window, gathered his courage, then pushed the curtains aside. Blue-white light flooded the room, and Joe stepped back in shock.

Danariel hovered outside.

Next to her, with quaking knees, Lilly teetered on the window ledge with his upper body concealed by a huge red brick. A muffled, panting voice ranted, just audible through the glass. "Sor help me, boy. If ya hadn't com to da winda dis toime, I would've put dis bloddy ting roit troo it!"

Joe opened the window, careful not to knock the cluricaun down. "What are you doing here?" he whispered. "People will see you."

Lilly dropped the brick, and it thumped in the grass below. The cluricaun's angry face shone a curious purple in Danariel's light as the tiny man began one of his outbursts. "Oooh, noice to see ya, Lilly. And it's a pleasure ta see you too, Danariel. What brings you to my humble dwelling? . . . Let os in, ya pickle-brained pillock!"

"Get inside." Joe grinned. "But be quiet. My mum might hear."

"Bloddy mammie's boy," Lilly muttered as he tumbled inside.

Danariel followed him gracefully. "Sorry to intrude, Joe, but we had to see you. We need your help."

Joe closed the window and sat on the end of his bed. He was about to speak when a shaft of light broke in through the gaps in his door and his mother's voice came from the landing.

"Joe? Are you all right? I thought I heard something."

"Fine, Mum. I just had a weird dream."

"You sure you're okay?" The shadows of her feet were visible at the bottom of his door. "Want me to get you a hot water bottle or mug of warm milk?"

Lilly pointed at Joe, hissing desperate laughter through clenched teeth as though he were being strangled. "Mammie's boy," he choked.

"Lilly!" Danariel spoke as quietly as she could.

"Honestly, it's fine, Mum. I just want to get back to sleep."

"Well, okay, then. As long as you're all right."

"Fine, Mum. Good night."

Joe puffed out a deep breath as his mum walked away.

"I'm very sorry, Joe," said Danariel.

"It's all right, but what are you doing here in the middle of the night? How am I supposed to help?"

"We don't know what else to do. It's Veronica."

"Mrs. Merrynether? What's wrong with her?"

"That's just it. We don't know. She's vanished."

"Vanished?"

"Yes. She hasn't been around for three days. The

first day we thought she may have been taking a longer time in the garden." Danariel shot an accusing look at Lilly. "She's had a lot of tidying to do in the last week after what happened with Cornelius."

"Nuts to you, fairy face," snapped Lilly. "Da stupid orld bint has probably jost wandered off somewhere widout her glasses."

"Lilly is feeling guilty, Joe. He thinks it's his antics that have driven her away."

Lilly pretended to be interested in one of Joe's socks on the bedroom floor.

"That's why he's here. It's why we're both here. I don't think Veronica has run away. She would never do that. I think something has happened to her."

"But I don't understand. What am I supposed to do? How would I know where she is?"

Danariel hovered down to Joe's knee. "We need you to go to the police. If she's reported as a missing person, they will try to find her."

"There's no point. They won't believe me."

"Why not?"

Joe looked sheepish. "I've already spoken to the police."

Lilly pulled Joe's sock off his own head. "Ya sporken to dem already? Watcha been op to? If it was about me, I—"

"No, it wasn't about you. There was an attack at the school by the Beast, and I . . . thought . . ."

"You think the Beast is from Merrynether Mansion?" asked Danariel.

Joe hesitated. "Yes."

"That creature has nothing to do with us," Danariel said.

"How do you know for sure? You've only been there a few weeks. And you have to admit it's a bit of a coincidence, isn't it?"

"Look," said Lilly. "Are ya goin' ta help os or not?"

"Of course I will, but the point is that the police laughed at me when I told them I thought the Beast came from the mansion. Do you think they'll believe me if I tell them Mrs. Merrynether's gone missing?"

"They would have to take your report seriously," said Danariel.

"Yes, I suppose it won't hurt to try, but what about Heinrich? Can't he do it? It would be more convincing coming from him."

"Have ya got any booze in here, boy?" Lilly had pulled a drawer out of one of Joe's dressers and was tossing the contents behind him.

"Lilly, he's a boy! Of course he doesn't have any drink."

"Not even a toiny drop o' sherry? Maybe a tipple of—"

"Lilly!"

"Vodka?"

"No!"

Lilly continued his search all the same.

Joe did his best to ignore the cluricaun for the moment. "Like I said, shouldn't Heinrich do something?"

"Heinrich refuses to get involved with the authorities. He's worried that the police will have to search the mansion. But he also hates to be seen by anyone because of the terrible burn marks on his face. He fears that he would have to meet the police face-to-face if he calls them."

"What? Isn't Mrs. Merrynether's safety a bit more important than that?"

"I think you underestimate exactly how strongly Heinrich feels about it. Apart from Veronica, you are the only person who's seen him for years."

"But she could be in danger!"

"I know, and it's driven Heinrich almost to the point of breakdown. He hasn't eaten, and he isn't even taking care of any of the animals. Kiyoshi, the new creature, isn't helping matters either. Heinrich can't cope with anything at all. He's a wreck."

"What are you going to do?"

Danariel looked up at Joe. "That's the other reason we came to you."

"Me? But I . . . You want me to—? No."

"We need you to talk to him. Bring him to his senses."

"But how would I know what to say to him?"

"I don't know, but you have to help us. You're the only other human we can trust . . . and you have a destiny, remember?"

Joe stared into space, shell shocked.

"We need you," Danariel insisted.

"Yes," added Lilly, standing by Joe's feet and staring up at him with a face as serious as a lit match in a firework factory. "*Oi* needs ya."

Joe looked at the cluricaun, doubly shocked.

"Oi needs ya ta find me some bloddy beverages. Are ya *sure* ya don't have a drop hidden somewhere?"

Joe shook his head dismissively. "There's really no one else?"

"No one," said Danariel. "Will you help?"

Joe sighed. "All right, but if I do help, you have to do something for me too."

Danariel's light flickered slightly as if she knew what Joe was about to ask. "Tell me what you want."

"I want to know everything. I want to know why I have a destiny. I want to know where all these animals come from, and I want to know what it's all about. If I'm part of something big, I want to know what it is."

The smile on Danariel's face fell into a contemplative, almost fearful, look. She nodded.

"Okay," said Joe. "I'll be there first thing tomorrow. I can't promise anything, but I'll do my best."

"Good," said Danariel. "Let's go, Lilly. Joe needs to sleep. He'll have a lot to think about tomorrow."

"Right ye are," said the tiny man, dragging a bulging sock to the window.

"Hey!" said Joe. "What are you doing with my sock?"

"Just a few tings oi moight be needin'. Dat's all."

"But—" Joe decided it would be futile to try to stop him. Instead, he walked to the window and opened it.

Danariel fluttered into the night, and Lilly struggled over the ledge after her.

The next morning was a bright start to what promised to be an eventful Saturday. Joe thrust some sandwiches, chocolate bars, and drink cartons into a carrier bag and, after saying a quick good-bye to his bewildered mother, hurried out of the house promising to be back in time for tea.

Joe ran through the forest, feeling the mixture of nervous excitement and trepidation building with every step. He wondered what sort of condition the vault would be in when he arrived. As the mansion came into view, something new caught his attention, something sprouting from the ground several yards away from the entrance gate.

Joe stopped. A large mound of dirt was heaped beside a gaping hole in the earth. It looked just like the one at the edge of the school grounds where Mr. Graves was attacked. At once Joe crouched and looked frantically for any sign of the Beast, but after a minute of careful observation, the sound of normal birdsong told Joe that the creature was long gone.

With cautious steps, Joe made his way to the hole and peered into the stinking darkness. Something enormous had burrowed deep, but there was no sign of a struggle or blood. Nevertheless, Joe had to suppress images of the great shaggy creature dragging the unconscious body of Mrs. Merrynether into its lair. Shuddering, Joe realized that they may well have to mount some sort of rescue party and venture underground to find her.

He looked up at Merrynether Mansion and wondered if it was safe to take Cornelius with him. Surely the Beast would be no match for a manticore. He hoped he wouldn't have to find out the answer. It wasn't certain that the Beast had taken Mrs. Merrynether anyway. Joe took one last look into the hole before hurrying off to the mansion.

NINETEEN

Heinrich looked most unwell when he answered the door. Although he was still a towering figure, he seemed to be stooping more than usual. His grey hair was a mess, and even the bags under his eyes had bags. The tiniest smile flickered across his lips when he saw Joe, but it was obvious Heinrich's mind was in a very distant place.

"Come in, Joe. I don't know why you chose to come back, but I am very glad you did." Heinrich retreated into the hallway, almost tripping over Archy the pig on his way.

Joe followed and shut the door. "How are you?"

The old man turned around and looked at Joe with wrinkled eyelids, as if he'd forgotten something. "Good. Yes. Good."

"I . . . um . . . heard that Mrs. Merrynether has gone missing."

"Missing. Yes." His confusion seemed to be mounting, and he stared at the ceiling. "Would you like a brew of tea?"

"Can you tell me what happened?"

"Happened?"

"Yes, to Mrs. Merrynether."

Archy ran around Heinrich's feet, snorting.

Heinrich made a halfhearted attempt to kick him out of the way. "Stop it, Archy. Ronnie will be . . . She will feed you when she gets . . ." He raised a hand to his head and tapped gently. "Not here. Ronnie's gone." He looked at Joe, suddenly alarmed. "Ronnie is gone, Joe. We . . . You must find her."

"Please just tell me what happened."

Heinrich nodded and bit his lip. It appeared he had momentarily regained his senses and was fighting hard to keep hold of them. "Come down to the vault, and I will explain there. Archy needs feeding."

When they opened the door to the vault, Joe was not surprised to see the place in a mess. A powerful stench of animal droppings from the enclosures assaulted him, and a variety of dirty rags, bags, and overturned bowls were scattered on the floor in the semidarkness. Somewhere near the back, Joe heard a rhythmic thud against the wall and caught a glimpse of something green. Could that be Flarp?

"I apologize for the mess," said Heinrich. "I have not been myself these last few days." He poured some crunchy objects into one of the dirty bowls and slid it under Archy's snout.

The pig received it with great enthusiasm.

At the sound of Heinrich's deep tones, a soft blue glow shifted inside the lightbulb at the center of the vault. Joe was pleased to see Danariel squeeze out from inside it and glide down toward them.

Heinrich pulled up his chair and dragged a stool near Joe, gesturing for him to sit, which he did.

"Hello, Joe," said Danariel.

Joe nodded his own greeting and then saw Cornelius approaching from the gloom.

Unchained and with calm magnificence, the manticore strolled toward them and settled beside Heinrich's stool, crossing its paws and holding Joe with his intense gaze.

Absently, the old man scratched Cornelius behind the ear.

Joe stood and edged away, touching his shoulder, remembering the wound.

"Cornelius is very sorry for what happened," said Danariel. "It was an accident."

The manticore purred in agreement and blinked slowly at Joe. Joe smiled and tentatively reached out to stroke his mane. The creature nuzzled against his hand.

"Danariel told me this morning that you will help us," Heinrich said.

"Yes," she added. "We must try to find Veronica."

Joe's stomach knotted as he thought of the tunnel

outside the mansion, and he slumped back onto his stool. "I think I know where she is."

"You do?" said Heinrich, leaning forward.

"I think she's been snatched by the Beast."

"The Beast of Upton Puddle?"

"Yes. Haven't you seen the tunnel it's dug just outside the gates? I think she's underground."

"No, no," said Heinrich. "That creature has never harmed anyone. It has damaged property and stolen food, but it has never harmed a human."

"It attacked Mr. Graves."

"Are you sure?"

"It drew blood on his arm, yes."

Heinrich looked thoughtful for a second. "Self-defense perhaps."

"But—"

"Even if it has started to attack humans, why Ronnie? She has the skill of empathy with animals. No, I believe this is the work of Argoyle Redwar."

"I agree with Heinrich," said Danariel. "Argoyle Redwar has been harassing Veronica for quite some time. I think he's getting desperate now and has resorted to kidnapping."

"But Joe does have a point," said Heinrich, reconsidering. "The Beast has actually attacked someone, and there is a tunnel outside . . . That would explain the smell."

"Smell?" said Joe.

"Yes, a few days ago, we kept noticing a peculiar

smell outside. At first we thought something was wrong with the drains, but she did say she was going to investigate. Perhaps she *did* encounter the Beast."

"I still think it's Redwar," said Danariel.

As the two of them continued to discuss the possibilities, Joe became increasingly distracted by the disturbance at the back of the vault. The rhythmic thumping had continued throughout their conversation, and Joe strained to look through the dim light to see what it was. "Is that Flarp over there?"

They all stopped to look where Joe pointed.

Heinrich nodded. "I am afraid so. The poor creature has taken Ronnie's disappearance as hard as the rest of us. He has been banging against that wall ever since we found out she was missing."

"Can't you put him somewhere? He might get hurt."

"I have tried to catch him, but he always flies away and returns to that same patch of wall. I don't know what to do, and the noise is torture, almost as annoying as . . . Oh, dear!"

"What?"

"I forgot about Kiyoshi. He has gone silent."

"Kiyoshi?" Joe leaned forward. "Is that the new patient?"

"Yes," said Heinrich, struggling to lift something off a large cushion from beside his desk. "Another patient I have no idea how to help. If Ronnie were here, she would know what to do."

Joe stared in fascination, almost revulsion, at the

sight of this new creature. It looked as if someone had taken several different animals and thrown them together to create a bizarre Chimera. Its predominant feature was very much like the shell of a giant tortoise but with subtly different patterns and white hornlike extensions jutting from the edges. Heinrich was using two of these as handles as he heaved the creature toward Joe. The sticky limbs dangling from the protective case had the wet sheen of an amphibian, and each leaf-green leg ended in a webbed foot with suckers for toes. As if the combination of reptile and amphibian were not strange enough, it had a mammalian head, not unlike that of a chimpanzee.

Heinrich was doing his best to keep the head upright as he grunted beneath the creature's weight, lowering it to the floor. At the top of the creature's head, a fleshy flap had fallen forward to reveal an opening the size of a bathtub's plughole. At first Joe thought it was some sort of injury, but when he saw tiny green scales around the rim, he knew it was part of the animal's unusual anatomy. A cloudy yellow liquid oozed inside the hole, and Joe noticed that some of it had dripped down the side of the creature's hairy head.

"What's that thing?" Joe asked with a grimace.

"A kappa," said Heinrich, gently tapping its cheek. "And it has been the bane of my life since it arrived."

"Why?"

The thing's eyes popped open. "*Why?*" it said with

the tone of a rusty door hinge. "*Why* is an utterance of great import to the noble art of chrestomathy. For without it, one would flounder helplessly in a sea of ignorance."

"That's why," said Heinrich.

"What did he say?" asked Joe.

"I have absolutely no idea. Even Danariel has trouble translating."

The kappa padded around ninety degrees to face Joe and studied him with lemur-like eyes. Its next words rattled from its mouth like bullets from a machine gun. "Australopithecus? Cro-Magnon perhaps? Certainly you have the anthropological characteristics of an advanced Neanderthal at least, though I must confess, some features may be idiosyncratic."

"Those are cavemen, aren't they?" Joe grinned "Are you insulting me? You're not so good-looking yourself, you know."

The creature popped its suckered toes up and down on the ground as if frustrated with Joe's answer.

"Your name's Kiyoshi, isn't it? Are you Japanese?"

"My species is indigenous to the land mass known as Kyushu; hence, the homogenous nature of my name, and since your inclination is to confabulate in matters of nomenclature, I would make a similar transaction."

"Wha—?"

"Yes, he comes from Japan," said Danariel, "and he wants to know your name too."

"Ah, right. Well, my name's Joe."

"Joe!" The kappa puckered its lips as if the name left a bad taste in its mouth. "A meager name reflecting a nugatory existence, no doubt. And you," said the thing, suckering its way to Heinrich. "You demonstrate not one whit of sagacity. I charged you with a single elementary duty, and your sole achievement is near speciocide."

"That sounded bad," Joe said.

"Yes, Kiyoshi believes I nearly killed him."

"Why? What did you do?"

"It is what I didn't do that upset him."

"Precisely." It squeaked, "One—" The beast's eyes suddenly closed as its head flopped forward. Some of the yellow liquid oozed over the edge of the opening, and Heinrich quickly nudged it under the chin. The eyes popped open, revealing what appeared to be mild confusion and frustration. "One . . .what was I saying?"

"Kiyoshi suffers from narcolepsy." Heinrich sighed.

"Don't *you* start," said Joe. "What does that mean?"

Danariel fluttered forward. "It means that Kiyoshi keeps falling asleep without warning."

"Oh."

"Gross incompetence," Kiyoshi grated.

"Yes," added Heinrich, trying to ignore the creature, "and for a kappa, this is deadly. You see that ugly hole in the top of Kiyoshi's head?"

"Couldn't really miss it, could you?" said Joe, pulling a face.

"Well, that is called the cranial vent. It contains a

fluid which is vital for his survival and endows the kappa with extraordinary strength and dexterity. Kiyoshi must avoid tipping his head forward with the flap open. Otherwise, all the fluid may leak out and his life would drain away. The trouble is, his tendency to keep falling asleep accompanies cranial incontinence, so you see, he needs constant supervision. We can't seal the flap closed either—the pressure would make him ill."

"Can't you just put a pillow under his head or something?"

"I tried that at first, but Kiyoshi won't sit still. Even inside one of the enclosures, he constantly wanders about. No, somebody has to watch him night and day. Danariel has been of some help, but even together, we are finding this difficult."

"And that's another reason you haven't been able to do anything else?"

Heinrich nodded. "I've had very little sleep and hardly anything to eat. I need either a way to cure him or more people to help."

"Which leaves us with a problem," said Danariel. "There are not enough people to go around. We need somebody to take care of the animals, specifically Kiyoshi. We need to deal with Argoyle Redwar. And, if you are right, Joe, we need to check the burrows for Veronica."

"I will go down the burrow with Cornelius to look for Ronnie. Anything to get away from him," Heinrich said with a frown at the kappa.

"That leaves me to do something about Redwar," said Joe.

"But what about the mansion?" said Danariel. "And who will make sure that Kiyoshi doesn't fall asleep?"

"We'll deal with that first," said Joe with a sly smile. "Lilly?" he called. "I know you're in here. It's about time you came out of hiding. We'll need your help."

TWENTY

"Good luck, and be careful," said Joe to Heinrich as they stood by the edge of the burrow. Night had descended on Ringwood Forest by the time they had worked out their plans, and the tunnel looked even less inviting than it had during the day. It smelled even worse than it looked.

"I shall be safe with Cornelius to protect me," said Heinrich, ruffling one gnarly hand through the manticore's red hair and shining a flashlight into the burrow with the other. "I am not so happy about leaving Kiyoshi in Lilly's hands, though."

"I think it's a chance we have to take," said Joe.

Cornelius lowered his head, gently butted the side of Heinrich's leg, and moved toward the entrance to the deep hole. A low growl rumbled from the beast's throat as he pawed the dirt impatiently and eyed his companion.

Beside Joe, Danariel hovered in the breeze, trying

her hardest to subdue the pulses of light shining from her body. On the other side of Joe, Flarp bobbed in the air, looking agitated.

"I think Flarp wants to go with you." Joe smiled.

"That would not surprise me. He has not been the same since Ronnie disappeared."

"This way," Joe said to Flarp. "I need you to be my lookout."

The large eyeball stared into the forest for a long moment and then drifted by Joe's side like a deflated jellyfish as they began their trip to Redwar Industries.

It didn't take long for them to emerge from the forest and creep toward the security gates of the huge industrial park. A road that circled the entire complex led to a floodlit gatehouse that imprisoned two zombielike security guards: one fast asleep, the other leafing mindlessly through a magazine. A huge metallic sign lit with harsh halogen lamps loomed above an enormous wiremesh fence.

R.I.P., it said in huge embossed letters across the top. *Redwar Industrial Park* shone in smaller imprinting underneath.

"Nice!" whispered Joe. "Makes you feel really welcome, doesn't it?" He took a deep breath and smiled at the seraph. "Are you ready, Danariel?"

"Just watch me."

"And you, Flarp? You've got to nudge me if you see anyone coming once we're in, right?"

Flarp seemed distracted, looking back into the forest.

"Flarp?"

"He understands, Joe."

"Okay. Let's do it. Go!"

Joe commando crawled through the grass toward the gatehouse. The slimy globble skirted the ground beside him, looking left to right. They stopped just before the tarmac.

Danariel flew like a tiny missile at the gatehouse, then zoomed upwards. She stopped far above the trees and hovered like a small blue sun directly in line with the fence.

A silent pandemonium broke out inside the gate house, bathed in sapphire brilliance, as the security guard with the magazine shook his colleague furiously by the shirt collar. Then both of them were waving their arms, pointing and grabbing for things. One of them found a mobile phone and pointed it at the UFO now darting from side to side, looking as mysterious as possible. The other guard looked like he was screaming in excitement as he pressed his hands against the glass and gawped at the shining visitor.

It was all Joe needed. While the two guards were held spellbound by Danariel, Joe darted underneath the car barriers and ran as fast as he could toward the main building. Two minutes later, Joe fell against the red granite of the enormous building, just around the corner from a set of glass doors that allowed entrance to the tower.

Panting more from exhilaration than exertion, Joe peered toward the security gates and saw Danariel performing a figure eight just above the trees.

Both guards stood outside babbling into their mobile phones.

Flarp spun round and round next to Joe, his soggy tendrils extended.

"Now all we need to do is get inside the main building. I wonder if there are any more security guards inside. Flarp, we haven't been spotted yet, have we?"

Flarp stopped spinning and just stared.

"I'll take that as a no."

The glass doors burst open.

Joe pressed his back against the wall as three more men in guard uniform ran outside, pointing and whooping at the strange phenomenon in the sky.

Flarp went to follow them, but Joe grabbed one of his tendrils and yanked him back. "Let's go," said Joe, pulling the globble with him through the doors. "Keep watch." He skidded along a white marble floor, leaving clumps of dirt behind him, and hurried to a direction plaque near the reception desk.

"Training Center . . . Lecture Theatre . . . Human Resources . . . Research and Development . . . Toxicology . . . Ah! Directors' Offices, twelfth floor. That's what we want. We should start with Redwar's office and see if we can find any clues."

Finding an elevator, Joe dragged the globble behind him like a frenzied helium balloon and stabbed the *12* button. The elevator hummed its way up to the offices. By the time it stopped, Joe had just about got his breath back. The doors slid open with a ping, revealing a darkened open office area. A few computers had been left on for the night, their cold electric light casting long shadows across the grey walls.

Joe edged out of the lift and whispered to Flarp, "Is anybody out there?"

The eyeball swiveled around, then butted Joe on the cheek before straining to the right.

Joe wiped Flarp's snotty grunge from his skin "Let's hope Redwar's office isn't that way, then. Can you see where it is?"

Flarp swiveled again, splodged Joe a second time, then strained to the left.

"Good. You lead."

They crept past several desks and into a corridor with a fax machine before seeing a series of wood-paneled doors. Redwar's lair was at the very end, naturally the most illustrious office entrance, with double doors made from expensive mahogany and shining gold handles.

Joe nudged one of the doors inwards and peeped through the gap.

Flarp butted the other one and swooped inside.

"Flarp! *Please* keep watch and stop getting so excited."

Flarp's drippy parts jostled as if in frustration; then it waited by the doors.

The office was much longer than Joe expected, and a line of stuffed heads ranging from antelopes to zebras gazed down at him with glassy indifference. Lowlight pin spots in the ceiling projected their haunting silhouettes across the width of the room, and Joe shuddered at the thought of Redwar admiring these morbid trophies. Before the creeping fear could take hold, he tore his gaze from them and made for Redwar's heavy desk.

There was only one drawer. It contained a stapler, a notepad, and a calculator—nothing incriminating. Joe scanned the office, trying to ignore the stuffed heads. Not one filing cabinet anywhere. No trays of paperwork, no piles of documents, and no secret maps revealing an underground dungeon that showed Mrs. Merrynether behind bars in a mildewed prison.

Joe shook his head and chewed at his bottom lip. "What was I thinking? What did I expect to find?" he said to himself. "Come on, Flarp. Let's get out of here before the security guards come back."

But Flarp had fixated on something at the other end of the office. In the center of the wall was a large oil painting of Redwar dressed in regal robes, puffing his flabby form out with a sideways pose of prideful majesty.

"Yes, ugly, isn't he, Flarp?"

The globble bounced off the portrait, leaving a sliding lump underneath Redwar's nose, making it look like he'd had a sneezing accident.

Joe stifled a laugh, then pulled at Flarp's tendrils. "Come on. We'd better go."

Flarp resisted and butted the portrait again.

"What is it?" Joe looked closer at the painting. "Is there something here I should see?"

Again Flarp threw himself at the picture.

"I can't see anything behind all that slime. Ah! *Behind.* Is there something behind the painting, Flarp? I bet there's a safe—the oldest trick in the book."

Joe lifted Redwar's portrait off the wall. Sure enough, a silver safe door was behind it. "Brilliant, but how do we get inside it?"

Flarp pushed to one side of the knob, drew back, and then attached himself to the wall next to the safe like a huge limpet. A second later he swiveled slowly clockwise and then stopped to focus on Joe.

"Of course! You can see right inside the lock. You can see the combination."

Joe mimicked Flarp's movements as he turned the knob clockwise and counterclockwise in a series of precise moves. A few turns later and the safe door swung open.

"Jackpot! Flarp, you're amazing!"

The globble plopped away from the wall and returned to the office door to keep watch while Joe brought Argoyle Redwar's secrets into the open. There were several packets, each containing items that looked like they belonged in an archaeological museum, but most of the valuables were in the form of paperwork, the majority extremely old and faded and written in strange languages. As Joe hunted for anything that would provide a clue about Mrs. Merrynether's disappearance, he became more and more convinced that Redwar had nothing to do with it. He hoped he was wrong. The thought that she had been captured by the Beast of Upton Puddle was . . . No, there had to be some other explanation.

Then something caught Joe's eye. A cold thrill ran down his back and all the way up again—a collection of small, black felt bags. Fearing the worst, but beginning to realize the horrible truth, Joe opened one of them. The familiar multicolored sparkle of diamonds glittered within. And with the bags, a pile of letters. Joe felt faint as he picked them up. He opened one at random.

Dear Jimmy,

It is with much regret that I write to you on this occasion. I have bad news. The cluricaun found a way to escape his enclosure again, and I fear that he may ruin things for us unless I find a more secure cage for him.

To add to my woes, last week Ronnie almost

discovered that I have been writing to you. In all the years we have been in communication, I have always been careful, but when trying to find Lilly, I left a letter on my desk and she almost saw it. So please understand the necessary precautions I must make from now on when I write to you.

As has become my custom, I enclose . . .

Joe could read no more. Feeling the blood rush from his cheeks, he sank to the ground. Letters from Heinrich to Argoyle Redwar. It was obvious now that the mysterious Jimmy was in fact a pseudonym for Redwar in case Mrs. Merrynether caught Heinrich red-handed. Heinrich could be forgiven if he was writing to an unknown relative, but to Argoyle Redwar? He would never be able to explain that. Joe's mind turned into a fog of fear, doubt, and horror. He had come looking for Mrs. Merrynether but found proof that Heinrich, her closest companion, was Redwar's secret mole, working against her all along.

But why? Not money. In fact, it seemed now that much of Redwar's financial success may well have come from Heinrich's continued gifts of diamonds. But where did Heinrich get those?

Flarp suddenly became agitated and darted toward Joe, then back to the door.

"The guards?"

Joe felt sick. He stood, threw everything inside,

and pushed the safe door shut. He stuffed the letter into his pocket. Quickly replacing the portrait, he followed Flarp out of the office and along the corridor. But this time, instead of heading for the lift, Flarp made for the stairs.

The guards were probably on their way up. Did they know intruders were in the building? Had Joe and Flarp tripped a secret alarm? Adrenaline pumped as Joe ran behind Flarp. Soon they would be outside and heading for Merrynether Mansion—safe.

No! Not safe—not anymore. What could be done about Heinrich? Should he be confronted? What if Heinrich was responsible for Mrs. Merrynether's disappearance? Should he hold back for now and talk to Danariel? The questions tumbled through Joe's mind as fast as he was running down the steps. Anger rose with every breath as he reached the ground floor, and Joe made a vow that as soon as they got back, he would get some answers. He'd start with Danariel.

Flarp continued to fly down the stairs beyond ground level.

"Flarp! We're right near reception. That's the way out. Where are you going? Where are the guards?"

But the eyeball continued down the stairwell, occasionally turning to see if Joe was following. With little choice but to do the same, he continued, biting down his frustration and anger with every step.

On they went through a labyrinth of corridors, labs, offices, and lounges until Flarp finally came to a halt, pressed against a set of white doors. A label above them read *Animal Section: No Admittance.* A card reader was embedded in the wall.

Flarp pressed himself so hard against the doors that Joe thought he might burst.

"What is it, Flarp? Is it Mrs. Merrynether? Can you see her? Is she behind these doors? We can't get inside. I think we need a pass or something."

Flarp plopped away, stared at Joe, and then retreated again as if changing his mind.

Confused, tired, and fed up, Joe decided not to ask again but simply followed his guide back into the corridor. It was plain that Flarp wanted him to see or do something, but whether Mrs. Merrynether was in there or not, Joe had no clue. And why would she be put in an animal section?

Joe stopped beside a workstation with a PC that had been left on. "I wonder," he said and started to look around the desk. "If this person's sloppy enough to leave their PC on, maybe they left an ID badge behind."

A few more seconds of searching and Joe realized he wasn't going to be that lucky.

"Perhaps I can get something from this instead," he said, sitting in front of the computer. Two minutes more and Joe had found an e-mail account and printed off some details.

"This'll do. I've got a list of names showing a few people who work here. It's a start anyway. Now let's get out of here, Flarp. I have to talk to Danariel—fast."

Twenty-one

It was past midnight by the time Joe, Danariel, and Flarp returned to Merrynether Mansion to discover that Heinrich and Cornelius had not returned. Joe had never been inside the mansion at night and, although it wasn't creepy, the whole place had a very different atmosphere than it did during the day. Even the vault seemed to have changed. Joe felt strangely detached when he set eyes on Heinrich's things laid out on the desk, as if he were looking at the belongings of a stranger. More than that—an impostor.

Flarp returned to his previous position: throwing himself against the wall of the vault. A patch of green slime covered one spot, looking as though it had stained the brickwork. Joe flopped to the floor and looked thoughtfully at Cornelius's empty enclosure. Was the manticore safe with Heinrich?

Danariel hovered in front of Joe's face. "You were

very quiet on the way back, Joe, and I can feel that something is very wrong. Are you all right?"

"No, not really." He frowned and glanced at Heinrich's desk. "How well do you know Heinrich?"

"I have known Heinrich for a very long time. At least fifty years."

"Fifty years? You knew him before you came here?"

"Oh, yes. In fact—"

Bicycle horns, bells, and bottles clashed in a rigorous Irish jig.

Joe clapped his hands to his ears, and Danariel shot into her lightbulb for cover. Only Flarp, who had no ears, seemed unimpressed by the racket and continued to bounce off the wall. Much to Joe's relief, the tune was over quickly. It was only then, as he looked closer at the wall just past Heinrich's desk, that he saw Lilly's latest masterpiece. A row of air horns squeezed between two long planks of wood, stripped from an enclosure, had been screwed into the brickwork. Underneath the horns, a shelf had been lined up with a long row of bottles, each holding different amounts of water. A pulley system with a tiny hammer designed to tap tunes out on the bottles hung next to them, now swinging from side to side, its job done.

And underneath all that, with a length of string tied loosely around his hairy head, leading to Lilly's insane musical instrument, was the exasperated Kiyoshi. To make matters worse, the cluricaun had fastened across the kappa's wide mouth a strip of duct tape with the words *SHUT UP* marked over it.

Joe smiled and shook his head. All his troubles were momentarily forgotten as he marveled at the mischief-maker's ingenuity. If the kappa were to fall asleep, his head would slump forward and yank the string, which in turn would trigger a musical nightmare before the creature lost any of the precious fluid from the hole in his head. Looking humiliated but nonetheless safe, Kiyoshi watched Joe as he approached.

"I'm so sorry we had to leave you in Lilly's hands," Joe said, trying hard not to laugh. He picked a corner of the tape and tried to peel it away without pulling the victim's hair out. No use. It was either quick and sharp or slow and agonizing, and Joe made his choice. A large clump of brown hair came away as Joe ripped off the tape. Kiyoshi howled, and Joe could have sworn he heard an Irishman chuckling as he rolled the tape in his hands and threw it to the floor.

"Are you all right?" Joe asked.

Danariel squeezed herself out of the lightbulb and returned to his side.

"All right?" the thing shrieked. "All right? In which crepuscular region of your picayune brain could you imagine that anything about my present condition is acceptable? That supercilious pygmy waited until I was in a state of slumber and then violated me. It is my informed opinion that such a recalcitrant creature should, indeed *must*, be incarcerated with others of his kind."

"I—"

"Do not interrupt. Did your mother not teach you elementary etiquette? As I was saying—"

"My mum!" Joe understood only part of what Kiyoshi said, but the *mother* word hit him like a rocket between the eyes. "She'll be going crazy wondering where I am."

Joe rushed to the phone, leaving the infuriated kappa to continue his squeaky rant. He dialed the number as fast as he could and waited for it to ring, frantically trying to think of an explanation that would satisfy. The busy tone gave Joe time to think. He replaced the receiver, lifted it again, thinking hard for an excuse, and then realized there was no dial tone.

A recorded voice said, "You have three messages. Press the star key to hear your messages."

"There are messages," Joe looked at Danariel. "Do you think I should listen to them? We don't know where Mrs. Merrynether or Heinrich are, and these could be important."

Danariel opened her arms and offered a single nod. Joe pressed the star key.

"Your first message was received at 4:33 p.m."

"Ah, hello, Mrs. Merrynether? I'm sorry to disturb you on a Saturday, but that swelling has reappeared on my . . . Oh, sorry. It's Betty here—Mrs. Bobbit? Yes. The, um, swelling. It's reappeared on my budgie's . . . Well, it's reappeared on my budgie again, and I'm rather worried.

Would you mind awfully ringing back? Thank you. My number is . . . erm . . . er . . . 81887542. Thank you so much. Bye . . . Bye . . . I hate these answer mach—"

"Your second message was received at 7:10 p.m."

"Oh, good evening, Mrs. Merrynether. My name is Rose Ashworth. We met recently when I came to pick up Joe? Actually, that's what I'm calling about. He told his mother he'd be back in time for his tea, but he hasn't come back home yet and . . . well, with all the talk about the Beast of Upton Puddle, I'm a bit worried. I was just wondering if he's with you. Please could you call me back as soon as possible to let me know? Thank you. I'm at 07199 656543."

"Your third message was received at 8:51 p.m."

"This is a message for Mr. Krieger. Container 1191248 has arrived at Hagworth central warehouse and is still awaiting pickup. Please contact us at 814233 as soon as possible, as the night shift staff is not prepared to take responsibility for zoological cargo beyond its allotted time slot. Thank you."

Joe replaced the receiver and puffed air through his cheeks. "Where do I start?"

"It sounds like arrangements were made to pick up another patient," Danariel said.

"That's what I thought, but how are we going to get it here? We can't leave it at the warehouse. And what am I going to do about Mum and Aunt Rose? They'll take turns at braining me when I get home."

"Indeed." Kiyoshi chimed in. "And who is going to prevent Betty Bobbit's budgie's bum boil bursting, hmm? Three tasks, and one child who is woefully maladroit."

Joe ignored him. "I'd better call that warehouse, then try Mum again."

He dialed the number and was put through to the same man who left the message. Five minutes later, after a difficult conversation made worse by Kiyoshi's continued verbal assault in the background, Joe agreed to wait for the staff to courier the cargo to Merrynether Mansion at considerable expense.

"Okay, that's sorted. They said the container will be here in about three hours, but I've just made the situation worse for myself. How am I going to tell my mum I'm not coming home yet?"

Joe found his way to Heinrich's chair and flopped into it to think.

Bottles tinkled as Kiyoshi freed himself from Lilly's contraption and padded toward Joe. "Ah, the disconsolate cry of the little boy lost."

"And there's Veronica too. We still need to help her," said Danariel, also ignoring Kiyoshi's taunts.

"Yes." Joe, feeling dejected, pulled out the list he'd printed from the computer at Redwar Industries. "I suppose I could start looking through this person's contact list. You never know who . . . Oh!"

Joe's focus had come to rest on a name he wished

he didn't recognize. He continued to look through the list, hoping to see someone else, anyone else, but that was the only one.

"What is it?" the seraph asked. "Do you know someone there?"

"Yes. Scott Duggan—head of security. That's Kurt Duggan's dad. Kurt goes to my school and beats up just about everyone. He doesn't like me very much."

"He's not likely to help, then."

"No, but he's the only one I know on this list."

Flarp's steady thumping against the wall didn't help Joe think, and the kappa's continued interruptions made matters even worse.

"Gastronomical desires may not be a significant priority for you at this juncture, but I require sustenance."

"You'll have to wait, Kiyoshi," Danariel said.

"What do you eat?" asked Joe absently.

"Children."

Joe raised an eyebrow at what he hoped was a joke.

". . . or Cucumis sativus," Kiyoshi said. "*Cucumber* to you."

"How about this, Kiyoshi? You think of a way to get Scott Duggan's security pass, and I'll find you some cucumber."

The phone rang, and Joe was almost grateful not to hear Kiyoshi's convoluted reply. He picked up the receiver, realizing at once that it could be his mother or his aunt. He froze.

The caller broke the silence. "Hello? Mrs. Merrynether?" It *was* his mother.

Panic-stricken and simultaneously irritated by the haughty expression on Kiyoshi's bizarre monkey face, Joe thrust the receiver at the kappa.

The thing's eyes widened as it stared at the mouthpiece. Fortunately, Kiyoshi was not shy of talking. "Greetings, spawner of maladjusted offspring."

Joe could still hear his mother through the earpiece pointed at the creature.

"Mrs. . . . . Merrynether? Is that you? Can I speak to Mrs. Merrynether please?"

"I am afraid Mrs. Merrynether is away on important business, Mrs. Copper. I am her secretary—Mr. Kiyoshi."

"Oh, I see. Well, I'm sorry to disturb you at this hour, but—"

"You wish to know if your son is currently located within our abode?"

"Yes. Is he? I'm not angry with him—just worried. Is he there?"

Kiyoshi's thin pink lips stretched into a smug smile. Joe wanted to crack him with the phone.

"No," said Kiyoshi, "but he did visit us this morning to procure some belongings he had left behind. He mentioned to us then that he would be staying with a school friend this weekend. I believe the young man's name is Kurt Duggan."

"Oh . . . Oh, I see. Well, thank you, Mr. Kiyoshi. You've put my mind at rest. Thank you."

"My pleasure, Mrs. Copper."

The phone went dead.

Openmouthed, Joe replaced the receiver. "What have you done?"

"High-order cognitive processing."

"What?"

Kiyoshi rolled his eyes. "An act of double avicide by geological means."

"What?"

"I think he said he killed two birds with one stone," said Danariel, raising her hands.

"He thinks that phone call solved two of my problems? How does that work?"

"The solution is—" Kiyoshi's head fell forward.

"He's gone again," whispered Joe, lifting Kiyoshi's head as gently as possible. It was surprisingly heavy. "Perhaps I can keep him this way for a while." The kappa's eyes stayed shut. "Okay, so how did he help?"

"Well, I'm not sure," said Danariel, "but perhaps Kiyoshi was going to suggest you really do stay at Kurt's place?"

"What? How? He hates me."

"There must be—"

"Wait a minute. He has the key."

"Key?"

"Yes. It's a long story, but Lilly gave me the key to the cellar trapdoor thinking I would get him some drink. Kurt Duggan got it off me, and I told him it was a key to my savings box hidden in the forest. I think Heinrich must have found out the key was missing and had the padlock replaced, but the point is, Kurt Duggan still has the old key. He's been hassling me since last Monday to give him a map to my savings box."

"I see. I think I know what you're thinking."

"Right. I'll go see Kurt tomorrow and tell him if he wants the map he has to cover for me *and* make sure I'm invited for tea tomorrow night."

"Do you think it will work?"

Joe tried not to think about the risks. "It has to. I don't know what else to try."

TWENTY-TWO

Joe woke with a jump. The sound of a buzzer echoed around the walls of the vault, and a burning sensation crept over his fingers. It took a few startled seconds for Joe to realize that after falling asleep cradling Kiyoshi's head in his hands, he'd jogged some of the cloudy yellow goo out of Kiyoshi's cranial vent and onto his skin when the alarm sounded.

"Aah!" Joe leapt to his feet, wrung his hands, wiped his hands on his trousers, and before he'd even considered what he was doing, he'd plopped his fingers into his mouth to suck away the burning pain.

Kiyoshi, having also woke with a start, looked up at Joe with a disdainful frown.

"Wok *is* gak htuff in your heg?" Joe asked, sticking his tongue out. "Ik's burnged ngy ngouf."

"Are you educated in adenology, chemistry, or herpetology? If not, I fail to perceive any value in providing you with an answer."

Danariel fluttered down from the skylight. "Joe, the delivery has arrived."

Joe swallowed. The burning in his mouth had settled into a peculiar tingling sensation. "Is that what the buzzer was about?"

"Yes, it's an alarm that lets Heinrich or Veronica know when someone knocks on the door."

"I'd better go up there, then. Can you keep an eye on Kiyoshi for a minute?"

Joe felt a lightness in his body as he made cautious steps toward the door. His mouth was dry, and he felt a curious sensation, like floating upside down in a vat of jelly with earmuffs on. What was in that head soup of Kiyoshi's? Had he poisoned himself? For a moment Joe thought he would pass out, but the world around him remained clear. He hardly noticed the door as he pulled it open. It seemed completely weightless. Running up the stairs, through the pantry, and along the hallway required no effort at all.

He opened the main door and was confronted by a tall man with a clipboard. The man looked so tired that the flat cap on his head seemed to weigh him down.

"Delivery. Sign and date here please." He pointed a nicotine-stained finger at an empty box on a piece of yellow paper, then handed Joe a pen.

"Can I see it first?" Joe asked.

"Sure." The man shuffled to the back of his van.

"Not much to see, though." He unlocked a padlock and swung the double doors open to reveal a large wooden crate covered in various warning labels and punctured with tiny air holes.

"What's inside?"

"How should I know? We never know. It's all very hush-hush." He tapped the side of his nose.

"What d'you mean, hush-hush? It's not illegal, is it?"

"Nah, I didn't mean like that. It's just a bit . . . weird. Merrynether's crates always get picked up from the middle of a field somewhere up-country. Nobody ever sees who drops them there, but we get instructions to pick them up ready for collection. Then some shifty-lookin' bloke with a hood, Mr. Kreiger I think his name is, comes to pick them up from the warehouse a few hours later and brings them back 'ere . . . Anyway, can't stand around chattin'. Delivery code's there," he said, pointing. "Got a fork truck or someone to 'elp?"

"Uh, no!"

"You'd better 'ave strong arms, then, boy. It's half past three in the morning, so don't expect me to start heavin' stuff about."

Joe stared at the man.

The man stared back. "I'll get the rest of the paper-work," he said eventually and sauntered to the front of the van.

Joe tested the corner of the crate. It felt as light as Styrofoam. "There can't be much in here," he called.

"Took a forklift to get it on, mate," the man shouted back, one leg dangling out the door as he rooted around for more documents.

Joe pulled at the crate again and found that he could lift it from the floor of the van without even trying. The van sprang slightly upwards as Joe proceeded to pull the crate clear and rest it on the ground.

The man came back with some crumpled envelopes. He frowned at the crate, then at Joe.

"How did you—? That must weigh at least two hundred kilos."

"Feels empty to me."

The man tried to lift a corner. It didn't budge. He looked around him, then squinted at Joe before looking around again. "Clever trick, that. How'd you do it?"

Unable to give him an answer, Joe simply winked, flexed an arm and pointed at his bicep.

"All right." The man smiled. "Have it your way, then. Keep your secrets. I'm off to bed."

When the delivery man had driven off, Joe lifted the crate again. He walked inside the mansion and, still holding the crate with only one hand, shut the main door.

"Awesome!" Joe said to himself. "Kappa juice. It must be the kappa juice."

As he carried the crate down to the vault, however, it grew heavier and heavier until finally he had to drop it just inside the door.

The kappa trundled to Joe, and Danariel flew in gentle circles above him.

"I feel like Superman," Joe said. "At least, I did a minute ago." Cold sweat beaded over his skin.

"The effects are not of a permanent nature," said Kiyoshi. "You should expect a brief period of hypothermic Meleagris gallopavo in precisely twenty seconds."

"Hypo- what?"

"Cold turkey," said Danariel. "You'd better sit down. It's not pleasant. Kiyoshi? Will you open the crate?"

Joe fell into Heinrich's chair and clapped his hands over his mouth. His insides felt like a washing machine on maximum spin with a full load of cold, wet towels, and it was all he could do to resist the urge to throw up. Hoping to distract himself from the impending vomit, he watched Kiyoshi stretch his amphibious legs out of his shell and grasp one side of the crate while keeping his head perfectly level. The kappa tore the wooden panels off with terrifying ease, and by the time the crate had been stripped down, Joe's temptation to gag had been replaced by the thrill of wonderment.

A beast almost twice the size of a crocodile lay coiled and sleeping amidst the splintered wood. Joe had no doubt it was some kind of reptile, but like everything else he'd encountered in Merrynether Mansion, it was different from any creature he'd seen in any book or TV documentary before. The creature's scaly skin had an oily black sheen that shimmered black, purple, and blue as its body rose and fell with its slow breathing. A large arrow-shaped head rested on a thick tail, and across its spiny back, two bony wings lay folded like closed umbrellas.

Joe made no effort to hide his excitement as he spoke. "Is that . . . Is it a dragon?"

"It's a—"

Kiyoshi spoke over Danariel. "Goodness, no! Consider the scale pigmentation and dimensions. Also take note of its claws." Kiyoshi thrust a suckered hand underneath the thickest section of the beast's body and lifted it with almost no effort. A formidable set of talons were tucked underneath.

"Two legs?"

"Indeed. Dragons are endowed with four."

"A dinosaur, then?"

"The etymology for the word *dinosaur* is Greek and means terrible lizard, so indeed, you may name it as such, but the true designation is *wyvern*."

"A wyvern. Is it dangerous?"

"Very dangerous." The answer didn't come from Kiyoshi or Danariel, but Joe recognized the accent instantly.

"Heinrich!"

Apparently the German giant had entered the vault while Kiyoshi had ripped the crate apart. Cornelius stood by Heinrich's side, head lifted proudly and barbed tail waving like a serpent behind him. Both looked exhausted. Heinrich had three bloody gashes across his right cheek, and his long coat had been shredded in several places. The manticore didn't look much better with his ruffled fur and bare patches where clumps had apparently been torn from his mane.

Joe eyed Heinrich. Part of him was overjoyed to see the old man again, but another part wanted to run as far from him as possible.

Danariel, still unaware of Joe's discovery at Redwar Industries, darted to Heinrich and planted her glowing body across the width of his face, her wings fluttering in delight.

Joe simply stared, unsure what to do or say.

"Hello, Danariel." Heinrich tried to smile. "Step aside, Joe. Snappel is heavily sedated, but she will be disorientated and afraid when I wake her. I must lead her to an enclosure before she is fully alert . . . Where is Ronnie? Did you not find her?"

Danariel flew down to greet Cornelius.

"No. What happened to you?" Joe asked, his voice monotone.

Heinrich threw a questioning glance at Joe, then crouched near the wyvern's head. "We entered the burrow and found a very big network of tunnels. It is a maze down there." He lifted the lizard's top jowl and examined a row of fangs. "We found no sign of Ronnie, but Cornelius caught the scent of the Beast and we tracked it down, hoping she would be near. We did our best to capture it, but it was too fast and strong. I was injured, and then it burrowed into the earth again."

Heinrich's voice cracked as he continued. "She could still be down there . . . hurt or . . ." He glanced around, fighting back grief. "I need rope and an apple."

"Like you said in the first place, I think she's with Redwar," said Joe, still cold in his response, "but we need to get into a restricted area."

"How?" asked Heinrich, finding an apple on his desk and a coil of rope hanging on a hook near Cornelius's enclosure.

"Leave that to me," said Joe, unwilling to give Heinrich any more information than he had to.

"Very well, but once I have secured Snappel, I am going back to the burrows to look for Ronnie. I cannot rest until she is found, and we do not know for sure that she is being held by Redwar."

"Do what you want."

"Are you all right? You seem a little . . ."

A heavy silence fell between them. All that could be heard was the steady rhythmic thump of Flarp bouncing off the wall and Cornelius's baritone purring as Danariel glided through his fur.

"Have you got somewhere for me to sleep with a locked door? If you're going out to look for Mrs. Merrynether again, I want to be here if you find her."

"Of course, but there is no need for you to lock the door."

Joe didn't answer. Weariness dragged at his eyelids. He desperately wanted to be at home in bed, swallowed up by his warm quilt. Absently, he watched Heinrich tie a set of complicated knots around the head and body of the wyvern and wondered why thoughts of sleep were sending nagging danger signals at the back of his mind. Sleep was good, wasn't it?

Kiyoshi!

"Where's Kiyoshi?" said Joe, instantly snapping out of his daydream.

Danariel launched into the air.

Heinrich stopped what he was doing and looked around.

"There," said Danariel.

Kiyoshi had fallen asleep by the side of Heinrich's desk, yellow stuff oozing from his vent.

Joe rushed over, tripped on a plank, and clattered to the floor, waking not only the kappa but the serpentine creature Heinrich was trying to secure.

"Great thundering ogres," Kiyoshi exclaimed. "What in the cosmos was that terrible cacophony?"

A roar rumbled through the walls of the vault, and Joe shuffled around on hands and knees to see the huge lizard rise clumsily from its coiled position. Fiery red eyes burned with apparent panic as it staggered, huge talons clacking on the floor as it fought to regain balance. Its wings unfolded and flapped like a great black tent caught in a high wind.

Heinrich pulled at the ropes, the veins in his head standing out as he struggled against the wyvern's strength.

"Whoa, Snappel. Careful, girl. Nobody's going to hurt you."

The creature's roar was followed up with a short, sharp burp. For a second the beast stopped moving and looked surprised at itself. Then in a sudden spasmodic jerk, it hiccupped and sent a jet of fire into the air, narrowly missing Heinrich's scalp. Snappel wavered, whoozy from the aftereffects of anesthetic, and Heinrich let go of the rope.

"You're about to see how she got her name," said Heinrich. He held the apple above his head and called to the creature. "Snappel! Look what I have here. A nice, juicy apple. Look!"

He waved it around for a second or two, then threw it into Cornelius's enclosure. With the speed of a heat-seeking missile, the wyvern shot into the manticore's old home and clamped her jaws on the fruit before it even came close to landing. The lizard flipped her head upright, snapped her jaws twice more, and then swallowed.

Heinrich slammed the door of the enclosure, but Snappel seemed unconcerned. With a final dazed look around, she collapsed into her former coiled position and closed her eyes.

"She'll be all right. We just need to cure her hiccups. It's why she's here."

Joe wanted desperately to ask a million questions about the new creature but could not bring himself to show any enthusiasm to Heinrich. "Good. Can you take me to my room now? I'm really tired. It's past four in the morning."

"Of course." Heinrich checked around, as if to see what else he needed to do first. "But don't expect me to be in when you wake up unless I have found Ronnie. I will make sure everything is secure before I go, but I will also leave a list of things that will need to be done in case I am back late. Can I count on you?"

"Me?" Joe laughed, unable to mask his bitterness. "I'm not the . . ."

"Not the what?"

Joe looked away. "Nothing."

"You've been different since I returned. Is it something I've done?"

Joe stared at Heinrich again, rage bubbling like lava. Should he confront him? Now, while Heinrich had no idea he knew about the deception, he seemed to be safe. But would that be the case if he challenged Heinrich? If the old man turned on him, would anyone jump to his aid?

"No," said Joe eventually. "I'm just tired."

TWENTY-THREE

Exhausted from the most eventful Saturday of his life, Joe slept through most of Sunday. He'd locked himself in one of the bedrooms of Merrynether Mansion and fallen into a deep sleep, oblivious to whatever was happening in the vault.

Together with Cornelius and Danariel, Heinrich was out for most of the day looking for Mrs. Merrynether. In the late afternoon, Heinrich returned, pale and haggard. With few words, he sent Joe home.

Joe was glad he didn't have to make conversation with him. He might even have felt sorry for him if he didn't know Heinrich was a traitor. Yet it was a mystery why Heinrich had such great concern for the person he had betrayed for so long. And why would he want to sabotage the practice he seemed to love so much?

Unfortunately, Joe was not the only one with questions. His mother drilled him for more than thirty minutes, wanting to know why he hadn't told her he'd be spending the weekend with the Duggans. While Joe was grateful for Kiyoshi's lie, answering her questions proved to be very difficult.

With the dawn of Monday, Joe woke at home feeling fresh resolve to get some answers, but first he had to survive another difficult day. Persuading his mum to let him go for tea at Kurt Duggan's house was hard enough, especially since he'd apparently spent the weekend there, but convincing Kurt was going to be much more of an ordeal. Nevertheless, no matter how nervous he felt or how hard the beating would be if things went wrong, Joe had to try. Mrs. Merrynether's safety depended on him.

Morning break came with the noisy rabble pouring out of the double doors to the school grounds. The cliques separated into their habitual huddles, some running to the playing fields, others to the common room. Kurt Duggan and his mob headed for their usual haunt.

Joe pulled a plastic bottle from his rucksack and examined the viscous, yellow gloop inside. "Here goes," he said to himself and poured the stuff into his mouth. Choking back the burning in his throat and wiping his watery eyes, Joe chased his nemesis. He didn't know how long the effect of the kappa juice would last, but hopefully it would see him through the next few minutes.

When the rest of the school was out of sight, Joe made his move. "Hey, Duggan! I need a minute alone."

The whole crowd stopped and turned to look at Joe. Duggan stood at the center, arms folded, face deadly serious while the others grinned and skulked like jackals waiting for a chance to pick at a carcass.

The thug sneered, waved a dismissive hand, and turned around, uninterested.

It wasn't the response Joe had hoped for.

He watched them walk on, his heart drumming harder as he psyched himself up.

"Now!" Joe shouted.

They stopped again.

This time Duggan's ape face was a hybrid of rage and surprise. "You what?"

"We need to talk."

"I need to smoke. *You* need to disappear before I fill that loud gob of yours with this." He raised a fist.

"It's about the map."

One of the jackals looked up at Duggan. "Map?"

"Forget it . . ." Duggan told him. "It's nothing."

"What's the matter, Kurt? Scared what they might do if they find out about your little secret?"

The bully's teeth flashed as he grinned with rage. "All right, you asked for it." He waved the others off and advanced on Joe.

The gang hesitated but left anyway.

"You think I'm stupid?" Duggan grabbed Joe by the shirt collar. "I know there's no map. There's no way you'd have kept it from me, not with the kicking you've been getting every day."

Duggan's knuckles pressed against Joe's chin as he tightened his grip.

"You're right. There's no map, but you've still got the key, right?"

"So?"

"So don't you want to know what it opens?"

"Are you going to tell me?"

"Yes, but there's something I want in return."

"No deal." Duggan dropped him and turned his back.

The tingling sensation in Joe's limbs faded as the thug walk away. A cold wave of nausea hung in his stomach. Time was already running out.

"I knew you were a loser," Joe said.

"Whatever."

Joe's legs began to buckle, but he chased Kurt and planted a fist squarely into the bully's back. "See? Loser."

That did it. Duggan turned and swung, exactly as Joe had been hoping for. The effects of the kappa juice had almost faded, but Joe caught Duggan's fist and twisted it in one lightning-fast reaction. Duggan sank to his knees with a frustrated cry as Joe held him there.

"Listening now?" said Joe, hoping Duggan wouldn't pay attention to his quaking legs or the sheen on his forehead.

"You're gonna get such a kicking when I get up," Duggan grunted.

Joe twisted a little more. His strength was waning,

but it was still enough.

"All right," yelled Duggan. "What d'you want?"

"What time does your dad get home from work?"

"Why?"

"Just answer me." Joe twisted a little more, his strength faltering.

Duggan winced all the same. "Just after four. Why?"

"I'm coming round for tea tonight."

"Eh?"

"I said I'm coming round for tea. Six o'clock. Got it?"

"Okay. Okay!"

Joe let go, and Duggan fell backward, his face a picture of confusion. He didn't say another word as he stood and jogged to his cronies, rubbing his wrist and frowning at Joe every few paces the whole way.

At six o'clock, Joe knocked on Duggan's door.

"Who's that?" came a screech from within. "Kurt? Get the door."

The door opened, and Kurt Duggan slouched in the doorway with a sour expression that changed instantly to shock when he saw Joe's face.

"You!"

"Yes, me. I'm here for my tea."

"But . . . I thought—"

"Kurt?" screamed a female voice. "Who is it? If that's your dad and he's forgotten his keys again, he can sod off!"

Kurt said nothing as his mother's slippered feet stomped toward them. Bright makeup that looked like it had been applied with a trowel exaggerated her contoured features. Her beehive peroxide hair brushed the top of the door frame when she approached, and a half-smoked cigarette waggled between her chapped lips as she said, "You selling something?" She looked at the large lantern he held.

"No, I'm a friend of Kurt's. He invited me for tea this evening." Joe offered the lantern, which began radiating a soft blue light through the patterned glass. "This is a present for you. It's a sort of night-light."

She took it. "Aw, ain't that lovely? Ain't that lovely, Kurt? Come inside, love, and have a sit-down in the kitchen. Don't mind the mess. Kurt never told me we was having company tonight."

She cuffed her son as they entered the house. A TV blared an Australian soap opera from the room next to the kitchen. Two cats screamed near Joe's legs as he sat at the table crowded with magazines, cups, and clothes.

"I didn't mean to be an inconvenience, Mrs. Duggan."

Mrs. Duggan admired the lantern in her hand. "Don't you worry, love. Kurt hardly ever brings his friends home. And you seem such a nice boy. What are you doing spending time with an idiot like him?"

"Mum!"

"I'll put this upstairs," she said. "It'll look nice on the windowsill."

Joe smiled to himself as she started up the stairs. Everything was going perfectly so far. When the lantern was in place, Danariel would pop out and look for a security pass that might let them into the secret areas of Redwar Industries. If she managed to find something, she would take it and then roll the lantern to the floor, creating a loud thud: the signal. Whoever found the lantern would see it pulsing and flashing as if it had short-circuited, and Joe would offer to take it home and fix it. That was the plan, but where was Kurt's dad? There was no chance of this working if Mr. Duggan was still at work with his security pass.

"I didn't get anything extra for dinner, but there are some frozen pizzas we can have," Mrs. Duggan called from upstairs. "Would that be all right, love?"

"Perfect," Joe yelled back.

Kurt glared, and Joe thought at any moment the bully's head might pop off to reveal a jet of steam.

"Mmmm, I love pizza."

Kurt growled but sucked it back in when his mother appeared again.

"Clear the table," she ordered her son. "And stick four pizzas in the oven. Your dad can have his warmed up when he gets in."

"But—"

"No buts. You do as you're bloody told. You can play on that PlayStation with your friend until your fingers fall off *after* you've done that but not a second before. And you'd better keep that noise down too—I'm watching the telly."

Duggan threw Joe a sadistic grin, apparently thinking they'd soon be alone, but Joe had other plans.

"Can I watch the TV with you, Mrs. Duggan?"

She raised her thickly lined eyebrows. "Really? Ah, bless him. Of course you can, love. Come in and sit down."

Joe followed her into the smoggy living room and sat in the armchair.

Kurt clattered in the kitchen, and Joe hoped his enemy hadn't done something hideous to his pizza. For the next twenty minutes, the crashing in the kitchen continued to escalate, competing with the TV as Mrs. Duggan gradually turned up the volume.

Kurt eventually appeared in the living room doorway. "Grub up."

"About bloody time," said Mrs. Duggan.

The three of them sat around the table, and Joe examined his food as carefully and as secretly as possible. He hoped by now Danariel had found something that would help them, but so far there had been no signal. He poked at his food and felt Duggan watching him, waiting for that first bite. The two cats sat either side of Joe's chair, waiting expectantly for treats.

"So . . . er . . ." Mrs. Duggan sparked up a cigarette.

"Joe . . . Joe Copper."

"Right." She puffed smoke across the table. "So,

Joe, you look like a clever one. Kurt getting you to do his homework for him, is he?"

"I wouldn't let that little runt near any of my stuff," said Kurt.

"That's no way to talk about your friend." She cuffed him around the head with her cigarette hand. A clump of ash landed in his hair.

"Don't take any notice of him, love. You just enjoy your dinner."

Joe took a reluctant bite of his pizza and almost gagged.

Kurt smirked.

There was no doubt—something offensive had been added to the sweet corn and peppers. He cut into another piece and tried to ignore Kurt's expression of glee as the fork approached his mouth.

The front door slammed. Joe was saved. As Kurt and his mum turned to look, Joe emptied the plate onto the floor and watched the cats move in for a feast.

"Bloody place," a male voice shouted from the door. Mr. Duggan stormed into the kitchen and threw a bunch of keys on the table. It came as no surprise to Joe that he looked like a larger version of Kurt.

"What time do you call this? You're almost three hours late, and your dinner's burnt," shrieked Mrs. Duggan.

"Don't you start, woman. If you must know, I just got the sack."

"The sack? Oh, that's just abso-bloody-lutely mar-velous. What did you go and do to get the elbow, Scott Duggan?"

"Me? It wasn't me. They had a break-in this week-end. Some vandals got into the building and wiped snot all over Mr. Redwar's portrait. He had the lot of us in his office trying to find out how it could've happened. Would you believe one of them actually said they saw a spaceship in the woods?" He shook his head. "Of course, nobody had an answer, and you know what that git's like. He fired every single one of us. Took all our keys, ID badges, and passes there and then and . . ."

With a sinking feeling, Joe realized there was no security pass to get his hands on.

Mr. Duggan pointed at Joe. "Who's that?"

Joe stared in shock.

"Never mind him," Mrs. Duggan said. "What are you going to do?"

"Do? I'll tell you what I'll do. I'm going to do a bit of breaking in myself. Maybe I'll smash up all his stuff. That'll teach him."

"And how are you going to do something stupid like that, Einstein?" Kurt said. "You won't even be able to get back in the building without a pass, let alone do any damage."

"Ah, well, that's where the old grey matter comes in, don't it? Something you weren't born with, boy." He tapped his head and looked accusingly at Kurt. "I'm head of security, remember? Had myself a second pass made up months ago and put it upstairs in the CD rack, just in case I ever needed it."

"You put a security pass in your CD rack?" Joe shouted and prayed Danariel heard.

"Who *is* that?" Mr. Duggan pointed at him again.

"I'm Joe Copper, Mr. Duggan. A friend of Kurt's."

"I don't care if you're the King of Pluto. Who invited you to come into my house and eat my food?"

"Scott Duggan, how dare you!" Mrs. Duggan stood and pointed a fork at him.

Thunk! Something heavy hit the floor upstairs— the best sound Joe had ever heard.

"What was that?" Mrs. Duggan asked.

"It sounded heavy," said Joe. "I hope nothing's broken."

"I'd better go and check," she said and stomped up the stairs.

The two Duggans stared at Joe like a pair of evil twins, though one was considerably bulkier than the other.

Joe smiled back. "That was a lovely tea. Thank you for having me, Kurt and Mr. Duggan."

"So you going to tell me about that key or not? You owe me big time, Copper."

Joe was spared as Mrs. Duggan thundered down the stairs, holding the lantern. It shone like a tiny blue sun and died to a faint glow before blasting another pulse of blue light.

"What the bloody hell is *that*?" Mr. Duggan was

pointing again.

"I think it's broken. One of the cats might've knocked it over. It isn't dangerous, is it?" Mrs. Duggan asked Joe.

"It shouldn't be . . . That is, if you always keep it upright. The gases inside it are a bit—"

"Hey!" said Mr. Duggan. "I asked a question."

"Well, perhaps you'd better have it back," Mrs. Duggan said, ignoring her husband and holding the lantern at arm's length as though it contained tarantulas.

"If you're sure."

"Oh, yes, yes. That's all right. It's the thought that counts, isn't it?"

"Well, all right, then," said Joe, edging toward the door. "Thanks again for having me."

"Come again soon," Mrs. Duggan said, and Joe stepped out of the house, trying to avoid Kurt's glare.

The sound of the door shutting came as a massive relief. Joe ran down the road and headed into an alleyway.

Danariel popped out from the top of the lantern.

"Tell me you got Duggan's pass. *Please* tell me you got it."

Danariel smiled, and from inside the lantern, she pulled out a plastic card with Scott Duggan's face printed on it.

"You're fantastic." Joe grinned.

"I do my best," she said, and they hurried to Merrynether Mansion.

TWENTY-FOUR

When Joe and Danariel arrived at Merrynether Mansion, Heinrich had just finished tidying the vault. He looked more haggard than ever and trembled as he eased into his chair. "Did you get what you needed?"

"Yes." Joe remained aloof. "I'm going to Redwar Industries now. We might have to wait about an hour until everyone's gone home, though."

"Good luck."

"I'll need Flarp again. He knew exactly the way to the restricted area. Danariel's coming too, like last time."

"Good . . . Joe . . ." Heinrich looked pained.

"What?"

"Something has . . . upset you. I wish you would tell me what I have done."

Joe swallowed, anger chewing at his insides. "I know about the letters."

"Letters?" said Danariel.

"Sorry, Danariel. I wanted to talk to you about it first, but I just didn't know what to do."

Heinrich lifted his great hands and clenched them. At first Joe thought the worst, but then Heinrich pressed his fists into his forehead, gritting his teeth in obvious despair. "Please forgive me."

"How could you do it, Heinrich? Mrs. Merrynether trusted you. She *trusted* you," Joe said, his anger plain.

Heinrich stared at the ground as his hands flopped down. "You don't understand," he whispered. "I had to . . . I had to. But I could not tell Ronnie. She—"

"Was it power, Heinrich? Blackmail? Why? Why did you do it?"

"It was . . . guilt." His lips trembled.

"Guilt? I don't understand."

"I have ruined everything. Everything!"

Joe didn't know why, but his anger melted away as Heinrich spoke. The man seemed so sincere. "How long have you been writing to him, Heinrich?"

"Years and years."

"But why? What's this about? I don't understand."

Heinrich lifted his head. His eyes were bloodshot. "I thought it would do no harm . . . I thought . . . And now I may never see her again." Heinrich's words surrendered to silent tears.

Danariel fluttered onto Heinrich's head and weaved her arms around in his matted grey hair, caressing his scalp with her tiny fingers. Joe saw pain in her eyes too.

"He is deeply hurt, Joe," she said, "but I can also feel that a burden has been lifted from him. Give him time to recover, and he may tell us more."

Joe looked at the old man. Any punishment he deserved seemed insignificant compared to his obvious torment.

"All right. Go get Flarp, and we'll rescue Mrs. Merrynether. She's the one who needs to deal with him anyway."

Flarp removed himself from the wall with some reluctance, but with a little extra persuasion, he was soon traveling with Danariel and Joe through Ringwood Forest, heading for Redwar Industries.

A gentle wind jostled the trees, and the calming sound of rustling leaves reminded Joe of a time when he would sit in these woods, untroubled by things like betrayal and kidnapping. Everything was so much simpler a few weeks ago.

"Danariel, I need to talk to you about Heinrich."

"Yes, what was all that about? What are these letters you mentioned?"

"When we came to Redwar Industries on Saturday night, I found something in Redwar's safe. There were loads of letters in there, all written by Heinrich and all of them with information about what's been happening at the mansion. He's the informant, and he's even been sending Redwar money—diamonds."

"Heinrich? A traitor? But I know him. He wouldn't."

"But he *has*, Danariel."

"Then Redwar must have some hold over him. Something else we don't know about."

"Could be. We'll have to talk to him when we get back. And this time, he'll have to tell us everything . . . Speaking of which, you told me *you* were going to tell me everything too. All that stuff about my destiny and—"

"Flarp!" Danariel zigzagged between the trees to catch up with the excited globble.

The gooey eyeball was heading deeper into the forest but stopped when Danariel caught up with him.

"What happened?" Joe called.

"He wants to go this way for some reason."

"Well, bring him back. I don't know what he's seen, but we need him with us."

Danariel playfully tugged at the globble's extremities. The eyeball, though apparently frustrated, followed.

"Do you think Flarp has seen something important?"

"He thinks it is. Globbles are hard to understand. Their thoughts are rushed and basic, but all I can feel from him is an urgency to go that way."

"He did the same thing last time we came out here. Perhaps we should go that way later."

"Perhaps."

They continued through the forest, back on track for Redwar Industries, continually pulling Flarp back with them until, a short way before they reached the gates, a scampering on dry leaves behind them caused them to stop. Joe thought it might be a rabbit or hedgehog, maybe even a badger. He squinted into the dimming light, hoping to get a glimpse, and smiled.

"What is it, Joe?"

"Nothing, really. I was just thinking about all the amazing creatures Mrs. Merrynether has shown me, and I still get excited at the chance of seeing a badger in a forest."

"That's why I like you. Would you like me to find whatever it was?" The seraph glided backward, bathing the foliage in silver light.

"No, that's all right. I . . . Wait. Did you see it?"

"See what?" Danariel twirled.

"Over there, in between those two trees."

Danariel flew where Joe was pointing, casting her light over the area and revealing a freshly dug burrow the size of a foxhole.

In the space of a heartbeat, Joe saw a flash of long claws, a glint of green eye, and a stretch of black fur before the thing scurried away. Any feelings of sentimentality had been snatched away and replaced with trepidation.

"It escaped into that hole," said Danariel.

"That wasn't a badger," said Joe. "It looked like the Beast of Upton Puddle but . . . much smaller."

"Are you sure?"

"Positive."

The two trees beside the burrow groaned as if

something huge had leaned against them, and without any more warning, the earth surrounding it collapsed and sent a spray of bark and soil into the air as a tangle of roots sprang upward. The tree wavered, then crashed into another before slamming to the ground.

"What happened?" said Joe, catching his breath.

Danariel fluttered around the caved-in earth. "It looks as though that creature caused a collapse when it burrowed away from us."

Joe puffed in surprise. "I suppose it would have to happen sooner or later. That Beast's been burrowing everywhere."

"But didn't you say it was too small to be the Beast?"

"Yes," Joe mused. "Look. It's happened over there too . . . and there. I can see at least four trees that have fallen down near some burrows. There must be loads of them."

"Heinrich did say it was like a labyrinth, didn't he?"

Joe thought about it, his fear escalating at the prospect of encountering several of these formidable creatures. "We'd better let the police know about this in the morning. Right now we should be concentrating on rescuing Mrs. Merrynether."

"Agreed."

Getting inside the building was much the same as before. Danariel performed her extraterrestrial light show above the gatehouse. However, this time the guards were better prepared. One fumbled with a night vision DVD recorder while the other busied himself making a series of phone calls. Regardless, just as before, Joe and Flarp entered the building without being seen.

The chorus of the *1812 Overture* blasted in Argoyle Redwar's office. Ms. Burrowdown sat in her chair, notepad and pen in hand, bespectacled gaze fixed firmly on Mr. Redwar as he waved his arms in rapture.

"Ah, there's nothing quite like the works of Beethoven, is there, Ms. Burrowdown?"

"Tchaikovsky," she muttered back.

"What?" shouted Redwar in time with a boom. "I can't hear a blessed word you're saying, woman. Speak up."

She waggled her head in frustration.

"Can you not picture those glorious cannons laying waste to Papillon's forces—driving their worthless army back to . . . to Germany? Why, that must have been a wondrous day for Churchill."

Burrowdown peered at Redwar in disgusted bewilderment.

Redwar, throwing his arms about and puffing his cheeks in time with the music, failed to notice the buzzer at his desk until the finale had completed. Breathless, he yanked the phone from its cradle. "Redwar! What?"

His tiny eyes sparkled with evil delight as he listened to the voice at the other end. "Do you have a shotgun? . . . Then shoot it, man! Shoot the wretched thing out of the sky . . . No, it's not an alien spacecraft, you fool . . . Shoot it!"

He slammed the phone down and hunched over his desk like an excited bulldog. "I knew they'd come back. They're here. We've got them."

"Ow many?"

"What?"

"Ow . . . Many?"

"Two. One's a boy; the other's a . . ." He grinned sadistically. "See for yourself. It's time we went to the monitoring room. We can oversee the whole thing from there. As soon as we have them cornered, we can send in security."

Flarp pressed against the doors of the restricted area. Glutinous strands oozed down to the corridor floor as the globble shuddered with the effort of squashing against the metal.

"It's okay, Flarp. We'll have her out of there any minute now."

Joe pressed Scott Duggan's ID card against the reader by the side of the door and watched the tiny red light flash green. Metal and stone ground in response.

"We're in," said Joe.

The doors swung inwards to a dark room saturated with a stench like unwashed socks and the sound of weeping. Flarp had already flown inside, racing toward the far end, swallowed by darkness. As Joe followed, pinspot lights illuminated a circle of space but not quite enough to show what lurked in the corners.

The hairs on his neck prickled as he closed in on the sobbing. "Mrs. Merrynether? Is that you?" Joe whispered, trying to ignore his instinct that the sobbing sounded too guttural, too liquid to be human.

More lights switched on as he reached the cool glass of a tall box. Then a whole series of lights flickered on to reveal an entire row of glass boxes against the wall, each containing a variety of animals Joe had never seen before.

"Argoyle Redwar has his *own* vault," he said, hardly believing his eyes.

The enclosure directly in front of him contained the ugliest thing he'd ever seen. Its shape was vaguely human, but the resemblance went no further than that. Its claylike skin covered in green, bubbling warts and boils made it look like somebody had scooped a pile of mud from the bottom of a stagnant river and tried to make a person out of it. The thing sobbed into a pair of clubbed hands, and as Joe approached, it lifted its head to reveal a featureless face. The pathetic visage lasted only a moment, though. As if in terror of Joe's presence, it squeezed itself against the back of its prison and melted like a lump of mouldy lard in a frying pan until it was no more than a rancid puddle.

Joe staggered back and gawped at the other enclosures.

Some had the same type of creature inside, all of them weeping. One had a sleeping serpent. Another looked like a tree in the shape of an octopus. But the one that really caught Joe's eye was the glass box Flarp had fixated on. Joe rushed to it, hoping, dreading, to see Mrs. Merrynether inside, but he didn't.

It was another globble. Each eyeball pressed against a side of the glass like a mirror image.

Joe felt a desperate urge to smash the glass and set the other globble free—to set all of them free. It was then that he noticed a black panel on one side of the container. Joe rushed to press the ID card against it. The glass front hissed into the ceiling, and Flarp's counterpart shot out of its enclosure, spinning and whooshing around them.

Joe looked at the other glass cases. Should he open them? These things could be dangerous. They might even hurt each other. But Joe couldn't just leave them here to suffer. What was Redwar doing with them? Where did he get them? And where—?

Thunk! The doors to Redwar's vault slammed shut.

"Attention, intruders," echoed a smug voice from a hidden speaker, "you are trespassing in a restricted area. According to health and safety procedures, Redwar Industries is obliged to keep you sealed inside your current location until such time that you can be apprehended by security. Thank you."

Joe's breath seized in his throat as he listened to

Redwar speak again, but this time in much more sinister tones. "Oh . . . and, young man, please don't expect to tell anyone the things you have seen in here today. If you leave this building, nobody except Mrs. Merrynether will believe you . . . That is . . . *if* you leave this building. And one last thing, boy. Don't expect a rescue from your little seraph friend either. Little blue lights in the sky make very easy targets for my marksmen. She looked just like a falling star when my men shot her down. The show's over, I'm afraid."

The Imprisoned Squonk

TWENTY-FIVE

Joe thought his blood had stopped pumping. He felt so cold. It was from shock, he knew, because his hands trembled and his vision was fuzzy, like looking into the night sky from the bottom of a revolving well. The weeping of the creatures in their enclosures mingled with Joe's own sense of loss, and the temptation to fall to sorrow was enormous.

But this was no time to pass out or allow grief to take hold. "I have to get a grip," Joe said to Flarp but more to himself.

This wasn't the first time he'd heard news like this. He was almost nine years old when the police came to the door holding their hats and frowning. His mum broke down before she'd even reached the armchair, and Joe? He didn't believe it.

His dad had left to drive to the shops in the neighboring village to buy a newspaper and some sweets. He did that every Sunday. And when he came home, he would walk in through the back door, put the paper on the table, and with a wink, he'd pass chocolate to Joe and his mum. But it didn't happen that day. The story about him swerving to avoid a dog in the road and hitting another car must have been true; he hadn't survived the collision.

Joe shook himself from the memory. He got through it then, and he'd get through this now.

Flarp and his new companion seemed to understand they were in grave danger. They bobbed in front of each other with their hanging tendrils twitching and their sticky skin rippling. Could they be communicating somehow? The other globble shot off behind them, Flarp following.

Joe didn't care what they were doing. However hard he tried, he couldn't ignore the terrible images in his mind: Danariel's fragile body twisting and turning as it fell from the night sky, her moonlight glow fading as life ebbed away. He blinked back tears and forced himself to look at the two globbles.

They had come to a halt by a set of empty enclosures, one of which had been cordoned off. The metal trims were twisted, and sharp remnants of reinforced glass poked out from the frame. Something with incredible strength had smashed the casing. Inside on the floor, some of the tiles looked much newer than the surrounding ones. Flarp hovered directly over them.

"What is it, Flarp?" Joe sniffed. "Is there something

under the floor?"

Flarp bounced off the tiles once, making a loud squelching sound.

Joe wiped his eyes, knowing there was no time to waste. He fell to his knees, blood gathering under his nails as he tried desperately to pull up the cold edges of the tiles. Eventually they came free, and under each one were sand bags: a shabby effort to fill a hole. Joe hauled one bag out, then another, his arms aching in protest. By the time he got to the third, faint footsteps beyond the vault told him security guards would be on him within a minute.

Flarp and his friend looked at Joe, then rushed to the cell containing the ugly creature that had melted earlier.

Bewilderment dampened Joe's grief when he saw inside. The creature had somehow rematerialized into the weeping, grotesque beast.

The globbles hovered in front of the card reader, and Joe realized what they wanted him to do. Dazed from wonderment and grief, he left the sandbags, went to the cell, and pressed Duggan's card against the reader to set the thing free.

The grinding of metal and stone told Joe the vault door was opening. The guards were nearly upon him.

Joe shook himself from his stupor and rushed to the damaged enclosure to continue yanking the bags out of the hole, hoping to find a way out.

The weeping creature had lumbered from its prison and sloshed against the doors, its club-like hands melting into the lock mechanism. Its bulbous head pushed against the surface of the metal. The globbles pressed too. Faster and faster, Joe removed bag after bag, clawing through layers of dirt.

"Flarp," yelled Joe. "I'm through. I'm through into a tunnel. Come on. Let's go!"

The two eyeballs raced back to Joe. He watched the other creature as it struggled to hold the door closed. A baton was forced between the gap, levering the door open, and Joe dived into the hole.

The darkness inside the earthy tunnel was like nothing Joe had experienced before. There was no light anywhere as he scrambled blindly forward, cutting his hands on sharp stones and scuffing his knees. Another turn and Joe felt the earth give way under his feet. He fell several feet before slamming into the earth, twisting his shoulder and cracking his head. A searing pain cut into his ribs. He couldn't breathe.

Warm slime enveloped the top of Joe's head and dragged his whole body. A scream left his lips before he realized Flarp, with his superior vision, was dragging him away from danger. The mad flight went on for five minutes with Flarp steering Joe through tunnels, twisting, turning, dipping, and climbing until finally the globble released him and flew upward.

Joe cleared the ooze from his eyes. Moonlight poured down. He clambered up and flopped, breathless, on the forest floor, thankful for the cool fresh air.

All he could hear were his own ragged breaths, pain jabbing his chest with each one. If the guards were still chasing, they wouldn't have much trouble catching him now.

Eventually Joe hauled himself up onto his elbows and looked at the hole he'd crawled out of. It was a burrow. There was no doubt now. The Beast of Upton Puddle, whatever it was, had escaped from Redwar Industries. Mrs. Merrynether wasn't deceiving him at all. The creature really hadn't come from Merrynether Mansion.

Thoughts of his time in the mansion and the hours he'd spent learning from Mrs. Merrynether came flooding back, and the full force of his failure to find her shot into his mind like a bullet. Tonight was more than just a failure. Danariel had lost her life. Joe felt numb as he stared into the dark burrow. What could he do now? Fresh tears stung his eyes, and with them, the pain in his chest and head grew worse.

On his own, Joe might have lain there for hours, but the two globbles had other ideas. Flarp hovered behind him, straining in one particular direction, apparently still desperate to keep moving. The other spun in circles, obviously overjoyed with its freedom. At least this nightmare had turned out well for someone. He thought of the strange warty creature that had helped them escape and hoped it was all right.

Flarp drifted in front of Joe, the center of his eye bulging toward him.

Joe drew a deep, shuddering breath. "All right,

Flarp. I know. Let's get back to the mansion." He struggled upright and examined his torn clothes. Dirty blood covered his palms, and his knees stung.

Flarp rushed into the forest, followed closely by his companion.

Joe trudged after them, trying to keep up.

Fifteen minutes passed before Joe realized they were not heading for the mansion. Several paces later, the eyeball stopped to hover above another burrow, close to yet another felled tree. Flarp stared into the dark entrance.

"Where have you taken me?" Tired beyond words, Joe ambled to the burrow and peered inside.

At once, everything became clear. All along Flarp was desperate to get to this place, not Redwar Industries. That had been Joe's idea. Not even Heinrich had realized why the globble was continually banging against the wall. He could see something nobody else could, but nobody took any notice.

Deep in the burrow, Joe could see a vague human shape curled up, motionless. His heart sank. Were they too late? Six days was a long time to be trapped. A human couldn't survive without water for more than three days. Was Mrs. Merrynether—?

"Joseph?" a hoarse voice whispered from the burrow.

Tears welled in his eyes. "Mrs. Merrynether? Is that you?"

"Yes, Joseph, it's me. I knew you'd come. I knew it."

"It really *is* you. Don't worry. We'll get you out of there."

But Joe looked around, not knowing how he would do that. "Flarp, go and get . . . get Heinrich. Understand? Go and get Heinrich."

The globble did something like a nod and then took off with his companion toward the mansion.

Joe edged into the hole and jumped down, ignoring the jarring pain in his chest.

Another form shuffled in the darkness as he landed, startling Joe and causing him to scuffle backward. Whatever it was, it made no advances. As Joe's eyes adjusted to the gloom, he also saw someone else lying next to Mrs. Merrynether. At first glance it looked like a very round human child, but as it raised its face toward Joe, it seemed more like a potato with a bulbous nose, cauliflower ears, and black beads for eyes. It wore ripped sackcloth that revealed a lumpy body. Four straight gashes stretched from its left shoulder to its chest, and Joe guessed it had been attacked by the Beast of Upton Puddle.

"Don't be alarmed by Thumbler. He's only a baby troll. Won't attack you," said Mrs. Merrynether, her eyelids half closed.

"He's hurt," said Joe.

"We both are." She nodded toward her right leg, and Joe balked. Blood had soaked through her long skirt. All he could see of the wound was an ugly gash starting at the lower part of her calf muscle.

"What can I do?"

"Not much. I don't know how long Thumbler has left, but I'm not sure I can hang on much longer. We've been surviving on a bottle of elixir I always keep on me, but I gave the last of it to my friend here this morning." She smiled at the troll who had closed his tiny eyes. "If it wasn't for Thumbler, I might be dead now."

"What happened?"

Mrs. Merrynether sighed and wrestled with her breathing.

"No," said Joe. "Don't worry. It can wait. Just rest. Heinrich will be here any minute. You'll see."

He held her hand.

"It's all right, Joseph. I need to talk. I have to stay awake. At least until I've . . . told you . . ."

"Told me what?"

"I have so much to tell you, Joseph—so much. I wanted to wait. Needed to tell you about all this years later, but now things are different. If I—" She coughed. "If I don't survive, Danariel will tell you everything you need to know. Heinrich will help too."

Joe pursed his lips. He had a lot to say too, and none of it was good. "It won't come to that," he said after a moment. "Tell me what happened."

"Later. There are other things much more important that have to be said."

"What could be more important than you?" Joe fought the welling tears.

"There's an island. Many islands, most of them hidden. You won't find them on any map. But one particular island is very important. The inhabitants call it Pyronesia."

"I've never heard of it."

"You wouldn't have. Many years ago, I was on an expedition with a large team. Heinrich was with me." She smiled. "We were heading deep into the Indian Ocean. There was a storm, and just when we thought we would all lose our lives, the island was revealed to us."

"Revealed? Couldn't you see it before?"

"No, the inhabitants have a way with minds. If they act collectively, they are able to convince travelers there's nothing there. You already know one of them."

"Danariel."

"Yes." Mrs. Merrynether didn't acknowledge the pain in his reply. "Many seraphim live on Pyronesia, but they are not alone. The island is like . . ." Her eyelids sagged, and Joe had to squeeze her hand to keep her awake. "The island is like a giant ark. It is home to a multitude of different species that most people believe are fictitious."

"So that's where all your animals have been coming from? Pyronesia?"

"Most of them, yes."

"But why? Why can't they be treated on the island? How did you become their doctor?"

Mrs. Merrynether coughed again. "It's complicated. For the moment, all you need to know . . . all you need to know is there are rulers on the island that hate humanity and want to destroy it. A small minority disagree with them and . . . asked for my help. I . . . agreed."

"By being a doctor? I don't understand."

Mrs. Merrynether said no more. Her head sagged to one side, and no matter how hard Joe tried to shake her, she didn't respond. He felt her wrist, checking for a pulse. It was weak and slow.

"Mrs. Merrynether," he shouted.

She didn't respond.

But something else did. A scratching came from farther down the burrow, followed by fast scuffling and the shifting of earth. At first, Joe thought it may have been Heinrich, but a flash of fangs and the gleam of a green eye shattered his hopes.

The Beast moved slowly toward them, its hot breath belching out in clouds, a growl rumbling from its chest.

"Get back," Joe shouted. He tried to grab both Mrs. Merrynether and the troll child in a futile effort to pull them back out of the monster's range, but there was no hope. He looked at the size of its talons and tried not to think about what they would do to him.

"Whether you're a traitor or not, Heinrich," Joe said to himself, "I need you. Please hurry."

T WENTY-SIX

As if in answer to Joe's plea, a ferocious roar bellowed into the burrow from above. Joe lay pressed against the dirt, sharp stones cutting into his back, the unconscious Mrs. Merrynether on one side and the unmoving form of the little troll, Thumbler, on the other. The Beast stopped to look up into the night, the slits of its eyes narrowing as the moonlight shone upon it. Two yellow catlike eyes stared back down at them but only for an instant. Joe braced himself as something bulky with red fur launched into the burrow, huge paws reaching, talons extended.

"Cornelius!"

A savage dance of crimson and charcoal hair played out in front of Joe as the two creatures grappled. Howls and roars rang, claws penetrated flesh, and he had to duck when the manticore's tail flailed in a tight arc toward the Beast. A large claw caught the spiky appendage before it made deadly contact. This fight would not be over quickly.

"Joe!" a familiar voice called from above. "Give me your hand." Heinrich's dark silhouette almost blotted out the light at the opening of the burrow. At his side, the two globbles bobbed in excitement.

"Heinrich, great timing! I've got Mrs. Merrynether down here and a young troll too."

"Reach up," Heinrich stretched a great hand, and Joe felt the strong fingers grasp his wrist and haul him out of danger.

The brutal battle continued in the burrow as Heinrich dropped inside to recover Mrs. Merrynether. Joe stared into the dark, unable to make out what was happening, but it seemed Heinrich was waving something like smelling salts in front of Mrs. Merrynether's nose while shielding her from the shower of soil exploding from the brawl beside them.

"I wish I could see properly like you, Flarp," Joe said.

"Perhaps I can help," someone else said.

A flood of silver-blue light filled the burrow, illuminating the action below.

A bloodcurdling howl ripped through the night as the distraction allowed Cornelius to strike a painful blow to the Beast. The wounded animal retreated, speeding through the tunnels the way it had come. Cornelius let it leave.

Joe turned around to see who had spoken, not daring

to believe what his eyes and ears had suggested. But it was true. Hovering in the air, just above Flarp and his friend, Danariel smiled at him.

"Danariel! But Redwar said you were dead."

She giggled. "You shouldn't take any notice of a man like that, Joe. He's about as good at telling the truth as his guards are at marksmanship."

"So you're not even hurt?" Joe's tears flowed freely now.

"Of course not," she said, drifting down to stroke his cheek. "I pretended to be hit right after I heard the first gunshot, then found a burrow and hid in the tunnels."

"I thought you were dead." Joe sobbed.

"Well, I'm fine, and you should be very proud. I don't know what happened to you since we had to separate, but Flarp has a new friend and we've found Mrs. Merrynether."

"I didn't do much."

Heinrich struggled out of the burrow with a delirious Mrs. Merrynether clinging to his back.

Cornelius leapt from the hole slashed and ruffled but alert. He roared in triumph as the other creatures gathered.

Heinrich jumped back into the burrow and appeared a few moments later with the limp troll.

"We're too late," he said. "This fellow is dead."

"Bring him with us," said Mrs. Merrynether, barely conscious. "Thumbler deserves a good burial. He gave his life for me . . . and for us."

The brief journey to Merrynether Mansion was silent. Each of them had thoughts to contend with, and although Heinrich looked overjoyed to see Mrs. Merrynether again, Joe saw trouble in the old man's eyes.

Emotions—grief, elation, fear, and uncertainty—balled together in Joe's mind, each one demanding its own special attention. Which to listen to?

Arriving at the vault didn't help Joe sort out his feelings much either. Left to their own devices, Kiyoshi and Lilly had launched into a full-scale verbal war. Meanwhile, Snappel the wyvern lay on the vault floor surrounded by apples from a split sack. Apparently she'd been let out of her enclosure, torn the cloth open, and then gorged a ridiculous amount of the fruit, leaving her bloated and incapacitated.

The scene would normally have amused Joe, but what he really wanted right now was a bath, relief from the throbbing in his head, and sleep.

He guessed Mrs. Merrynether felt far worse. Heinrich helped her to his chair and brought her a plate of biscuits with a mug of tea and a fresh bottle of elixir. Fresh blood trickled onto the floor from the wound in her leg, but Heinrich was already unrolling gauze from a first aid kit and attending to it.

Joe sat by the wall and watched the warfare near the back of the vault. Kiyoshi, so involved in his dispute with Lilly, seemed not to have noticed them as they walked in. The disgruntled kappa was trundling up and down the length of the vault, trying to locate Lilly, who was, as usual, shouting his abuse from a hidden location.

"May da devil himself trow up in dat stupid horl in da top a ya head."

" . . . and furthermore," Kiyoshi said over Lilly's insult, "you are nothing but a pilgarlic, sir, and your argumentative methods are nothing more than fragmented galimatius. I am quite certain your motivation is to distract me from the real matter at hand—namely, why you chose to release the wyvern. However, you need not concern yourself with explanations. I see no further advantage in debating our current predicament with an inebriated leprechaun."

"Leprechaun? Leprechaun? How dares ya!" An empty beer can bounced off the floor next to Kiyoshi. "Oi'm a cluricaun, and don't ya forget it."

"Far be it for me to ultracrepidate. I know exactly what I'm talking about. There is absolutely no difference between you and a leprechaun—you are both classified as belonging to the Maddus midgetus irritabilius class."

"You jost made dat up."

"I did not!"

"You can kiss moi shoiny pink—"

Snappel hiccoughed, and a puff of fire belched into the air, singeing Kiyoshi's hair.

"I say!"

"Quiet!" Mrs. Merrynether's voice shattered the

bickering. She slammed the bottle of elixir onto Heinrich's desk, making the half-eaten biscuits jump on the plate. Clearly the food and drink had boosted her strength. "We have urgent issues to discuss. Heinrich, see to . . . Is that a wyvern?"

"Her name is Snappel, Ronnie. I'll get her back in her enclosure."

"Will you help him, Kiyoshi?" Mrs. Merrynether asked.

"May I remind you that I am a patient in your care and not a mindless bulldozer to be employed for your kinetic requests. However, I am pleased to see your safe return. I will do as you ask."

While Heinrich and the kappa manhandled the incapacitated lizard into its enclosure, Danariel bustled the two globbles to the back of the vault and into their own pens for the night.

Joe stepped forward. "Mrs. Merrynether." His heart raced with the burden of what he needed to say, and his headache surged. "Before you tell us anything, there's something you should know."

He stared at Heinrich, who froze in the middle of dragging the wyvern's tail inside the enclosure. "Are you going to tell her, or shall I?" Joe said.

Heinrich returned Joe's stare, and silence fell as they searched each other's soul.

Heinrich's gaze dropped to the floor. "I should attend to Kiyoshi. He is falling asleep."

"If you don't tell her, I have to."

"Tell me what?" Mrs. Merrynether looked at each of them.

"Heinrich?" Joe pleaded.

The old man didn't look up. Instead, he concerned himself with positioning the kappa in such a way that his head was resting on the tip of the wyvern's tail.

"Mrs. Merrynether . . . Heinrich has . . . been writing letters to Argoyle Redwar for years. He's the one that's been passing on information, and he's even been sending him money."

Heinrich dropped the wyvern's tail and looked up. In the space of a heartbeat, his expression changed from remorse to fury.

"What? You lying filth!" Heinrich spat. "I would never—"

"It's true," said Joe, shocked by Heinrich's fury. "I saw the letters with my own eyes in Redwar's safe, written by his own hand."

"Ronnie. Don't believe him. It is not true."

Mrs. Merrynether opened her mouth but didn't speak.

"It *is* true. Mrs. Merrynether, I know you haven't known me very long, but—"

Heinrich launched forward like an enraged bull, his fingers outstretched and his eyes murderous. Cornelius jumped between them and bellowed at Heinrich, his tail arched over their heads. At the same time, an empty beer bottle rebounded from the back of the old man's head.

As quickly as the rage showed on Heinrich's face, a new expression of distress replaced it, followed by utter confusion. He staggered back for a moment, gazed tearfully at Mrs. Merrynether, then ran for the vault door. He paused with a hand on the doorknob. "I'll see to it that you regret saying such things."

No one stopped him as he ran up the steps and out of the mansion. Silence came again for a full minute.

"I'm sorry, Mrs. Merrynether. I didn't expect him to act like that. He seemed so . . . sorry about it all when I confronted him before."

"I . . . can't believe it."

"We think Redwar must have some sort of hold on him. Blackmail, perhaps."

"Not Heinrich, no. He was always such a noble man. So strong. How did you find out about this, Joseph?"

"We broke into Redwar's building thinking he'd kidnapped you, but instead of finding you, we found his safe. He's been keeping all of Heinrich's letters and putting them in there."

Mrs. Merrynether nodded ruefully. "It's all starting to make sense. I don't know why Heinrich did what he did, but . . ." Her voice trembled as she placed one hand on his desk, as though she could somehow reach the old man through the wooden surface. "But I already know what Redwar was trying to find out from him."

Joe paused to give Mrs. Merrynether a moment to compose herself. "Do you think Redwar wants your animals? He's got his own vault with his own creatures in it, you know. That's where the Beast of Upton Puddle came from. It escaped, and we used its tunnels to get out too."

"I already know about Redwar's terrible prison."

"You do?"

"Yes." Mrs. Merrynether nodded toward a body encased in cloth close to the door. "The Beast of Upton Puddle wasn't the only creature to escape Redwar's prison. Thumbler escaped too."

"Oh!" Joe looked at the floor. "I'm sorry."

She nodded. To Joe, it seemed all the strength she had recovered was fading fast, her skin turning almost grey. Yet he could still see determination in her eyes, as though she had to set aside her troubles to deal with something that was too important to ignore.

"So what is it that Redwar wants?"

"He wants to know the location of Pyronesia. All this time he's been trying to get his hands on this mansion just to find the island's location. He's come close by discovering some of the smaller islands, which is why he has some exotic species, like the Beast, but he's never been able to find the main island."

"So why didn't Heinrich tell him where it is?"

"Heinrich doesn't know its location any more than I do."

"But you were the ones who found it, weren't you?"

"Yes, but once we left, the location was blinded from us. They cannot afford for the world to know of their existence."

"So the island must still be safe, then."

Mrs. Merrynether sighed heavily. "That's the news I was about to tell you all before Heinrich . . . ran away. Thumbler escaped from Redwar Industries to pass on some information he overheard. Somehow, Argoyle Redwar has discovered Pyronesia's location and is making preparations to go there as soon as possible."

"What's he going to do when he gets there?"

"I have no idea, but he is power hungry, greedy, and from what I heard from Thumbler, he has a terrible hatred for anything that isn't human. Considering what he and his people will encounter on that island, this can only end badly. We have to stop him or find a way to get there first."

"So what *will* Redwar encounter if he gets there?"

"That's what I wanted to talk to you about in the burrow, but now that we are back and safe, it can wait until tomorrow . . . Thank you for finding me tonight," she said, grasping his hand. "I owe you my life."

"It was Flarp that found you. We would have found you earlier if I'd paid attention to him sooner."

"But you came looking. That's what matters to me. At least someone is still loyal to me." She grimaced as she moved her wounded leg. The blood had already soaked through Heinrich's bandage.

"We have to get you to a hospital," said Joe.

"Oh, don't worry about me. I know things about

medicine most doctors would sell their own mothers to find out. But you don't look so good yourself, young man. Perhaps it's you that needs the hospital."

"I'm all right," Joe lied. "Are you sure I can't call an ambulance for you?"

"No, no, I'm out of danger now that I've had my elixir and something to eat. We should both get some rest. What time is it? I've lost all track."

Joe looked at his watch. "It's quarter to twelve." He shook his head. "I have to get home. I've pushed my luck way over the edge this time. Mum is going to ground me for sure."

"Make sure you show that bump on your head to your mother. It's the size of a golf ball, and you might have a concussion."

"I'll be fine," Joe insisted with a smile, but it wasn't a happy gesture. "Do you think Heinrich will be back soon?"

"He'll come back," she said solemnly. "He has nowhere else to go."

"But you can't trust him."

Joe regretted stating the obvious when he saw how his statement had cut into her. It took her several long moments to form a reply, which sounded far from confident. "Heinrich and I go back a long way. We'll work this out somehow."

Danariel drifted from the far end of the vault to hover over Mrs. Merrynether's shoulder, one hand touching the old woman's cheek.

"So much to do." Mrs. Merrynether sighed.

"You must rest, Veronica. Is there anything I can do to help you?"

Mrs. Merrynether looked doubtful, but she nodded. "I need you to do one thing for me. It won't be easy."

"Anything."

"Find Lilly. If we can't find a way to keep Redwar here in Upton Puddle, we're going to need Lilly's help. In fact, we're *all* going to have to pull together before the next few days are over."

Cornelius the Brave

TWENTY-SEVEN

Argoyle Redwar slammed his phone down. "Gumble will be here in twenty minutes to sort out that debacle in the restricted area."

He leaned on the desk and massaged his forehead. Even with the lights set to low in his office, they were still bright enough to aggravate his headache.

"What 'bout police?" muttered Ms. Burrowdown.

"What? Oh. We'll just have to keep him away from them when he gets here. I don't want that idiot blabbing if he gets scared. God knows we've paid him enough money to keep him quiet, but people say stupid things when the pressure's on . . . Damn them! Who called the police anyway?"

"Mr. Bacon. Out walking his dog. Heard gunshots."

"And they're still talking to security?"

"Think so."

"I don't like this at all. If they start sniffing

around—"

"Shouldn't worry. They aren't s'picious. They don't know anything."

"Maybe not, but that boy does. Have those bungling idiots found out who he is yet? I want to know everything about him."

"Name's Joseph Copper. Goes to school at Clarkdale. Lives in the village with his mother. No brothers or sisters but has an aunt, Rose Ashworth."

Redwar leaned back in his chair and wrestled his fat arms behind his head. He gave Ms. Burrowdown a sideward glance, watching her as she turned over the page of her notepad and scratched her forehead with her pen.

"It must be the same boy we saw at Merrynether's place. That's why he had one of those blasted fairies with him."

"And the eyeball."

"What? Oh, yes, that thing as well. Damn them all, I wasn't expecting Merrynether to do something as drastic as this. That ugly little troll must have convinced her to mount a rescue operation. But why use the boy?"

"Expendable."

"Perhaps. It's certainly her style." Redwar paused in thought. "But, no, I think there's something else going on. Perhaps she hasn't taken our bait."

"Need to wait."

"Wait? How long has it been since that troll escaped?

More than a week, I'm sure."

"Only arrived at the mansion a few hours ago."

"Really? What's it been *doing* all this time?"

"Doesn't matter." Ms. Burrowdown shrugged. "It's there now. Not moving 'bout much, though."

"Are you sure the bug is still attached?"

"Don't know. That's why we should wait."

"All right. We'll give it another day or two before we try something else."

Burrowdown scribbled something on her pad. "What about Copper?"

Redwar stroked his chin as if he had an imaginary beard. "The boy? Hmmm. Well, I'm hoping nobody will believe him if he says anything; nevertheless, I don't want to take any unnecessary risks." His lips spread into a callous smile. "I'll have someone . . . invite him to see me."

Burrowdown leered in approval, then turned back to her notepad.

Much had happened in the last few hours on Joe's street. Usually at a quarter past twelve his neighbors would be tucked up in bed fast asleep, but not tonight. Small groups stood in the road busily discussing, pointing, and looking generally angry. A police car and several service vans were parked a few doors up from his house, and a huddle of workmen had gathered around a section of road that looked like it had been flooded.

"Joe!" came the voice of his mum. She marched toward him, slightly hunched with her arms folded close to her body to hold back the chill of night. "Where have you been? I've been worried sick."

"What's been going on?" asked Joe, looking around the road for clues. Then he saw the answer.

One of the men in overalls moved aside. He held a bent manhole cover, and a flood spilled across the road.

"Never mind that," she said, grabbing her son to steer him toward the house. "Why didn't you tell me where you were? I called the Duggans, and they said you left hours ago. I couldn't even call you because your mobile phone is broken. Where have you *been* all this time?"

She stopped just outside the door and held him at arm's length. "You look terrible. Are you hurt?"

"I'm okay, Mum. What happened to the road?"

"There's blood on you!" She pulled Joe into the house. "Get inside in the warmth. I want to have a proper look at you and make sure you're all right before I go."

"Go? Where are you going?"

"Is that our missing pumpkin, Jane?" a familiar high-pitched voice called from the kitchen.

"Yes, he's back, Rose. Could you get the first aid kit? I think he's hurt." She took him to the kitchen and sat him in a chair. "What happened to you, Joe?"

"Oh my!" Aunt Rose said as she heaved herself from her chair. She puckered her lips and examined Joe as if he'd accidentally pulled the pin out of a hand grenade and swallowed it. "Oh my! Oh my! Look at you. Just look at you. That's a terrible large bump, that is." She planted a soggy kiss on Joe's forehead, wrung her hands, then bustled up the stairs.

Joe's mum ran some warm water into a bowl. "Are you going to tell me what happened, or is this going to be a one-way conversation?" she said with her back still turned.

Joe bit his lip. What could he tell her? She wouldn't believe most of it.

"I left Kurt Duggan's house at about seven, I think."

"Go on," she said, turning around with a damp cloth in her hand. "Did you go into Ringwood Forest?" She glanced at him.

"Umm . . . yeah. I . . . got attacked."

His mum dabbed at his face, and Joe felt the sting of something salty in the cloth. "I can see that."

"Attacked?" Aunt Rose almost fell down the stairs on the way down. "We should call the police at once, Jane. At once!"

"Let's hold on a minute first." Joe's mum held out a hand to receive the first aid kit. "Who attacked you, Joe?"

Joe flinched when she pressed the bump on his head. "I fell into one of those burrows, and the Beast came after me."

"Oh, goodness," said Aunt Rose, finding her way back to her chair and fanning herself with a newspaper.

"They said it was the Beast that damaged the sewers, you know. It's probably made tunnels all the way under the street. Oh! It could pop up in the garden any minute! Do you have a shotgun, Jane?"

"How did you get away?" Joe's mum asked.

"I got rescued by a friend of Mrs. Merrynether's. Heinrich Krieger."

"Off with your shirt . . . And how did he know you were there?"

Joe removed his shirt, feeling a sharp pain across his chest as he lifted his arms. A large blue-red bruise had spread across his shoulder. "I called for help, and he came," said Joe, wincing as his mum touched his skin.

Alarm flashed in her eyes. She gave him a look Joe recognized very well: she knew he wasn't telling her everything. "You must have been quite close to Mrs. Merrynether's place, then . . . Does it hurt here when I press it?"

"A little bit," Joe said. "Did you say you were going somewhere? Is it Nan?"

"Yes, it's Nan. She's had another fall. That's why Aunt Rose is going to look after you while I'm away. I should have left four hours ago. Rose, would you run Joe a bath please?"

"Of course, dear." Aunt Rose hurried upstairs, and soon Joe heard the sound of running water.

"I'm really sorry."

Joe's mum pressed a bandage against his head. "You should have called me."

"I haven't had a chance to fix my phone."

"Didn't you say you called that Mr. Krieger?"

"Not with my phone, no."

"So how, then?"

Joe looked at the floor. It was getting harder and harder to explain things without mentioning any of Mrs. Merrynether's creatures. What if he did tell her? Would she assume he was lying? And what about Redwar? Shouldn't he say something about him? Joe's stomach churned as though all his troubles had somehow found the perfect place to sit and stew.

"Joe? I asked you a question." She knelt directly in front of him. "How did Mr. Krieger know you needed help?"

Joe hesitated, thinking about what to say.

He was rescued when Aunt Rose ambled into the kitchen. "They've got a dog unit out there now. I saw it all from the bedroom window. I told you it was the Beast, didn't I, Jane? I saw them shove a black hairy thing into the back of their van. I don't think it was very happy."

"They've caught it?" Joe turned, shocked.

"Yes, didn't look like much of a Beast to me, though. Everyone's been talking about that thing as if it was as big as a bear. This thing looked more like a . . . well, like a dog, if you ask me."

"But it *is* as big as a bear," said Joe. "I've seen it three times."

"Well, things can look different in the dark," his mum

said. "Whatever size it is, at least they've got it now."

"I suppose so," said Joe uncertainly.

"Right," said his mum decisively, "I have to be off. Rose, you're sure you'll be all right taking care of Joe while I'm away? I shouldn't be more than a few days."

"We'll be fine." Aunt Rose grabbed Joe's cheeks and pinched them.

"Good. Make sure he doesn't leave the house except for school—or the hospital if that bump on his head gets worse."

"Mum! You're grounding me?"

"You came home late on more than one occasion, you've been back to Merrynether Mansion, and on top of all that, I know there are things you're not telling me. Of course you're grounded."

"But—"

"Don't worry, Jane. I'll make sure he's all right."

"Thanks. I don't know what we'd do without you."

"Oh, it's a pleasure. Give your mum my love, won't you? We'll see you when you get back. Now come on, young Joe. It's about time you got in that bath. Don't forget your shirt."

Joe had been asleep only two hours when the commotion began. It took a high-octave scream and the sound of smashing crockery for him to realize that something was terribly wrong. Yells of pain from at least two men, heavy bumps, swearing, and more smashing crockery came from downstairs as Joe leapt from his bed and turned the light on. It took less than half a minute to throw on the clothes he should have put in the wash, and without another thought, he grabbed the heaviest thing he could find: a golf club that used to belong to his dad.

He almost fell down the stairs in his haste but quickly realized the intruders had got more than they bargained for with Aunt Rose in the house. Like a champion discus thrower overdosed on sugar, she threw plate after plate at two brutish men dressed in black, cowering by the broken back door. And with each launch came a word of acidic rebuke.

"Twenty-   "

Crash!

"Three . . ."

Smash!

"Years . . ."

Thunk!

"Married to . . ."

Crunch!

"A drunken . . ."

Whoosh!

"Wrestler . . ."

Swish!

"And you think . . ."

Thwak!

"You can take . . ."

Smack!

"Me on?"

No more plates.

"Run, Joe!"

One thug lay whimpering on the floor surrounded by shards of china. The other, wide-eyed with shock or terror or both, saw his chance and lunged forward. Joe swung his golf club, cracking both shins, and the howling man fell to the ground.

"I said run!"

The other man had already shaken the debris from his clothes and staggered to his feet. He stepped over his partner and grabbed for Joe. Four meaty knuckles connected with the attacker's cheekbone before he could make good with his efforts, but before Aunt Rose could gloat over her victim's goggle-eyed collapse, the other man had already grasped her ankles. She toppled on him like a mountain of suffocating blancmange, screaming and flapping her arms in a frenzy.

"Run," she yelled again as a brown sack covered her head, muffling her next words. "Get out of here! Call the police!"

Joe was about to swing the golf club a second time, but as he lifted it, a hand grasped the end.

"Oh, no, you don't. You're coming with us."

A puffy bruise had already formed across the man's eye, but Joe knew now that it was going to take more than one of Aunt Rose's punches to stop these men. Joe yanked at the golf club, but the man landed his fist squarely on the side of Joe's head, connecting perfectly with the bump that already throbbed.

"Somebody wants a word with you, boy."

But Joe hardly heard what the man said. Tiny yellow lights sparkled before his eyes as the world became a nauseating, echoing cyclone. He let go of the club and staggered backward, avoiding the man's grasp through sheer chance, and scrambled out of the kitchen with the scowling enemy a mere arm's length behind. Fearing that the pain and shock would shut his mind down at any moment, Joe flailed, throwing anything he could reach behind him as he launched at the front door. It worked. The phone, yanked off the wall, took the cord with it and tripped the man.

Joe made it to the pavement before he fell, his consciousness slipping away.

"Bill," yelled the man. "Give us a hand quick. He's getting away."

"Busy!" came the struggling response.

Joe could do nothing but lie in the road, wishing for a miracle, hoping maybe someone in the street would see him, but in the small hours of the morning, there was no chance. Not even the neighbors were peering through their curtains to find out what was happening. It seemed they'd all had enough drama for one night with the burst water pipe.

Something hard caught Joe's hand as it flopped by his side—something small and round he'd left in his pocket. He pulled it out, barely able to focus, and as he realized what it was, he wondered if his miracle had come.

It was the cap of the bottle he'd used for the kappa juice. Joe thrust it in his mouth, searching the edges with his tongue, desperate for the foul taste that might be his salvation. Two tiny drops assaulted his taste buds. Joe's vision began to clear as a man's silhouette filled the doorway and lunged toward him. Two hands grasped his shoulders.

But it was too late. The kappa juice had given Joe just enough energy to fling the man backward and stand up. Feeling the strength in his veins fading already, Joe took off, letting his legs guide his faltering body away from the house, down the road, and into Ringwood Forest.

Through the trees he ran, relying more on instinct than sight as his mind slipped into dark chaos. The blur of trees and moonlight swirled as he staggered on, overwhelmed by pain, lashed by branches, almost believing his flight would never end.

At last he fell hard against the doors of the one place he knew he could rely on more than anywhere else—Merrynether Mansion.

TWENTY-EIGHT

Consciousness returned to Joe with tangy thirst. Gurgling complaints from his stomach told him he was hungry too, especially with the aroma of a roast wafting into his nostrils. Joe held his eyes shut, enjoying the smell, vaguely aware that some horrible reality was about to force its way into his thoughts and spoil this moment of comfort. Roast onions, sizzling beef, and . . . yes, definitely pork sausages. Was it Sunday? Who was cooking? Not Mum; she'd gone to see Nan. And Aunt Rose was . . . Aunt Rose!

Joe sat bolt upright and opened his eyes. Golden late-afternoon light streamed through a window at the other end of the room, but this wasn't his bedroom. A small crowd surrounded him. The two globbles and Danariel floated on either side, Mrs. Merrynether stood by the door with Archy the pig, and Kiyoshi sat at the end of his bed with his legs tucked inside his shell.

"Good evening." Mrs. Merrynether smiled.

Joe shook his head and tried to recall his last memories. Aunt Rose had been nabbed by two of Redwar's men. He'd been hit hard by one of them, and he'd run away. The last thing he remembered was collapsing outside Merrynether Mansion and someone pulling him through the door.

"How are you feeling?" Mrs. Merrynether asked.

Joe tentatively reached for the bump on his head. It was gone, and so was the pain. "Much better, thanks."

"You're very welcome. Are you hungry?"

"Yes. But, Mrs. Merrynether, I—"

"That's a good sign. You'll need to eat something solid after being out for this length of time."

"What d'you mean? How long have I been asleep?"

"I'll leave the others to explain. I'm going to serve up dinner, and I'll see you in the dining room once you're dressed." She smiled again and left the room.

Joe saw a fresh set of his clothes folded on a chair by the window and wondered how they'd got there. A glass of water sat on the table next to his bed, and he guzzled it.

Danariel fluttered down to sit cross-legged on top of Kiyoshi's shell, much to the kappa's irritation. "You've been unconscious for almost three days," she said.

"Three days? But I can't have been. What about—?"

"I am afraid our photomantic companion is quite accurate," said Kiyoshi, popping a green hand out of his shell and extending a suckered index finger as if teaching a class. "You have been in a state of neurological challenge for almost thirty-one hours. During that period, you have volunteered utterances one can describe only as linguistic absurdity."

Danariel giggled. "He said you've been unconscious and talking in your sleep."

"I have? What did I say?"

"Lots of things. Most of it didn't make sense, but you managed to let us know Redwar's men had broken into your home and were looking for you."

"Did I say anything about Aunt Rose?"

"Yes, we know what happened. Redwar's men have kidnapped her, hoping to get to you. As soon as we heard you talking about it, Mrs. Merrynether asked Lilly to get his . . . associates to check. The whole house has been tidied, but there's no one home. We managed to get some of your things here, but—"

"Has anyone called the police?"

"Of course not," said Kiyoshi. "No evidence remains for the local constabulary to perform a satisfactory examination. Any action on their part would be mere futility."

"Then if nobody else is going to do anything, *I* have to," said Joe, jumping out of bed and grabbing his clothes off the chair.

Danariel stood and pirouetted on Kiyoshi's shell. "What are you thinking of doing?"

"I don't know," said Joe, jumping into his jeans,

"but we know Redwar's to blame, so—"

"Do you happen to remember any of your dreams?"

"No." Joe pulled his T-shirt on slowly, trying to remember any images from his time asleep. "Why? What's that got to do with anything?"

The kappa turned in time with Danariel, trying to swat the smiling seraph off his shell but failing. With a grunt, Kiyoshi faced Joe. "It is clear from your choice of words during your time of somnolence that your dreamscape has been subjected to excessive psycho-netic influences. You have been a witness to the Tree of Sanctuary on Pyronesia, a symbol unknown to the unenlightened but romanticized in the racial memory of all human culture and transcribed in mythology and legend throughout the ages."

"I do keep having a dream about a massive tree with loads of eyes on it, but what's that got to do with Aunt Rose?"

"You said you wanted to do something," said Danariel.

"I do." Joe laced up his shoes.

"Argoyle Redwar has left Upton Puddle. He took your Aunt Rose with him."

"He took my aunt with him? But Mrs. Merrynether said Redwar wanted to go to Pyronesia. Why does he want to take her there?"

"We think his real intention was to take you, but instead, he decided to take your aunt as a hostage."

"She might be hurt. What if Redwar—?"

"Your aunt is in no immediate peril. I was able to discern a communiqué sent directly to us in old Morse code late last night."

"Morse code? How? Where from?"

"It was brief," said Danariel, "and I'm sure Kiyoshi would love to explain in great length how he knew about the message, but he can do that later. It seems she was taken on board a boat, but she has already managed to escape her cell and will contact us again once they've reached land and it's safe to communicate."

"Really? She's amazing," said Joe, relieved. "I can't wait to hear how she managed that."

"There's more. We only know the small amount of information Thumbler passed on to Mrs. Merrynether before he died, but he overheard Redwar talking to his secretary and it seems they have secured an army."

"He's going to *invade* Pyronesia?"

"It seems likely."

Joe slumped in his chair. "What are we supposed to do against an army?"

"Nothing. It's what the Pyronesian Conclave will do that we need to worry about."

"Who?"

"The Conclave are the rulers of the island. If Redwar attacks, it could provoke a terrible war that will reach far beyond the boundaries of Pyronesia."

Joe shook his head. "Like a world war or something? Are the Pyronesians really that powerful?"

"Yes, like a world war. And, yes, they are very powerful."

Joe stiffened. "And we have to go there? What are we supposed to do? What will *I* do?"

"There's been a lot of planning, and plenty has been done while you've been asleep." Danariel smiled. "Come on. It's time you had dinner. I'm sure Veronica will tell you more while you eat."

Dinner was a strange affair. Joe had never been in the mansion's dining room or tasted any of Mrs. Merrynether's cooking. The room, designed to accommodate extravagant banquets and enthrall its guests with fine art and intriguing sculptures, had long been abandoned for that purpose. There was no question it had been well looked after, but now only one square table was positioned in a corner of the hall, surrounded by the necessities to feed two people. It seemed a very lonely place, and Heinrich's absence was obvious.

When Mrs. Merrynether came into the room with two plates of steaming food, Joe felt something in the atmosphere. Mrs. Merrynether's smile was strained when she set their meal on the table. She sat opposite him.

Joe salivated at the sight of the food, which wasn't roast beef or pork sausages but was smothered in thick gravy and smelled like something from heaven.

"What are these?" Joe prodded at something that

looked like a brown carrot with a yellow tip.

"Try it."

He pressed into it with his knife and felt the skin split. Clear juices ran out, and Joe loaded his fork with a generous chunk. Usually, he would have been cautious about trying something new, but his hunger gnawed with such persuasion that he thrust it in his mouth and chewed. His taste buds tingled as he munched and the flavors oozed over his tongue. "It's like lamb but with a sort of orangey thing going on."

"It is rather like lamb, isn't it?" she said, cutting into her own food. "But you won't find any meat on these plates. Not that I'm against eating meat, of course. It's just that we're rather short in the larder at the moment, so I had to improvise with some of the garden vegetables."

"This is a vegetable?"

"We call it flubbage. Its proper name is Flatulensia stenchorendous. Be careful not to cut into the—"

A wet raspberry noise ripped through Mrs. Merrynether's words as Joe's fork pierced the yellow end.

"Bulb," she finished.

"It . . . It farted!" Joe stared at it, shocked.

"Yes, rather embarrassing at dinner parties. I tend to avoid serving them usually, but they taste wonderful, and as I said, we're rather short at the moment."

Joe pushed the offensive vegetable to the side of his plate and tentatively cut into what he hoped was a potato. He wondered if it might scream, squeal, or perform some other offensive act. "Don't tell me these come from Pyronesia too?"

"Absolutely. Flubbage grows around the cliffs on the north side of the island. Very nutritious. Rich in fiber but a bit gassy."

Joe nodded and bit into his potato, relieved to discover it actually was a potato. "So, speaking of Pyronesia, Danariel said we have to go there to stop Redwar."

Mrs. Merrynether's smile fell. "Yes."

"She said he has an army."

"Thumbler said that, yes."

"And Danariel said something about the Conclave going to war if he provokes them."

Mrs. Merrynether stared at her food, avoiding Joe's eyes. "That's very likely, yes."

"And are you going to let me know where I fit into all this?" Joe felt unnecessarily angry, as if he sensed Mrs. Merrynether was hiding the truth from him. A slight tremble altered his voice as he continued, "Danariel said I had a destiny, but if Redwar and the rulers of Pyronesia are going to start up some big war, what am I supposed to do about it? I don't even know anything about this island or who lives there, and I've only ever seen armies on the TV."

"Joseph—"

"Why me? Aunt Rose got kidnapped, and I . . . I ran away. Redwar almost killed Danariel because of me, because I didn't listen to Heinrich, and now even *he's* gone because of me."

"Heinrich betrayed us, Joseph," she said quietly. "You did the right thing by telling me. It's a lot easier to stay quiet than to stand up for what's right. What you did was very brave."

"I don't feel brave. Like I said, I ran away when they took Aunt Rose."

"Sometimes running away *is* the brave thing. Did you want to stay and help?"

Joe hesitated as tears blurred his vision. "No. I wanted to run."

"But did you run because you were scared or because you knew you couldn't help?"

"I . . . don't know."

"Yes, you do. But right now you're scared. You hate the idea that your destiny is connected with this war, and you think you can't help, so it's easier to convince yourself you're a coward and turn away. But you're *not* a coward, Joseph. You *can't* turn away."

Joe said nothing.

"The truth is that I don't know what's going to happen. But what I *do* know is that if a war starts on Pyronesia, it won't stop there. The whole world will be a ball of ash in less than a year, and if Danariel and her people think you have a part to play in preventing that, I think we should trust her . . . We have to go."

Joe sighed and rubbed his eyes. "I do trust her."

"Then you'll go?"

"It's better than school." Joe managed a smile. "How do we get there? You said you don't even know how to find it."

"I rather hoped Danariel would be able to tell us. After all, she lived on the island for a very long time before she came here."

"Did you meet her on the island? Danariel told me she knew Heinrich before she came to Upton Puddle."

Mrs. Merrynether took a long drink from her wine-glass. "What else did she tell you?"

"Nothing. We didn't get to finish our conversation."

She took a deep breath. "Good." She breathed out. "That's a story for another day. Now finish up your food. I've got something to show you in the garden that will help us get to Pyronesia. I think you'll like it."

The rest of the meal passed with lighter conversation. Mrs. Merrynether filled Joe in on other things that happened while he was asleep: Flarp's eyesight was improving now that she'd got the balance right for his new ointment. Kiyoshi was not cured of his sleeping fits, but she found just the right herbs to direct some of the kappa's strength into keeping his head flap shut. No more precious fluid would be leaking from his cranial vent. Even Snappel's fiery hiccups were cured; she simply needed a different brand of apples.

Joe listened intently, and after mopping up the last drops of gravy on a thick slice of bread, he rubbed his belly, satisfied and ready for the surprise in the garden.

TWENTY-NINE

Mrs. Merrynether's garden looked a little less manicured than it had last time. The grass was longer, and the flowers were wilted as though they were heavy with apathy. Still the garden had a grandeur that demanded a certain reverence. Had it not been for Redwar's ugly tower spoiling the view beyond the trees, the garden may have even looked cheerful.

Mrs. Merrynether and Joe walked past the glasshouse, and Joe couldn't help but admire the vine-covered statues again: huge creatures frozen in stone and set on a wide plinth—manticores, seraphim, dragons, and Joe even recognized a wyvern this time, though it had been made to look much less magnificent than the dragons.

"Who made those?" Joe asked.

Mrs. Merrynether stopped and nodded toward the stone figures. "Those?"

"Yeah."

"Ahhhh." She smiled wistfully. "A very old friend. He died a few years ago."

"I'm sorry. I bet whoever it was must have come from Pyronesia, right?"

Mrs. Merrynether sucked in her bottom lip. "And how would you know that?"

Joe pointed at the manticore. "That really looks like Cornelius. Whoever sculpted these knew exactly what a manticore looks like, and there aren't many of those in the London Zoo."

"Good point. Do you like them?"

"I love them. Especially that one." He pointed to the central statue with the magnificent dragon looking skyward and the seraph doing the same. He was just about to ask if dragons really looked like that when his eyes fell on the creatures ringing the perimeter of the plinth, sprinkling water at the dragon's clawed feet. His stomach knotted as he realized he'd seen them before for real. "Mrs. Merrynether, what are those things?

"Those sad-looking creatures?"

"Yes."

"They're called squonks. Oddly enough, you won't find many of those on Pyronesia, but there are lots of them populating the surrounding islands."

"I've seen some," said Joe, his voice cheerless as he recalled the events in Redwar's vault.

"Redwar Industries?"

"Yes, how did you—?"

"Something else Thumbler told me before he died. Squonks are dejected enough creatures already, even without Redwar's torture cells. There's a very old legend about how the ancient dragons from an age long ago tried to make themselves into the most beautiful creatures on the earth. Dragons are proud beasts, powerful but vain, and they hated imperfection of any kind. So much so that they vomited out their ugliness and created the squonks."

"That's gross!"

"Yes. The story goes that the squonks were so distraught by how they looked that they spent all their lives crying, and that's how the oceans of the world were created—by the tears of the squonks. Most of them melted into the sea, and the rest fled to the outer islands in fear of their creators, the dragons."

"That's so horrible."

She patted Joe's shoulder. "It's just an old story the Pyronesians used to tell to explain why the squonks are the way they are."

"One of them helped me escape from Redwar."

"Yes, they may be pitiful creatures, but they are good-natured."

Joe sighed. "I wish I could help *them* escape."

"Maybe you will one day. But for now, we have a bigger priority."

"Pyronesia."

"Yes. We need to leave as soon as we can. The

quicker you come with me, the quicker we'll get there. Come on." She winked.

Mrs. Merrynether led Joe through a rickety gate at the far end of the garden. They passed through a field of grazing animals that looked like cows but with long, floppy ears and tiger-striped hides.

"Norblers," Mrs. Merrynether casually informed him.

They walked into another field surrounded on all sides by tall poplar trees. In the center was the most peculiar and amazing vehicle Joe had ever seen.

"That *has* to be Lilly's work." Joe grinned.

"Spot on. Take a look."

Joe, unable to contain his excitement, burst into a sprint toward it, laughing as he ran, taking in every bolt, strap, wheel, handle, knob, and gadget holding the enormous machine together.

The whole thing, taller even than Merrynether Mansion from its exquisitely curved base to the tip of its giant mast, had been constructed almost entirely of varnished wood and brass. It reminded Joe of the *HMS Victory*—Nelson's breathtaking flagship that he'd seen on a trip to Plymouth when he was just six years old. It was a piece of history that pulled in hordes of awestruck tourists every day. In the center of Mrs. Merrynether's field, this ship, not supported by ocean waves but by a genius work of wooden scaffolding, looked even more impressive.

Along the upper gun deck where a Viking longboat might have secured its oars, Joe marveled at six dragon-like wings made from shaved tree trunks and leather membrane. They swept outward in pairs from either side of the ship, flat against the grass like giant waxy flippers. A ring of decorative black cylinders like cannons poked from the back of the ship where Joe expected to see a rudder or propeller; he guessed they had more to do with propulsion than weaponry, though he had no idea what might be used to power them.

A vivid image of this titanic machine, steered by those massive wings, hurtling through stormy clouds and leaving a fiery jet stream in its wake, burst into his mind's eye. But how could this behemoth even get off the ground? Joe found his answer when he looked farther behind the ship. Extending from the back, almost reaching the trees bordering one part of Ringwood Forest, a tangle of ropes led to the deflated form of the largest air balloon he'd ever seen. As if to remind everyone who had built this amazing piece of workmanship, the canvas had been dyed in green, white, and orange stripes, ready to proudly reveal the Irish flag once it had been inflated.

"Awesome," Joe shouted as he ran up a ramp to the quarterdeck. A huge cabin, almost the size of Mrs. Merrynether's vault, had been built into the stern with barred windows that revealed tentacles and bulbous eyes from within. The familiar odors of Mrs. Merrynether's vault wafted on the breeze from the cabin, and Joe realized all the animals had been moved into this enormous sky boat while he'd been asleep in the mansion.

"Awesome," Joe said again.

For a fleeting moment, he glimpsed movement just behind him to his left. He spun round, convinced he'd spotted a sleeping cluricaun using a beer bottle as a pillow, but all he could see was the empty container spinning slowly in a small puddle.

"Lilly?" said Joe. "Where are you? This is . . . This is . . . awesome! I know you're good, but how did you build it so fast?"

Mrs. Merrynether climbed onto the deck to join Joe. Archy the pig trotted out from behind a coil of rope to receive an ear-scratching from his keeper.

"I think you'll find Lilly had a little help from his drinking friends," Mrs. Merrynether said with a cheeky smile. "They did have a good incentive, though."

"What did you do?"

"Nothing much. Danariel told him that the world's oldest brewery and distillery was in danger of destruction and that if he helped out, the owners would make sure he had all the whiskey he could ever drink in ten lifetimes. It's not so far from the truth. They make a very interesting drink on Pyronesia that is a lot like whiskey, and if a war does break out, nowhere on the island will be safe—including the distillery."

Taking in the spectacle, Joe said, "It's like a modern-day Noah's ark."

Mrs. Merrynether walked toward the cabin. A sailor's wheel had been positioned on a platform just in front of it. Directly in the center of the large wheel, an envelope had been attached.

"What's this?" she said, opening the envelope and pulling out a letter. She read it and handed it to Joe. "A parting message from you-know-who."

Joe read it, imagining the little red face and the angry eyes.

Dear losers,

The boys and I spent many a long hour building your stupid machine when we could have been drinking. May she fly high, sail fast, and rain down a fiery and painful death on the filthy philistines that dare to deprive the world of a fine brew.

Yours truly,

Lilly

"Have you seen the name plate?" said Mrs. Merrynether. "I think it's in honor of you."

Joe walked to the cabin door to read the brass plaque nailed above: *The Copper Celt.*

"Me?" He brushed his fingers across the shiny finish. "He's put my name on it?"

"I told you he liked you, didn't I?"

"I didn't think he liked anyone."

"Well, I think this proves otherwise. Are you ready to take her on her maiden voyage?"

"Do cluricauns like to drink?" Joe grinned. "What are we waiting for?"

"Well, one or two things," she said, pointing down into the opposite side of the field.

Joe had been wondering where the others were. Now he knew what two of them were doing. Cornelius, the fearless manticore, was galloping like a frightened kitten away from Snappel, the wyvern.

"What's going on?"

"Just watch. It's been quite entertaining."

The great reptile bounded awkwardly after Cornelius, half hopping on her claws and half flying, her wings raking through the air. After a few skips, the wyvern stopped, belched fire, and splayed her wings outward, the black skin stretching taut between the bones. Like a blanket trapped in a powerful gust of wind, the wings fluttered and made a loud ruffling noise. Cornelius had stopped to watch and catch his breath as Snappel strutted like the dominant rooster in a farmyard, roaring and flapping, but the manticore only had a few moments to rest. After another flourish of her wings, the huge lizard strode after Cornelius again, gathering pace with each heavy thump of her claws, and the manticore galloped away, bellowing as the chase began again.

"That's been going on all afternoon," said Mrs. Merrynether. "I think she's feeling a little amorous."

"She fancies Cornelius?" Joe laughed.

"He is rather a magnificent beast, though, don't you think?"

"But she's a wyvern."

"There are some cases where different species can breed, you know. Tigers and lions, for example."

"Yeah, but they're both cats. That's . . . that's a reptile." Joe motioned to Snappel who had again settled into her extravagant courting display. "How long will it go on?"

"Oh, not for much longer. Danariel will be out in a minute to put a stop to it. She's been getting the last of our occupants settled into the ship. Sorry, she has a name now, doesn't she? The *Copper Celt*."

"Are Kiyoshi, Flarp, and his friend already on board?"

"Present and accounted for," came the squeaky voice of Kiyoshi as he waddled in from the cabin doorway. "Our cycloptic friends will be making our acquaintance shortly."

"Good," said Mrs. Merrynether. "And is Danariel nearly finished? We need her to deal with Snappel. I don't want them too worn out. We need both of them to drive the wings."

"She sent me to inform you that all preparations are now complete. We may begin our quest."

"So when Cornelius and Snappel are on board, we can leave?" Joe asked.

"Absolutely," said Mrs. Merrynether. "Look. There she goes now."

Joe looked back toward the insane courting ritual. Danariel had entered the scene with a flood of silver-blue light, flitting between the exasperated manticore and the lovesick wyvern. The seraph weaved a hypnotic spiral in front of Snappel until the distraction lured her in the direction of the *Copper Celt*. Cornelius took cautious steps a few paces behind.

A minute later, all three had stepped onto the deck. Snappel had apparently curbed her affection for the time being and was now more interested in the ropes attached to the balloon.

Joe dropped to his knees and stretched his arms toward the shaggy red beast. "Come here, Cornelius."

Cornelius trotted to bash his great head into Joe's cheek and receive a hug. Joe scratched behind one of his ears, and as he dug his fingers into the soft fur, he saw Flarp rush out of nowhere. The slimy globble whipped around in a tight circle, with even more childish excitement than usual, sending rivulets of green grunge outward like a lawn sprinkler.

"Welcome aboard." Danariel beamed at Joe and landed gracefully on the tip of the sailor's wheel. "Ready to go?"

"Whenever you are." Joe let the manticore go and got to his feet. "How do we get this thing moving?"

"Lilly left a few instructions, which I read this

morning. Snappel is dealing with the first part of take-off. Flarp here will help me with navigation . . . Flarp?"

Flarp rushed to the very tip of the *Copper Celt*, followed by his companion globble, and plopped onto the end of a long pole that stretched out ahead. It was the most bizarre figurehead Joe had ever seen.

Claws scraped the deck behind him, and Joe turned to see Snappel stooping over Kiyoshi. Her long black tongue reached into the kappa's cranial vent and scooped out a generous dollop of kappa juice.

"Kiyoshi will need to rest awhile to recover," Danariel told the rest of them, "but it will make Snappel's job far easier."

Snappel reeled as if she'd been hit by an avalanche, then thundered over the edge of the boat to land on the grass next to the open end of the deflated balloon. With a rush, she flew inside, lifting the vast canvas high above the *Copper Celt*. There was a moment of thrashing and maneuvering inside before a bright flash of flame illuminated the interior. There was another blast and another until the balloon expanded and rose, driven by the heated air inside it. Soon the Irish flag, stretched in a huge pear shape, dominated the horizon, and the ropes groaned against their fastenings as the *Copper Celt* struggled against gravity.

"She needs a little help," Mrs. Merrynether told Cornelius.

The red giant bounded to a section directly behind

Flarp's figurehead pole where two lion-sized tread-wheels waited. He leapt inside and charged, turning the wheel. Belowdecks, the thunk and clank of machinery fired into action.

Snappel flew to the manticore's side, landing inside the other wheel and turning it with her kappa-powered muscles. Responding with the yawn of stretched wood, the six wings lurched, beating the ground and air with a ferocity that grew as Cornelius and Snappel increased their speed.

Joe jumped and whooped as the huge ark drifted gracefully from the field. Somewhere belowdecks toward the back of the ship, excited animals howled and hooted as a thunderous bang fired up the cannons, propelling the *Copper Celt* with a burst of speed. Soon he could see the whole of Mrs. Merrynether's vast estate and the huge wooded area of Ringwood Forest below them.

"Flarp has seen Pyronesia," Danariel called above the roar of cogs and pulleys. "Take the wheel, Joe, and I will give you instructions. I can feel which direction Flarp is pulling."

"Me? Take the wheel?" Joe felt such a rush of excitement he could barely stand.

"Of course. Lead the way. Steady as she goes, sou' by southwest . . . Two turns of the wheel, Cap'n."

Joe grasped the wheel. The cool breeze swept across his face and ruffled his hair as the sun sank behind the trees. He knew he was heading into dangers even his dreams could not conjure, yet he had never been so happy in his life.

"Let's go and get Redwar," he shouted as he spun the wheel.

THIRTY

Night came quickly. A full moon bathed the deck with velvet white, and the faint but rhythmic creak of the wooden beams of the *Copper Celt* made Joe feel as though he had sailed into a monotone dream. Even the wind seemed reluctant to convince Joe he was awake. He felt only the faintest of breezes as he rested his chin on the edge of the stern, gazing below at what he believed must be the Mediterranean Sea. He had no idea how high or fast they were flying, but occasionally the silken carpets of cloud far below broke to reveal dark expanses of water.

Behind him, the others slept. Mrs. Merrynether had said the balloon would keep them on course until morning. Flarp had remained steadily focused in the same direction as the gentle air currents, and so it was an opportunity for all of them to rest. Cornelius lay curled up next to his treadwheel, purring in rhythm with Snappel's smoky snorts as she lay on her back, claws stretched upright. Kiyoshi, now able to control the flap in the top of his head, lay close to the cabin entrance, dozing and muttering what sounded like algebraic equations as his sticky feet twitched.

Even Danariel had fallen asleep. Joe had never seen her that way before, and it fascinated him to watch the gentle pulses of light radiate in rippling patches in time with her breathing.

Joe sighed. This was a time of tranquility, a pause in time granted by the gods before he was plunged into a war he knew almost nothing about. The prospect should have terrified him, but here in the sky, caressed by cool, pure air with an atmosphere of serenity warming him, ugly thoughts seemed too distant to disturb him.

"A penny for your thoughts?" Mrs. Merrynether drew up beside him, peeping over the edge and folding her arms under her chin.

A moment later, Archy trotted over to her side.

Joe cocked his head. "I thought you were asleep."

"Me? Oh, no. I can't sleep for longer than four hours a day."

"Four hours? I'd be dead on my feet."

"It's been even less than that since . . . Heinrich left."

Joe fell silent. He studied the clouds, noticing every pattern as they churned in slow motion, melting into saddened faces that soon became unrecognizable before slipping from view.

"Mrs. Merrynether." Joe pursed his lips as he considered his question. "Why do you think Heinrich betrayed us?"

She stared at the sky for a long time.

"Truly, Joseph"—she released a long sigh—"I simply don't know. I thought I knew him better."

"Has he ever done anything like this before?"

"Never. I sometimes sensed a feeling of guilt from him, but in all those years, Heinrich never once gave me cause to mistrust him."

"Sounds like you've known him a long time."

"More than fifty years. We met on an expedition to the North Pole in 1950, and I remember how he held the team together when we lost contact with our base camp. The rest of the team stayed confident for a while, but it was Heinrich who had the real survivor's instinct. He kept us going, kept us focused." She nodded, clenching her teeth as a tear shone in one eye.

"We didn't stay lost for long, but I knew back then that I would always want that man to be on my team wherever I went . . . Always."

"That doesn't sound like Heinrich to me, Mrs. Merrynether. He always seemed so . . ."

"Defeated?"

"Yes, defeated. That's it."

She stared through Joe and smiled, but there was no humor there. "He was never the same after Pyronesia."

"Something happened to him on the island?"

Mrs. Merrynether narrowed her eyes a little and frowned. "Do you remember when I told you how Heinrich got his face so terribly burnt?"

"You said it happened in a forest fire."

"I'm sorry, Joseph. I lied. The truth was too . . ."

Joe said nothing, waiting for her to continue.

"Finding Pyronesia was an incredible discovery but there were signs that the trip was cursed right from the moment we left. Soon after we departed, we discovered a stowaway—a boy called James, the son of one of the couples on the team. We should have taken him back straight away but decided against it because it was too inconvenient. We thought he'd be safe if he stayed on the boat: a decision I will always regret.

"Even when the weather turned and one of the crew almost drowned in the storm, we still decided to go on. There were seventeen in the beginning, every one of us an expert in our field, and between us we'd been just about everywhere you can think of in the world. We thought we were prepared for anything, invincible. But then we landed on the island." She shook her head.

"When the island was revealed to us and we set foot on that beach . . . well, you can't begin to imagine how excited we all were. It was like finding Atlantis or the Ark of the Covenant. The whole island was full of species everyone believed were extinct or mythical. We found dodos, manticores, trolls—just about everything you can think of—and we were all so caught up in our champagne toasts and so engrossed in our plans of success that we became careless.

"As if it wasn't enough to make the biggest zoological discovery of the century, we were suddenly the richest people on the planet. The cavern walls were covered almost entirely in diamonds. Most of us were still so excited by the animal life we didn't much care, but two of the party—Gloria and Donald Merson—decided to fill their pockets. They stocked up diamonds in as many crates and sacks as they could, but they didn't realize what lived in those caves. Halfway through the fourth crate, they were attacked. Care to guess what by?"

Joe shook his head, mesmerized by Mrs. Merrynether's story.

"Baby dragons, Joseph. Baby dragons attacked us. Before we knew what hit us, five of the team were burnt to a crisp. It was absolute chaos. Some of the team ran but got picked off on the way out.

"I . . . lost my husband that day."

"I'm so sorry."

Mrs. Merrynether touched Joe's shoulder. "Oh, it's all right. I learned to live with that pain a long time ago." She paused to give Joe a curious look, as if she didn't quite believe her own words, then spoke quickly. "It's what we realized next that I find harder to live with. The others panicked. Gloria and Donald shot two of the dragons, even brought one of them down, but what they didn't know was that their son, James, the stowaway, had sneaked into the cave behind them.

"That poor boy watched his mother and father get burned alive by one of the adult dragons when it came to rescue its offspring. He was only seven years old."

Mrs. Merrynether didn't look at Joe when she continued. "The whole cavern seemed to fill up with smoke and fire, and I was the closest to the entrance . . . so I ran. I thought they'd all been killed—I really did—but when I got near the cave exit, I heard Heinrich call for help.

"I knew I couldn't leave him, so I went back. And, so help me, while I was thinking of only myself and running away, Heinrich . . . he . . ."

She choked, then looked Joe in the eye. "Heinrich shielded that little boy from one of the dragons. That's how he got burned, Joseph. He got burned saving that boy's life while I was running away."

She stared down at the ocean.

Joe waited a moment or two, then asked, "How did you escape?"

"Escape? We didn't escape," she said quietly. "We were confronted by one of the adults. She was only trying to protect her young, but we'd killed one of them. She was about to take her revenge, and if I hadn't done something there and then, I wouldn't be talking to you now."

"What did you do?"

"I used the boy. James."

"You . . . used him?"

"Yes, to my shame, I didn't consider what that poor

lad was feeling. I didn't stop to think that he'd just lost both of his parents. All I could think of was survival, so I told Heinrich to bring the boy to me.

"I had no idea whether the dragon could understand me or not, but I spoke to it anyway. I told it I was sorry that one of the young dragons had died but that we also had young. I showed James to the dragon and begged for mercy so that no more innocent lives would be lost."

"Did it understand you?"

"Perfectly."

"And it let you go?"

"Not exactly. It let Heinrich and James go. The two of them were taken to the boat and sent back to England, but Heinrich was never the same after that day. He had to stay in the hospital for a very long time, and during his recovery, he was interrogated repeatedly by the police about what happened. He never broke. Never told them about the island—to protect me, I think. He just told them that everyone was lost in a horrible accident.

"James was adopted, and both Heinrich and I vowed we should never make contact with the boy. Somehow he had to heal, and our presence would only have kept that wound open. The police told us that James was too traumatized to speak about what happened. Without any more evidence, the case was eventually closed."

"And what happened to you on the island?"

"Do you remember me mentioning to you that

many seraphim live on Pyronesia?"

"Yes."

"Well, that's who the Conclave are. The seraphim and the dragons are the rulers of that island. As you know, the seraphim are skilled at sensing the thoughts of any living thing, so I was taken to them to face judgment for my crimes. They would know my true intentions."

"So they found out you were innocent."

"Innocent, yes, but they still held me responsible for what happened, and I was sentenced to a lifetime of servitude. They knew of my skill as a veterinary surgeon and told me I must spend the rest of my days healing their sick to make up for the loss of the hatchling.

"That's where I learned my empathic skill with animals. The seraphim taught me how to use my mind in ways I never believed possible, and I learned some amazing surgical techniques during that time.

"That's how I met Danariel. She told me how the Conclave had a deep-seated mistrust and hatred for humankind and that our disastrous expedition only fueled their paranoia. She told me plans were being made to destroy the world by fire. Danariel, of course, did not share their point of view, and neither did a few of the other rulers. They wanted to build an army in secret to reform the Conclave but knew they could never achieve this on the island—the rest of the Conclave would surely detect the conspiracy as numbers grew."

Joe said, "So they found a way to get you back

to England to build an army where you wouldn't be found out?"

"Exactly right. Danariel and a few of her friends were able to convince the rest of the Conclave that I would function better in my own environment. There was a lot of resistance to that, but Danariel can be very persuasive when she needs to be.

"So I was sent back to England, and whenever an animal was sick or injured, it would be sent to me on the condition that if anything ever went wrong, I would be brought back immediately to continue my sentence on Pyronesia."

"And how many years ago was all that?"

Mrs. Merrynether sighed. "Too many . . . and I know what you're thinking. You want to know what sort of army we managed to get together in all this time."

"Actually I was wondering how dragons talk, but yeah, that's a good question too. What about the army?"

"There isn't one. The truth is, everything went quiet. I got back to England, found Heinrich, and we set up the practice in the most secluded place we could find, which turned out to be Upton Puddle. I fooled the clinical community into thinking my ability was a harmless confidence trick intertwined with proper training and called it the Merrynether Technique. I had everything I needed. The Conclave even sent me diamonds to fund the clinic.

"But anyway, the idea was that sick animals who

were not happy with the Conclave would be sent to me. I would heal them, recruit them, and keep them at the Merrynether estate as long as needed. But as the years went by, the Conclave mellowed toward the outside world. They became far more introverted, bickering among themselves, so our plans for a coup faded. I still wanted to help but thought the real danger had passed. Danariel and I decided someone else should be able to continue after I had gone in case things looked bad again." She raised her eyebrows.

Joe gulped. "Me?"

"Yes. You."

"But I'm—"

"Perfect for the job. You're compassionate, intelligent, resourceful, and above all, you have a love for nature. Anything you don't know, we can teach you. Besides, Danariel is convinced you're the one we want, and I trust her judgment."

"Will you teach me the Merrynether Technique?"

"I'll teach you everything you need to know, but it might not be relevant anymore. We have to survive the island. Redwar's own army on Pyronesia is sure to stir up the Conclave. They'll sense his hatred, and I have no doubt their plans for destruction will surface again. And there's another problem too."

"What?"

"Thumbler."

"The baby troll?"

"Yes. We've brought his body with us so that his family can give him a proper burial, but the repercussions may be huge. If they find out Redwar has been taking animals from the surrounding islands and torturing them, there's no doubt they'll join the Conclave in wanting all-out war with the rest of the world."

"What can we do?"

"I have no idea yet. It's a handful of us on a boat and a few sympathizers on Pyronesia against two armies—the Conclave and Redwar's soldiers. And if I know Argoyle Redwar, he won't have wasted a moment to start the hostilities. We may already be too late."

THIRTY-ONE

Joe slept restlessly that night. The smallest dip in altitude or the faintest stirring of creatures from belowdecks woke him each time he drifted off. And then the questions came again.

How could they stop Redwar?

What if they were attacked when they reached the island?

When would he see Aunt Rose or his mum again?

Would he even survive?

No answers came as he stared into the pitch black. Claustrophobic fear pressed against him. Frustrated, Joe switched on his lamp, another one of Lilly's fascinating inventions. Amber light flickered over the walls of his cabin, generated by tiny, luminous creatures jostling inside a glass bowl. Joe stared at the lamp, rubbed his eyes, and smiled. The switch appeared to start up a clockwork device in the casing that vibrated tiny fibers, which in turn caused the tiny things inside the lamp to leap as though they were being tickled. Joe was sure he could faintly hear them giggling.

The cabin was surprisingly comfortable, considering it had been designed by the mischievous cluricauns. Joe kept expecting some manic Jack-in-the-box to spring out from the closet or his bed to fold up while he slept, but everything was perfect. Oak beams, brass door-knobs, a minibar packed with every kind of alcoholic beverage, and even a luxurious bathtub.

Already he missed Lilly. Why didn't he want to come along? Perhaps the little cluricaun understood the danger that Mrs. Merrynether was heading toward and wanted no part of it. Perhaps he just wanted the mansion and all the wine to himself. Whatever his reason, it didn't feel right without him. Joe leaned back on his pillow, stared at the wooden ceiling, and counted the cracks in the beams—anything to take his mind off his troubles. It would be a long voyage.

Three days and nights passed as they journeyed to Pyronesia, but the trip was far from boring. Flarp redirected the *Copper Celt* on numerous occasions to avoid being spotted by other aircraft, and sometimes they came dangerously close to being discovered. Joe wondered what a giant ark with six wings and a huge balloon would look like on the news. But it was important they were not seen. Any outside knowledge of their journey that revealed their destination would be disastrous, so both Danariel and Flarp had put every effort into staying as far away from land as possible.

As each day passed, the animals became increasingly agitated. Belowdecks, the creatures grew louder at mealtimes, and Snappel had even stopped chasing Cornelius, concentrating only on keeping the *Copper Celt* airborne. Sometimes she had to take flight within the enormous balloon, billowing clouds of fire inside, to increase their altitude. Other times, she would happily run inside her treadwheel to help Cornelius with the wings. But all the time, Joe could feel a certain uneasiness from the creatures as they went about their duties. Even Danariel had become sullen, and Kiyoshi seemed to be inventing the most ridiculous words just to distract everyone from his own apparent feelings of apprehension. It was only on the final evening before they landed that Joe had learned to set aside the tension.

As the evening waned, Joe was in his favorite position at the captain's wheel, fingers clasped around the varnished grips. The gentle whoosh of the *Copper Celt's* wings beat on either side of him in hypnotic rhythm, like the blades of a giant's cooling fan in slow motion. Cornelius and Snappel loped inside their treadwheels, their talons complementing the wings with their own percussion.

They'd made a course correction and headed west,

directly into the fierce shimmering sun as it melted into the horizon. Joe knew he shouldn't look directly at it, but he was captivated by the titian clouds breaking either side of the lowering sun and the sparkling reflection across the water. He almost forgot Danariel had seated herself on his shoulder; she'd been so quiet— quieter than she had been all day, and her glow seemed a little subdued, as if she were subconsciously trying to hide from something.

"Beautiful, isn't it, Danariel? I wonder why the sun gets so red when it sets."

Danariel made no attempt at an answer, but Kiyoshi almost fell over himself to provide one. "The effect of which you speak is known as Rayleigh scattering. The particles of light projected by our native celestial companion are perceived differently by our optical organs as they penetrate the earth's ionosphere, mesosphere, stratosphere, and troposphere. At an angle of zero degrees to the observer, the light travels through less atmosphere, but at an angle of ninety degrees, the light is forced through a much denser section, thereby causing a refraction which our neuroreceptors interpret as red."

"So it's like looking through a pane of glass and then turning it on its edge." Joe grinned.

Kiyoshi paused, almost indignant. "Yes."

Joe laughed and looked at Danariel, but it was obvious her thoughts were distant. "Are you all right? You haven't said much all day."

"I'm sorry. I've been feeling some unusual thoughts from Flarp in the last hour."

Joe squinted toward the end of the stern pole. The big, slimy eye seemed disturbed. He still strained to the west, but every few seconds, he flinched and pulled back as if they were approaching something he didn't like.

Mrs. Merrynether, standing at the stern with her hands behind her back, also watched the globble with concern. "We must be getting close," she said.

"What can Flarp see?" Joe asked.

"Too hard to tell," said Mrs. Merrynether. "Danariel, what are you getting from him?"

"Broken images. He sees . . . I think he sees fighting. He keeps repeating one word over and over . . . hurt, hurt, hurt."

"Redwar."

"No. Something else. This isn't like a war. It's more like a minor skirmish. Possibly within the Conclave. I don't know."

Mrs. Merrynether left the stern and walked toward Cornelius and Snappel, who were busy on their tread-wheels. She signaled them to stop, and as the wheels slowed, the beating wings lulled into silence.

"So what do we do?" asked Joe. "What's the plan?"

"Well, my original plan was to go to the Conclave and try to warn them about Redwar before he arrived. I was hoping to avoid a conflict, but it sounds as if something is happening that we might not want to get involved with." She shook her head and muttered, "Terrible timing. Just terrible."

"But surely we can't let that slow us down," said Joe. "Don't we still have to get there before Redwar?"

"Of course, but if the Conclave are having their own dispute, they're much less likely to pay attention to anything we have to say, hmm?"

"I suppose. But even if they *are* in a good mood, d'you think they'll listen anyway?"

Mrs. Merrynether shot a concerned look at Danariel, and Joe didn't have to look at the seraph to know she was responding in kind. He could feel it ebbing from her.

"They have to," said Mrs. Merrynether.

Joe leaned forward. "But what if—?"

"Veronica!" Danariel leapt from Joe's shoulder, shot toward the stern pole, and hovered just above Flarp, pointing at the setting sun. "Dragons!"

Joe peered into the distance. At first, the five tiny black V shapes looked like gulls, but as they came closer, he realized they were bigger. *Much* bigger.

"The Conclave?" Mrs. Merrynether's voice sounded tight.

"I don't know," said Danariel, "but their attention is on us. No doubt about it."

"Do they feel hostile or friendly? Indifferent? Curious? Do they recognize any of us? We need to know more."

Danariel lifted her hands. "They are masking their feelings very skilfully."

"Everyone," said Mrs. Merrynether. "It is very

important that you conceal any feelings of guilt or fear you may have." She marched up and down the deck. "We are visiting Pyronesia with peaceful intent to warn them about Redwar. They must suspect nothing that could lead them to the knowledge of those who are against the Conclave."

Joe watched the massive beasts as they swooped closer—a beautiful yet terrifying sight. Fear was not an easy emotion to conquer under the circumstances, yet it was one he was becoming more and more acquainted with. Each time he'd felt its paralyzing touch in the last few weeks, the stakes were higher.

He had to keep his cool.

The five dragons flew in an arrowhead formation, their wings sweeping the air with slow grace, in perfect timing with each other. Joe remembered how he felt the first time he saw Snappel and how amazed he was at seeing such a magnificent lizard, but Snappel was a mere newt in comparison to these hulking monsters. Yet there was definitely a resemblance—the same oily sheen to the obsidian scales, the same triangular head structure, and even the same tail—but whereas Snappel had only two legs sprouting from her body, the dragons had four, each of them tucked neatly against their bulky frames as they weaved through the sky. The dragon flying at the center of the formation was twice the size of the others and four times the size of Snappel. Its long neck, rippling with sinew and muscle, arched and shuddered as it snorted a ring of thick soot into the air that snaked around the balloon. The acrid stench of sulphur bit into Joe's sinuses, causing him to retch as the cloud dispersed.

"We've no chance," cried Danariel. "They know. Their minds are full of anger. They're going to attack."

"Belowdecks," screamed Mrs. Merrynether as the dragons swept in.

Joe looked up as he staggered away from the wheel, his eyes watering from the sting of smoke. One of the smaller dragons tore into the balloon above, thrashing at the canvas with huge talons and snatching at the lines with nightmarish teeth. A blur of black wings streaked from Joe's left as Snappel roared into the air, screeching at the attacker. Cornelius followed her, tail flailing like a rotor, razor claws extended, and wings beating the air in mighty strokes.

"No," yelled Joe, crashing to the floor before he could reach the cabin entrance.

Mrs. Merrynether had already got to the door, holding the exasperated Kiyoshi, who was shouting insults nobody would understand at the dragons. She made to come back for Joe but fell backward when one of the other dragons blasted into the deck between them. Splinters and fiery clouds erupted around the leathery wings of the beast as it straightened like a demon ready to rain hell upon them.

At the same moment, Danariel raced forward, shining like a nova, darting in front of the dragon in twists and turns. But the distraction only lasted long enough for Joe to clamber to his feet and fall backward, just out of range of the monster's claws as it gouged an enormous chunk from the bow.

The dragon swatted Danariel aside just as Flarp shot out of nowhere to splat directly into one of the dragon's eyes. He dropped out of range, under the enraged beast's legs as it clawed at the snotty blemish and then zipped to Mrs. Merrynether to drag her by the head through the cabin doors.

Not daring to look behind him, Joe shuffled on his hands and knees across the broken deck, screaming, choking against the bile in his throat, feeling the torn wood bite into his palms. He felt a sudden lightness as the *Copper Celt* lurched downward. With nobody driving the wings and the balloon ripped into streamers, there was nothing keeping the ship in the sky.

Almost lost in the chaos and finding nowhere to go beyond the stern, Joe turned onto his back, waiting for death as the huge beast stamped across the deck toward him. Above, the shredded remnants of the balloon swirled in the rushing air and one of the other dragons was getting the best of Snappel and Cornelius.

On the far side of the ship Joe caught a glimpse of the three remaining dragons, one of them the fearsome leader, rushing forward. The image was blotted out by the dark shape of Joe's pursuer. With none of his friends left to rescue him, Joe clamped his eyes shut as the enormous jaws of the dragon yawned open above his head. At least it would be a quick death.

Thirty-two

A rush of hot breath reeking of sulphur raised goose bumps on Joe's skin as he screamed. Then it was gone, replaced by icy wind sucking the air from his lungs as he fell with the ship. Joe snapped his eyes open, hardly believing he was still alive. The dragon that lunged at him had been snatched away, buffeted aside by its larger comrade. As the *Copper Celt* plummeted, dragging a stream of debris in its wake, the two dragons fought. At first Joe thought the larger dragon wanted to assert its dominance over the other to steal its meal, but through the cyclone of wooden shrapnel, the battle looked far too vicious to be normal rivalry. Before the world became a blur of smoke, ash, sky, and water, Joe saw the leader tear a fatal lump from the neck of its victim and toss the limp body away. The sky roared with the cries of death, and the wind whipping through the remains of the *Copper Celt*'s balloon howled in sympathy.

A flash of orange-smeared green flapped around Joe as he tumbled, and with the wild hope of survival, he grabbed for fragments of canvas. Cloth burned his palms, slipping through his grip, but the moment to hold on was gone. The last of the ship had passed below him. Joe glimpsed two of the other dragons ripping into another as he flipped over, facing the world underneath.

Out of nowhere, a land mass had appeared: a huge crescent-shaped island ringed by unspoiled beaches and smothered with the rich green of healthy forest. Soon the *Copper Celt* would be spread in a million pieces across that land and Joe with it. But before he could fully consider what it might be like to hit the ground from such a great height, a set of scaly claws grasped his waist, scooping him upwards. The claws were too small to belong to one of the dragons but had the same oily sheen. Joe realized Snappel had just rescued him from a bone-crunching death.

Joe grasped the smooth talons, as if holding on to the wyvern's claws would provide a little extra security. Thick blood like cherry syrup slid against his fingers as he held on tight. A metallic odor soured his nostrils, and Joe noticed many of Snappel's scales were torn. Joe wished the wyvern could speak. At least then he might be able to find out if she was in serious pain, and she might even be able to tell him what happened to Cornelius.

As if in answer to a prayer, the manticore's regal

form sped below them toward the falling ship. Apart from two unsightly gashes in his right wing, Cornelius appeared unharmed.

The *Copper Celt* continued its fateful plunge toward the island, and Joe saw only three of the original five dragons. They had taken positions around the edges of the ship, tearing into the hull with their huge talons and fighting the ark's descent with ferocious strokes. Cornelius joined them, adding his own efforts to prevent the crash. Snappel dived too, her grip tightening around Joe's body as the *Copper Celt* came closer.

A rush of blood to the head almost caused Joe to pass out as the wyvern swiveled him with a single claw. With the other, Snappel latched the side of the cabin. Joe's ears buzzed with the combined cries of all five beasts as they strained against gravity.

And then came the almighty crash. An explosion of poles, buckled beams, and brass girders laced with a fountain of sand and seawater blasted into the sky as the *Copper Celt* broke upon Pyronesia's shore. Joe caught sight of the largest dragon as the impact launched it from the ark. Rolling and flailing, it cut a huge wedge into the sand.

Joe was thrown violently from Snappel's grasp onto the remains of the deck. Debris rained around him as he nursed yet another bruise forming on his head.

Snappel waggled her head and blinked her inner eyelids, then stretched out the membranes of each wing in turn to check for damage, but Joe noticed the trembling in her legs and a stream of dark blood pooling on the deck's remains.

"Thanks, Snappel," said Joe. "I thought I was a goner!"

The wyvern snorted out a puff of smoke, then fell onto the deck in a heap. She was still conscious, but an awful moan escaped her jaws.

"Snappel," Joe cried. He scanned the deck, frantically looking for someone or something to help the injured wyvern. The crash had tipped the *Copper Celt* toward its right side, so anything loose had slid into crumpled piles that overflowed onto the beach. Wailing, shrieking, and howling gathered in volume from the lower decks. The horrible truth dawned on Joe that Snappel was not the only creature injured as a result of the impact.

Among the splintered beams and balloon fragments, Cornelius trod carefully toward one of the three dragons that had helped crash-land the *Copper Celt*. The dragon had not survived the impact. The magnificent body sprawled against a rocky outcrop, a long gash in its side revealing pink innards and its neck twisted back. By its side stood the largest of the dragons, its head bowed in apparent mourning. The other dragon that Joe saw thrown into the sand limped over too.

Why the dragons had turned against each other during the attack was a mystery to Joe, and although he wanted to find out more, Snappel needed help— and quickly. Joe was about to call out for help when he heard the collapsing beams and splintering wood below the skewed deck. The whole ark shuddered, and the noise drowned out the screams of the wounded.

Joe climbed the deck to the upturned side to look over the edge. An enormous breach had appeared in the lower part of the hull. A crowd of animals spilled out from the hole, milling, striding, and leaping onto the sand. Joe spotted Mrs. Merrynether among them, and already Danariel had set about trying to herd the crowd into one area.

Joe cupped his hands around his mouth and called, "Mrs. Merrynether. We need help. Snappel's hurt."

She looked up, trying to locate the source of Joe's voice, then saw him. "We'll have things sorted out down here momentarily." The tone of her reply sounded far less confident, but she continued, "I'll come to Snappel right away and take a look at her. If you're mobile, check around the deck to see if there are any wounded that need help, will you? We need to get organized and gather them all in one place. Danariel will help you in a minute or two, and Kiyoshi should be near you too."

Joe gave her a thumbs-up and slid down the width of the deck, looking around for signs of other animals.

Kiyoshi had just crawled through a gap in the boards to meet Joe, his strange monkey face wrinkled in concern. "You are granted my servitude through the duration of this emergency. I will assist you in any way possible."

"Thanks, Kiyoshi."

Joe looked around. Apart from Snappel, the deck was clear. He turned to watch the two dragons stooped over the dead dragon on the beach. He saw Cornelius also watching from a distance. The right wing of the smaller dragon hung limply by its side, broken by its impact with the beach.

Mrs. Merrynether had asked Joe to look for any wounded, and this certainly classified as an injury. With a tightly held breath, Joe walked toward the huge lizards before fear could stop his feet from moving. He stopped a mere ten paces from the leader. A gust of air, possibly the beast's breath, passed across Joe's face, carrying a prickly heat and a strong smell like burnt meat, but he resisted the urge to step back.

"Excuse me," Joe said, his voice sounding a little too insignificant for his liking.

The lead dragon tilted its head toward Joe with the sleepy motion of someone disturbed from a world of sorrow. It fixed him with its fiery reptilian eyes for a long moment.

"Is there anything we can do to help?" Joe asked. "For that dragon's broken wing?"

The dragon continued to stare, then lowered its head flat to the ground, arched its back, and released a roar so loud that Joe fell backward and sat in the sand. Kiyoshi backed off too. The beast took one step before the other dragon unfurled its good wing to hold the leader back. Brief growls were exchanged, and the leader focused on Joe. Too fearful to look away, Joe stared back but decided to say nothing else.

Kiyoshi, however, took the opportunity to speak, his voice dripping with sarcasm. "Our apologies if our pestiferous interruption has disturbed your time of omphaloskepsis. Unfortunately, we—"

"Not helping," hissed Joe as the dragon shifted its dangerous gaze to Kiyoshi. "Why don't you go back to the ship and have a look in the lower decks for some more wounded, then try and gather them. If they're seriously hurt, you could give them some of your kappa juice to help them recover."

Kiyoshi glared at Joe, then scuttled off.

Joe shook his head and looked back at the dragons. Thankfully, they had refocused on their fallen friend.

"You'd better lie low for a bit," said Danariel, now hovering beside him. "They're not exactly happy to see us."

"Why?" whispered Joe. "What have we done? What was all that about up there?"

Danariel flew down to face Joe, but then she twitched her head as if hearing something behind her. Joe caught a glimpse of a scowl on her face as she turned on the dragons.

"And if you so much as try and touch him, I'll make sure you regret it." She paused, then spoke again. "I may be separated from Gnauserous, but don't presume my influence over her is gone. I meant what I said. If you hurt this boy, you *will* regret it."

The lead dragon bellowed and puffed a huge ball of smoke.

Joe stared at the tiny seraph. He had never seen her act so aggressively before. "Danariel," he whispered, "what's going on?"

She turned, her face now apologetic. "So sorry. I forgot you can't see or hear them. It seems they didn't think about that either."

"See who? And who's . . . Gnauserous?"

"Do you remember why I came to Merrynether Mansion? Do you remember what my ailment was?"

Joe scratched the bump on his head. "No, remind me."

"You shouldn't be able to see me, remember? Everybody can see me, but nobody should be able to see a seraph unless two things happen."

"Right," said Joe. "I remember now. You have to believe the seraphim exist, and you have to know the seraph's name."

"Exactly. Now, I know you believe in the seraphim, but you don't know the names of three seraphim that happen to be in our presence right now."

"There are three here? Now?"

"Oh, yes. There were five earlier, but the other two fled. Of the remaining three, one is unconscious and the other two are mourning over the fallen, alongside their kin-ties."

"What's a kin-tie?"

"I'll explain in a moment. First, I think it's best to

make sure you can see and hear them." She pointed at each dragon in turn. "Alariel, Semeriel, and Tabariel."

As Danariel spoke each name, a flash of light appeared near each dragon, revealing beings similar to Danariel but each with its own subtle difference in color. The one identified as Semeriel lay next to the dead dragon, her eyes closed and her violet-blue pulse very weak. Tabariel, the seraph closest to the leading dragon, had a faintly apple-green glow, and so did the other, though his was a fraction deeper.

"Amazing," said Joe. "I can see them now. Are the seraphim connected to the dragons somehow?"

"That's right, but it's actually a lot stronger than a simple connection. You could say each dragon has a spirit and its spirit is the seraph. The dragon and the seraph are separate, but they are also one."

"Oh," said Joe, nodding and pretending to understand. "How did they . . . Has it always been like that?"

"No. There was a time when seraph and dragon were united as a single being. Nobody really knows how or why that changed, but there's an old legend about it. It tells of an ancient Pyronesian king who lost his queen to a terrible illness. The physicians did all they could to save her, but when they failed, the king became so angry that he ordered every doctor to be executed."

"That's insane."

"Absolutely. Even the king thought so when he finally came to his senses. He grew so distraught at what he'd done that he decided he never wanted to be angry again, and so he went to the highest mountain on the farthest land to be alone for twenty years. At the end of that time, he vomited the rage from his spirit, which created the first dragon. He himself became the first of the seraphim."

"Weird. It sounds a bit like the story Mrs. Merrynether told me about the squonks."

"Ah, yes, about how the oceans of the world were created when the dragons wanted to get rid of their ugliness."

"That's the one. Do you think any of them are true?"

"They're just old myths." She laughed. "Like the ones the Greeks invented when they wanted to explain the laws of nature through metaphor."

A seraph drifted to Danariel and grabbed her arm. "I told you to remove that human from my sight. I might not agree with Gnauserous and her plans, but that does not mean I have any love for these . . . abominations of nature."

"Well, Tabariel, you'd better get used to this one," she replied, pointing at Joe. "He might be our best hope for a peaceful solution."

"Was he worth the death of three dragons?"

"Are you blaming *him* for their deaths? Surely you can't hold this small boy responsible for that ugly display in the sky. Are you going to tell me what that was about?"

Tabariel's lips thinned as he looked down at Joe, then back to Danariel. "I'll tell you but not here. We need to find somewhere safer for everyone to stay . . . if there *is* anywhere."

"The old Nesting Caverns."

Tabariel looked at the sky. "Yes, the Nesting Caverns will be adequate for the time being, but we must move quickly. It's dusk already, and it will be dark within the hour. Gnauserous will likely send a larger contingent to deal with you now that you have managed to survive. I cannot believe you came, Danariel. What did you think you could achieve by coming here with—?"

"As you said, we should discuss this in a better place." Danariel turned back, then faced Joe. "Come on. We need to get everyone gathered, including the wounded. We have to make a trip along the beach before we're attacked again."

THIRTY-THREE

The journey from the ruined ark to the Nesting Caverns was mercifully short. Once the wounded had been gathered, makeshift stretchers were fashioned out of the remaining balloon canvas, and a generous dose of Kiyoshi's kappa juice enabled the others to transport everyone to safety. Passed out from supplying so many, Kiyoshi had been carried in one of the stretchers, mumbling in his sleep about the joys of eating cucumber.

Twilight brought the chirruping of a thousand insects. The sky darkened to a murky blue, a cold wind following. Joe entered the caverns, grateful for the rocky shelter. He carried one end of a stretcher that held an animal resembling a rabbit but the size of a husky. Several dozen oil lamps lit the cavern, the stuttering flames creating an orange glow against the glittering walls. Joe guessed this was the very same place Mrs. Merrynether had spoken about.

The cavern was huge. At some time in the past, volcanic activity had formed a tall mountain, but much of its interior had been gouged out and burned away by the nesting dragons who had clearly returned year after year for millennia to nurture their young. Joe stood in one of the hub areas, a vast chamber with scores of tunnels leading away from it. Clusters of sparkling diamonds lined every surface except the floor, which was carpeted with the broken shells of countless dragon eggs.

Joe looked around for Mrs. Merrynether as he lowered the stretcher. Flarp and his friend hovered by the entrance as lookout. Snappel waited underneath, her right leg bandaged by Mrs. Merrynether's expert hand. Kiyoshi lay asleep nearby, his limbs neatly tucked inside his shell. Danariel hovered with the other seraphim, engaged in a heated discussion. Deeper into the cavern, the various animals had been rounded up by Cornelius, who paced the crowd, growling and swishing his barbed tail to keep them in order.

Joe thanked the long-legged animal that had taken the other end of the stretcher as he lowered it near the herded group. Then he continued to look around for Mrs. Merrynether. He spotted her sitting on a wooden crate by herself in a darkened part of the cave, Archy curled up by her feet, asleep. Mrs. Merrynether seemed unconcerned by the needs of the creatures around her. Her brow even more wrinkly than usual, she stared ahead in dreamy thought.

Joe sat on the floor next to her. "Hello. You all right?"

She continued to stare ahead. "No."

Joe waited a moment. "Want to talk about it?"

She let out a long sigh and scanned the rocky surface of the cave floor.

Joe held one of her hands. "There are still some wounded animals. They're all over there." He pointed toward Cornelius, who was thumping the ground beside a group of boisterous imps. "Will you show me how to help them?"

She squinted through her glasses at the group. "Of course I will help, Joseph. I was just taking a minute to think things through. That's all."

"Okay. I'll be over there when you're ready."

He went to pull away, but Mrs. Merrynether tightened her grip and looked at him with a curious sadness in her eyes. "You're a good lad, Joseph Copper."

Joe smiled. "Thanks. Will you tell them that?" He nodded toward the two dragons standing side by side in another part of the cavern. Their fallen comrade lay stretched out behind them next to a line of six other creatures killed in the crash. At the far end was the tiny body of Thumbler, the young troll, neatly tied up in what looked like a ceremonial cloak.

Joe immediately regretted drawing Mrs. Merrynether's attention to that area of the cave.

"We're lucky there weren't more deaths," she said.

"I'm sorry," said Joe, looking down.

"Right where Thumbler is now—that's where Gloria and Donald Merson were burned alive all those years ago." She motioned to the left. "I found my husband's body right over there. And just beyond that tunnel—that's where I watched four more of my team die . . . Now I'm afraid it will happen all over again when the Conclave get here. I have made such a terrible mess of things and put you right in the middle of it all."

"None of this is your fault, Mrs. Merrynether."

"I should never have come."

"But you had to."

"Did I? Where is Redwar? He isn't here, is he?"

Joe stopped to think about that. She was right. So far they had not seen or heard any sign of him or his army.

"And look at my army!" Mrs. Merrynether waved at the crowd of animals around her. "My task was to amass a force that could overthrow the Conclave and keep the world from being thrown into a war it could never win. I've had all these years to do that, and I've done nothing . . . Nothing!"

"That's not true. You've—"

"And now I've brought us all here, ready to be—" She stopped, horror in her eyes.

Joe hunted for the right thing to say, but before he could think of anything useful, Tabariel, the green-hued seraph belonging to the largest dragon, drifted to them and faced Mrs. Merrynether.

"Veronica Merrynether. The years have not been

kind to you."

She looked up and huffed, as if the greeting was exactly as she expected. "Hello to you too."

"Danariel assures me your presence on this island is necessary, but she has yet to offer us a good enough reason for your arrival."

"Then am I to understand Argoyle Redwar has not come to Pyronesia threatening to destroy you all?"

"Danariel also mentioned this man, but you are the first outsiders to come to Pyronesia for decades. Am I expected to believe this Redwar has a way of detecting us and even threatening us?"

"I heard from a reliable source this was the case"—Mrs. Merrynether let her eyes fall on Thumbler's body—"though I seriously doubt Redwar has the means to endanger any of you, even with an army."

"Then why did you come?"

"Our intention was to stop him and his army before he made any contact with the Conclave. We were afraid he would precipitate an all-out attack on the rest of the world."

"And so he would have. Gnauserous has been growing restless these last few years, and when Danariel eventually left to see you, all Gnauserous has been discussing with the rest of the Conclave is when to begin the attack. The arrival of someone like Redwar would give Gnauserous the perfect excuse to begin the war, as it was with your arrival."

"Our arrival?" Joe interrupted.

"Yes, yours. How do you think Gnauserous reacted when the globbles saw an enormous ark heading toward Pyronesia? She sent me out to destroy you. For years I have managed to conceal my support of the rebellion, but now my involvement is plain. I had to kill two of my kin to keep you safe, only to find this pathetic gathering you came up with to oppose the Conclave. What have you been *doing* all this time? Is this the best you could do?"

Mrs. Merrynether had never looked so downcast. "We . . . I thought the Conclave had . . . mellowed."

"Mellowed. Do you think a thousand years of hatred and paranoia could be calmed in such a small span of time?"

"Well, what have you been doing, then?" Joe said, feeling a righteous anger bubbling within. "Why should it be up to Mrs. Merrynether to stop one of your own? If you don't have the courage to stand up to her, that's your own problem, isn't it?"

The lead dragon, deeper in the cave, stamped a claw and roared a ball of fire.

Tabariel's glow deepened to indigo.

"Thank you, Joseph," said Mrs. Merrynether, "but Tabariel is right. The Conclave's hatred for humanity was inflamed when I brought the team here all those years ago. I have a responsibility, and I have not fulfilled my part in this."

"No," insisted Joe, eyeing the seraph. "He can

stamp and complain all he likes. What happened all those years ago was a big misunderstanding, and even if there were a couple of greedy people on the team, you can hardly hold the whole of humanity responsible for what they did."

The seraph stared back at him, and Joe thought he saw a flash of a smile. "Brave words, boy. I happen to agree with you, which is why I am part of the rebellion, but don't ever accuse me of cowardice again. There are too few of us in opposition to Gnauserous to make a stand at this time. Acts of bravery will most certainly result in our destruction."

"But what about earlier on? Didn't you say what you did would make your involvement with the rebellion plain?"

"Exactly. And now perhaps you understand my anger. I have risked everything and"—he waved a tiny hand—"gained nothing."

Joe looked at Mrs. Merrynether.

She looked back but said nothing.

"Who is this Gnauserous anyway?" Joe asked. "I heard Danariel say something earlier about being separated from her but still having some influence."

"The boy doesn't know?" said Tabariel, staring incredulously at Joe. "I thought his presence on this island meant you had chosen him as the—"

"Stop!" said Mrs. Merrynether.

"The what? What have I been chosen as? I thought

you said you wanted me as your successor for your practice? What's going on?"

Mrs. Merrynether shot an angry glance at Tabariel before resting her tearful gaze on Joe. "I do want you as my successor, Joseph, but . . . that role carries a dreadful responsibility—something I wanted to tell you when you were older so that you could decide for yourself whether—"

"What responsibility?"

She sighed. "I told you only a portion of the truth earlier. You remember when I told you about the boy James Merson and how I showed him to the dragon to beg for mercy?"

"Yes."

"That dragon was Gnauserous, the Queen of Pyronesia and the head of the Conclave. She wanted to destroy mankind even before the catastrophe that killed most of my team and led to the death of one of her young. But by pleading my case to her, I unknowingly invoked an ancient Pyronesian law. Before war is announced, a chosen representative from each side must meet to see if a peaceful resolution can be found.

"I was taken to the Conclave, but when I made my plea, Gnauserous would not accept it and still wanted to go to war. Fortunately, her kin-tie did not agree, and after a bitter dispute among the Conclave, war was avoided and Gnauserous's seraph separated from her that day."

"Danariel."

"Yes, Danariel."

"But where do I fit into—?"

A minor commotion broke out near the entrance to the cave as Flarp zoomed inside, tendrils wriggling. Snappel was hopping, flapping her wings.

"What's up?" asked Joe. "Is something coming?"

Flarp backed toward the entrance.

Joe and Mrs. Merrynether followed, Tabariel zipping beside them. Night had fallen like a dark cloak across the island. Joe marveled at the moon lighting Pyronesia's landscape—until a cloud of V shapes blotted out the white disc.

"Is it the Conclave?" Joe asked, wondering if he really wanted to hear the answer.

"I will find out," said Tabariel.

A gale almost knocked Joe over as the enormous dragon leader flew overhead and into the night, Tabariel on its back. A small crowd had gathered at the entrance, tensely anticipating the confrontation.

There was a moment of shared fear, nervous growls, and high-pitched chirps as the other dragons formed a ring around the rebel; then relief settled as their dragon joined the rest and headed down toward the Nesting Cavern.

Joe counted eighty-seven dragons when they landed on the beach. None of them were quite as large as Tabariel's dragon, but each of them looked formidable. It was hard to see properly in the moonlight, but Joe noted that they all had different colorings and markings. Ranging from the deepest black to the palest blue, each of them had slightly different scaly growths on their hides, which Joe thought might be an indication of age or rank.

From the peak of the crowd, Tabariel fluttered toward Joe and hovered before him, looking grave.

"Who are they?" Joe asked.

"The time has come to make a stand. The gathering you see is the full force of those who will resist Gnauserous and the Conclave."

"There are loads of you. Surely you can easily take over."

Danariel came to rest on Joe's shoulder. "You underestimate the size of the Conclave. They have ten thousand dragons at their disposal, and they aren't the only creatures populating Pyronesia."

"So why is it time to make a stand? We're outnumbered a hundred to one."

"We have no choice," said Tabariel. "Your arrival on this island started a chain of events, and now we are all exposed. If we do not resist or make a plea, Gnauserous will have all of us destroyed anyway and begin her campaign against the world unhampered."

"So is that it? That's the plan? To fight with no chance of winning?"

"The time for war has not yet come. We have made our plea before the Conclave for representatives from each side to meet. They must first try for a peaceful solution before war is announced."

"So that's good news, right?"

"No. It is merely for show. She will call the meeting. If she wins, she will go to war. If she loses, I suspect she will find a way to manipulate the law and start hostilities anyway."

"So what's the point in even trying?"

"We can buy some time to plan," said Danariel. "It's all we have. If we're really lucky, the rest of the Conclave might even persuade Gnauserous that war is a bad idea, but that would depend on the skill of our representative . . ."

Mrs. Merrynether, who had quietly joined them, broke the silence. "Then take me to the Conclave. I brought this calamity here. I should be the one to represent us."

"No," said Tabariel. "You *know* it cannot be you. You are a sentenced criminal in the eyes of the Conclave and would not be heard. No, surely this is the real reason you brought the boy."

Joe's stomach leapt as he turned toward Mrs. Merrynether. Her eyes betrayed the pain of guilt before she looked away.

"Joseph Copper," said Tabariel, "as the only other representative of the human race on this island, will you come with us?"

*T*HIRTY-FOUR

A strange feeling of destiny sent thrills across Joe's skin as he traveled to meet the Conclave. Dawn came with a stormy sky, but the sun shone through the clouds, as if to expose the dread he had been trying to conceal in the dark of the night. Mrs. Merrynether had insisted he be allowed to sleep before being taken to the Conclave, but Joe could not even close his eyes when the time came to rest.

From the moment he accepted his role as humanity's representative to meet Gnauserous, he experienced feelings that threatened to overwhelm him. He remembered the heaviness of responsibility when he'd found out about Heinrich, and he recalled the twisting and turning inside his belly when Mrs. Merrynether had gone missing, but none of that had prepared him for this. What lay before him now was quite different, and he wondered how many other people in the long-forgotten ages of the world had been burdened with the knowledge that their actions could change the course of history. All at once, he felt like the unexpected hero of the hour but also the most insignificant speck of dust, swept along in a cyclone of events over which he had no control.

In a curious way, Joe's journey to the Conclave mirrored his feelings exactly. There he was, the brave knight fastened into a saddle, riding on the back of a giant reptile, the cold wind stinging his eyes and numbing his face as they swooped through the clouds toward his destiny. Or was he the speck, manipulated into being just another disposable pawn of a war he knew nothing about, clinging in sheer terror to the back of a monster leading him to his death?

Below, the beach had turned to dense forests and then to bony mountains as they raced onward. To his left and right, a host of twenty dragons flew in majestic harmony, perfectly aligned in order of size, each beating its wings in time with the others. Joe felt a cascade of emotions. Whether they would be expressed in tears, cheers, or screams, he had no clue, but as the confusion rattled his thoughts like marbles in a tin box, he clutched at the leather handles, fighting to keep a calm mind, staring at the green mountains below.

"You will need to quiet your soul before you face Queen Gnauserous."

Joe turned, startled from his thoughts. Tabariel

had drawn alongside him, his delicate wings flickering as he matched their speed.

"Easy for you to say."

"But true nonetheless."

"It doesn't make it any easier. I don't have a clue what to do or say. And anyway, I can't just switch off how I'm feeling, can I?"

Joe studied the seraph's face and envied what he saw. Old and stern but softened by ethereal green light, the seraph had the face of a warlord who had seen a thousand battles. Tabariel's face twitched into a scowl; then he shook his head. "Merrynether has taught you nothing."

"There hasn't been much opportunity."

Tabariel hovered closer, his intense gaze burrowing deep, and Joe felt prickly indignation at the sudden intrusion. He allowed the seed of emotion to have a foothold and quickly felt it sprout into anger, believing that to be far better than the fear and despair he might have felt otherwise. The resulting outburst was a little more aggressive than he had planned.

"Get out of my head," Joe shouted. "I'm done being controlled and . . . and told what to think and feel. I'm done with people tricking me, and most of all, I'm done being used. Just leave me alone!"

"I am trying to help you calm your thoughts."

"I don't want your help. You're the one who wants mine, so if you want *me* to be a representative, you'd better let *me* deal with how I feel, all right?"

"Your anger is directed at those you love. I can feel that."

Joe stared directly ahead, focusing on the slow rhythmic movement of the dragon's shoulder blades, hating the seraph for being right and still wanting to hold on to his anger. Anger at Heinrich for betraying everyone, anger at Mrs. Merrynether for not telling him all the truth, and anger at Danariel—she surely must have known too, yet she persuaded him to come to Pyronesia to fulfill his *destiny*. Joe's pulse quickened, and his breathing grew harsher with each stinging thought.

"I trusted them," he said.

"And they have let you down?" Tabariel said.

"Mrs. Merrynether didn't tell me I might die when I agreed to come with her to Pyronesia."

"Nobody is going to let you die. I will protect you."

"Now you're doing the same. You can't make promises like that. You don't know what's going to happen. But that's not why I'm angry anyway. She didn't give me the opportunity to choose this. None of them did."

"Perhaps you are missing a greater point, Joseph."

"Like what?"

"I know Merrynether's mind. There is no deception in her thoughts, only the torment one finds when faced with impossible decisions. Merrynether is a skilled surgeon, not a great leader or tactician, but she has a heart filled with good intent, and that is what you must trust."

Joe was about to mutter a phrase he'd heard somewhere about the road to hell but was interrupted by a call from his right.

"The Tree of Sanctuary signals our approach." The voice came from Alariel, whose dragon had broken formation to push ahead.

Joe edged forward, straining to peer around the neck of his dragon. Shock surged through him when, straight from the dream that had invaded his sleep, a gargantuan tower loomed from the peak of the tallest mountain into the clouds. Seemingly carved out of wood, it stood like a tree uprooted from a planet of giants and thrust into the island. The gnarled trunk, wider than an office block, weaved and twisted up out of sight. Its wild branches, each the size of a runway, extended in all directions. Its rootlike foundations clutched at the mountainside. Joe knew what he would see next as they drew closer. True to his dream, the branches ended with clusters of pea-green orbs that could be mistaken as leaves from a distance, but closer up, Joe recognized them as families of swiveling eyes restrained by long fibrous cords.

"Globbles." Joe gasped. "The eyes are globbles."

"Of course," said Tabariel. "They are the eyes of the island. Day and night they observe everything everywhere. If anything threatens to come close to the island, the Conclave sense their fervor and investigate."

The group of globbles leashed to the closest branch

strained toward them like excited puppies pulling on leads to greet their master, but the dragons flew below, heading for the base of the tree with an archway as large as the entrance to a castle. Joe wondered what lay in wait within. It was with some relief that he realized a newfound awe had overwhelmed his anger—for the moment anyway.

"Magic beans," Joe mused as their dragon extended his legs like the undercarriage of an aircraft.

"Beans?" Tabariel asked.

"Just an old fairy tale my mum used to read to me when I was younger."

Joe's face met hard scales as the dragon thudded onto the mountain rocks. A moment later, a flurry of dark wings rustled all around as each of the other dragons landed.

"I sense great unease among the Conclave," said Tabariel as they began a slow march toward the archway. "The pains of civil war are upon them, and each of them knows deaths will be unavoidable. Only one of them remains confident of the future."

"Gnauserous," said Joe.

"Yes. She alone is looking forward to the war."

"She's actually looking forward to it? Surely the other seraphim can sense she's evil, and if none of the others agree with her, why don't they just get rid of her?"

"Understand this, Joseph Copper—she is *not* evil," snapped Tabariel, halting the dragon. "She looks forward to the war because she sees it as a final end to the division on Pyronesia and a decisive step forward to cleansing the earth. Unlike the others, she is true to her convictions and is confident of her judgment."

"You're starting to sound like you agree with her."

"I do not, but that does not mean I think she is evil. She has always been a fair and righteous leader, but in this matter, I believe her to be mistaken and so I have made my stand."

"How can you think she's fair and righteous if she wants to destroy every human being?"

"Enough. Save your words for Gnauserous. It is she you need to convince, not I."

Joe fell silent as they reached the arch. He looked over his shoulder to take in the view one last time. The tree's shadow stretched across the land like an open claw. He wondered how far its reach would extend after today.

Prepared or not, Joe was about to face his destiny. Entering the Tree of Sanctuary was a moment of awe Joe knew would stay with him for the rest of his life. The floor alone was a breathtaking sight. Its polished slabs, encrusted with gold and diamonds, were interlocked to create a mammoth mosaic. Joe could not see properly from his viewpoint, but it seemed to portray a story, much like tapestries he'd seen in a stately home once. But the floor was only the beginning.

The craftsmanship of no cathedral, stadium, or palace would ever compare to what had been performed on the inside of this tower. It looked like the inside of a giant walnut, every ridge and wrinkle a sweeping arc or gilded column. Golden fittings at every node and junction gleamed in the firelight of a thousand torches, which lined the circumference a hundred feet above.

Between the torches at regular intervals, twelve enormous forked tongues carved from dark wood stretched out like pathways from the wall. Directly above each one, a circular mouth, decorated with ivory fangs large enough to fit a tube train inside, faded into murky tunnels apparently to chambers deep within the mountain. The tunnel opposite the entrance was much larger than the rest, and the tongue was far longer, sweeping down to ground level like some sort of medieval death slide. Above each opening, seraphim names were engraved in gold.

"The Conclave are coming," said Tabariel.

Nervous anticipation tormented Joe as they all gathered at the bottom of this vast hall. Joe's dragon settled into a seated position at the center, and the others held back, waiting near the entrance.

"Stay exactly as you are. Do not dismount," Tabariel whispered.

Joe craned his neck, looking upward, and felt as if he were at the bottom of a gigantic well waiting for water to engulf him. But instead of water, flames came. From each of the mouth-like tunnels, a jet of fire roared above to meet at the center like a miniature sun of churning flame.

Joe pressed himself into his dragon's hide, the intense heat beating down, and then it was gone, vaporized into a sooty mass that dispersed into floating ash.

A low rumbling followed, soon becoming the distinct marching thump of heavy claws on thick wood. With the simultaneous precision of practiced ceremony, eleven reptilian, age-mottled heads appeared inside the hall, each protruding from a different tunnel. The dragons marched forward with exact timing and solemn grace and halted at the center of the tongues, stretching their old necks upward as if reaching for something in the heavens. It was time for the twelfth dragon to appear.

From the largest tunnel, Gnauserous came. Her bloodred scales rippled as she slid from the opening and eased her bloated belly onto the wood like an aged monarch waiting to be entertained after a heavy feast. For a moment, her cold green eyes settled on Joe before she stretched her neck upward in unison with the others.

Joe waited, feeling his muscles tremble now, but the ceremonial entrance was not over. A hot wind rushed through the tunnels, howling with power, meeting in the center just as the fire had. The sooty remnants of the ball of flame scattered like confetti, swirling in torrents around the hall, and Joe shielded his eyes until the storm died down. Through gaps in his fingers, he saw seraphim fly from the tunnels with the same meticulous ritual as the dragons but faster. Each hovered directly in front of its respective dragon, arms and wings stretched out and heads tilted upward.

At once, a flash of recognition came to Joe and his mind rushed back to Mrs. Merrynether's garden, to the magnificent statue of the dragon. The stone had been sculpted in the same positions that these dragons and seraphim now assumed. But something was missing here. There were other stone creatures surrounding the dragon and seraphim in Mrs. Merrynether's garden. He remembered the weeping squonks at the base of the plinth.

A loud grinding of stone directly ahead disturbed his thoughts. A door had opened at the back of the hall. Two lumbering beasts, wearing brown rags and vaguely resembling oversized humans, stepped out. They struggled beneath the weight of an enormous glass ball that contained a swirling mass of milky-green fog, eventually lowering it to the ground directly beneath Gnauserous. Once the glass had been steadied, they slouched back through the doorway.

"It's a Speaking Glass," Tabariel whispered. "Since her separation from Danariel, she has to use one of these to talk."

Joe looked up again at Gnauserous and saw that she was the only dragon that did not have a seraph.

"Oh. Should I speak to the dragon or to the glass?"

"Say nothing until I tell you. Let me do the talking for now. We need to buy time for Merrynether and the others."

At that moment, each of the dragons spat another jet of fire upward. Once the air had cooled again, they stretched their wings to form a giant umbrella. The seraphim, including Tabariel, spoke in unison. Booming in accord with the others, a clear female voice rang out from the glass ball.

"May the light of understanding call The Four.

"May the unity of The Four bring us wisdom.

"May the joy of wisdom bring us peace. So may it be."

As the dragons folded their wings against their bodies, Gnauserous lowered her head to look at Joe. Her voice vibrated loudly from the glass sphere. "This is the human representative, Joseph Copper?"

"It is," said Tabariel, fluttering in front of Joe. "I had hoped, Majesty, that as a common courtesy, you would allow us to show him the hospitality of our city and refresh him before engaging in discussions of war."

"No," she hissed. "The hour is late, and it would be unwise of me to allow our opponents the luxury of time to form a strategy against us."

"You would deny this boy the chance to rest and prepare a defense? Such attitude defies the spirit of our laws and ignores the precepts declared by our ancestors. I beg that Your Majesty—"

"Do not lecture me on loyalty to authority, Tabariel. You who have deserted the Conclave to stand with these miserable creatures. You who have spurned those who gave you power."

A muttering of agreement from the other seraphim echoed around the cavernous hall.

"I would spurn any power that seeks only to serve itself," Danariel said. "We ask—"

"Enough! Too many have died even today because they defied the wisdom of the Conclave. There must be no further delay in resolving this conflict, so let the formalities be dispensed with. The human child will present his case before the Conclave. If he cannot provide adequate defense for his kind, he and all who support him will be eradicated and peace will be restored before the end of the coming cycle."

The seraph belonging to a pale dragon two places away from Gnauserous glided into the center to address the others.

"I agree with Gnauserous in that there must be an end to hostilities, but Tabariel is right. This is only a boy. If we are to commit ourselves fully to the law, should we not seek a more appropriate representative?"

The seraph returned to her dragon and was replaced by another, slightly larger and shining in a darker hue.

"The laws do not state any restrictions to age. The only requirements are that a representative must be a willing participant and must also be unanimously chosen by all the defendants who seek a peaceful resolution to a declaration of war."

"Then the requirements are met," said Gnauserous. "The boy's presence with us indicates his willingness, and Veronica Merrynether has clearly brought the boy to fulfill this purpose. I presume there are no other humans present on the island who are aware of the war declaration?"

There was a brief silence before Tabariel replied. "No, Majesty—no other humans are present on the island."

"Then let the boy come forward to provide his defense."

THIRTY-FIVE

Joe had never felt so small. He climbed off the dragon's back and stood at the center of the hall. He wished Danariel could be with him, offering words of wisdom. Or perhaps Kiyoshi, who would confuse the Conclave with discourse so complicated it would take a hundred dragon scientists a year to work out what had been said before passing judgment. Or perhaps Cornelius and Snappel, who could storm in and clear a path for him to escape while they fought against the bewildered Conclave. Even Flarp's excited presence whizzing around the hall, sliming his accusers, would have helped.

"Speak!" boomed the voice of Gnauserous from the huge glass ball.

Joe swallowed. It felt like he'd tried to eat an entire egg without cracking the shell and got it lodged in his throat. He could feel Tabariel's gaze boring into the side of his head, willing him to say something, anything, but he couldn't speak.

"The fate of your kind rests on your shoulders, and you say nothing?" said Gnauserous.

Joe's legs melted to jelly, and his teeth chattered. Shoulders hunched, expecting a blast of fire to consume him at any moment, Joe peered above him with one eye closed, looking directly into the fierce eyes of the dragon queen. Everything else faded. There was no sound. No feeling in his body. All he could see were the two eyes staring back at him like stagnant, green pools split by dark rifts. And in those rifts Joe saw his own cowering, pitiful form reflected back.

Joe stared at himself. Was this who he really was in the face of death? In the face of injustice? Was this how an ambassador for humanity should look? The image blurred as tears formed a hazy screen over his eyes. He knew this was not what he wanted to be, knew he was about to let down more than six billion people, but bone-crushing terror pressed him to the floor. The hard stone sent a juddering crack through his kneecaps.

A voice echoed behind him. Tabariel's response no longer held the edge of respect that it had earlier, only blind anger. "What are you *doing*?"

At first Joe thought Tabariel was shouting in rage at him, chiding him for his weakness and cowardice, but the seraph continued. "Have none of you any honor at all? Or are you so afraid that you must attack a child who has not even had a day's training in resisting such things?"

At once, the oppression lifted from Joe. The fear

was still indented on his mind like the pain of swallowing a jawbreaker and still feeling its bulge in his throat even though it was no longer there. He struggled to his feet, still staring at Gnauserous, still feeling the quivering in his legs, but at least knowing now that not all of it was his own weakness.

"His lack of preparation is not our concern," said the queen stiffly. "Too much is at stake to take any chances, even if this is just a boy."

"With every action and every word, you confirm your dishonor. Why don't you simply attack and be done with this charade? Why even bother—?"

"Tabariel!" one of the other seraphim behind Joe shouted. "Don't tempt her. You know she'll do it, so don't fall into her trap."

Gnauserous roared, and raucous rage-filled words rebounded from the walls as the seraphim and dragons began their tirade. Thirty-two voices screamed for dominance, and Joe could pick out each one and hear each word. Wincing under the wrath of a debate that had no doubt been argued with the same venom time and time again, Joe looked around the great hall, seeing the dragons weave their necks like charmed snakes, seeing the seraphs dart and pulse with glaring lights as they shook fists to make their bitter points. At least the quarrel was buying some of the time they needed, even if it was short-lived.

The squabble was broken by Gnauserous as she

reared up, belched a huge fireball, and stamped her front claws into her platform. The thunderous noise resulted in sudden silence. Joe watched, painfully aware that he still had said nothing.

"No more." said the glass ball. "The time for discussion is over. The boy has not provided a defense, and therefore—"

"Charges!" shouted Joe, knowing there would be no other opportunity.

"What?" hissed Gnauserous.

"Charges," Joe repeated. "If you're going to destroy everyone, and I'm supposed to have something to say, you'd better tell me what it is we've all done wrong . . . Your Majesty."

Stillness settled inside the hall as Gnauserous glowered at the tiny figure in the center of her lair.

"Very good, Joseph," whispered Tabariel. "Excellent."

Gnauserous lowered her head to the level of Joe's, an acidic stench on her warm breath. The voice came slowly, tauntingly, from the sphere. "You wish to know why I am declaring war on your species?"

Joe held his ground. "Yes."

"The crimes of humanity are numerous. Any one of them is enough to justify eradication."

"Then I want to know all of them," said Joe, feeling that he'd got the ball rolling rather nicely. "Right from the start, right up until today. I want to know every single crime."

"Ridiculous! Your principal crime is existence. All humans are evil. Your kind is nothing but a germ, a rampant disease that has spread across the skin of the world and infected it. A lush and beautiful earth it was once, but every day you plunder it, then squander what you steal, only to blacken the skies with poison. Would you give measles or influenza the chance to survive if it invaded your body, or would you purge your blood with medicines before it caused more suffering?"

"Measles can't talk, but if they did, I'd at least listen to—"

"All living things speak, Joseph Copper, but human arrogance presumes that ears are the only way in which their speech is heard. Were it not for the seraphim, we would be as mute to you as the bacteria you destroy without hesitation. If dragonkind were at the mercy of humans, we would not be given the privilege of a hearing such as this."

"You're wrong. Not everyone—"

"Gnauserous!" The shout came from a seraph that had darted into the hall from behind Joe. "The globbles have seen many ships approaching the island. An army is coming."

"What?" said Gnauserous. "How can that be? They cannot possibly know we are here."

"I don't know, Majesty, but they have come upon the water. There is a battleship, several cargo ships, and we sense from the globbles many men wait to land on the beach with weapons. What should we do?"

"There is no longer any need for debate. I do not know how they have discovered us, but the humans have made the first aggressive move, and we will respond in kind. After the eradication of these invaders, we will turn our attention to the rest of the world. Kill these traitors that stand before me now, including the boy."

The rest of the Conclave, both dragons and seraphim, looked at each other, as if adjusting to the gravity of Gnauserous's order before acting.

Tabariel yanked Joe's ear, the pain jogging him from shock. "We don't have much time. Climb onto my dragon. Quickly!"

Still shaking, Joe clambered up the leather straps surrounding Tabariel's dragon and pressed against the scaly skin as the beast reared into the air, dodging two of the Conclave and bellowing flame. A yell of pain exploded from Joe as the dragon rocketed through the hall's entrance, almost yanking Joe's arms from their sockets. But Joe grasped tight, watching in horror as a blur of tooth, talon, and wing rushed around him in clouds of smoke and fire. With his ears popping and the skin pulled tightly across his face, Joe fought to stay conscious as Tabariel's dragon spun upward into the sky like a shot from a gun. Dragons raced on either side, some allies, some not. Blue sky became thick forest as the world turned upside down.

"Hold on tight and close your eyes," yelled Tabariel,

who clung like a limpet to the dragon's neck.

Joe did exactly as he was told as they zigzagged between trees at impossible speed to outrun the enemy dragons. With every desperate turn, Joe felt the whip of a branch or the scorch of a fiery blast, until at last they skidded to a halt on the beach closest to the Nesting Caverns.

"Run," said Tabariel. "We will meet you in the caves if we survive."

Joe threw himself off the back of the dragon, hitting the beach so hard that the wind was knocked out of him. He strained for breath, turning onto his back. Several dragons collided, kicking, clawing, and screeching.

Joe spat grit and blood and ran for the caverns, almost falling face-first as he wrestled to gain pace on the shifting sand. Less than two minutes later, Joe collapsed into the entrance, wishing he could not hear the deafening shrieks behind him. His throat burned with each exaggerated breath.

There was no one there to greet him. They had all moved on.

Outside, the skirmish reached its climax as eight dragons writhed amidst coils of sulphur and spraying blood. Two fell, joining a line of serpentine bodies dashed across rocks and strewn along the shore like beached fish. The occasional wing or tail tip lifted and quivered in the throes of death as the other six victorious dragons selected a place to land. One simply slumped, too injured to move on, but the other five limped toward the cavern.

Joe was unsure if these five were on his side or the Conclave's, but Tabariel's appearance soon set his mind at ease.

"We escaped," he said, "but the Conclave will send more. We must find out where Merrynether and the others have gone."

"Perhaps they left us a message."

Tabariel raised a hand and cocked his head. "I can feel somebody reaching out to me. Somebody must have stayed behind to wait for us while the others searched for a new location."

Tabariel hovered deeper into the cavern, lighting the walls green as he went, and Joe followed, his feet crunching on broken eggshells. They didn't have to search long before Danariel's own moonlight luminescence mingled with Tabariel's glow from one of the tunnels.

Danariel smiled briefly. "Tabariel, Joe, good to see you both. What happened? We thought it would be at least two days before you returned."

"Good to see you too, Danariel, but I am afraid the news is not good. Gnauserous is taking no chances. She loosely follows the law to keep the rest of the Conclave subservient but has already ordered our deaths."

"So suddenly? But she—"

"Wait," said Tabariel. "There's more. Strangers have come with an army. Perhaps it is this Argoyle Redwar you expected."

"Redwar," Danariel said, nodding slowly.

"It *must* be him," said Joe, "but nobody seems to know how he managed to find the island. Aren't the Conclave able to stop people from seeing it?"

"Yes," said Danariel, "but while you were away, we found something. Let me show you."

She floated a little way down the tunnel she had come from and pointed to a dirty brown rag on the ground. Joe decided not to get too close when he smelled its repulsive stench. Then he recognized it.

"That's Thumbler's coat, isn't it?"

"That's right. Veronica has a potent combination of herbs and chemicals to preserve bodies for a lot longer than usual. She planned to get Thumbler here, prepare him for the trolls' ritual burial, and take him to them. She wanted to personally explain what happened—a big risk, knowing how trolls are at the best of times."

"Doesn't smell very preserved to me," said Joe, pinching his nose.

"No. It's how we discovered something was wrong. Veronica realized a foreign element must have reacted with the chemicals she used for preservation and, sure enough, she found something inside Thumbler's coat that she hadn't noticed before."

Danariel drifted down and picked up a black disc. She passed it to Joe. It was the size of a large coin and had tiny square markings along its edge. Small perforations revealed silver innards on one of the faces.

"This is a homing device, isn't it?" said Joe.

Tabariel buzzed in a tight circle. "A traitor. He led your enemy straight to us."

"He wasn't a traitor," said Danariel sharply. "Thumbler was a tortured prisoner, and Redwar used him. He fed false information to Thumbler, who thought Redwar already knew the location of the island. They fitted him with a bug and let the poor little troll escape so he could warn Veronica. And we all fell right into his trap."

Joe stamped a foot. "We rushed here to stop him but led Redwar straight where he wanted to go."

Danariel sighed. "Veronica was furious with herself. We tried to convince her the chemicals probably stopped the bug from working, but we all knew it was too late."

"Where is she now?" Tabariel asked.

"She went with Snappel to Hallowbear Tor, the troll colony. She's hoping to persuade them to join our cause."

"What chance has she got?" asked Joe.

Danariel looked at Tabariel before answering, her expression less than hopeful. "It will be dangerous. Trolls are fickle creatures. But they aren't treated very well by the Conclave, so there is a small chance they might help."

"And if they do help," Tabariel joined in, "then the wyverns may help too."

"The wyverns?"

"Yes, the wyverns live with the trolls. They are treated with equal disdain by the Conclave, and to our shame . . . most dragons on Pyronesia treat wyverns with the same contempt."

"Why?"

"Because, although wyverns are similar to dragons, there are physiological differences. Ridiculous, I know, but they are seen as a lesser species because they are smaller and have two legs rather than four. But it's more than that. They are also considered far less intelligent."

"I see."

Tabariel's aura diminished slightly for a moment, like a bulb on the verge of burning out. "But what of the others? Where did the rest of my dragons go with your . . . army?"

"Semeriel suggested that we move to the Mourning Gorge," Danariel said.

Tabariel balked. "Semeriel suggested *that*?"

"Yes. I was unsure at first, but I suppose it is the safest place on the island from the Conclave."

"Safe from the Conclave, yes, but perhaps not safe from . . ."

"Not safe from what? What's in there?" Joe asked.

Both seraphim hovered for a moment, avoiding direct eye contact with each other.

"Come on. What's the big problem with the Mourning Gorge? What's inside?"

"It's haunted," said Tabariel abruptly.

"Haunted?"

"Yes. Haunted."

"I didn't think ghosts were real," said Joe. "But then I suppose a few months ago, I didn't think you were real either."

"They aren't real," said Danariel with an edge to her voice. "It's just a tale. That's all. Nobody has ever actually seen a ghost there."

"But they've been heard," said Tabariel.

"I don't think I want to hear more," said Joe. "I don't care what's there. If that's where everyone else is, that's where we should go."

"Of course," said Tabariel. "We should leave at once before the Conclave come for us again. I will check on our dragons, and then we must be on our way."

*T*HIRTY-SIX

Joe had never seen a ghost and felt more than a touch of nerves at the idea of hiding in a haunted cave, but for the second time in less than a day, Joe gulped down his fear and endured another dragon flight toward an uncertain end. Another sandy beach peeped out from behind a crumbling cliff edge before Tabariel's dragon banked toward a dense forest area. Joe wiped his eyes as the sudden rush of air forced tears from them, but he kept a solid focus on their destination. Through gaps in the vast cloak of leaves below, Joe could make out what had to be the Mourning Gorge: a great split in the ground stretching for miles on either side, deep enough to hide a fair-sized tower block, dark enough to make bats think twice.

"Is that what I think it is?" Joe asked.

Tabariel, who was sitting next to Danariel on the top of his dragon's head, swiveled round to look down at Joe.

"The Mourning Gorge, though some call it the Gate of Sorrows."

"Great," said Joe, "so I should expect to have plenty of fun when we get there."

"At least you'll be with friends again," said Danariel.

Warmth filled Joe when he thought of Mrs. Merrynether and the others waiting for them—but only for a moment. Anger gushed back with the memory of how the old lady had got him into this situation. Danariel too. He looked at the seraph, and when she turned to look at him, he knew she could feel his pain. He wanted to say something, wanted to tell her just how betrayed he felt, but there was such a depth of compassion in her eyes that his anger slid away like salt through a sieve.

"Lie flat. Cover your head," said Tabariel, and at once they were crashing through the leafy layers, branches cracking away from them as exotic birds scattered in panic. A jolt, followed by four nearby thuds told Joe all five dragons had landed.

They stood at the edge of a chasm, peering into unfathomable depths.

As it had so many times before, Joe's curiosity got the better of him. "I know I said I didn't want to know earlier, but . . . is it really haunted?"

Two answers came from both seraphim at the same time.

"Yes."

"No."

Joe pressed his lips together and squinted at each of them in turn. "Why do people *believe* it's haunted?"

Tabariel fluttered upward, then stared into the blackness. "Nobody has been there in many years and with good reason. The last time a seraph came here looking for alternative nesting grounds for her dragon, she went mad. She spoke of . . . of humanlike creatures that stood before her one moment and were gone the next. And their disembodied wailing was so disturbing that she fled in terror. After she told the Conclave, she never spoke again and slowly degenerated into a reclusive soul that eventually starved her dragon of life."

"A ghost story. That's all that was." Danariel sniffed.

"What do you think is in there, then?" Joe asked.

"I have my suspicions."

Joe waited, hoping for more.

Danariel glanced at Tabariel, then looked away. "It doesn't matter, but we'll find out soon enough, won't we?"

One of the other dragons swooped from the edge of the chasm, its leathery wings stretched out, riding the thermals, circling downward into the darkness as it looked for signs of the entrance. It breathed a jet of fire on the other side of the gorge not far below, momentarily lighting up a teardrop-shaped gouge that split the slate-colored rock face into an opening large enough to hold Merrynether Mansion. Several tracks had been etched by years of water erosion from the forest above, making natural but dangerous paths to the foreboding cavern. It looked as though the trees had wept for this great wound cut into the island.

"That's where we have to go," said Danariel, drifting from the dragon's head and pointing toward the cave.

"No wonder they wanted to go there. It must be really hard to get to by foot. Do you think the others are really in there?"

"Let's find out."

Tabariel nodded, remaining quiet, straight-faced, and seeming more than a little nervous.

They dropped to the teardrop cave, which was barely visible in the dim light of the gorge, and landed just within the gloomy mouth. Tabariel and Danariel, along with the other four seraphim, hovered inside, gingerly edging into the dark and lighting the mossy-green walls with their presence.

The five dragons fidgeted at the edge of the cavern, shifting their claws on the stony surface. Joe patted the side of Tabariel's dragon, trying to comfort the beast, but Tabariel shot an irritated look in his direction as if this was an unwelcome distraction.

As the six seraphim moved deeper inside, Joe stared at the smoothed walls at the edges of the cave, straining to see the details in the dim light. Something didn't look right, and it took him a few confused moments to work out what it was. Tiny trickles of water ran up the grooves in the wall, converging into bubbling streams, all the way up to the surface. Up!

There was very little time to puzzle over this. Something green, wet, and extremely excited shot out from the darkness and smothered Joe with the zeal of a dog whose master had just brought back a bone the size of a whale.

Joe dismounted the dragon, laughing as he tried to fend off the exuberant globble and wiping slime from his left ear.

"Get off!"

"Flarp, you incommodious mollusk!" came a squeaky voice. "Much as I am cognizant of the attraction of familiarity regained, I must insist that you forsake this course of action and withdraw unless you wish to become the first unwilling victim of a most unsightly hecatomb."

"Kiyoshi," cried Joe as Flarp rushed backward into the cave, still watching him.

The monkey-headed tortoise waddled into view, surrounded by a group of dragons and seraphim all eager to greet Joe and his companions with relief and delight. Cornelius was among them, swishing his barbed tail with pleasure. All the animals previously held in Mrs. Merrynether's vault, with the exception of Snappel, who was out looking for the trolls with Mrs. Merrynether, were inside this new refuge.

"And the rest of you, please follow me," said Kiyoshi.

Kiyoshi turned and led the way into the darkness.

The large shell bobbed along as the kappa continued inside, leading everyone down through a tall passage that eventually opened out into an even wider area. The walls were smooth and wet, and the ground no longer crunched under Joe's feet but squelched as though he were walking through a bog. The air, crisp and cool, was heavy with the strangest smell—an odor he recognized but couldn't quite place, like unwashed socks.

Shadows stretched and contracted, faded and sharpened, like phantoms fleeing from light as the seraphim flitted between the dragons. It was enough to unnerve the strongest of minds, and Joe could easily understand why this place had a spooky reputation, but it was not the smell or the shadows that bothered him so much as the feeling that he was being watched.

"Your return is as unexpected as it is gratifying, Joe," said Kiyoshi, revealing his teeth.

"Thank you, Kiyoshi. I could've used your talent with words today. Things didn't go well with the Conclave. They didn't really give me a chance to defend myself, and then they chased us all the way back to the Nesting Caverns before our dragons managed to fight them off."

"I see."

"Any news from Mrs. Merrynether? Danariel said she went looking for trolls with Snappel."

"Indeed she did, but contrary to your aspirations, no communication has been received aurally, visually, or telepathically."

"You could've just said no." Joe grinned.

"Omniloquence should never be discouraged."

"Whatever you say, Kiyoshi. Do you—?"

"Hush," said Tabariel, rushing one finger to his lips.

The other animals were quiet and tilted their heads from side to side, as if they were trying to hear something. A melancholy wail echoed somewhere distant, somewhere deeper under the earth.

"What was that?" whispered Joe.

"I warned you," said Tabariel. "This is called the Mourning Gorge, remember? It is haunted here."

The wail repeated twice more, then changed to great heaving sobs as other faraway mourners joined in. An eerie stillness descended in the cave, as if Joe and his friends were uninvited guests at a wake. The vault creatures huddled against the walls, the dragons lowered their heads as if scolded, and the seraphim stopped moving, their lights diminished.

Icy fear crawled through Joe's stomach, but as he shifted a foot, ready to creep to the nearest wall for cover, he noticed something even more disturbing. The boggy water had gone. Joe peered at his feet but could not see properly in the low light. His shoes no longer sloshed in the fetid water that was there when he first entered the cave. Instead, he heard only the soft crunch of tiny pebbles.

Something moved. Joe caught a glimpse of a black

shape deeper in the cave, vaguely human. With a terrible cry, it melted away. Others saw it too, and like an invisible wave, panic spread from creature to creature, starting closest to where Joe saw the apparition and ending at the dragons nearest the passage exit. All of them fled in fear, drowning the weeping with screams and stamping feet. All of them, that is, except Joe. With dawning realization, he knew what they had encountered.

"Come back," Joe shouted after them.

The light faded as the seraphim darted from the cave, and Joe wrestled with his fear as the darkness closed in.

"Come back," Joe repeated, a little weaker this time. The cold fear had not left him, and though he was not usually afraid of the dark, he had to battle with his own temptation to run in blind panic. The fact that he could not see anything at all helped him stand his ground but added to the creeping sensation that something monstrous was looming like a specter of death. He crouched to the floor, folding his arms around his knees.

"I know what you are. I know what you are. I mustn't be afraid," he whispered to himself.

A ball of silvery light returned to the cave, much slower than it had left. Danariel had come back, her expression a repeating slideshow of dread, shame, and resolve. Kiyoshi and Cornelius trotted apprehensively underneath, bathed in the seraph's ghost light. There was no sign of Flarp.

"Joe, where are you?" hissed Danariel.

"Over here."

"I'm so sorry. I didn't mean to leave you," she said. "I thought you'd be behind us. Just follow me, and we'll get out of here."

"I . . . I don't want to come just yet."

"Young man," Kiyoshi chided, "perhaps there is a fracture in my malleus, incus, or stapes, because I do not believe my auditory nerve interpreted your words correctly. Or perhaps you have a dopamine deficiency in your hypothalamus. Are you mad? Is that it?"

"I think I know what this place is," said Joe.

"It's a haunted cave," said Danariel. "Let's go." She turned to leave.

"I'm not going. And you're not either."

"Dementia! Neurosis! Lunacy!" Kiyoshi cried.

Cornelius roared and promptly flipped the kappa onto his back.

The frustrated creature wheeled his limbs, rocking in a circular motion like an overturned beetle, and the flap on top of his head quivered as Kiyoshi struggled to hold it shut. "Cornelius! Cornelius! You hairy ignoramus! Return me to my correct posture immediately. Cornelius!"

Joe laughed as he heaved the heavy kappa onto his feet. "I think Cornelius agrees with me."

The kappa blew a raspberry at the manticore and turned his back on Joe. "Very well. Do as you must."

Joe drew a deep breath, feeling a spike of courage after their moment of comic relief. "Right. Follow me, but be as quiet as you can. I don't want to frighten them off."

"Frighten off whom?" Danariel asked.

"They're squonks. I'm sure of it."

Joe edged toward the place where he'd seen the human shape melt away.

"Squonks?" She sighed. "I admit, I have suspected this is a home for squonks for some time, but I've never really done anything about it. None of us have. I think we've always kept thinking of this place as haunted because it's easier than finding a way to help them."

"Well, I can't ignore them. If it wasn't for one of them, I wouldn't have escaped from Redwar's vault."

They stopped and looked at the ground. Danariel's glow highlighted small holes in the rock.

"I think we frightened them," said Joe. "I saw water running up the side of the gorge, and I bet that was some of the squonks running away. They probably live in here and melt through these holes when they're threatened. I bet there's another big cave underneath us."

"You're probably right, Joe, but we have no way of reaching them."

Joe sighed as he stared at the holes. "Hello?" he called. "Don't be frightened. I just want to talk to you."

All he heard in reply was the same continual crying.

"I want to help you, like you helped me once."

Still they wept.

"Why are you all so unhappy?"

"Sisyphean nonsense," muttered Kiyoshi.

"They are reputed to be incredibly shy creatures." Danariel shrugged. "Nobody has ever managed to talk to one. That's another reason they've been ignored."

"Well, Redwar has several of them locked away that he got from the surrounding islands," Joe said. "He must have had contact with them somehow."

Then an idea struck him. "Hello down there. I think I know how I can help you. I don't know why you're always unhappy, but perhaps I can help cheer you up. I've seen some of your own in a building near where I live. They're being held prisoner by a man called Argoyle Redwar, but if you come and talk to me, I promise I'll try to set them free."

At first, there was still no response other than the wailing. Joe was about ready to admit defeat, but just as he had made up his mind to leave, he noticed a swelling of murky water around the holes by his feet.

Like a muddy snowman melting in reverse, the dirty water began to pile up in grimy globules, clumping together in squirming lumps. The three of them backed off as the squonk coagulated into a grotesquely animated mannequin. It had no face, no fingers, no feet, no eyes, but somehow it faced them as if it could see them. A series of tiny bubbles formed and popped in the center of the largest blob that Joe thought could have been its head, and a long, slow sound like sewage being sucked into a sinkhole gurgled from it. "Ugly me," it seemed to say as it melted from a standing position into a seated lump.

"No," said Joe, "I'm sure you're very . . . handsome . . . for a . . . a squonk."

Joe looked and nodded at Kiyoshi, Danariel, and Cornelius, his eyes widening to encourage them to say something.

Cornelius whumped his tail into the ground.

"Oh . . . oh, yes, very good-looking," said Danariel.

"Aesthetically, I appreciate that anthropomorphism of liquid-based—"

Joe kicked Kiyoshi's shell to shut him up.

The squonk gurgled again.

"Ugly me . . . Kind you."

Slowly, like chocolate porridge poured from a bowl, it dissolved into the rock and joined its brothers in the chamber below.

"Wait!" said Joe.

"Nice try," said Danariel. "I think we should go now."

"But why can't we get everyone back inside? We've made contact now, and we know they won't hurt us."

"Somehow I doubt the others will be—"

"What?"

"Something's not right outside."

"The Conclave! Have they come for us?"

"Flarp was going insane outside earlier, as though he'd seen lots of different things at once and didn't know which one to look at. At first we thought he was upset when the other globble went back to the tree, but I think it's more likely that he's seen the Conclave. It was only a matter of time, after all."

THIRTY-SEVEN

Another day on Pyronesia approached its end. The dazzling sun baked the mountains on the far side of the island as Tabariel's dragon flew Joe out of the gorge. He shielded his eyes from the fiery glare, then marveled at the spectacle above. A kaleidoscope turned in the sky, bat-like silhouettes wheeling against the deepening blue. With his usual talent, Joe counted them quickly and saw one hundred fifty-five giant lizards circling overhead. He took courage in the fact that more of the Pyronesian dragons had decided to defect, but were there enough to take on the Conclave's forces? Joe doubted it. Danariel had told him the Conclave had thousands of dragons under their command.

Tabariel landed them on the side of the gorge closest to the beach, at the edge of a dense woody area a mere mile from the cliff edge. In the hope that the gorge would provide some protection, not only by its reputation but by

the enormous chasm, the other dragons had already begun transporting Mrs. Merrynether's creatures there.
With very little time to prepare for the inevitable attack,
Danariel did her best to herd them behind trees and
inside burrows. It would make little difference against
dragons attacking from the air, but Tabariel said it
would at least protect them from a ground attack, as
they would not easily be able to cross the gorge.

All the while, Flarp zigzagged between the trees in
a panic-stricken state, seeing death approaching from
the horizon. Soon Joe saw it too: an army of dragons
visible only as an amorphous black swarm streaming
from the mountains.

"They are coming," said Danariel. "Flarp is confused, seeing many things at once. He wants to tell us
so much, but his thoughts are too muddled even for me
to decipher. I'm sure of one thing, though. There are
many more this time—enough to make sure we have
no chance of survival or escape."

"What will we do?" Joe asked as he jumped from
Tabariel's dragon onto the grass.

"*You* will stay here with the others," Tabariel said
firmly. "The rest of us will try to reason with the Conclave's army. We have no hope of victory against such a
force, so reason is our only ally now."

"But what if they won't listen?"

Tabariel rounded on Joe, frustration boiling into
anger. "Then we will all . . ."

Joe stared, wide-eyed.

Tabariel faltered, mellowing as he continued. "Then we will all have to accept our fate. None of this should ever have happened. You should not be here, the dragons should not be at war with each other, and the fate of the world's future should not hang on such a fragile thread.

"More than anything, I wanted a peaceful solution. I believed that by this time Merrynether would have amassed an army with which we had the power to negotiate, but that was not to be. Now those of us on Pyronesia who cast our responsibility onto her shoulders must pay the price for our cowardice."

Joe hardly knew what to say.

The seraph hovered closer, placing his miniscule hands against Joe's chest. "Others may have deceived you for what they believe to be a noble cause, and perhaps it is, but I will not lie to you now, Joseph Copper. Make peace with whatever deity you believe in, because today Gnauserous will not rest until she has her way. I have known her for centuries, and I have never seen her as determined as she is now."

Deep primordial fear squeezed Joe's throat. Though the seraph continued to talk, Joe could no longer hear his words. A frost had coated his thoughts, a numbing realization that he was going to die—and soon. He would never see his mother again. Never see Aunt Rose again. Never sit in Ringwood Forest, listening to the birds. There would be no more visiting Merrynether Mansion. No growing up . . .

His mind wandered to a conversation he once had with Danariel. He was worried about Cornelius, worried about death, and she taught him to see things differently. Perhaps she was preparing him for this very day. Oddly, it was a fond memory, and the warm reminiscence of happier days melted the frosty fear that threatened to paralyze him.

"You're smiling," said Tabariel, bemused.

"Yes," said Joe absently.

"Anyone who can face death with a smile will always be a friend of mine. Farewell, Joseph Copper. May we meet in another life. And farewell, Danariel. I wish you luck."

Danariel nodded solemnly and touched Tabariel's cheek.

The warrior seraph turned away, gripped the scales on his dragon's head, and raced into the sky. Joe watched them until they disappeared into the cloud of rebel dragons circling above. A few seconds later, they dispersed and formed a huge phalanx hovering like a massive umbrella. Pride rushed through Joe, but then he saw the swarm that approached. Even Joe could not count them.

"Do you think we have any chance at all?" Joe asked Danariel.

She stared at the two armies for a long time before

answering, "No."

Joe took a long breath. It was the answer he expected. What he didn't expect was a sudden thump on his back.

Cornelius had butted his great head against Joe, then stood at his left, looking up at him with those strange cat eyes. The manticore shook his scarlet mane, ruffled his wings, struck the grass with his tail, and bellowed a loud roar. It was not said in words, but Joe knew Cornelius had given his own resounding reply to the question: a wholehearted yes. Joe clenched his teeth, feeling yet another rush of pride.

"You're the bravest friend I've ever known," Joe said. "If you think we can win, then so do I."

"If I may be so bold as to make an observation?" said a squeaky voice to Joe's right. Kiyoshi had waddled over, his shell gleaming in the waning light.

"As long as we can all understand it." Joe grinned.

"You spoke of chance and probability, did you not? The odds of a victory with a ratio of one hundred fifty dragons against five thousand are approximately thirty-three to one. The odds of your being the one human child chosen to be on this island out of two billion others is two billion to one, yet here you stand. By my calculations, surviving this battle will be mere probabilistic trivia compared to the gargantuan leap you have already made. Victory is confidently at hand."

Joe eyed Kiyoshi, widening his grin. "I'll take your

word for it."

Together they watched the ominous cloud of dragons fly toward them, and Joe wondered how long it would take for the two armies to clash. Five minutes? Fifteen? An hour? How long before the claws of some dark lizard snatched him from the ground to squeeze the life from him? Again Joe tried to distance himself from grim thoughts of death and oblivion—not only his own but all his friends' as well. It would surely do no good to think about such things.

A white light flashed somewhere near the beach where the *Copper Celt* had crashed, shocking Joe from his thoughts. A shuddering boom followed a few seconds later, and he took a step back as the distant concussion thudded against his chest. "What was that?" he asked.

Danariel shook her head as another white flash lit up close to the first.

Again, the shock wave came.

"Look," said Danariel. She was pointing at the dragon cloud. A sizable portion of it had veered toward the explosions. Streaks of grey curved across the darkening sky, impacting Gnauserous's army, and a mass of dragons dropped like black rain.

"That must be Redwar's army," said Joe. "He didn't waste any time picking a fight, did he?"

"He's an idiot," said Danariel as more dragons fell from the sky, lit by another white blast. "He doesn't stand a chance against so many. All he'll succeed in doing is enraging Gnauserous. It's just what we wanted to avoid."

"I don't suppose Redwar knows how big the dragon army is," Joe said. "On the bright side, it's keeping them occupied. Gives us a chance to—"

"To what? We have no way to resist them."

Joe shrugged, unsure of an answer.

Danariel sounded uncharacteristically low, as if her last remnant of hope had been smashed, ground into dust, and blown into the sea. And Joe saw why. Even though much of the dragons' attention had been diverted to deal with Redwar, the remaining numbers still outmatched their own by at least five to one, and the battle on the beach was sure to fuel Gnauserous's campaign to go to war against the rest of the world. All was lost, and Joe watched the distant skirmish in despair.

Could he really be watching the beginning of the end? The end of everything? Surely not.

"We're not giving up," said Joe with a slight lift of his chin. "And you're not either. Got that? We've still got our own dragons and . . . and who knows? Tabariel might still be able to bring the rest of the Conclave round. And we've still got a little bit of time to sort out some defenses, haven't we? Surely we can think of *something*."

Danariel stared at him with a look of such love drowned by defeat.

"Your optimism may be of little service," said Kiyoshi. "Observe the trees on the opposite side of the gorge."

Joe peered across the chasm, squinting as the light continued to dwindle. Through the dark gaps between the trees, things shuffled. Tall blue-grey things with no necks, flat heads, and broad snotty noses. One by one, they lumbered into sight, lining up at the edge of the rift, gormless grins spread wide over their ugly faces as they hollered abuse at Joe and his companions. "Bluh! Bluh! Bluh!" they chanted.

Cornelius roared back, pacing the edge of the cliff.

"Trolls," said Danariel as if she'd been expecting them from the moment they arrived on the island. "Gnauserous must have sent them hours ago."

"Didn't Mrs. Merrynether go to see the trolls? I thought they'd be on our side."

"She went to see the trolls at Hallowbear Tor. These trolls are servants of . . . They are enslaved by the Conclave. Gnauserous only ever brings them together as an army on rare occasions, and they are considered expendable."

"Well, at least they can't get to us from over there."

"Don't underestimate them. They aren't as stupid as they look."

And as if to confirm Danariel's warning, two of the largest trolls faced each other. One pointed at the trees closest to the edge of the gorge.

"Bluh?"

"Bluh, bluh . . . bluh."

"Bluh."

The first troll loped to one of the tallest trees, the knuckles of one hand dragging along the grass, the other reaching inside the back of his loincloth to scratch his rear end. "Bluh!" it shouted to the other one and started headbutting the tree trunk repeatedly.

Other trolls, apparently excited by the idea of bashing something, shuffled over and joined in, occasionally headbutting a comrade by accident.

"Are they doing what I think they're doing?" Joe asked.

"We'd better think of something fast," said Danariel.

"Bluuuuuuh! Bluuuuuuuuuuuuuuh!" shouted one of the trolls.

Creaking and snapping, the brutalized base of the tree yielded to the pull of gravity. A torrent of melon-like fruit rained from the branches into the gorge as the tree swooned with a deafening crash. The trolls had made their bridge across the gorge.

Cornelius launched onto the trunk, roaring.

"Cornelius, no!" called Danariel. "There are too many!"

But the scarlet beast didn't listen. A spray of poisonous darts sent many of the trolls running for cover into the woods before the manticore had even reached the other side. With claws raking through the grass as he landed, Cornelius broke into a gallop, chasing the panicked trolls like a sheepdog rounding up sheep. But not all of them ran. Some made for the makeshift bridge.

"Belliferous obsequious buffoons," cried Kiyoshi, scuttling toward the tree. By the time he'd disappeared under the branches, four trolls had already stomped onto the trunk, crossing the gorge. Leaves rustled as the kappa pushed the tree away from the edge and it plummeted into the abyss.

Four cries of "Bluuuuuuuuuuh" echoed from the depths. Across the gorge, the remaining trolls flew into a rage, some thumping and stamping on the grass, some tossing the tree's fallen fruit across at Kiyoshi.

"Two can play at that game," said Joe. "Quickly, Kiyoshi, your kappa juice."

Kiyoshi bowed his head and opened the folds on top to reveal the mustard-colored liquid. Flinching as one of the melons exploded near his feet, Joe dipped his fingers into the gloop, stuck them into his mouth, and allowed the burning fluid to do its work.

"Joe, they're trying again," said Danariel, who fluttered around his head.

Joe stopped only to glance at the trolls as he ran to the tree nearest him, ramming his shoulder into the trunk with a fresh burst of kappa strength. It shuddered, dropping a few of its fruit, and Joe hugged it and began shaking it ferociously. The rewarding sound of many more ripe fruit pounding the grass followed, and Joe hurried to collect as many as he could fit into his arms before running to the edge of the gorge to drop them in a pile.

By that time four more trees had been felled and a stream of trolls had already begun lolloping across. Screams and shrieks told Joe that Mrs. Merrynether's animals had abandoned their hiding places in favor of a panicked stampede to no place in particular. For a flash, Joe felt the hysteria almost push him away, but this was no time to lose control.

"Danariel, try to keep the others calm. Kiyoshi, go for the closest tree."

Without question, Danariel darted toward the fleeing crowd, beaming brightly.

Kiyoshi scuttled away to grasp at the branches of the closest tree bridge.

Joe scooped up one of the melons and launched it like a yellow cannonball at the trolls on one of the other trees. At the same moment that the brutes tumbled off like ninepins, Kiyoshi tossed the other tree into the gorge. Two down, two to go, but three of the monsters had already reached their side, lurching forward with huge grimy hands outstretched. Three more trees were being felled as Kiyoshi trotted to another, but soon he was surrounded by a scrum of trolls.

"Kiyoshi," Joe yelled, but already his view was blocked by a grinning duo.

"Bluh!" they grunted as they lunged for him.

Still feeling the buzzing sensation of kappa juice in his blood, Joe knocked one of the trolls on his back but did not escape the grasp of another, then another and another. Three trolls had him in their grasps, and even with his kappa strength, Joe could not resist them.

"Cornelius," yelled Joe, knowing the manticore was still roaring and battling on the other side of the gorge, but hoping for a miracle.

A curtain of fire tore across the grass, close enough to singe the edges of Joe's hair. Among the flames, two enormous winged reptiles thundered into the ground, locked in vicious combat, sending spumes of soil and grass over Joe's head. The trolls fell over each other in desperation to put distance between them and the dueling dragons.

Joe was left lying in the dirt, his muscles burning and skull aching.

The two lizards struggled desperately, their back legs kicking at each other's undersides and their formidable jaws locked around each other's necks.

More dragons came. Those loyal to the Conclave either swooped at the creatures Danariel was trying so hard to conceal or attacked their traitorous kin who had dared to side against Gnauserous. Those opposed to the Conclave dived down to snatch trolls from the ground and throw them kicking and bellowing into the depths of the gorge. More trolls poured across the gorge to replace them, waving clubs and stamping feet, overjoyed at the chaos that had been unleashed around them.

Amid it all, Joe scrambled toward the trees, expecting some great foot or claw to crush him at any moment. There was no sign of Kiyoshi, Danariel, or Cornelius, and where had Flarp disappeared to? All Joe could see was a blur of fighting, and once again, he considered the fact that he might not live to see the next day.

THIRTY-EIGHT

It took more courage than Joe believed he had to throw himself back into the thick of the battle, but remembering he still had some of Kiyoshi's kappa juice flowing through his veins helped a great deal. He could do nothing about the dragons swooping and diving from above, but he decided it was time to send a few of those ugly trolls packing.

A few well-placed punches incapacitated two of the enemy, and Joe was relieved to see Cornelius rejoin the fray on his side of the gorge, competently dispatching several of the clumsy creatures with combination attacks of claws and poison barbs. Much faster than he expected, Joe realized the trolls were no longer a danger. He wouldn't have noticed if not for the flash and glare of the warring dragons above his head, but many of the trolls had fled, sensing the carnage in the sky would soon bring havoc to the ground. Other trolls were rolling in the grass, groaning in pain like giant babies, but strangest of all was the crowd that had gathered in a big circle, mesmerized by something at their feet. Stealing a quick glance above him to check for more falling lizards, Joe decided to risk an investigation.

Cornelius came alongside Joe, proud of his victory, and together they trod carefully to the silent crowd of trolls. Just a few feet away, from the center of the audience, a familiar voice creaked.

"My dear fellow, forgive my impertinence, but the proportional ratio of your zygomatic bone and maxilla in relation to your mandible suggest to me that you and the rest of these unfortunates are suffering from a condition known as mandibular prognathism. There is, of course, no cure for structural mutations of this nature, but one can be made significantly more comfortable if one endeavors to undergo a course of treatment by a qualified trolluscatherapist."

"Bluh!" One of them clapped his hands.

The others continued to stare in fascination.

"Indeed! And you," Kiyoshi said, pointing a suckered digit at another troll. "I watched your abominable technique as you propelled Citrullus lanatus at a forty-five-degree trajectory across the gorge. Greater precision can be achieved if one utilizes spin at a lower angle."

Danariel landed gently on Joe's shoulder.

"They're hanging on every word," whispered Joe.

"They see him as a child," she said.

"A child? Why?"

"Trolls are very different from humans. They're born with a sort of race memory that makes them very smart and knowledgeable while they're young. Unfortunately, they get more and more stupid as they get older until they're complete imbeciles. They're very impressionable when they reach full idiocy, which is why Gnauserous is able to control them so easily, but whenever someone like Kiyoshi comes along, they're fascinated—probably because he reminds them of their youth."

"So do you think they'll be on our side now?"

"Probably, yes."

Joe was about to break into the scrum and say something to Kiyoshi when a fireball exploded into a tree just behind them.

A wounded dragon slammed into the burning tree, moving in woozy delirium.

The trolls scattered, shocked out of their infatuation with Kiyoshi, but Joe stayed there, unsure where to run.

The whole area became a field of fire. Bushes, trees, and grass ignited as the dragons brought their feud to ground level. Streaks of fire tore through the night sky as though the skin of the world had been cut with hot knives.

The friendly dragons were greatly outnumbered, and Joe was reminded of the futility of their fight. The trolls had been dealt with for now, but the Conclave had too many dragons. Their resistance would be over in a matter of minutes, and he doubted Redwar would be able to stand against the bulk of the Conclave's forces for long. The enemy had as good as won, and with Mrs. Merrynether's slightly inconvenient "army" removed and Redwar dealt with, Gnauserous would take her ruthless campaign to the rest of the world.

Joe crouched and covered his head, squeezing his eyes shut, unable to prevent a scream of terror from bursting forth. Claws scuffled all around, and tongues of heat lapped on all sides. Joe felt too terrified to stay but too terrified to run. He screamed again, waiting for either an agonizing death by fire or a sudden death by a dragon's bite.

Joe felt the peculiar sensation of something sticky grasping the top of his head. Wet tendrils clung to his neck, dragging him to his feet and to safety behind a rocky outcrop. Flarp had returned. But at the same moment that Joe thanked the globble for saving his life, another peculiar thing happened. Water surged halfway up his leg, then splashed down again into the grass, pooling into a muddy quagmire a few feet from him.

Flarp rushed in circles as the pool grew like an unplugged bathtub draining in reverse.

Joe was just at the point of thinking he was losing his mind. Fire raged around him; dueling monsters shrieked in the night sky; multitudes of beasts, mainly trolls, staggered in confusion; and a murky lake seemed to be forming into a life of its own.

"What's going on?" Joe yelled at Flarp, knowing the frantic eyeball could not answer. There would have been no time for a response anyway. The pool of liquid exploded upward, looking remarkably like a giant hand, and fell like a flood against the burning trees, instantly putting out the flames. The water formed again, rising, bubbling, boiling, and twisting into a huge creature the size of a small office block made from a collection of mud balls. The enormous figure stomped on other burning trees, dowsing the flames but only bending the branches as though each stamp of its watery feet were carefully aimed waterfalls. With arms like geysers, it swatted the Conclave dragons from the sky.

"Squonks," shouted Joe in sudden elation as he realized what he was seeing. "They all dissolved and joined to get in on the fight. I can't believe it."

But the good news didn't stop there. A shout came from above and behind him.

"Joseph! Don't move!"

"Mrs. Merryncther! Is that you?" He whizzed round and looked up, trying to see where she had called from. He was amazed to find her on Snappel's back, clinging to her neck, as they tore through the night sky. Behind her was a small army of wyverns carrying trolls who brandished clubs, slings, tridents, and various other deadly weapons. Some of the wyverns landed in the mud, running in groups to attack the remaining hostile dragons like packs of scaly turkeys pecking at alarmed crocodiles. The remaining trolls on the other side of the gorge ran when their slightly smaller counterparts, screaming war cries, leapt from the backs of the wyverns.

Ten minutes later, the battle was over. Kiyoshi hopped in victory as his troll fan club formed a hand-holding ring around him and danced in jubilation. The last of the dragon rebellion, wounded but very much alive with pride, circled above, snorting fire rings as Snappel led the wyverns in weaving loops around their new allies.

The brave squonks, still so shy, had returned to their solitary cave. Joe, grateful beyond words at their involvement, sat in the sodden grass hardly believing they had survived.

It was a huge relief to see that all his friends were safe and sound. Cornelius strutted, roared, and leapt, occasionally looking at Joe and sharing something that he was convinced was a smile. Danariel had also returned, talking to Mrs. Merrynether with great animation while Flarp whizzed in a dizzy figure eight around them.

" . . . and then he socked two of them in the eye. You should have seen him, Veronica." Danariel pointed at Joe. "A true leader and a real hero—nobody braver."

Mrs. Merrynether looked at Joe with what could be nothing other than love, but Joe saw a terrible guilt mingled with the tears of happiness she wiped from her eyes. "A hero," she choked out.

"I wasn't really. I just ran about hitting things

without thinking, and I wouldn't have done it without Kiyoshi's kappa—"

Mrs. Merrynether ran over and hugged him so tightly he couldn't puff the last word out.

"I am so very, very sorry, Joseph." She wept.

"Why?"

"I have let so many people down, but I think deceiving you to bring you to this island is the worst thing I have ever done." She finally let him go. "I am so very glad you are still alive."

Joe looked down at her: a tiny woman, perhaps the oldest he'd ever seen, bursting with so much energy; it was a shame to see her waste it all on regret. And with such celebration happening around him, he could never hold any kind of grudge against her.

"I know why you did it." He shrugged. "It's okay."

"It isn't okay. But fate has been kinder to me than it ought to be. I don't deserve to have you forgive me, Joseph Copper." She touched his cheek.

They turned toward the raucous celebrations, but before Joe could join in, he heard the thrumming engine of a jeep pulling up on the hill behind them. He swung around. The jeep parked, and two figures got out and walked toward them, one tall and stooping, the other short and stout. The tall one spoke. It was a man, and Joe could hardly believe his eyes.

"Ronnie? Joe? I . . . It's me . . . Heinrich."

And with him stood Aunt Rose.

On the beach, weaving through the wreckage of the *Copper Celt* and heading toward the Nesting Caverns at high speed, another jeep bounced across the sand. Four people sat inside, dressed uncomfortably in camouflage uniforms. Not far behind them, the chatter of gunfire and the whoosh of rocket-propelled grenades rent the air as they fled the scene. Sweating in the driver's seat, Argoyle Redwar throttled the wheel as though it would fly away if he let go. Ms. Burrowdown sat in the passenger seat with an expression so sour she looked like a disgruntled pug sucking splinters through a straw. And being thrown around in the back like puppets in a bouncy castle, Kurt and Scott Duggan fired shots wildly at two dragons chasing them.

"My God, man! Are you planning to hit anything with that, Duggan, or do you just like the sound of gunfire?" Redwar shouted.

"Perhaps if you drove straight for two bloody minutes, I might be able to get a"—whump!—"clear sodding shot!"

"Mr. Redwar's doing best 'e can," said Burrowdown.

One of the dragons swooped in, hooking the side of the jeep with a talon, briefly lifting the vehicle's wheels from the sand. The jeep roared like a crazed animal as Redwar, screaming, leaned into the pedals. Kurt Duggan, who had been given a shotgun by his father, let off both barrels at the creature's claw. The recoil sent him sprawling back, but the dragon roared and released its prey, darting backwards into the sky, leaving the chase to its partner.

"See that, Dad? I got it! I got it!"

"Yeah, big deal. Your mum could've killed it at that range with her tongue."

"It's more than you did. You can't even—"

"Shut up and shoot," cried Redwar. "There's still another one after us."

The other dragon had soared overhead, then hovered ahead of them, taking advantage of their distraction to pause in readiness to unleash fiery death upon them.

Redwar's face bulged with fury. "Shoot! Shoot! Shoot! We're almost there, damn it."

The jeep juddered over a rock as Redwar tried to swerve around the reptilian obstacle. Kurt screamed. Scott aimed his semiautomatic rifle at the beast's mouth and pumped eight shots into it. The dragon turned its head, screeching in agony as a torrent of fiery sulphur arched through the air to their right, sizzling into the sea. They drove straight through the cloud belching from the water as the dragon staggered and fell dead into the sand to their left.

"I bik my kung!" Kurt wailed.

"Yes!" Scott raised his gun above his head, shaking it triumphantly.

"Don't congratulate yourself just yet, Duggan. That other one might come back, and they may send more after us," said Redwar, racing toward the cave entrance.

"I bik my kung!"

"Shut up, boy," said Kurt's dad, making his point with a slap to the head. A look of pure contempt curdled his features. "I brought you along to show you the ropes, teach you a few things about being a real man, so stop whining and reload like I showed you."

Redwar brought the jeep to a stop just inside the cavern, left the headlamps on to illuminate the cave, and got out. Ms. Burrowdown and the two Duggans followed.

"Just as I remember it," muttered Redwar. "But this time *I'm* the one in charge."

"Diamonds," said Scott Duggan, ogling the sparkling walls.

"Indeed, Duggan. Diamonds. Lots and lots of diamonds, and they're all m— ours."

Duggan pointed his rifle at Redwar. "No way. I didn't take this job for a nice little picnic on the beach, and you aren't paying me enough for what we've had to handle so far. I'll be taking this lot, not you."

"You moron. Exactly what do you think you're going to do? You need me to get off this island, and what do you think the rest of my men will do when they see me at gunpoint?"

Duggan chewed his bottom lip and squinted. He looked upward as though he might find the answer lurking somewhere on the top of his head where he couldn't quite see it.

Redwar turned to Ms. Burrowdown. "Didn't he used to be our head of security?"

"Yep."

"I thought I fired him after all that nonsense with the break-in."

"Yep."

"Then why was this meathead employed as my bodyguard?"

"Interviewed and hired by Mrs. Young last week. She didn't know Duggan was fired."

"Young? Who's Young?"

"New personnel manager."

"I thought Chatterly was the personnel manager."

"Fired."

"Blast! Fire Young as soon as we get back."

"Oi!" Duggan waggled his gun. "The diamonds?"

Redwar turned to point a chubby finger at Duggan but froze when a rumbling shook the cavern. Fire swirled above their heads, and they threw themselves to the ground, swatting their skin.

The other dragon had returned, and it must have used the mountain tunnels to find a back way into the cavern. From the entrance to a cloudy hole, a serpentine head the color of evergreen slid into view, its jaws stretched wide open.

Redwar scuttled backward like a fat crab in overalls, cutting his hands on shells with every move. The others cowered against the wall.

"Wait!" Redwar screamed. "Don't kill me. We can make a deal. We can end the hostilities between us today if you just listen to me. I am in command of the forces attacking you. Some of my men have been ordered to plant powerful bombs around your island. The war ship was just a diversion, I swear. If you spare me, I will tell you the location of every single bomb."

Great drops of sweat rolled over Redwar's skin as he waited for a response. The dragon had stopped its advance and appeared to be sizing him up.

Redwar blinked several times as if something had flown up his nose. "What?" he said. "Did you do that? I thought I imagined a name. Makariel, was that?"

A seraph popped into view before Redwar's eyes. "Tell me now. No deals," said the seraph.

"My men will cause such destruction on this island it will be nothing but ashes if you choose to ignore me."

"But you will die."

"And so will you." Redwar stood now, jutting his chin, brushing powdered shell from his army clothes. The seraph held him with a cold gaze, apparently thinking it over, and the dragon leaned its head back, puffing slow streams of smoke from its nostrils.

"I have another proposition for you," the seraph said.

A distant, ear-splitting explosion boomed outside, causing a powerful tremor, and an orange glow lit the cave entrance.

"A demonstration of your intentions?" The seraph's voice was low and menacing. "If any damage has been done to the Tree of Sanctuary, I will paint the walls of this cavern with what remains of your broken body."

The dragon's head snaked forward, the jaws opening even wider.

"No, no," panted Redwar. "I have no idea what that was, I swear. My men would not dare to detonate any of the bombs without my permission."

Scott Duggan had edged his way to the entrance. "Remember that big war ship of yours?"

Redwar held his breath as Duggan spoke again.

"Well, bits of it are flying through the air. I don't think there's much of it left."

THIRTY-NINE

"Noah's beard! What in the world was that?"

Mrs. Merrynether squinted through her spectacles at the cloud mushrooming a few miles from shore. Everyone had been so overcome by Heinrich's reappearance that the massive explosion was even more of a shock.

"That'd be our brave Heiny," said Aunt Rose. She grabbed his hand and squeezed it against her chest as though it were a cuddly toy, then beamed at Joe. "And Joe! My word, I'm so relieved to see you're still in one piece, dear. Quite a place, this island, isn't it?"

Joe rushed over to give her a hug. "I'm so glad you're safe."

Mrs. Merrynether shot Joe a glance of puzzlement before placing her hands on her hips and questioning Heinrich. "You have a lot to explain, Heinrich Krieger, and you'd better start now before I—"

"Before you what?" Aunt Rose stepped forward, her

hands also on her hips, making her look like a cannon-ball with handles. "If it wasn't for Heiny, you'd all—"

"Let me tell you a few things about *Heiny* here." Mrs. Merrynether pointed a finger as though it were a magnum.

"Ladies, please! Rose, let me explain everything to Ronnie. It is very important. And, Ronnie, hear me out. I beg you."

Deep breaths were drawn all round before Mrs. Merrynether nodded stiffly.

"Thank you, Ronnie. The explosion you saw was Argoyle Redwar's war ship. With the help of Joe's aunt, I blew it up."

"You blew it up?" said Joe. "But we thought you were working for Redwar."

"That is where you are completely mistaken. Argoyle Redwar is not who any of us thinks he is. On the day you accused me of helping Mr. Redwar, I went mad with despair. I was very hurt, and I could not understand why you would tell such lies about me."

"But they weren't lies. I saw—"

"Please let me finish. I know now that you did not lie, but I did not lie either. We were all deceived. I wrote my letters to a man named James Merson."

"James Merson?" said Mrs. Merrynether, aghast. "But we agreed he should never be contacted."

"Wait," said Joe. "Wasn't James Merson the boy whose parents died on this island all those years ago?"

"Yes," said Heinrich. "James Merson and Argoyle Redwar are the same man, Joe."

"What?" cried Mrs. Merrynether and Joe together.

"Yes, it was he who contacted me many years ago by letter, claiming he had been abandoned by his foster parents and needed help. I decided to help him by writing back and sending him one of our diamonds. We kept in contact for years and years. Each time, he had a new reason for needing more money—his new foster mother was sick and needed an operation or he wanted to buy a new house—and I . . . I kept sending him more diamonds. I had no idea he was building a business empire with it. I grew more and more guilty about not telling you, but I thought you would be angry and send me away."

"Oh, Heinrich, I would never have sent you away, but you're quite right: I would've been very angry with you. I *am* very angry with you."

"How did you find out about him?" Joe asked.

"That night when I stormed out from the mansion, I went to find James Merson at the address I was posting the letters to. I wanted to prove my innocence, but obviously I did not find him. Instead, I found a private school run by a man named Toby Burrowdown. It was difficult to get information from them, but eventually I found out that they were forwarding my letters to Argoyle Redwar at Redwar Industries. It was then that I suspected they were the same man and he had assumed an alias."

"But why would he do that?" Mrs. Merrynether asked.

"I found that out when I confronted him."

"You went to see him?"

"Yes. He was surprised to see me, and I think he took a certain amount of delight in telling me he was going to destroy everything I held dear. He assumed a new name so that we would not suspect who he was when he set up his head office in Upton Puddle. He wanted to get closer to us so that he could find out the location of Pyronesia by any means necessary. He knew we would never tell him, especially if we knew who he really was.

"He is a very bitter man, Ronnie. He told me it was true that his foster parents abandoned him. They could no longer bear to hear his stories about the dragons and the island, so they sent him to a boarding school to be cared for. They thought all he needed was to be disciplined. Eventually he was released, and that's when he sought me out. When he had a big enough business empire and enough money from me, he funded expeditions to find the island, but the seraphim kept it hidden from his sight, as they do to all who come close to finding them. All Redwar could find were some of the smaller islands close to Pyronesia, which is where he found some of the rare species he keeps locked in his vault."

"And now he wants to get revenge on the dragons that killed his parents," said Mrs. Merrynether.

"And to become even richer," said Heinrich. "He

knows this is where the diamonds come from, and he wants to take the island by force. He managed to bribe a lot of people within the government and the military to get what he needed. Many of the men on those boats are mercenaries."

"The idiot! He has no idea what he's started by coming here. But how did you get to the island with him?"

"It was not hard to convince him I was on his side. I found it uncomfortable to lie to him, but I told him I wanted revenge for the way the dragons had disfigured me and would gladly help him. It was then that he told me he'd found out the exact location of Pyronesia, and I asked to come along. I did not realize he tricked you into going so that he could follow, but I came in one of the boats and joined the crew, hoping to stop him and find you."

"That was when he found me," said Aunt Rose. "He learned they had me as a prisoner on board. He sneaked me out, bless him." She gave Heinrich a warm smile, and he blushed. "After that, we pinched some of their explosives and rigged them up with a timer when all the fighting started. Then we escaped, saw there were more dragons fighting on the other side of the island, and guessed you might be involved. Looks like we were right."

"Remarkable," said Mrs. Merrynether, twinkles lighting her eyes.

"Heinrich's my hero," said Aunt Rose. "There's never been a man to match him since my Fred was alive, God rest his soul. I'm not letting this one get away."

Heinrich smiled sheepishly at Mrs. Merrynether and shrugged.

"I'm thrilled for you both," said Mrs. Merrynether, grinning.

Joe smiled as Danariel fluttered over, glowing brightly and planting herself across Heinrich's face. An admiring crowd surrounded Heinrich.

"I hate to interrupt your reunion, but our troubles have only just begun," came an exhausted voice from behind them. Tabariel collapsed at their feet, his glow distinctly subdued as he lay in the grass.

"Tabariel, are you all right?" said Joe, stooping to pick up the seraph, who felt as cold as a garden frog.

"Kalladrad is dead," Tabariel said quietly.

Like a flying brick, it hit Joe that Kalladrad must be the name of Tabariel's dragon, the noble beast Joe had come to know over the last few days.

"I'm . . . so sorry," Joe said. "Is there anything I can do?"

"Not for me, no. I will recover from the shock in a little while, but no seraph is quite the same when his dragon is killed. We fade away in time."

"Are you sure there's nothing we can do?"

"Never mind me. You must all prepare yourselves. Tonight's battle was a mere scuffle compared with what is to come. Gnauserous is regrouping her forces. Redwar's army is no longer attacking. He has joined her."

"What?" said Mrs. Merrynether. "The Conclave hate humans. Why would Gnauserous side with him?"

"I don't know, but whatever the reason is, Gnauserous will put up with Redwar only as long as she has to. She probably considers it much easier to take on one group than two at a time. Once she has finished us off, she will deal with Redwar. Then she will turn her attention to the rest of the world."

"How long do we have?" Joe asked.

"They will most likely attack at dawn. I doubt she considers us much of a threat, but Gnauserous is not foolhardy. She will consider her strategy carefully."

"So we have a few hours to prepare," said Heinrich.

"Prepare?" said Mrs. Merrynether. "Prepare what? That last fight took all we had. If Gnauserous knew how few of us are left, I doubt she would bother to wait at all."

"Mrs. Merrynether is accurate in her assessment," said Kiyoshi. "We have only nineteen dragons, sixty-three wyverns, one hundred twenty trolls, and a hand-ful of us left. The squonks may help, but that cannot be guaranteed. The enemy still commands thousands of dragons, several hundred trolls, and now they also have a small army of heavily armed human mercenaries."

"So what do we do? How do we stop them?" Joe asked.

"Should we run? Try and warn the governments before they attack?" Heinrich suggested.

"It would take too long to convince the outside

world," said Mrs. Merrynether. "And soon their numbers will be even greater when a new nest of dragons hatch later this year. Somehow we have to find a way to end all of this on the island, but I have no idea how."

Joe looked at Danariel, a grave solution becoming painfully obvious to him, and he decided to put a voice to it before he was able to change his mind. "We have to kill Gnauserous. She's the one most determined to go to war, so without her, we might be able to change the Conclave's mind."

Danariel stared at Joe, her angelic face expressing both grief and resignation. Silence fell, so strong, so tangible, Joe thought it would crush the noise of the celebrations behind them. With the death of her kin-tie, Joe had just offered Danariel a slow and lingering death.

"You'll need me to flush her out," she said eventually, casually. "She may not come at all, but if she does, she won't be easy to find among so many dragons. I can help to pinpoint her, but it's all very risky. Even if we succeed, the Conclave might decide her death should be avenged."

"But it's a better chance than no chance, right?"

The silence fell again, but this time Aunt Rose broke it. "I agree with Joe."

Everyone looked at Mrs. Merrynether.

With terrible regret in her eyes, she was looking at Danariel. "Yes. It would seem to be our only choice. Heinrich? Do you agree?"

Heinrich gazed at his feet for the longest time before uttering the quietest of agreements.

"Then we're all agreed," said Mrs. Merrynether, lifting her head slightly. "Gnauserous is our target."

"It's the best chance we have," Danariel said with a philosophical smile.

As the hour ended, the celebrations died away, replaced by growing solemnity as the dwindling army made preparations for the next battle. Heinrich had brought some provisions from the boat: first aid kits, grenades, land mines, explosives, but most important of all, two crates of cucumbers, which were given to Kiyoshi to replenish his cranial fluid.

The kappa set to work gobbling up as many as he could until he was fit to burst; then he forced more down until his tired monkey face had turned almost the same color as his amphibious limbs. While he ate, Heinrich siphoned kappa juice from Kiyoshi's cranial vent and sealed the potent liquid in tiny plastic bottles ready to feed those who would have to fight.

The trolls buried land mines at regular intervals along the edge of the gorge. Grenades were stacked in piles behind the cover of rocks, and Mrs. Merrynether used the first aid kits to patch up the wounded dragons and trolls. The night passed with grim wordlessness as they all went about their business, counting the cost of their fallen comrades as they buried the dead, hoping by some miracle they might somehow survive what was expected to be another massacre.

As dawn's first light glistened gold across the mountain-tops, Joe patted down the dirt around the last of his trip wires that would detonate a pack of explosives. He looked at the others, who appeared to feel the same as he did. All he wanted to do was curl up somewhere in a comfy bed and fall fast asleep for a year, but he knew that couldn't happen, especially not today. An old phrase came to mind that seemed appropriate—"I'll sleep when I'm dead."

He smiled ruefully, knowing he was probably not alone in his thoughts, and then he saw Danariel, quiet and mournful as she sat cross-legged at the base of a burnt tree. The look on her face told him she was grieving over all the seraphim who had suffered the loss of their dragons and were now wilting before her in the hollow of the gnarly tree trunk. Joe imagined them bunched together, mourning over the loss of their dragons and beginning their slow journey toward death. Tabariel would be among them now, coming to terms with his own future, and he could see that Danariel was thinking she was already part of that heartbroken group.

Joe sat next to her.

She looked at him with a bright but unconvincing smile. "Hello, Joe. Everything ready?"

"I suppose so. There's not much else we can do."

"No, I don't suppose there is."

Joe stayed quiet, staring at her tiny face and admiring the perfectly formed features. The subtle glow pulsing across her skin reminded Joe of the calming patterns of a lava lamp he used to own. It was hard to believe a creature like this could ever die.

"How long will you have . . . if we manage to . . . you know, stop Gnauserous."

She sighed, looking again at the seraphim Joe could not see. "Difficult to say. Some seraphim can carry on for scores of years before they pass away, but most die sooner."

"I wish there was another way."

"There isn't," she said quickly. "Besides, everyone here must face death today. I'm no worse off than anyone else, and it may be that none of us survive this day."

"Well, we'll soon find out," said Mrs. Merrynether, who walked toward them. "Flarp has seen them coming."

FORTY

Flarp's warning of the Conclave's approach didn't prepare Joe for the sight over the mountains. As if to herald their coming, the rising sun seared the landscape in a blaze of deep yellow as it peeked over the snowy tips. In the sudden glare, a dark writhing mass spread in the sky like a splash of black ink in a pail of water. Then it shifted. Thousands of tiny dots, each one a powerful dragon, converged into the shape of one almighty dragon with wings outstretched and neck pulled back like a cobra about to strike. It was a deliberate show—an intimidating vision that sent a wave of ice from Joe's head to his feet.

"How long before they reach us?" Joe gulped.

"Twenty, maybe twenty-five minutes," said Mrs. Merrynether grimly, "but they won't attack yet. The ground forces will strike first. They'll be sent in to soften us up, and then when that's over with, and if we're still alive, they'll turn this whole area into an inferno."

All Joe could do was nod. He couldn't take his eyes from the leviathan hovering in the distance.

"And there they are," said Danariel, "right on schedule."

On the other side of the gorge, two armies marched toward them, one from the east and the other from the west. Just as before, but in far greater number this time, an army of trolls lumbered between the trees on the eastern side. Some were naked apart from tiny loin-cloths; others were clad in leather armor festooned with chains and wore helmets decorated with crooked spikes. A smaller army came from the western side that looked much more familiar: men. A profound sadness came over Joe as he watched them surge forward, so eager to bring death and destruction, so proud of the weapons they carried. For a fleeting second, he could almost understand the Conclave's desire to destroy humanity.

"Get to cover," yelled Heinrich.

"And keep our dragons and wyverns out of the way for now," shouted Mrs. Merrynether. "We'll need them if those dragons decide to join in."

Rocket-propelled grenades screamed across the gorge. They were far louder than Joe had expected, but in a way he was glad of the noise. It drowned out the sound of his own fearful cry as he ran. All but their own brave trolls headed for deeper cover within the woods. In less than a minute, they were safely hiding behind rocky coverings and ledges they had identified earlier, and Joe peeped over the top of his rock, watching through showers of dirt the unfolding battle.

Half of the trolls, each having drunk a measure of Kiyoshi's kappa juice, leapt across the length of the gorge as if the chasm was a crack in a pavement. Two were knocked down into the gorge by rockets, but the rest made a rush for the army. Cheering erupted when some of the trolls managed to sweep aside five, then ten, then twenty of the mercenaries, but the celebration quickly stopped as they were gunned down by a line of camouflaged soldiers.

The rockets stopped, but Joe soon realized the barrage was a diversion so that bridges could be quickly placed across the gorge without any resistance. The larger trolls, hungry for war, stampeded like crazed bulls across to Joe's side. The ugly behemoths rushed forward unchecked, but there was no sense in running now. Joe had expected this. With a sudden spike of adrenaline, he gulped back a bottle of the kappa juice.

Two heavy explosions thundered out as a trip wire sent a bunch of the blue-skinned thugs sprawling. Overhead, Joe saw several grenades fly at more of them. A series of blasts echoed across the gorge as Joe waited for the flood of strength to take over his body; then he ran out to meet the rest of them, screaming his own defiance as he swung a troll's club around his head.

Heinrich ran alongside him, screaming too, and

Cornelius launched into the air, firing barbs.

One of the trolls actually turned and ran when he saw the trio come at him, but two others didn't, and Joe had to knock them aside.

A full forty minutes of chaos dominated that small part of the island as the battle took its course. There seemed to be no opportunity to locate Gnauserous among the dragons. All their time was taken up in staying alive. With casualties mounting on both sides, the fighting became more and more desperate.

Kiyoshi lay exhausted, almost unconscious and hidden inside an old tree trunk, unable to produce any more juice. Mrs. Merrynether and Aunt Rose did their best to get the wounded trolls to safety to be treated, but even Danariel with her soothing tones could offer no words of comfort for the failing troops. Joe could almost sense the despair. Even if they somehow survived the assault, this was just the first and easiest part of the Conclave's strategy. The real army was above them, a host of dragons brooding like angels of death.

"We need Snappel and the wyverns," cried Joe, trembling with the exertion of wrestling a large troll to its knees and knocking it out. He was on his third bottle of kappa juice now, and the burning in his veins had become almost unbearable.

"We have to hold out," said Mrs. Merrynether. "No!"

"Yes! We *can't* hold out any longer without help. We need the wyverns."

Mrs. Merrynether shook her head and looked at the gorge.

The enemy trolls had beaten back most of their own, the trip mines were gone, and now the human army jogged across, searching out points of cover.

Joe saw the dejection in Mrs. Merrynether's eyes.

"We're beaten," she said. "Beaten."

"It isn't over till the fat lady sings," said Aunt Rose, tightening a bandage on the knee of a wounded imp. "And I haven't sung a single note yet."

Joe grinned, more out of pride than pleasure, but before he could add his own comment, a roar of water caused everyone to duck. A majestic wall of muddy liquid poured upwards from the gorge, twisting like the cords of a colossal water rope. It searched the air; then individual watery fingers lanced downwards on top of individual trolls, sweeping them away in a violent flood to the gorge.

"Squonks! They're back!" Joe whooped and clapped.

Mrs. Merrynether's face flinched into a smile.

At the same moment, another flood erupted from the depths of the gorge, but this one was very different. Joe thought some gargantuan machine had sprayed a stream of slime up onto the island, but soon he realized he had seen an invasion of individual gooey-green eyeballs shooting upward like mushy peas from a fire hose, jostling with each other in rampant excitement.

As the panicking enemy fled in confusion, the globbles,

led by Flarp, picked out their targets and attacked.

"Clever little fellow," said Mrs. Merrynether. "So that's where he's been disappearing to. He started his own little rebellion and got all the globbles from the Tree of Sanctuary to come with him. They must have been hiding in the caves with the squonks."

"Go, Flarp," yelled Joe, punching the air.

The remaining trolls on his side of the gorge picked themselves up, renewed by the unexpected reinforcements, and headed back to the fight. Joe felt a strong urge to join in, but there was no more kappa juice and he wouldn't stand a chance without it.

Pandemonium continued as soldiers ran around with green cyclops heads, flapping their arms as the globbles sucked at their shoulders, driving the confused men in circles around each other. Some of the men had fainted, and their feet were dragged through the grass. Others had just about managed to escape and were hollering at each other to wipe the gunk from their skin and get to cover. Trolls waded in, soldiers ran for their guns, and Flarp was mowed down by a spray of bullets.

"No," screamed Joe.

The green blob flopped into the dirt, trembling, full of tiny metal lumps.

Heinrich rushed over, braving the battlefield, and scooped up the eyeball. He sprinted back and handed the wounded hero to Mrs. Merrynether.

Joe wanted to look, wanted to do something to

help, but there was no time: the dragons, seeing that the battle had swayed away from their advantage, chose that moment to launch their own devastating attack.

A dozen dragons broke from the cloud and cork-screwed down to the fighting mobs, bellowing fire without caring if their own side was scorched. Trees ignited instantly, and the great mass of squonks rose to protect the woods, trying to dowse the flames, but more dragons answered with an inferno that sent the watery creatures tumbling away. The mucky water splashed against the grass and separated into individual squonks that gushed to the safety of the gorge, defeated.

Even the globbles could not hold their ground for long. One by one, the soldiers managed to rip the green blobs from their heads and rattle off gunfire to send them flying away.

Joe slumped against one of the few trees that had not been turned to charcoal.

Cornelius limped toward them, one of his magnificent wings bent awkwardly.

The land around them was strewn with the bod-ies of trolls, soldiers, and various other beasts Joe could not recognize. Not even the greenery had escaped. The trees looked like old witches' hands with twisted black fingers, smoking with the aftermath of a firestorm.

It was just as Mrs. Merrynether had said. The ground forces had done their job, and now the drag-ons would sweep down at their leisure, picking off the last survivors like vultures swooping in to tear at an old carcass.

Even as Snappel led the wyverns in to take on the enemy, Joe could no longer muster the optimism he'd felt earlier. A few of their own dragons and perhaps a hundred wyverns taking on thousands? It was hopeless. They didn't even see Gnauserous among the myriad of winged lizards, let alone strike her down. Danariel knew she was there but could not pinpoint her.

They all looked at each other in silence, their future catching up with them. Mrs. Veronica Merrynether, Heinrich Krieger, Rose Ashworth, Kiyoshi, Danariel, Cornelius, and Joseph Copper—RIP. Flarp might already be dead; Joe couldn't tell, but it certainly looked that way. The helpless eyeball lay on a dirty mat like a punctured green basketball, staring upwards, not moving.

A cry came from the edge of the gorge.

"We surrender." It was a familiar voice that caused them all to look round. Seven figures ran toward them, dodging blasts of fire. One of them had tied a grubby white handkerchief to a stick, waving it furiously.

"Is that who I think it is?" asked Mrs. Merrynether.

"Yes," said Heinrich.

Joe was unable to read what Heinrich was feeling by that short answer, but his face had darkened.

"Argoyle Redwar," said Joe.

And with the sweating fat man came Ms. Burrowdown, Scott and Kurt Duggan, and three other soldiers struggling with bulging sacks containing who-knew-what.

"You've got a nerve," said Mrs. Merrynether.

"My dear woman," puffed Redwar as he stopped in front of them, hands on knees. "There really is little to be gained by pointing fingers. We are all facing the same threat now."

"Struck up a bargain with the Conclave, did you?" she said. "All went terribly wrong, did it?"

"I suggest we find a way off this island—and quickly," said Redwar.

"We're not going anywhere," said Joe. "Not until we've found a way to stop the Conclave coming after the rest of the world."

"Are you mental?" said Kurt Duggan, the words bursting from slimy lips, the green grime a sure sign he'd been violated by a globble only minutes before. "We're all going to die if we stay here."

"Shut up, boy." Scott Duggan slapped him.

"The boy's right," said Redwar. "We have to leave."

A line of fire whooshed behind them as if to underline Redwar's statement.

"Why have you come to us?" said Heinrich flatly. "Surely you have your own transport."

"All gone. Blown up," muttered Burrowdown.

Heinrich smiled mirthlessly.

"Unfortunately, that's true," said Redwar. "We don't have a single ship we can use, so we need to use your transport, whatever and wherever that is."

"We crashed," said Mrs. Merrynether smugly. "You're stuck here just like we are. And you'll die just like we will."

A horrified silence fell among Redwar's group.

Another burst of fire startled them as dragons landed nearby, breathing a river of flames above their heads to flush them out from their rocky cover.

Snappel and several more wyverns tried to come to the rescue, and Cornelius limped forward, but none of them were a match against five hulking dragons. One of the monsters tore chunks of rock away, exposing the terrified group, and the others formed a circle around them.

This was the end. Joe felt the world around him slip into a dreamy haze as fire rippled the air and curious odors filled his nose—an odd tangy smell like sewage and a sharp but subtle whiff of alcohol. This had to be how the final moments of delirium and hallucination warped the brain of someone who was about to die. Joe even thought he heard a faraway melody of drumbeats and pipes, something like an Irish jig. An angry voice with a harsh accent blasted like a demolition ball through the walls of his confusion and despair.

"May ya wings torn inta snot rags and arl da devils of hell blow deir filty noses on ya! Get 'em, lads!"

Like a storm of muddy rain, a waterfall of feces and other unpleasant items shot like hot meteors from above.

Joe covered his head but could just about see the dragons squirming as the hideous refuse stung their hides and clung to their wings. Redwar fled the scene with Burrowdown and the others right behind him. Joe thought about trying to stop them but reconsidered, believing there to be little point. When the downpour finished, Joe looked up through steaming clouds of stink. He had never been so elated in his life.

A vast army flew over. Hundreds and hundreds of great ships just like the *Copper Celt* sailed to meet the dragons hovering over the island, guns blazing. Lowest to the ground, making for a landing, was one of the largest. The enormous boat plowed through a line of trees and churned up the dirt as it slowed to a halt a little way from them. Lilly stood at the helm, a fancy megaphone held to his tiny lips.

"Is dat you down there, Joe boy? Where's dis brewery the beasties are tryin' ta deproive us of?"

"Fell for it, didn't you, Lilly?" shouted Joe. "But if you and the others take care of these dragons for us, we'll build the biggest brewery you've ever seen in your life."

"Ya mean ya got no booze? I get arl me mates tagedder, and dere's not one drop of amber nectar? Roight! Now oi'm *really* angry."

Above their heads, a war of fantastic proportions raged. Dragons soared and wheeled while the sky boats fired dung, sewage, rotten food, compost, and all manner of smelly horror from cannons. Cluricauns parachuted to the island, chuckling and firing catapults at trolls as they drifted to the ground.

"Snappel," said Danariel quickly. "The dragons have been caught off guard, and I know where Gnauserous is. Take me with you, and bring every wyvern you can find. We're going to rid the world of its greatest enemy."

Joe watched as Snappel led a swarm of the feisty lizards with Danariel into the heart of the battle.

"All we can do now is wait and hope," said Mrs. Merrynether.

"At least we *have* hope now," said Joe.

"We have more than hope," said Heinrich, smiling at Lilly, who had left his boat to approach them. "We have a whole army of cluricauns at our side."

"We only came for da party" said Lilly, gritting his teeth. "Tort dere'd be some free booze if we saved the day."

Kiyoshi stirred at the sound of Lilly's voice. "There are many more admirable pursuits than your never-ending endeavors to attain a state of crapulence through alcoholic poisoning."

"Did monkey face just swear at me, den?"

"I merely stated that—"

"And oi'm merely gonna—"

"Stop it!" said Joe, holding back a laugh.

Kiyoshi closed his eyes, settling into a doze, the words "coprophagous midget" on his breath as he crossed his arms under his chin.

"There must be thousands of you," said Joe. "Where did you all come from?"

"It doesn't take long for us ta build up an army

if we need ta, especially when beer's at stake. Oi just spread da word."

"Look," said Heinrich, pointing. "I think something is happening."

Above them the great swarm of dragons had dispersed, exploded apart by fire. From the core of the hot cloud, Gnauserous burst forth, her great body weaving in a cyclone of smoke. She snatched, clawed, and buffeted a series of dragons that came at her from every direction. She swiped, smashed, and ripped at wyverns that attacked from above. One of the cluricauns' sky boats splintered into fragments as Gnauserous thrust her horned head into it. Through it all, Danariel shone like a tiny supernova, clinging to her former kin-tie's head, using whatever powers she had to throw the great dragon's mind into confusion.

The plan appeared to be working. Despite her ferocity, the queen could not sustain her defense. As Snappel closed in to attack, more dragons and wyverns swarmed in until a final, piercing death cry echoed across the island.

The Queen of Pyronesia had fallen.

A troll in the *B*attle of *P*yronesia

FORTY-ONE

"Be ready," said Mrs. Merrynether. "We don't know how the rest of the dragons will react."

A stream of cautious dragons approached their side of the gorge as the battle above petered out. The fleet of cluricaun boats dispersed, either landing somewhere on the island or choosing to head back to England.

Joe ached in places he hadn't even realized were there. Until this moment, a combination of adrenaline, kappa juice, and the consistent expectancy of death had kept his mind off how he felt physically, but now his body was screaming.

The approaching clutch of dragons, two of which he recognized from his audience with the Conclave, seemed unthreatening. They moved slowly, almost respectfully, between the charcoaled trees toward Joe's small group. It was still not a good time to relax, though. Joe had no idea what their intentions were.

Danariel drifted beside Joe. He tried to ignore the fact that her glow had diminished since Gnauserous's fall.

"Hold your ground, Joe. They want to talk."

She told Joe the names of the seraphim that flew with each dragon, and they appeared before Joe in their various orbs of color.

The seraph belonging to the largest and oldest of the dragons approached. A turquoise tint surrounded the seraph as he hovered a few feet away from Joe's face. "Many have died," he said.

A lump of remorse caught in Joe's throat, but he tried to keep his voice even. "I know."

"Your kind has always brought destruction, but never before has it ended so terribly. Our queen fell today."

"Your queen wanted to kill all of us. We only wanted to protect ourselves."

"And Gnauserous only wanted to protect Pyronesia. She knew every inclination of the human heart dwells upon evil all the time. It was only a matter of time before that evil touched this island. Our queen was merciful once, but Argoyle Redwar's return forced her to act.

"Even as we speak, Redwar is making his escape from Pyronesia, taking with him a spoil of diamonds from our Nesting Caverns. All he wanted was wealth, and he didn't care about who he would kill to get it."

"No," said another seraph. "His intentions were far worse. He planned to kill every dragon on this island.

We had to remove explosive boxes placed at the Tree of Sanctuary."

"So you see," said the first seraph. "Mankind is evil and should be removed. Gnauserous was right."

"No, she was wrong," Joe said. "Not everyone is evil. Some people are good, and some are just . . . bad. I don't think anyone really knows why."

"Does your society not destroy things that are evil? Why do you allow human beings that are evil to go on living and poison your culture?"

Joe glanced at Mrs. Merrynether with an expression that begged her to help him.

She stepped forward to address the dragons. "You cannot expect—"

"Are you the chosen representative for humanity?"

"Well, no, but—"

"Then be silent and let the boy speak."

Mrs. Merrynether grimaced in apology to Joe and stepped back.

Joe took a deep breath and stared at the seraph, feeling the weight of the world pressing down on the top of his skull. A fork in the road lay before the whole of mankind, and Joe stood at the junction, holding the signpost. He tried hard not to think about that as he considered the best way to answer his inquisitor.

"I don't think you can put people in categories like good and evil. Even evil people aren't evil all the time, and good people sometimes do bad things, don't they?

What do you do with dragons or seraphim that do evil things?"

"We destroy them. Evil has no place on Pyronesia."

Joe glanced at Mrs. Merrynether and the others. Each was silent with motionless tension, and Joe could not tell if they thought he was failing or succeeding. Even the wind had stopped, as if the island were waiting to see how he would answer. How could a twelve-year-old boy reason with beings thousands of years old and much wiser than he? Nevertheless, all he could do was try.

"Look. You can't go around just killing people because they don't fit in. You can't just . . ." He trailed off as he looked from the seraph to the dragon. Something important fell into place in his mind, as if a key had been turned in a lock.

"You can't just cut the bits off that you think are wrong or evil. My dad died a few years ago, and because of that, I used to be afraid of dying too. Then I met Danariel, and she showed me how not to be scared of death. I used to wish I could get away from how death made me feel . . . as if I could somehow cut death off of me or cut out the bits that made me scared, but you can't. At least, humans can't. We have to live with it, and sometimes it can help us to appreciate what life is really about."

"What you say makes no sense. When something fails in the human body, do you not cut it out or replace it?"

"That's different. You can't cut out bad thoughts like a dodgy appendix."

"And that is why humans should be destroyed."

"No, we shouldn't. Part of being a good person is learning how to say no to evil thoughts. Some people are just better at it than others; that's all. I suppose it takes a bit of practice."

"You speak nonsense. If there is evil, it should be cut away. That is the way things have always been on Pyronesia, and that is the way the world should be."

"If that's true, then all dragons should be destroyed."

An angry murmuring rumbled out from the dragons, and Joe could almost sense waves of anxiety from Mrs. Merrynether and the others.

"Dragons are not evil," the seraph said, remaining calm.

"If your history is true and what you say is right, then *all* of you are evil. I heard the story of how dragons were created. Your ancient king went to a mountain for twenty years after having all his doctors killed. He got rid of his hate, and it turned into the first dragon. So all you are is a race of hate, something evil discarded by an old king."

"A ridiculous legend, nothing more." Then Joe took a chance, but he had a hunch he might be right. "But all of your big ceremonies in that Tree of Sanctuary are built on those legends, aren't they?"

The seraph looked suspicious. "Without adherence

to the great laws, our society would be meaningless, but that does not mean we believe in myths and legends."

"So what was that thing you all said when I was in there? Something about the four?"

"May the light of understanding call The Four. May the unity of The Four bring us wisdom. May the joy of wisdom bring us peace. So may it be," the seraph said solemnly.

"I bet you don't even know what The Four are, do you?"

"How dare you question our—"

"Do you?" Joe had lost all sense of fear now.

"They represent the four spirits of ancient time when our people were lost and without direction. They—"

"Yes, but what *are* they?"

The seraph said nothing, but Joe could sense he was bristling with frustrated anger. His dragon's claws extended into the burnt soil, etching its disapproval into the earth.

"Want to hear what I think?" said Joe, praying he was right, hoping desperately they would think he was too. Joe guessed a few scientists would have a good belly laugh at his expense if they heard what he was about to suggest. But the really important thing was that the dragons believed it.

"I think the legends are true and that you really did all come from humans originally. I think your ancestors tried to get rid of everything that was evil and that was how the dragons and seraphim came about. And I think you wanted to get rid of all your ugliness, just like in the legends, and that's where the squonks came from. I don't know what the fourth creature is, but I bet your ancestors also realized they made a big mistake and wanted to put you all back together again somehow. What else could they mean by 'May the unity of The Four bring us wisdom'?"

The turquoise light from the seraph rippled like an angry heat wave. "Gnauserous has had many dragons sentenced to death for uttering such blasphemy, but to hear such things spoken by a human boy is more than we can bear."

The seraph's dragon arched its spiny neck and drew a guttural breath.

Joe hunched his shoulders and thrust his hands into his face, waiting for a swell of flame to consume him, but before the dragon could act, Snappel launched between them with her wings outstretched in a protective canopy, Heinrich yanked Joe backward, and Danariel zipped into the air, shouting for them to stop.

Joe sat in the dirt, shaking.

"Listen to what he says," she shouted. "Doesn't he say the same thing as Azariel so many years in the past? I watched in shame when Gnauserous had her executed, all because the Conclave are too terrified to accept what is so obvious. Should we continue to bury the truth in fire and remain in denial, or is this the time for our kind to rise above its fear and act with nobility?"

"But to accept such a thing would mean that dragonkind was spawned from human iniquity. Our law would dictate our destruction."

"Then maybe it's time to change your laws," said Joe, pushing past Snappel's wings to face the dragons. "I don't think any of you should be destroyed. I think you're all amazing."

"He's right," insisted Danariel. "It's the only way forward. Either we stop this now or everything ends in fire and blood. The island would no longer be secret. The world would be a burnt cinder, and you would have destroyed your creators. In your hearts, none of you want that."

A thoughtful silence settled over the small crowd. Snappel dropped back, and Joe looked around. The dragons were no longer circling in the sky. During the debate, all of them had landed on the other side of the gorge, gathered in multitudes but all watching quietly, and Joe guessed with awe that thousands of seraphim, invisible to his eyes, surrounded them, watching and waiting for the Conclave's decision.

Then a new revelation struck Joe.

"Danariel is the last part of Gnauserous you have left, isn't she?" he said, breaking the silence. "Doesn't that make *her* your queen now? Shouldn't you be following *her*?"

The seraph still had no answer other than the look

of confusion, shock, and embarrassment flickering over his tiny features. Then after a deep sigh, he spoke. "The Conclave has much to discuss. There will be no more war today, but for the truce to hold, one problem remains—Argoyle Redwar. He knows where we are, and he must be stopped. As long as he has power, Pyronesia cannot remain hidden. One day soon, war is sure to come again."

"We'll deal with him," said Mrs. Merrynether firmly.

The seraph nodded, then fluttered to Danariel.

"You must stay with us. If you are our queen, we need you."

"I know," she said, looking not at the seraph but at Joe with a forlorn smile.

Joe swallowed. "Do you have to?"

"No," she smiled. "But I should. Don't worry, though," she said, stroking his forehead. "We will see each other again. You're the human ambassador, remember?"

Joe sighed. "I suppose so."

FORTY-TWO

Leaving Pyronesia was a curious affair. On the island, Joe hadn't even considered what he would do if he got back home. He hadn't expected to be leaving at all. He thought he'd be dead by now, one of the first casualties of a war to end all wars, but it hadn't happened that way. Somehow, against the amazing odds, he had survived. Somehow, they had all survived. Danariel had stayed on the island with the Conclave, hopefully convincing them that humans should be allowed the chance to go on living. Without Gnauserous, she wouldn't enjoy the same longevity that the other seraphim had, but Mrs. Merrynether assured Joe she had a few good decades left in her yet.

Even Flarp had recovered. Joe had been convinced the poor globble had slimed its last on Pyronesia when he'd been gunned down, but once again, Mrs. Merrynether had set Joe straight. Globbles had no nervous system, they felt no pain, and all they really did was look at things all day. After the bullets had been popped out of his green skin, Flarp was up and about, whizzing around as merrily as ever.

Cornelius's damaged wing had been repaired, Kiyoshi had fully rested, Snappel's wounded claw had completely healed, and Heinrich, having heard Aunt Rose accept his offer of marriage, was suddenly a new man.

Yes, they'd all been very lucky indeed. On the long journey back in Lilly's airship, Mrs. Merrynether had insisted it had nothing to do with luck but everything to do with Joe. She'd told him, with the twinkles of tears in her eyes, that there could be no braver boy on the whole planet and that it was he who had inspired such fierce devotion from everyone he met—man, woman, or beast. And she'd told him he would grow up to be a fine man, if he wasn't already.

Joe had smiled and blushed but held those words close, hoping he would not let her down.

If leaving Pyronesia had been an unexpected event for Joe, arriving back in Upton Puddle turned out to be even more surprising. Though Joe felt mildly triumphant that they had managed to avert disaster on a global scale, they were not out of the woods yet.

After bribing one of the cluricauns to take him home in one of their airships, Argoyle Redwar had left several hours ahead of them on his way back to Upton Puddle, and none of them had the slightest idea how to put an end to his hateful campaign. Having left the island with more diamonds than most human beings had ever seen, Redwar needed only to bribe more people, hire another army, and expand his growing empire to be ready to launch another attack on Pyronesia. Even without Gnauserous, Joe guessed it would take very little to provoke the Conclave into war. Joe doubted the greedy businessman would ever understand the danger he or the rest of the world faced because of him.

As the airship settled over the Merrynether Estate to make its landing, the serious debate about Redwar appeared to have no resolution in sight.

"Oi say we stick some fireworks up his backside and send the fat git to da moon," Lilly said, making a final spin on the ship's wheel.

"A most astounding machination," Kiyoshi commented, "but with two calamitous shortcomings. Firstly, your lack of comprehension concerning the laws of physics is rivaled by that of only the most basic of protozoan life forms. Secondly, the combustion required for thrust would be negated by the reduction of oxidizing agents once the explosive has been inserted in—"

"Let's test it in the turtle first," Lilly drew a big lug from his pipe and blew a ball of smoke in Kiyoshi's face.

"We should go to the police," said Aunt Rose.

"And what would we tell them?" asked Mrs. Merrynether. "Anything close to the truth would sound ridiculous. Besides, even if we could convince them by showing them proof, the last thing we want is for Pyrone-sia to be revealed. No, we have to deal with him ourselves."

"But how?" asked Heinrich as they made their way from the ship to the mansion. "He is too powerful."

They were lost in thought as they walked through the fields and into Merrynether Mansion's enormous garden, searching for an idea of how to stop Redwar. Unsurprisingly, Joe noticed Lilly had disappeared minutes after they had disembarked, even though the mischievous cluricaun appeared to have walked down the ramp with the rest of them. Joe stopped for a moment, first looking for Lilly, then surveying the untended garden, the trees, and the sky. Something was different, but he wasn't sure what.

"Dorty, rotten, stinkin', short-arsed, smelly, fat boggers," yelled Lilly.

The cry came from the entrance of the mansion.

Joe whirled around, surprised that the tiny man had decided to reveal himself. It took a moment for Joe to register what Lilly had found. The cluricaun held a note, jumping with fury on a huge pile of glimmering jewels next to three emptied linen sacks.

"Oh my stars," said Aunt Rose with her hands smacked to her mouth. "Those are diamonds, they are. Great big sparklers, make no mistake."

Lilly screwed the note up and threw it as far away as he could, still cursing and jumping. Grinning, Joe rushed over, picked up the note, and read it out loud.

Dear ~~Maximus~~ Lilly,

You said there'd be booze if we helped you. There wasn't a drop on that whole miserable island. We'll give you ten days to build the brewery you promised. The fat bloke's diamonds will help if you need to buy a little help.

Fond regards,

The Clans

The others spent several minutes laughing, and Joe guessed Lilly would have burst several blood vessels if he'd stuck around for the ridicule, but the cluricaun had vanished, leaving Redwar's spoils behind.

"Well, that's Redwar's finances dealt with," said Mrs. Merrynether, "but we still need a way to stop him. I think we should pop inside. I'll make each of us a nice cup of tea, and we can work something out. Agreed?"

The others nodded, but Joe squinted at the tree line again, the puzzlement returning as he wondered why it looked so different. Then it hit him like an arrow between the eyes. "Where's the tower?"

"What?" said Mrs. Merrynether.

"The tower. Redwar's tower. That great big eyesore. Where is it? It's usually just over there."

Mrs. Merrynether frowned, Heinrich scratched his head, and Aunt Rose crossed her arms.

"I think we'd better take a look, don't you?" said Mrs. Merrynether. "Let's get everything sorted out here, and we can be on our way."

Three hours passed while they secured the animals comfortably in the vault with fresh bedding and food. Joe had called his mum on her mobile, reassuring her that all was well but that he and Aunt Rose had quite a tale to tell when she returned home next week.

The rest of the time, they speculated on Redwar's tower, and none of them had been able to think of a satisfactory reason for its disappearance. They considered everything from secret dragon attacks to convenient asteroid showers, until eventually the time came to find out the real reason.

Reluctantly, Heinrich stayed at the mansion to make sure the animals were settled, with Aunt Rose more than happy to keep him company.

Mrs. Merrynether and Joe headed to Redwar Industrial Park.

"It feels like ages since we were here last," said Joe as they started along the footpath next to Ringwood Forest, "but it's only been a few days. I wonder if anything's happened while we've been away. Apart from the tower disappearing, I mean."

"Well, what about that, for a start?" she replied, pointing ahead.

The entrance to the woods that Joe knew so well had been taped off. Signs with bright red warnings had been mounted on boards either side, and traffic cones had been lined up to dissuade inquisitive people from venturing inside.

"Of course," said Joe with dawning realization. "I suppose it was only a matter of time before they cordoned off the whole of the forest. With everything else that's been happening, I'd completely forgotten about the Beast of Upton Puddle."

Mrs. Merrynether stroked her wrinkly chin and peered over the top of her spectacles at the forbidden entrance. "Do you think the police would mind if an old animal surgeon like me had a look around?"

"Is it safe?" Joe asked, grasping Mrs. Merrynether's elbow and staring into the shade of the forest.

"Safe? Goodness me, no, but we haven't exactly worried much about that in the last few days, have we?"

They crept between the trees, watching closely for signs of movement, and it was then that Joe realized there was no movement at all, save the slight jostling of leaves above them in the breeze. It was an eerie thing to walk through a forest and hear no birdsong. Usually the cheery chirping of an occasional blackbird or wren would call out and a casual walker trudging through the woods might not even notice, but when the sound of wildlife had gone completely, the silence felt horribly unnatural. Joe had noticed this when the Beast first started to appear, straight after its escape from Redwar's vault, but now the silence seemed to have filled the entire forest.

As they moved deeper in, signs of the Beast grew in number. First they stumbled across the familiar burrows the creature had been digging. Then they saw fallen trees and wide areas of sunken ground. Two oak trees had fallen against each other to form a crooked arch. But the real shock came when three pairs of emerald eyes shone at them from inside a dark hole between them. To Joe's horror, Mrs. Merrynether crouched and held out a hand toward them and began to make soft clicking noises at whatever was hiding in the blackness.

"Come on," she said gently.

"What are you doing?" Joe whispered, alarmed.

"It's all right. Watch."

Joe stood perfectly still and dared not blink as he watched the hole. First a furry snout appeared, twitching and wet; then, like a frightened child dipping a toe into a swimming pool for the first time, a creature wobbled into the light. It stood on a pair of short, fluffy legs with a pair of enormous claws held close to its breast. It shuffled a little closer, its gleaming eyes bright with curiosity. Two more creatures, slightly smaller than the first but identical in every other respect, slunk up behind the first, trembling with either cold or fear; Joe couldn't be sure.

"Come on," she coaxed them again. To Mrs. Merrynether's disappointment they chose not to come any closer but darted into the safety of their hole and vanished.

"What were they?" Joe asked.

"I had my suspicions but couldn't be sure until just now. When I first heard a description of the Beast, I believed it to be a Sasquatch but couldn't work out what it could be doing here in Upton Puddle."

"A Sasquatch? But aren't they from America?"

"Most of the sightings have been in Canada, actually, but their true home is one of the smaller islands close to Pyronesia. When I heard that the Beast had become violent, I began to doubt my original idea. The Sasquatch is a gentle creature and very solitary, so it didn't seem likely that it was one of those. Of course, at that time, I had no idea Redwar had been taking creatures from those islands, and I knew we didn't have a Sasquatch, so I concluded it must be something completely different, especially after it had attacked me."

"But it is a Sasquatch, right? And those were baby Sasquatches we just saw?" Joe smiled and nodded at the hole.

"Exactly, and that's why the Beast became violent. She was pregnant and reacting according to her protective instincts. She must have gone almost insane, trapped inside Redwar's vault, but she managed to escape and then ended up hiding in Ringwood Forest."

"So where is she now? Shouldn't she be with her babies?"

"From what I've learned, the Sasquatch is a prolific breeder and they have huge litters—up to thirty cubs,

Danariel told me once. There could be little Sasquatches digging around all over the forest, and the mother could be absolutely anywhere, probably out gathering food."

"Won't they be in danger, though, especially with the area cordoned off? The authorities probably want to track it down because it has attacked people."

"Well, we'll just have to get them to safety before anyone finds them, won't we?"

"How? We don't know how many there are, and they could be anywhere."

Mrs. Merrynether tapped the side of her nose. "You leave that to me. It won't be hard now that I know what we're dealing with, and I've been in this line of work for a very long time. You just have to look for the right information in the right places and have the right tools at the ready."

Still eager to find out what had happened to the tower, they continued through the forest until eventually they reached the perimeter of Redwar Industrial Park. The sight that greeted them was as shocking as it was welcome. Among a throng of busy crowds stood the pitiful remains of a business park in ruins. Joe thought the whole site had been bulldozed, but a closer look at the ground surrounding the rubble revealed an enormous dip in the earth. It looked as though something had scooped up Redwar's entire building, crumpled it like a piece of waste paper, punched a gaping hole in the dirt, and used it as a humongous trash bin.

"I think our hairy friends have been busy," said Mrs. Merrynether.

A plethora of people bustled around the edge of the enormous crater like termites vacated from their nest. Some were police trying to round people up, some were council workers in hardhats and bright orange coats, others looked like government agents in sharp suits hiding behind dark glasses, but the majority appeared to be employees of Redwar Industries.

Joe hurried to three men who were in hot debate. Mrs. Merrynether followed.

"What happened here?" Joe asked when one of the men paused for breath.

"You're kidding, right?"

"Yeah, where have *you* been?" said his friend.

"Sorry," Joe answered. "It's just that we've been away for a few days, so we haven't a clue what's been going on."

"Scandal. That's what's been going on," one of them said with a slow nod. "See over there?" He pointed through the crowd. "That's Mr. Redwar. He did a vanishing act just about the same day the whole building collapsed. They reckon it was the Beast that did most of the damage but that he did the rest to claim on the insurance."

"Yeah," said another, "he's not getting away with it, though. Just about the whole of the county was waiting for him, I reckon. The moment he turned up this morning, the police came; then the health and safety mob;

then those government blokes; and after that, most of the village showed up to have a good look."

The first one laughed. "They've been grilling old Redwar and taking statements and evidence from people for at least three hours. The old fart's been going mental. I thought his head was going to blow off a minute ago." He pointed and laughed even harder. "Look at him go."

Joe thanked them. He took Mrs. Merrynether's hand, and they pushed their way through the heaving crowd to get a closer look at their nemesis. He and Ms. Burrowdown stood at the center of a ring of people still dressed in their camouflage gear, covered with bruises, scratches, and dirt from the ordeal on Pyronesia.

Joe realized he must look equally bedraggled, which was probably why everyone gave him a wide berth. Worrying what other people thought was the last thing on Joe's mind, though, as he watched the fiasco unfolding before him.

Every possible vein throbbed at the sides of Argoyle Redwar's overripe head as he stamped, cursed, and throttled invisible necks and screamed his fury at the officious group. "You cannot do this. I know my rights. I—"

"According to section fifteen, paragraph eight of the Public Declarations Act, you don't have any rights at all, Mr. Merson. Redwar Industries was covered contractually under the name Argoyle Roderick Redwar, and you are *not* that man."

"But I . . . Who are you, young man?" He turned on Ms. Burrowdown. "Who is he?"

"Graham Chatterly," she said.

"Chatterly? Didn't we fire him?"

"Yes, you did," said Chatterly, "and I got a job with the Home Office. Much better there, I have to say."

"How dare you—?"

"You are also under suspicion of several allegations of cruelty to animals," said a smartly dressed woman handing him a brown envelope. Gumble, the twice-fired animal keeper, stood next to her, holding Redwar with a smug sneer.

"Piffle," Redwar puffed. "I'll have you for slander, Gumble." He threw the envelope to the mud and ground his heel into it, provoking some noisy abuse from the surrounding crowd.

"You'll be doing nothing of the sort," said another familiar voice. Mr. Huffney, a man who—judging by the huge bags under his eyes—still found it hard to sleep at night for fear of nightmares about cluricauns firing balls of rancid dung at him, pushed his way into the circle. He wore a smile almost as smug as Gumble's. "Remember me, Mr. Redwar? I took a job as a health and safety inspector for the government after you fired me, and I'm very curious to know what sort of chemical compounds you've been dumping into the forest since you've been here."

"That's another slanderous lie. I'll not hear any

more of this. I'll have my head of security escort you off"—he passed a defeated glance at the rubble where his site used to be—"my land."

"Your head of security? Him, you mean?" Huffney pointed at Scott and Kurt Duggan as they were led away into a police van, screaming and swatting invisible things away from their heads.

Catching Kurt's eye as the bully was thrown inside, Joe gave him a wink.

"But this is ridiculous. I don't have any toxic waste."

"Really?" Huffney flared his nostrils and gestured to the ground. Puddles of filthy water bubbled around Redwar's feet, as though a bog had suddenly risen to spoil his shoes.

"What the—?" Redwar squawked and stepped away from the sludge. He waved his arms, moving from rage to near hysteria. "Would anybody else like to join in? I'm sure there are plenty more laws I've broken."

"How about treason?" said a gruff voice.

"Treason?" Redwar left his hysteria and slipped into horror.

A tall man in a dark blue uniform with a stern face and a short haircut to match strode into view. "Sure. Conspiring to bribe, to threaten, and to falsify documents to secure your own private army and steal a ship belonging to the Royal Navy, which you then managed to sink. I'd say that would put you behind bars for good."

No sound came from Redwar this time as his jaw

dropped like a puppet's mouthpiece. He looked at Ms. Burrowdown, who tossed her notepad into the dirt and walked off without another word.

Redwar was led away to a police van, handcuffed and shell-shocked.

With everyone watching, Joe was the only one to notice the dirty puddle Huffney had referred to as toxins. A sludgy face formed at its center, lifted slightly, then winked before dissolving into the slime.

An hour later, Joe stepped into the vault of Merrynether Mansion and beamed as the reality of their success began to wake up within him.

Archy the pig trotted forward to greet Mrs. Merrynether when she came in, and she smiled at Joe with a victorious look in her eyes that told Joe there was no longer anything to worry about.

Kiyoshi sat at the center of a beanbag munching on a cucumber, staring intently at Lilly, who had decided to stay for some whiskey before drawing up his plans for the construction of Ringwood Brewery.

Cornelius sat sphinxlike in the center, using Flarp for poison barb target practice as the frolicsome globble zipped and bounced in front of him. Snappel crouched next to the manticore with her long tail stretched affectionately over his back as he fired his shots, and Joe relished the deep throaty sound of purring that alternated between the pair of them as they enjoyed each other's company.

But perhaps the sight that warmed Joe most was the other couple in the room, grinning with carefree contentment. Heinrich sat at his desk, with Aunt Rose standing behind him, her huge arms resting gently on his shoulders.

Joe spun around, taking in the whole familiar space. "So," he said, rubbing his hands together, "what will our next patient be?"

MEDALLION
P R E S S

Be in the know on the latest Medallion Press news by
becoming a Medallion Press Insider!

As an Insider you'll receive:
· Our FREE expanded monthly newsletter, giving you more insight into
Medallion Press
· Advanced press releases and breaking news
· Greater access to all your favorite Medallion authors

Joining is easy. Just visit our website at
www.medallionmediagroup.com and click on
Super Cool E-blast next to the social media buttons.

---

medallionmediagroup.com

MEDALLION
P R E S S

Want to know what's going on with your favorite author or what new releases are coming from Medallion Press?

Now you can receive breaking news, updates, and more from Medallion Press straight to your cell phone, e-mail, instant messenger, or Facebook!

Sign up now at www.twitter.com/MedallionPress to stay on top of all the happenings in and around Medallion Press.

For more information
about other great titles from
Medallion Press, visit

medallionmediagroup.com